Brooklyn

GIRLS

GEMMA BURGESS

Brooklyn GIRLS

PIA

Quercus

First published in the US in 2013 by St. Martin's Press,
175 Fifth Avenue, New York, N.Y. 10010

This edition published in Great Britain in 2013 by

Quercus Editions Ltd
55 Baker Street
7th Floor, South Block
London
W1U 8EW

A CIP catalogue reference for this book is available
from the British Library

ISBN 978 1 78206 733 7

1 3 5 7 9 10 8 6 4 2

Printed and bound in Great Britain by Clays Ltd, St Ives plc.

FOR **YOU**

CHAPTER 1

Never screw your roommate's brother.

A simple rule, but a good one. And I broke it last night. Twice. Oopsh.

At least the party was awesome. I'll try that excuse if Julia is pissy. And if her house is trashed. Which I'm pretty sure it is.

I'm not exactly surprised. I like parties, I'm good at them, and it was August 26 yesterday. And on that date, I always drink to forget. This year, I did it with whips, chains, and bells on.

My bare ass keeps brushing against the wall as I squish away from Mike. Don't you hate that? Doesn't random hookup etiquette demand he face the other way? I wish he would just leave without me having to, like, talk to him.

I wonder what Madeleine, his sister, would say if she found out.

She'd probably ignore me, which is what she always does these days. I wish Julia hadn't asked her to move in.

Julia, my best friend from college, inherited this house when her aunt passed away. So Julia invited me, her little sister Coco, and Madeleine to move in. And then we needed a fifth, so I asked my friend Angie. We're a motley crew: Coco's the Betty Homemaker type, Angie's all fashi-tude, Julia's super-smart and ambitious, and Madeleine's uptight as hell. And me? I'm . . . well, it's impossible to describe yourself, isn't it? Let's call me a work-in-progress.

We moved in two weeks ago. It's a brownstone named Rookhaven, on Union Street in Carroll Gardens, a neighborhood in the borough of Brooklyn in New York City. None of us has properly lived in New York before.

Carroll Gardens is a weird mix of old people who've probably lived here forever, young professionals like us who—let's face it—can't afford to live in Manhattan, and a bunch of yupster couples with young kids. There's a real neighborhood village vibe with all these old, traditional Italian bakeries and restaurants next to stylish little bars.

I like stylish little bars.

I like my bedroom, too. I've had a lot of bedrooms in my life—twenty-seven, if you count every room change at boarding school and college—but never one quite like this. High ceilings, windows looking out over the front stoop, wall-to-wall mirrored closets. Okay, the mirrors are yellowed and the wallpaper is a faded rosebud print that looks like something out of an old movie. It just *feels* right. Like this is how it's supposed to look.

That's kind of Rookhaven all over. If I were feeling nice, I'd call the décor vintage and preloved. (Old and shabby.) I'm just happy to be in New York, far away from my parents, in the most exciting city in the world, with a job at a SoHo PR agency. My life is *finally* happening.

Can I be honest with you? I shouldn't have slept with Mike. Not when things are already, shall we say, complicated with Madeleine. Casual sex only works when it's with someone you can never see again. But, as I said, it was August 26 (also known as Eddie Memorial Day, or Never Again Day). And on August 26, shit happens.

What is that damn ringing sound?

"I think that's the doorbell."

Gah! Mike! Awake! Right here next to me. I peek through my eyelashes. Like Madeleine, he's ridiculously good-looking. I guess it's their Chinese-Irish DNA. Good combination.

"Erm . . . someone else will get it," I murmur. My breath smells like an open grave. Not that it matters. Because I don't like him like that. Even though last night I—ew. God. Bad thought. But hey! So what? So the whole sex thing was a bad idea. There is no reason to feel stupid Puritan guilt about one-night stands. I am a feminist. And all that shit.

The doorbell goes again.

"Pia . . . Come here, you crazy kitten," Mike says, pushing his arm under me.

"I better get the door. It could be someone important!" I say brightly, slithering down around him and falling onto the dark green carpet with a thump.

I wriggle into my panties, trying to look cool and unbothered as I put on the first T-shirt I see. It belonged to Smith, a guy I dated (well, slept with a few times) in college. The back says, "I brake for cheerleaders . . . HARD."

I pull on my favorite cutoff jean shorts and Elmo slippers and stuff my cell phone in my pocket.

"I'm glad you brake for cheerleaders," says Mike. "They're an endangered species."

"Um, yup, totally!" I say, and slam the door behind me, cutting him off. Mike! God! Nightmare!

I close my eyes, trying to remember last night. It's worryingly hard. I was feeling meh after Thompson (this cockmonkey I've been dating, well, sleeping with) ignored my text (*Hola. Bodacious party. Bring smokes if you can . . .* Good text, right? Ironic use of passé slang, trailing ellipses rather than a lame smiley face, etc.). And rejection is not a good look for me. Not on August 26.

So I drank more. And more. And then more.

I remember dancing. On a table, maybe? Yeah, that rings a bell. . . . And I think I was doing some '80s-aerobics-style dance moves. The grapevine. Definitely the grapevine. I was having fun, anyway. I don't usually worry about much when I'm having fun.

And Mike was doing one-handed push-ups, really badly, and making me laugh, and then I stumbled, and next thing I knew Mike's lips were on mine. Now I *love* kissing, I really do, and he is pretty good at it, and I was trashed, so I suggested we go to my room. And then . . . oh, God.

Nothing burns like hangover shame.

The person at the door is really dying to get in. *Dingdongdingdong-dingdong.*

"Coming!" I shout, picking my way over the bottles and cigarette butts on the stairs.

I hope it's not the cops. I don't *think* there were drugs at the party, but you never know. Once time at my second boarding school I thought that my boyfriend Jack had OCD, which was why he arranged talcum powder in little lines, and as it turned out— Wait. Back to the nightmare.

I open the front door and sigh in relief.

It's just a very old man. His face is like a long raisin with pointy elf ears, on the top of a tall and skinny body.

"Young lady, where is your father?" he says in a strong Brooklyn accent. *Fadah.*

"Zurich," I say, then add, "Sir." (And they say I don't respect my elders.)

"Are you a relation of Julia's?"

"Fu— I mean, gosh, no."

"Well, that figures. I didn't think Pete remarried, and you're definitely a half-a-something."

Seriously? "I'm a whole person, not a half. My mother is Indian, my father is Swiss. Please come back later." I try to close the door, but he's blocking it.

"I need to speak with Miss Russotti."

"Which one? There are two. Russotti the elder, also known as Julia, and Russotti the younger, also known as Coco."

"Whichever is responsible for the very loud party that went on till 5:00 A.M. and caused the total cave-in of my kitchen ceiling."

I gasp. He must live in the garden-level apartment under our house. My mind starts racing. How can I fix this?

"Oh, I am so sorry, I can pay for the ceiling, sir, I—"

"I take it that there were no parents present?"

"I think my roommate Madeleine has babysitting experience, does that count?"

"Don't be smart with me."

"I've never been called smart before," I say, twisting my hair around my finger, trying to get him to laugh a little bit. No one can stay angry after they laugh, it's a fact.

His expression warms slightly, then falls as though pushing the crags and crevices into a new shape was too much effort. "Just get Julia."

"Yes, sir. Would you like to wait inside?"

"If you think I want to see what this house looks like this morning, you've got another think coming."

"Is it think or thing?"

"It's think."

"I'll go get Julia."

I run up the stairs, jumping over the leftover party mayhem, and knock on Julia's bedroom door.

"Juju?" I peer in.

No Julia, just Angie and some tall English lord guy she met in London at the Cartier Polo (yes, seriously). I saw them making out in the laundry room last night after a game of "truth or dare," which Angie renamed "dare or fuck off." Man, I hope they didn't screw on the washing machine. My laundry is in there. I keep forgetting to take it out, and it goes all funky with the heat, so then I have to wash it again and— Oh, sorry. Focus.

"*Angie!* Wake the hell up!"

I shake her, but she just gives a little snore and buries herself deeper into the bed. She looks like a fallen angel with a serious eyeliner habit. And she's *impossible* to wake after a night out.

Julia will lose her shit if she finds out about this. She and Angie haven't exactly bonded. My bad: I talked Julia into letting Angie move in before they'd even met, because Angie's folks got her a job as a PA to some food photographer woman in Chelsea and she needed a place to live, and Angie's been, like, my best friend since I was born. (Literally. Our moms met in the maternity ward.)

Then Angie walked in, said, "It's a dump, but it's retro, I can make it work," and lit a cigarette. Julia was not impressed.

"Angie! Get. The hell. Up."

"Pia?" She peers up at me through her long white-blond hair. "I had to sleep here, there was a threesome in my bed."

"Ew," I say, grimacing, as I pull Angie onto her feet. "Help me. Major crisis."

"You're such a fucking drama queen. Hugh. Dude. Get up."

Hugh climbs out behind her unsteadily. He has a very posh English accent. "Tremendous party." *Pah-teh.* He's very handsome, like a young Prince William, with more hair.

As soon as he leaves, Angie licks and smells her hand to check her morning breath. "Yep, pretty rank. What's wrong, ladybitch?"

"Everything. We have to find Julia."

"Roger that." Angie's still wearing her tiny party dress from last night and slips on a pair of snow boots from Julia's closet. "You have a hickey on your neck."

"How old school of me." I grab Julia's foundation to dab over it. "Ugh, why is she wearing this shade? It's completely wrong for her. Sorry, off topic."

We head upstairs. Angie stares at her closed bedroom door. "God, I hate threesomes."

"Totally. It's just showing off."

Angie smirks, then karate kicks her door in. "Show's over, bitches! Get the hell outta my house."

Two girls I've never seen before and a tall dark-haired guy I vaguely recognize from college saunter out of Angie's room.

"Pia, babe!" says the guy, putting on his shirt. "I tried to find you all night! Remember that party back in junior year? A little Vicodin, a little tequila . . ."

I shudder. Now I remember him.

"Leave," snaps Angie. "Now."

"Bitch," he calls, walking down the stairs.

"Blow me!" she calls back, then heads into her room. "Fuck! I'm gonna have to burn the sheets."

I hear a hinge squeak. It's Madeleine, coming out of the bathroom in a pristine white robe, her hair wrapped perfectly in a towel-turban.

"Morning!" I say, smiling as innocently as I can.

She pads to her bedroom and slams the door. Typical. Good thing I didn't add, *By the way, your brother is naked in my bed.*

I trudge up the last flight of stairs, finally reach Coco's attic room, and knock. Julia must be in here. There's nowhere else to go.

"It's me . . ." I open the door slowly.

Julia is sitting on the bed, still wearing her clothes from last night yet sportily immaculate as ever, next to Coco, whose blond bob is bent over a plastic bucket and—oh, God. She's puking.

"Coco!" I say. "Are you sick?"

"Clap, clap, Sherlock," says Julia.

"I'm fine!" Coco's voice echoes nasally in the bucket. "So fine. Oh, God, not fine." Noisy, chokey barf sounds follow. "Wowsers! This is green! Oh, Julia, it's green, is that bad?"

"It's bile," says Julia, rubbing Coco's back and glaring at me. Furious and sisterly, all at once. "I need to talk to Pia. Try to stop vomiting, okay?" She has a deep, self-assured voice, particularly lately. It's like the moment she graduated, she decided it was time to *act adult at all costs.*

"Maybe I'll lose weight," Coco's voice echoes from the bucket.

I follow Julia to the tiny landing at the top of the stairs, closing Coco's bedroom door behind us. I feel sick. Confrontation and I really don't get along.

"I am sorry," I say immediately. "I guess you're angry about the party, and—"

"You sold it to me as a 'small housewarming,'" interrupts Julia. "This place was like Cancun on spring break, but less classy."

I hate being told off, too. It's not like I don't *know* when I've screwed up. Or like I do it on purpose. And I never know what to say, so I just gaze into space and wait for it to be over.

"I *said* no wild parties. When we all moved in, that was the rule." God, Julia is scary when she wants to be. "What the fuck were you *thinking*, Pia?"

"It just sort of, um, happened. . . ." I say, chewing my lip. "And I'm sorry about this, too, um, there's an old dude at the door? He said his ceiling caved in? I'll pay for it! I have the money and—"

"Vic?" says Julia in dismay. "I swear to God, Pia, I can't live with you if you're going to fucking act like this all the time. I mean it!"

She's going to kick me out of Rookhaven?

"I won't!" I exclaim. "I'm sorry! Don't overreact!"

"Start cleaning up!" she shouts, thundering down the stairs.

She's going to kick me out. I thought I finally had somewhere that I could call my own, somewhere that wasn't temporary, and somewhere I might actually not have to wear shower shoes. Yet again I am the master of my own demise. Mistress. Whatever.

I walk back into Coco's room. "Can I get you anything, sweetie? I've got rehydration salts somewhere."

"No," she croaks, smiling cherubically at me from the pillow. "I had fun last night. You were so funny."

"Oh, well, that's good." What the hell was I doing?

There are hundreds of books on Coco's floor. I think they're usually in the bookshelves in the living room. They're all old and tattered, with titles like *What Katy Did* by Susan Coolidge and *Are You There God? It's Me, Margaret* by Judy Blume. I loved *What Katy Did,* I remember. The sequel, *What Katy Did at School,* was one of the reasons I thought boarding school would be awesome. Stupid book.

"Why are these here?" I ask.

"I didn't want them to get, um, you know, trashed at the party," says Coco. "So I picked up all the ones that my mom loved the most and brought them up here."

"It must have taken you a while," I say.

"Every time I made a trip, I had a shot. . . ." Coco starts puking again.

"Hey, ladybitches," says Angie, sauntering in with an unlit cigarette propped in the side of her mouth.

"For you, Miss Coco." Somehow, Angie has found an icy-cold can of Coke.

"Wow, thanks! I normally drink Diet Coke, but—"

"Trust me, Diet Coke is bullshit. Okay kids, I am officially over this post-party chaos thing. Let's clean up."

At that moment, my phone rings. Unlisted number. I answer.

"Hello?"

"Pia, it's Benny Mansi."

Benny Mansi is the director of the PR agency where I work. My parents know his family somehow and got me the interview back in June. I started working there last week. Why would he call me on a Sunday? Is that normal? Perhaps it's a PR emergency!

I try to sound professional. "Hi! What's up?"

"Are you aware that there's a photo of you on Facebook, dancing on a table topless and drinking a bottle of Captain Morgan rum?"

WHAM. I feel like I just got punched.

"Um, I—"

"Pia, we're letting you go before your trial period is over."

WHAM. Another hit.

"You're firing me . . . for having a party?"

"Captain Morgan is one of our biggest clients," Benny says. "As my employee, you represent the agency. You're also Facebook friends with all your brand-new colleagues. You were tagged, they saw it. I applaud your convivial approach to interoffice relations, but that sort of behavior is just . . . it's unprofessional, and it's completely unacceptable, Pia."

"I know." A wash of sickly cold horror trickles through me, and I stare at the yellowed glow-in-the-dark stars on the sloping ceiling in Coco's room. They lost their glow long ago. . . . Oh, God, I can't be fired. I can't be fired after *one week.* "I'm so sorry, Benny." Silence. "Did you . . . tell my, um, father?"

He sighs. "I e-mailed him this morning. I didn't tell him why." I don't say anything, and his voice softens. "Look, Pia, it's complicated. We made some redundancies a few months ago. So hiring you, as a family friend, really upset a few people, and that photo . . . my hands are tied. I'm sorry."

He hangs up.

I can feel Coco and Angie staring at me, but I can't say anything.

I've lost my job. And I'm probably about to get kicked out of my house. After one week in New York.

My phone rings again. It's my parents. I stare at the phone for a few seconds, knowing what's on the other end, what's waiting for me.

I wonder if Coco would mind if I borrowed her puke bucket.

I need to be alone for what's about to happen, so I walk back out to the stairwell and sit down. I can hear Madeleine playing some angsty music in her room on the floor below, mixed with Julia's placating tones and Vic's grumbly ones from down in the front hall.

Then I answer, trying to sound like a good daughter.

"Hi, Daddy!"

"So you've lost your job already. What do you have to say for yourself?"

My voice is gone. This happens sometimes. Just when I need it most. In its place, a tiny squeaking sound comes out.

"Speak up!" snaps my father. He has a slightly scary Swiss accent despite twenty years living in the States.

"I'm . . . sorry. I'll get another job, I will, and—"

"Pia, we are so disappointed in you!" My mother is lurking on the extension. She has a slight Indian accent that only really comes out when she's pissed. Like now.

"You wanted the summer with Angie, so we paid for it. You wanted to work, so we got you a job. You said you had the perfect place to live, so we agreed to help pay rent, though God knows Brooklyn certainly wasn't the perfect place to live last time I was there—"

"You have no work ethic! You are a spoiled party girl! Are you sniffing the drugs again?"

They've really honed their double-pronged condemnation-barrage routine over the years.

"Work ethic. Your mother is right. Your total failure to keep a job . . . well. Let me tell you a story—"

I sink my head to my knees. My parents have the confidence-killing combination of high standards and low expectations.

They also twist everything so it looks terrible. They told me if I got good grades they'd pay for my vacation, and that I'd never find a job on my own, *and* they offered me an allowance, so of course I said yes! Wouldn't you?

". . . and that is how I met your father and then we got married and had you and then lived— What do you say? Happily ever after . . ."

Yeah, right. My parents hardly talk to each other. They distract themselves with work (my dad) and socializing (my mother). They met in New York, where they had me, then moved to Singapore, London, Tokyo, Zurich . . . I went to American International Schools until I was twelve, and then they started sending me to boarding school. Well, boarding school*s*.

"Life starts with a job, Pia. You think we will always pay for your mistakes, that life is just a party. We know you'll never have a career, but a job is—"

"A reason to get up in the morning!"

"And the only way to learn the value of money. Do you understand?"

I nod stupidly, staring at the wall next to me, at the ancient-looking rosebud wallpaper. At the bottom the paper has started to peel, curled up like a little pencil shaving. It's comforting.

"Pia!" my mother is shouting. "Why are you not listening? Do we have to do the Skype again?"

"No, no, I can't, my Skype is broken," I say quickly. I can't handle Skyping with my parents. It's so damn intense.

"We are stopping your allowance, effective immediately. No rent money, no credit card for emergencies. You're on your own."

"What? B-but it might take me a while to get another job!" I stammer in panic.

"Well, the Bank of Mom and Dad is closed unless you come live with us in Zurich and get a job here. That's the deal."

"No way!" I know I sound hysterical, but I can't help it. "My friends are here! My life is here!"

"We want you to be safe," says my mother, in a slightly gentler tone. Suddenly tears rush to my eyes. "We worry. And it seems like you're only safe when you're with us."

"I *am* safe."

"And we want you to be happy," she adds.

"I am happy!" My voice breaks.

My father interrupts. "This is the deal. We're vacationing in Palm Beach in exactly two months, via New York. If you're not in gainful employment by then, we're taking you back to Zurich with us. That's the best thing for you."

The tears escape my eyes. I know I've made some mistakes, but God, I've tried to make it up to them. I studied hard, I got into a great college. . . . It's never good enough.

How is it that no one in the world can make me feel as bad as my parents can?

"Okay, message received," I say. "I gotta go."

I hang up and stare at the curled-up rosebud wallpaper for a few more seconds. Then, almost without thinking, I lick my index finger and try to smooth it down, so it lies flat and perfect against the wall. It bounces right back up again.

With one party, I've destroyed my life in New York City. Before it even began.

CHAPTER 2

When Julia comes back upstairs moments later, pink with fury, my stomach flips over. I hate fighting. And Jules is really good at it. She should have been a lawyer.

"You destroyed our neighbor's ceiling," she snaps. "Destroyed. A piece of plaster fell on his sister's head this morning. She's eighty-six-fucking-years old, Pia!"

"Is she okay? Oh, my God, I can't—"

"She's fine," says Julia. "It was only a tiny piece. But Vic is *pissed*."

"I'll pay for it, I promise!" I say. "I have, like, sixteen hundred dollars. He can have all of it." It's all I have in the world, and the last of the money from my parents, but I need to convince Julia not to kick me out. "I'm sorry, Julia, I didn't know it'd get so out of control."

"What were you *thinking*?"

"I just . . . I thought it would be fun, that everyone would have a good time." I can't tell her that I was drinking because it was August 26. I never talk about Eddie to anyone. Only Angie knows the story, only Angie saw me that day. "Seriously, Juju, I never meant to hurt anyone . . . or destroy the old guy's, I mean Vic's, ceiling."

"Vic and Marie have been here *forever*. Since long before I was born, or my mom," says Julia. "They're like family, okay?"

Suddenly, I understand. Her mom grew up here, and she died of breast cancer about eight years ago. Her dad has cocooned himself in silent grief ever since, and then her Aunt Jo passed away, so I guess Vic and Marie—and Rookhaven—are sort of a last link to her mom. No wonder she feels so protective.

"I'll fix the floor damage," I say, reaching out for Julia's hand. She doesn't resist, which I take as a good sign. "And I'll get them flowers to say sorry. Today. And I will not let anything bad happen to this house again. I cross my heart."

Julia takes a deep breath and leans against the wall, closing her eyes. She looks exhausted, and it's not just from the party. Her job—trainee in an investment bank—starts at 6:00 A.M. every day, and she doesn't get home until past 7:00 P.M. every night. It's step one in her plan to take over the world. She's so exhausted, she's actually kind of gray. And she's not even hungover.

"I had fun last night, by the way."

"What?" I say.

She opens one eye, a tiny grin on her lips. "It was a great party. I had fun. Right up until Coco started to do a striptease in the kitchen."

I clap my hand over my mouth. "No way."

"I carried her up here. Anyway, don't tell her. She doesn't remember. I always think it's better that way."

"Oh, I know," I say. "You never flashed an entire bar your Spanx on Spring Weekend."

"Totally. Goddamnit, I wish I'd been wearing a thong that night."

We grin at each other for a second, remembering. That's the Julia I know and love. The girl who works hard and plays hard, too. And the girl who always wants to make everything right. But I can't tell her what happened with my job and parents just yet. I need to process it (uh, pretend it didn't happen).

"Hang on a moment." Julia narrows her eyes at me. "Bed hair. Panda eyes. And stubble rash. Peepee, you got action last night!" she exclaims.

"I did not! And don't call me Peepee!"

"Have we made up?" coos Angie, peering out from Coco's room. She wraps her bare leg around the door, lifting one snow boot–clad foot up and down like a meteorology-loving stripper. "Are we all friends again?"

"Those are my boots," says Julia. "Why are you wearing them?"

"Are you planning on skiing soon? I think not." Angie sashays past us down the stairs. "It's August. I'll return them in pristine condition as soon as the house is clear of party debris, okay, Mommy?"

Julia rolls her eyes and heads downstairs. "Start cleaning."

Angie flicks the finger at Julia's retreating back.

"Real mature, Angie."

"Suck my mature."

"I'm hungry."

"You're always hungry. Let's clean."

Somehow, being hungover and giggling with Angie cheers me up and helps squash my what-the-sweet-hell-am-I-going-to-do-now thoughts. She keeps making little moans of dismay at each new inch of party filth, and pretty soon we've both got the giggles.

"When I have my own place, there will be no carpets," I say. "Carpets are just asking for trouble."

"Did anyone lose a shoe? And why did we invite someone to our party who wears moccasins?"

"Is this red wine or blood? No. Wait. It's tomato sauce. Weird."

"You wanna talk me through the hickey, ladybitch?"

I catch Angie's eye and bite my index finger sheepishly.

"You had the sex? You little minx . . ."

"With her brother," I whisper, pointing at Madeleine's door. "Bit of an oopsh."

Oopsh is our word for a drunken mistake.

"Oopsh I kissed the wrong dude, or oopsh I tripped and his dick landed in my mouth?"

I crack up. No one does crass like Angie. She looks like a tiny Christmas angel and acts like a sailor on a Viagra kick. "Or was it more like, oopsh, I'm riding his face and—"

"Too far! That's too far."

"Sorry."

"Don't tell Jules, she'd just have to tell Maddy, and it'd be a whole thing."

"Absolute-leh, dah-leng," she says, in her best imitation of her mother's British accent. "You were totally kamikaze last night."

"It was August 26. That's International Pia Goes Kamikaze Day, remember? Crash and burn."

There's a pause. "Oh, dude, I'm sorry. I totally forgot. Eddie."

I can't bring myself to look at her. Only Angie saw me that day, only Angie knows how bad it was. She always calls me a drama queen, but she knows that misery was real. You don't fake that kind of breakdown.

"I don't want to talk about it," I say.

Angie keeps cleaning. "Fuck him, Pia. Okay? Fuck him! It's been four years!"

I nod, scrubbing as hard as I can. It has been four years since we broke up. And I really should be over it. Then, thank God, Angie changes the subject.

"So I'm gonna move out to L.A. after the holidays," she says. "I don't really belong here in Brooklyn, you know?"

This news just makes me feel even sadder. There's no point arguing with Angie. She does whatever she wants. Instead I scrub harder and, stair by stair, stain by stain, we make it downstairs. Angie puts on some music, and we clean to the post-party-appropriate strains of the Ramones. I can hear Julia and Coco throwing out empty bottles in the kitchen and, every now and again, shrieking when they find something nasty. Oh please, God, no drugs or used condoms. Just spare me that.

"What time did the party finish?" I ask Angie.

"About five. Lord Hugh and I saw out the last of the party people just as the sun was coming up."

"He seems . . . Lordesque."

"He's very Lordesque." She nods. "He also knows his way around a washer-dryer."

"Did you guys do a"—I pause and grin at her—"full load?"

"Just a half load. Then we rinsed. Very thoroughly. Oh, look. Half a spliff. How nice."

We make it to the first floor, and help Julia and Coco finish up the kitchen, which primarily involves de-stickying every surface. Nothing does sticky like forty-year-old linoleum.

"That was intense," says Julia, wiping her forehead with her arm. "The laundry room flooded. That's what made Vic's ceiling collapse."

"I'll fix it," I say again.

"Oh, I know you will."

"I cleaned the bathrooms," says an icy voice. I look up, and see Madeleine, carrying a mop and bucket. "They were absolutely revolting."

"Thanks, Moomoo," says Julia. Madeleine rolls her eyes at Julia's nickname for her—she professes to hate it—and pushes past us to the sink, giving Julia's ponytail an affectionate tug. She's so nice underneath that cold-and-controlled exterior, just not to me, not anymore.

Okay, the Madeleine story, in brief: we were friends once. Really good friends. In fact, she and Julia and I were pretty much inseparable for freshman year. We're all very different, but somehow we just . . . clicked, in an opposites-attract kind of way.

Then, suddenly, at the end of freshman year, Madeleine got crazy drunk for the first time ever and, out of nowhere, told me she hated me. I was holding her hair back so she could throw up, and she just said over and over again, "I hate you. I hate you, Pia, I hate you." Then she passed out. The next day, I tried to talk to her, she shut down, and we've been in a cold war ever since. And now her brother is naked in my bed.

Hmm.

Between you and me, I wouldn't have moved in if I'd known Madeleine was going to be here, too. Jules was probably hoping we'd make up, that the five of us will become best friends and start swapping traveling ya-ya pants, or whatever. I can't see that happening. Particularly given that Julia's now busy making her own little cold war with Angie.

An hour later, the whole of Rookhaven is clear of party fallout, not including hangovers.

"Perfect," says Julia, smiling as she looks around the living room.

"C'mon, Ol' Rusty hasn't been perfect since the Eisenhower administration," says Angie.

"Don't call this house Ol' Rusty," snaps Julia. "If you hate it so much, you can always leave."

"Who said anything about hating it?" says Angie.

"I like it just how it is," I say.

"I *love* it. And I love Brooklyn. I'm a lil' Brooklynista." Angie smiles sweetly at us all.

"Can we get some food, please?" I say to distract them from their almost-argument. "I'm starving."

"I'm making French toast!" That'd be Coco. She's been trying to force-feed us comfort food since we moved in. "Everyone in the kitchen!"

"I'll just be a minute," I say.

Time to deal with you-know-who.

"Hey." Mike is groggily stretching in my bed. He looks a lot better clean-shaven and in a pressed shirt. "Where've you been? You wanna snuggle?"

I laugh. "Snuggle?"

"All the cool kids are doing it. C'mon . . ."

I put on my aviators and take a deep breath. "Mike, your sister will kill me if she finds out about last night. Let's just pretend it didn't happen, okay?"

"Okay. Fine." Wow, he's bratty when things don't go his way.

"I'm serious. She doesn't like me as it is."

"She doesn't?"

"No . . ." Suddenly I realize that talking to Mike about his sister being a bitch isn't the smartest move. "Um, you know. I'm probably misinterpreting it."

"Maddy's pretty hard to read," he says. "She never lets her guard down. Even with me, and I'm family. I think it's insecurity."

I fight the urge to roll my eyes. I am so sick of people blaming everything on being insecure. It's not a get-out-of-jail-free card, you know?

"Whatever. We're all in the kitchen. Wait ten minutes and you can leave without being seen."

"Why don't I just climb out the window and shimmy down the drainpipe?"

"That would be perfect! Do you think you could?" I say, just to see his reaction. "Kidding. See ya."

Thank hell that's over with. I have more important things to worry about. Like being unemployed, broke, and cut off from the so-called

Bank of Mom and Dad (pay interest in guilt!) with the threat of being forced to leave New York in exactly eight weeks.

If a kitchen could be grandmotherly, then this one is. It's huge, yet also 1960s-sitcom-rerun cozy. The kind of kitchen in which cakes and cookies and pies are always baking, you know? My mother *never* baked.

As we're sitting around the kitchen table, listening to Lionel Richie and eating Coco's amazing French toast with bacon on the side, I finally tell the girls everything. About the Facebook photo, work, and even my parents.

"In a nutshell, I destroyed Rookhaven, and I'm unemployed, unemployable, and broke," I say, pushing my food around my plate miserably. "I don't know what to do. Who gets fired after one week? I'm such a fuck-up. . . . If I don't get a job, my parents will make me go live with them."

"You can't do that!" Somehow, Angie manages to look cool even talking through a mouthful of bacon. "You'd never survive! Your parents can't make you do anything."

"Yes, they can!" I say. "I've never stood up to them. I just do what they say, and then avoid them."

"Sounds healthy," Julia says.

I shrug. Is anyone's relationship with their parents healthy?

"I can't believe you were fired!" says Coco. "That must have been awful." She reaches over to give me a hug. For the second time today, I have to blink away tears. I swear I want to cry more when people are nice to me than when they're mean.

"Yuh," says Madeleine. "Who would have thought dancing topless at a party would backfire like that?"

"I was wearing a bra!"

"Pia, it was a sheer bra."

"Stop it, Maddy." Julia forks another piece of French toast onto her plate. I notice she hasn't said anything about not wanting me to move out.

"Listen, I have loads of cash, you won't go hungry . . . or thirsty." Angie picks up a piece of crispy bacon with her fingers and dips it in a pool of maple syrup, and then lowers her voice. "And I think the laundry room flooding might have been our, uh, my fault. I'll help pay for it."

"I can loan you money, too," says Julia quickly, her competitive nature kicking in.

"Don't be crazy." I can't accept charity. I won't. "If I need money that badly, I'll go to a bank. Get a loan."

"Are you crazy? Take a loan? You'd have some bananas interest rate, and the loan would just get bigger and bigger and you'd never be able to pay it back! So you'd have no credit rating! It would destroy your life!" Wow, Julia is really upset about the idea of a loan.

"Okay, jeez, I won't go to a bank," I say. "Anyway, that's really not the point. The point is, I need a job. And I just have no idea what I could do."

"What was your major?" asks Coco.

"Art history."

"Art . . . historian?"

Everyone at the table giggles.

"Yes, I chose a very impractical major. No, I don't know why."

"Probably because it sounded cool," says Angie, flashing me her best I'm-so-helpful smile.

I raise an eyebrow at her. "Not helping."

"I could see you working at a fashion magazine," says Coco, hopping off her chair. "Who wants more coffee?"

"Me please!" say Julia and Angie in unison, and frown at each other.

"I'm not a writer," I say. "Anyway, it would be all *Devil Wears Prada*–y. And the models would make me feel shitty."

"Besides, it's really hard to get a job in anything related to fashion," says Angie. For a second, I wonder if she knows that from personal experience. Before I can ask, she picks up her phone to read a text.

"And I need to earn money, *now*," I say. And, I add silently, it's a fact: the cooler the job, the worse the money. My salary at the PR agency— not even that cool compared to working in, like, fashion or TV or whatever—was thirty-five thousand a year, which, if you break it down and take out money for rent and bills, works out to about twenty-five dollars a day. I mean, a decent facial in New York is at least a hundred and fifty. How could anyone ever survive on that salary and still eat, let alone have a life?

Julia is in fix-it mode now. "Let's make a list of your skills and experience. What did you do at the PR agency last week?"

I think back. "I pretended not to spend all my time e-mailing my friends, sat in on meetings about things I didn't know anything about, and watched the clock obsessively. I swear I almost fell asleep, like, twenty times, right at my desk."

Everyone (except Madeleine) laughs at this, though, honestly, it was kind of depressing. Am I really meant to do that for the rest of my life?

"If you need fast cash, get a fast-cash job, girl," says Julia. "Waitressing. Bartending."

I blink at her. "Manual labor?"

Madeleine makes a snorting sound of suppressed laughter. I ignore her. I said it to be funny. Kind of.

"With that kind of princess attitude, you're screwed," says Julia.

"I want a real job. Something that will impress my parents, which means something in an office. Something with an official business e-mail address."

"So e-mail your résumé to PR recruitment agencies in Manhattan," says Julia. "Then wow them with how bright and smart and awesome you are. Any PR agency in Manhattan would be lucky to have you!"

"Okay." I love having a bossy best friend sometimes. It makes decision-making much easier.

CHAPTER 3

"Pia Keller?"

I stand up, smiling the hi-I'm-totally-employable smile that I've perfected during my previous fourteen recruitment agency interviews.

Bridget, the consultant who reluctantly agreed to "discuss options" with me, smiles thinly and offers a boneless handshake. My mother judges women on their shoes, but in the past week, I've learned to judge women on their handshakes. Limp is not a good sign.

I follow Bridget out of the reception area down a narrow hallway to a tiny meeting room. For a second, I consider turning around and walking out. I know exactly what's about to happen, and I almost can't bear to go through it again.

But I need a job. Fixing Vic's kitchen ceiling cost just over twenty-two hundred, which I split with Angie (she insisted, though I'm not sure the flooding was caused by her and Lord Hugh; the plumber said a drain was blocked with cigarette butts), and the last ten days has sucked up the five hundred dollars that were left, just on food and the subway and tampons and shampoo—you know, *stuff*. It is as painfully obvious as it is painful: New York is an expensive city. I have, as of this very second, exactly eight dollars to my name. And nothing left in my checking account. At all.

So walking out of this interview is not an option.

"Take a seat." Bridget takes a small bottle of sanitizer out of her pocket and rubs a glob between her palms. "Why don't you tell me about yourself?"

"Well." I try to look confident, and not like I am broke and desperate. "Um, my name is Pia Keller, I'm twenty-two years old, and I have a degree in art history from Brown—"

"Why art history?"

"I'm fascinated by the way that art reflects the political-social climate in which it was created," I say. That sounds good, right? "Sadly, it's not that useful, unless you want to be an art historian!" I smile. She doesn't. They never do. I should really drop that line.

"And your internships?"

"Uh, well, my parents live overseas, and we're a really close family, so I spent vacations with them, which unfortunately didn't leave much opportunity for internships." As you can probably guess, this isn't entirely true. I just never knew what kind of internship I'd want to do, and Angie always had something fun planned, so I joined her instead.

"And now you want to work in PR. Why?"

"I love public relations! I like helping to channel information to people through the right mediums, I like—" I pause, trying to remember again why I thought I'd like PR (because it sounded fun and I didn't know what else to do?). "Helping companies, I mean, brands, build the right image, and organize events that create a buzz in the marketplace, and make a difference to modern society." Oh, Pia. You utter tard. That was pathetic.

"Here's my problem, Pia." Bridget clasps her hands together like she's praying. "You are very young. You have no relevant qualifications. You have no experience. You have no skills. You are fundamentally unemployable."

"Um—"

"Why would any company pay you a monthly salary when you can't help them make money? Not to mention the time and human resources they'll waste training you. And they have no way of knowing if it'll even be worth it." She holds out her hands, palms up, as if testing for rain. "No experience. No job."

Every single interview I've had so far has ended right here. "But I can't get experience unless I have a job!" I can't keep the panic-squeak out of my voice. "What am I supposed to do?"

She offers a smug smile. Some people are inordinately happy to tell other people that they're screwed, have you ever noticed? "It's a tough market. It's the same across advertising, marketing, digital media . . . the roles are only going to the very best and brightest."

"Not me, then," I say, trying to get a smile.

A smile-free Bridget stands up. "Before you go, we have a ritual here that every candidate creates a digital intro of themselves, no matter how unpromising they are."

"A . . . what?" Unpromising? Bitch.

"A digital intro. For our records," she says, leading me into an open-floorplan office. She claps her hands to get the attention of her colleagues. "Everyone! This is Pia. Dave, do it!"

A guy with overly gelled hair points a digital camera at me. "Who are you? And what are you looking for?"

As the entire room stares at me, their expressions ranging from uninterested to indifferent, pure fear washes through me.

I *hate* public speaking. Even if my voice shows up, I hate myself for being so hopeless. It's like I'm standing beside myself saying "you are *such* a moron" the whole time.

I can't do this.

"Go!" says Dave.

"My name is," I start, and my voice breaks and disappears. My brain is *thumpety-thumpeting* as Dave's words ricochet around. *Who am I? And what am I looking for?*

"Speak up!" shouts Bridget.

I clear my throat quickly and start again, mumbling and racing through the words. "My name is Pia Keller. I'm twenty-two years old." They're all looking at me, all thinking how stupid I am. I want to look smart, I want them to remember me. Oh, God, the pressure. "And I'm looking for a job . . . I mean, I'm looking for a *career* . . . that, uh, I can love."

What a stupid thing to say, Pia. "That's what I . . . that's what . . . I'm . . . yeah."

Shut *up*.

Dave sits back down, making a little "Yikes!" face that he probably thinks I can't read. In the soul-crushing moment of silence that follows, I feel a shame so strong, it's painful.

Seconds later, they swivel back to their laptops. I am gone, forgotten, an irrelevant blip in their day. Another dumb graduate who can't string a sentence together.

At the elevators, I try to smile as I grasp Bridget's boneless hand.

I'll never get a job.

I'll never make any money. I won't be able to pay the rent for Rookhaven, not that it'll matter, because my parents will turn up and force me to move to Zurich with them, and get a boring-as-hell job, and I'll be alone, forever, for the rest of my life.

As the elevator doors close, I suddenly feel like the air is being sucked out from around me. I fall against the wall, trying to catch my breath. *Oh, God, please no, not a full panic attack, not now. . . .*

Then my stomach lurches and my face tingles and I know *exactly* what's going to happen in about three seconds.

I'm going to puke.

I press every button and the elevator lurches to a halt on the fifth floor, and I run out, frantically looking for a bathroom sign. Where is it, oh, shit, I'm going to be sick, I know it, I know it. . . .

A split second later, I throw myself onto my hands and knees, vomiting in an empty umbrella basket in front of an office doorway. It's an acidy, watery gush that I can't control, and when it's all out, I wipe my mouth with the back of my jacket arm and lean my forehead against the wall, panting with relief.

Why, hello, anxiety vomit. We meet again.

At least it wasn't a full-blown freak-out. I haven't had one of those in a couple of years, and not a really big one since, yep, you guessed it, August 26.

I look back down at my puke basket. I can't leave that here for someone else to clean up, right? It's gross.

Five minutes later I'm walking as confidently as I can out of the building onto Broadway, carrying a stolen umbrella basket of puke.

So.

Another stunning success of a meeting.

Yay me. Way to go.

As I always do when I'm in Manhattan, I look up, between the buildings reaching into the sky over my head. Have I mentioned that I *love* big cities, and New York most of all?

I do. The people, the traffic, the noise, the bars, the restaurants, that indescribable and chronically over-referenced *buzz*. . . . I love knowing that something is always going on, right around the corner.

I was born here, but we left when I was a little kid. So I never had that chance to *own* New York the way people who are born-and-bred do. I've never owned anywhere, really. I never belong.

I walk down Broadway, looking at all the people rushing past with cool faces and occupied minds. How did they get to where they are today? What do they have that I don't? Why does everyone else seem so *calm* about this whole adulthood thing? All I feel is panic, a tight flutter in my chest at the thought that I might not be able to do what everyone else finds so easy. . . . I might not be able to make a life for myself, a real life. Ever.

Maybe I should focus on what I want my life to look like, I muse, as I drop the stolen basket of puke into a garbage bin. Positive visualization, right?

I want to work hard, love my job, and be good at it. I really do. I want to earn my own money. I want a home (walk-in closet a must) of my very own, that no one can take away from me, and I want to keep my friends forever. Oh, and I want to date gorgeous guys, and one day do the whole marriage-babies thing, and so on and so forth.

How do I get from here to there? I'm jobless, penniless, and covered in puke.

I wish I could press fast-forward.

Sighing heavily, I begin my walk all the way back to Brooklyn. I can't afford a cab and it's too hot for the subway. My feet start blistering right after Canal Street, so I buy a pair of three-dollar sandals and hook my heels over the handle of my bag. I now have five dollars left. What can I get with five dollars? A couple of Jell-O shots? This is it. It's over. Then my stomach growls, so I spend my last five dollars in the world on a Fage yogurt and a Luna bar. No point in buying a cookie. A sugar crash would not improve my day.

When I'm walking over the Brooklyn Bridge, with Manhattan on one side of me and Brooklyn on the other, I make a decision. I have no money. I have no future.

I will just call my parents and tell them I'll move now.

Why does that feel so wrong? I feel like, I don't know, like maybe I am supposed to be here. Like maybe I *belong*.

As I'm walking past a long stretch of grass outside some old memorial, I see a homeless woman. Old, gray-haired, stooped, and, despite the heat, she's layered in grubby winter coats, and cardboard boxes are tied to her feet. Maybe I should offer her my sandals. I'm nearly home already, why not just walk the rest of the way in bare feet?

We make eye contact, and I smile at her. And for a second, I think she's going to smile back.

Then she opens her mouth.

"*You!*" she screams. "Go home! You're not welcome here!"

I immediately look away and keep walking. When I peek back, I see that she's started to walk toward me. I quicken my pace, and hear her cackling with laughter.

"I'm comin'! I'm comin'! Run!"

So I run.

As fast as I can.

But I don't know where I'm running to. Shit, where am I? I take the first left. Oh please let me find people. I don't even know where I'm going, another corner and— *Yes!* People! I always feel safe in a crowd. I try to run down Court Street, then some woman shoves me, jabbing me hard in my boob with her elbow. I gasp in pain, start sobbing uncontrollably and stop running. Big, fat tears are coursing down my face and I'm breathless and hiccupy, half from running and half because I'm scared and desperate and I just bombed yet another job interview and I don't know what's next.

I feel like I'm at the edge of an abyss. Do I turn around and go back, or do I jump and see what happens?

Then a cab pulls up next to me.

A guy in a suit gets out. He's so good-looking that I'm jolted out of my misery. Tanned skin, dark hair, the deepest blue eyes I've ever seen, and good eyebrows, eyebrows that almost make me wonder if he does something to make them so nice. . . . I can't help it. I stare.

Here's the weird thing. As if sensing my stare, the guy pauses, too, turns his head, and our eyes meet. My heart thumps so strongly, I put my hand up in front of it, almost automatically. Shit, maybe I'm having a heart attack.

The guy gives me a slow, easy smile and I smile back, thinking, *You're perfect.* I feel the strangest sense of déjà vu, like I've met him before, a genuine click of recognition.

And yes, that's a totally stupid thing to think.

"Hi," he says, his voice breaking halfway through. It sounds so strange that we both laugh. Then, one of my heels falls from my bag onto the sidewalk.

The guy immediately crouches down, picks it up, and, still on one knee, hands it to me. Like Prince freaking Charming. If I had a voice, I'd make a Cinderella joke. So instead, I lean over and take my shoe, my mouth still hanging open in stupid wonder.

Prince Charming frowns and is just opening his mouth to speak, when—

"Can you help me out, for God's sake, you ridiculous man?" shouts a female voice with a British accent, and boom, the spell is broken. He immediately turns to help the woman out of the cab: a brunette as gorgeous as he is, in tight jeans, heels, and a silk top, trailing scarves and bags in that effortlessly messy London way. *Girlfriend.* He has a girlfriend.

As soon as I see her, I put my head down and walk away, and I don't stop to see if he looks after me. I can hear her voice echoing down the street as they walk into Sweet Melissa Patisserie. "And I was like, why, you know? And— Ooh! Waffles! Bliss! And he said, look, darling, you always knew it was going to be like this—"

And then they're gone. The perfect man . . . and his perfect girlfriend. I still feel an endorphin rush from smiling at him, is that weird? It probably is. Not to mention shallow, after the end-of-days hysteria of a few minutes ago.

Then I glance up at my reflection in a store window and let out a wail: I am a mascara-stained, puke-puckered sweat rat. *Urgh.* Why do I only ever see cute guys when I look like an armpit?

Anyway, I can't do serious relationships. I haven't since the whole Eddie meltdown. Even my casual hookups have a tendency to bite me in the ass. (If you know what I . . . never mind.) I've ignored three texts and two calls from Mike since that Sunday. At least Madeleine hasn't found out about it. (Yet.)

"Well, if it isn't Little Miss Whole Person," says a voice. I look up. It's Vic, the raisiny old guy who lives downstairs.

"Hi! I mean, good evening! Mr.— uh—"

"Vittorio Bartolo," he says, with a flourish. "Call me Vic."

"I'm Pia . . . Pia Keller. And I'm really sorry, again, about your kitchen ceiling." I haven't seen him since that morning; Julia took over as a go-between. "Is it all, um, okay?"

"It's perfect. Thank you." He grins, and all those craggy crevices I noticed last Sunday morning move around his face again. Suddenly I have the feeling he found the whole thing kind of funny. "I'm sorry I called you a half a person the other morning. I didn't mean to offend."

"You didn't. How's your sister?"

"Marie's fine," he says. "She's with her grandkids over in New Jersey. She spends half the week with them, half with me. It makes her feel popular. So, are you going to tell me why you're huffing and puffing like you're gonna blow the house down? Oops, sorry. Wrong choice of words."

"Ha," I say. Quite the comedian, isn't he? "Um, I need a job. I need to make money."

"Welcome to New York," he says amiably. "It's nothing to cry about. Just get on with it. Your future is waiting for you."

"What if I can't? My life in New York will be over before it's even started."

"Not for nothing, but the way I see it, the only people who make any money in this world are entrepreneurs," he says. "Come up with an idea for a business, make it work, sell it on."

"That sounds doable . . . except the selling-it-on part. And the making-it-work part. Oh, and the coming-up-with-an-idea-for-a-business part."

Vic erupts into a wheezy laugh. For a second I'm scared he's going to collapse a lung.

"Actually, when I was fourteen, I tried to start a business," I say, remembering. "I made one-of-a-kind ripped jean shorts from second-hand jeans I bought real cheap on eBay, and sold them as customized vintage on Etsy."

"I don't know what any of that means."

"Yeah, no one did. They weren't that great. I sold about half of them." I sigh, remembering the dozens of dilapidated cutoffs falling out of every drawer in my room for months. Angie was supposed to help me out with the customizing part—she's good at stuff like that—but she flaked out on me. "And when I was eleven I tried to start a kids' club. We were on vacation in the south of France, and my idea was I'd organize activities for the younger kids staying in the same town. . . . Kind of like a party planner. But the other parents didn't believe that I was responsible enough to look after their kids so it, y'know, didn't take."

"Well, that sounds like it would have been a great idea."

We grin at each other for a second.

"You hungry?" he says, pointing down Court Street. "Esposito and Sons. Best rice balls in the neighborhood. We can talk about your career prospects on the way back."

Esposito's is an ode to the if-it-ain't-broke school of décor, and outside the front is a statue of a grotesque pig wearing a butcher's apron.

"Wow," I say. "Old school."

"It's been here since 1922," says Vic.

Everyone in Esposito's sings out "Vic!" when he comes in.

"Quite the celebrity," I murmur, almost to myself.

"I prefer neighborhood personality," he cracks back.

Vic orders four pork rice balls, an Italian sub, and a square of lasagne.

"You got it, chief," snaps the guy behind the counter. "Marie's away, huh? How's your cholesterol these days?"

"You breathe a word about this to my sister . . ."

I grin to myself, looking at the prepared food lined up behind the glass. This must be Vic's secret vice.

The counter guy turns to me. "What about you, Miss Pakistan? You want somethin'?"

"Miss Pakistan?" I repeat.

"Sorry. Miss World, is that better?"

Don't you just love being singled out for the color of your skin? But he'd probably call me Miss Sweden if I was blond. That's what I tell myself, anyway.

Counter guy is getting impatient. "C'mon, what'll it be, sweetie?"

This is like being in someone's home and refusing food they prepared just for you. But I haven't got any money left. Not a dime.

"Um, no, I'm . . ."

"You a friend of Vic's?"

"Yes," I say, at the same moment that Vic says, "Neighbor."

"Well, you're a lucky girl. Vic will look after you. Here you go, sweetie. On the house."

Minutes later we're walking out, a rice ball the size of a grapefruit in my hand.

"Great place," I say, taking a bite. "Oh, wow, this is so good!"

"It's the best. So, here's a thing. My nephew Angelo has a restaurant over on Smith. Bartolo's. My brother started it fifty years ago."

"Really?" I say, brightening.

"He'll give you a job. It's a real neighborhood restaurant. People there are good tippers, too. If you walk me up there right now, I'll introduce you," he says.

"Wow, thank you so much!" A waitress! I could be a waitress! My no-manual-labor stance of ten days ago looks pretty stupid right about now.

"It won't make you a fortune, but it's better than sitting on your keister moaning about life. Long as you're not afraid of a little hard work."

"No! I mean yes, I'm not, I mean— *Thank you*. I'm not afraid of hard work! That would be awesome!"

We walk slowly up Union Street, passing Rookhaven, toward Smith Street, enjoying the balmy evening.

"So, how ya settling into the place, anyway?"

"Um, fine."

I'm not sure what he means. I never settle; I just sleep somewhere for a while and then life changes and I sleep somewhere else.

I gaze up at the Brooklyn brownstones around me, at the trees arching up into the blue sky above our heads. Every house, every stoop, every window, is similar yet unique, with little individual touches from owners past and present. It's like everyone who's ever lived here has left their mark.

"Union Street is so beautiful," I say. "It feels personal, in a way that most streets never do. Every house is a home."

He nods. "It has character. That's why I never left, even when it was not an area that you'd want to be in, let me tell you. . . . My parents moved here from a little town called Pozzallo, in Italy, in 1922. A lot of people from Pozzallo came here; they even named a street after us."

"No kidding. Your parents moved all the way from Italy?" I say in surprise as we turn right onto Smith and keep walking. "Right here to Carroll Gardens?"

He grimaces. "Not Carroll Gardens. It's South Brooklyn, it's always been South Brooklyn. Not Carroll Gardens, not Cobble Hill, not BoCoCa."

"Yes, sir."

"My mother and father landed on Ellis Island in 1927 when they were just twenty-one years old. The trip was their honeymoon. They lived in the Lower East Side at the start, but got out of there real quick. Eventually, my father bought Rookhaven with his brother. Two families, five kids each, can you imagine? In that house?"

"No kidding. Then what happened?"

"Well, my father was killed in France in 1944."

"Oh, I'm so sorry," I say quickly.

"That's okay, it was a long time ago." Vic gives me his craggy grin. "His brother moved to Jersey. And my mother and her sister turned the place into a boarding house. We took in lodgers, mostly ex-servicemen."

"Wow." I wonder who was in my room. It's strange to think about decades—centuries, even—of people coming to New York to start their lives, just like we are. It's like nothing ever changes, not really.

We pause at Sackett Street and Vic gestures down another idyllic row of brownstones, pointing out where his cousins and friends lived.

"And my first girlfriend lived there." Vic points to a brownstone with high bay windows and rosebushes outside.

"Beautiful roses," I comment.

"I gave her that rosebush as a present on our second date."

"Nice move! So, what happened? You broke up?"

"I married her. She died."

I try to think of what to say, but can't, so I just link my arm through his instead. His arm feels a lot stronger than it looks. He must have been a big guy when he was young.

"And here we are!" he says a minute later. We're outside a stone-covered restaurant with a sign reading BARTOLO's in curly 1950s type-face.

Manual labor, here I come.

CHAPTER 4

After three days of working in the restaurant, my back aches, my feet are blistered, my ears are ringing with children's screams, and my hair smells like garlic.

But I'm earning money.

And that's what I need to do to stay in New York, with my friends, and start my life. I don't know what's next, but right now, I need this job to survive.

I'd never even have considered eating somewhere like Bartolo's before. And guess what? I *love* it. The entire place was designed, fitted, and decorated by Vic's brother and Vic a long time ago. As a result, the floor is uneven and worn, the plates and cups are all mismatched from sets bought long, long ago. There's a bad hand-painted mural of Italian countryside on the back wall, and Frank Sinatra, Tony Bennett, and Perry Como play on a never-ending loop.

But the restaurant has that same neighborhood warmth I noticed in Esposito's. Customers don't come here just because they've been told to by some ad campaign or because it's the flavor of the month. They come here because they know the food is good and the welcome is warm.

"*Pia!*" Angelo runs into the kitchen, where I'm gossiping with his cousins Ricky and Vinnie, the chefs. "Why the heck do I keep finding you in here? I need you on table three!"

"Sorry!" I flash my best smile.

"She was just helping us with the arugula salad." Vinnie finds arugula salad hilarious; it's the only new addition to the menu in the past decade. Meanwhile, apparently every other restaurant in Brooklyn is breeding organic hybrid lettuce in their backyard.

Actually, they were telling me all about Jonah, the cute bartender (think cowboy meets surfer, extra blond, extra hot). Tonight's our first shift together, and we've exchanged a few eye-meets, but I'm also detecting a little something between him and one of the other waitresses, Bianca (pinch-faced punk-hipster hybrid with a hot pink buzz cut on one side of her head and attitude to match—the kind of girl who just doesn't like other girls). According to Vinnie, nothing's ever happened between Bianca and Jonah. Ricky thinks she made a move last weekend and got rejected. (I swear to God, dudes are the worst gossips. I love it.)

At table three, a very pretty young mom and dad are sitting with their two kids and finishing up their pizzas. The little boy, who must be about three or four, is telling a story.

"And then, Mom? Mom? Mom? Mom, there was this dog, and the dog was sniffing"—he's so excited he can hardly get the words out—"and then he *pooped!*" He squeaks and falls off his seat giggling. I laugh and bend down to help him up.

"Oh, thank you," chorus the parents. They're both dressed in impeccable Brooklyn chic. I'm pretty sure his jeans cost more than I'll make tonight and her jacket definitely does.

"Gabe, no poop stories at the dinner table," says the mother, fighting to keep a straight face.

"I can't believe you just used the phrase 'poop stories,'" says the father in a low voice.

The dad turns to the little girl. "Pia, honey, no iPad while we're eating." She frowns and ignores him.

"Is your name Pia?" I say to the little girl, who is older than Gabe and has two little pigtails that look like she tied them herself. She nods shyly. "That's my name, too! We're like twins. Would you like to see the dessert menu?" I drop my voice to make it sound like a big secret. She nods again and puts the iPad away. I love kids. For six to eight minutes at a time.

"Oh, boy! Dessert!" squeals Gabe.

"Thank you." The mother smiles as I clear the table and hand them the kids' dessert menus. She can't be much older than thirty, I think with a jolt. That means she probably gave birth when she was about twenty-three. That's next year. Holy shit, I'm running out of time to be a young mom.

"Table five," hisses Angelo as I take the dirty plates to the kitchen. "More breadsticks."

"Thank you, new girl!" exclaims one of the men at table five, a paunchy guy with a strong Brooklyn accent, just like Vic's.

"No more bread for you," snaps the woman next to him. "Angelo! Easy on the carbs for this one!"

"I just do what I'm told," calls Angelo, whizzing past us without stopping.

"That's because he remembers me saving him from Conor Barry's fist back in the fifth grade!"

Half the tables in here tonight seem to have known Angelo, Ricky, and Vinnie for their whole lives. Brooklyn is the world's biggest village. Perry Como's "Papa Loves Mambo" comes over the music system, and I fight the urge to sing along.

I smile at table five. "Are you ready to order?"

"We'll have the sausages and peppers, the chicken romano, the double garlic spaghetti, a big white pizza for the kids—don't worry, Ricky will know what I mean. Keep the garlic bread coming, and tell Vinnie: extra sage and onion salt."

"You got it," I say. Ordering off-menu in a tiny trattoria. Ballsy.

"I want juice!" screams the freckled kid next to him.

"Last time you had juice you started drooling and humping the table," says Carb Guy. "No."

"He's sugar sensitive!" exclaims his wife.

"He's a sugar junkie," says Carb Guy.

I struggle not to laugh (waitressing is the best people-watching, ever) and write everything down. I smile at them all as I repeat it, and they smile back. I head to the kitchen to hand in their order with a goofy grin still stuck on my face. I never expected to love waitressing so much. It's sort of like paid socializing.

"Miss! Excuse me, miss?" I turn around and see a table waving at me frantically. They're not in my section, but their waitress, Bianca, has disappeared. I hurry over with a smile.

Two men, two women, all somewhere in their forties, wearing T-shirts and too-short shorts. They're surrounded by shopping bags that they've tied together with a shoelace—in case someone steals one, I guess? Tourists, without question, staying at a local hotel to avoid the expense of staying in Manhattan. Immediately I steel myself. There've been four or five similar tourist-filled tables over the past few days, and each time, they treat me like a second-class citizen. I'll give you one guess why.

"How may I—"

"Menus?" says one of them loudly, a man with "Pete's Gym" written on his cap. He's sweating profusely from the energy it takes his body just to exist. "We need *menus.*"

"We want to *order?*" enunciates his wife carefully, a frowsy blonde with a non-ironic fanny pack. She makes a big square in the air with her hands.

"Menu! Hungry!" says Pete's Gym again, pointing to his mouth and making a *chompy-chomp* motion with his jaw.

I smile tersely, turn around, and grab them some menus. If they're going to assume I don't speak English, I'm not going to bother to correct them. I drop the menus off with a smile and head back to the kitchen to get the first rounds of garlic bread for table five. Then I run the desserts over to table three, where Pia, the little girl, is now singing a song about mud.

"Thanks, Pia!" she shouts.

"No problem, Pia!" I call back.

I head back to the tourist table, as Bianca still isn't around. They order, still shouting and enunciating their words as though I'm an idiot. I just smile and write everything down. There is no point in rising to it.

Then I hear this:

"Lordy, there are so many of them in New York," murmurs Fanny Pack. "I wouldn't feel safe, I really wouldn't. . . ."

They think I'm threateningly exotic-looking, possibly Middle Eastern, probably Muslim, and therefore, I pose a threat to national security. I should be used to it, but my heart starts hammering with anger/anxiety/ [insert your extreme emotion of choice HERE], and before I can say anything, I'm bumped out of the way by Jonah, the hot bartender.

"Good evening, folks! I'm Jonah, and I'm here to take your drinks order. *You* sir, look like the kind of man who would be in charge of wine." Jonah's Texan drawl makes the out-of-towners feel right at home. "Am I right?"

"We don't drink." Fake Nails smiles at Jonah like he's the second coming of Billy Graham.

"Four large Diet Cokes," says Pete's Gym.

"No ice in mine," interrupts the other guy, staring at my boobs. Sheesh, I hate that. "They try to cheat you out of the drink with extra ice," he adds, not quite under his breath.

"No ice in any of them," says Biggest Fattest, winking at Boobs Guy.

"Very good, sir, and may I say, inspired choice." Jonah is really oozing Texan charm now. "Aspartame is exceptional this time of year. I'll send your waitress right over with them. . . ."

Jonah grabs me by the waist and hustles me away.

"Where the hell is Angelo when you need him?"

"They said . . . they were—" I'm stammering with rage as we get to the bar.

"I know. Well, I don't know, but I can imagine."

"How?" I snap. "Tell me, blondie, how often do you get mistaken for a crazy jihadist?"

"Calm down, princess." Jonah fills up four glasses with Diet Coke. "They're just ignorant. Bianca!"

"Wha'?" says Bianca, sauntering in from the back, followed closely by the smell of cigarettes. "I was on the phone with my business manager."

"Cosmo?" says Jonah. "He's a loan shark. Don't big him up."

"He's nice!" exclaims Bianca, punching Jonah playfully. Flirting for beginners.

"Please tend to your table," I say through gritted teeth.

"Chill," says Bianca, picking up the tray of drinks.

I glance at Jonah. "My name is Pia, by the way. Not princess."

"I know," he says, flashing a whiter-than-white movie-star smile. "Princess suits you."

I look over. Bianca is serving the Diet Cokes. Everyone at the table is leaning forward, whispering to her intently, glancing over at me.

I can't breathe, I feel sick, oh shit, I think I'm having an anxiety attack. Not again, please God. . . .

Bianca walks back toward us, mouth pursed. "What did they say?" I manage to ask.

"Ignore them."

"Tell me what they said."

She sighs. "They asked to make sure you didn't touch their food. Forget about it, it's not a big deal."

I stare at her for a second. How can she say that? "Yes, it is. It's always a big deal."

You know, I'm used to the comments, the assumptions that I don't speak English, the constant "where are you from?" question. It's annoying, and it's just the way it is. I don't look like everyone else. I get it.

But this is more than that. This is racism. When I was younger, attitudes like theirs scared me and made me feel sick. Then it upset me, so I would pretend I hadn't heard and run away.

Not this time.

I've had a really bad couple of weeks, and, yeah, my problems are all of my own making, but I'm doing the best I can to make my life better. I don't need this shit. People can judge me on my inexperience, my princess attitude, my lack of sound decision-making skills when under the influence of tequila. . . . Judging me on my skin color is wrong. And that's all there is to it.

"Call me . . . irresponsible," croons Sinatra over the music system.

Taking off my little white apron and putting it on the bar, I walk leisurely and deliberately over to their table.

I lean over, hands on my knees, and start talking, in my sweetest voice.

"I'm American, you morons. I was born in New York, I have an American passport, and the reason I look like I do is that I'm half-Swiss and half-Indian. Indians are Hindu, not Muslim, and the two religions are completely opposed to each other. Whether I am Muslim, Buddhist, Orthodox Greek, or worship at the altar of Spongebob fucking Squarepants, I still have the right to serve your meal without getting this racist abuse. Moreover, none of it would be any of your business, because it's a free country. And you?" I turn to Boob Guy. "These were not invented for your visual pleasure. Get your filthy eyes off them. And get the hell out."

I stand back, flushed and trembling.

With barely a murmur, they leave the restaurant, shuffling out as fast as their chafing thighs can carry them.

Oh Jesus. I just kicked out paying customers. I don't know where Angelo is, but it won't be long until he hears. I'm fucked.

"You okay?" says Jonah, who is suddenly standing behind me. I wonder how long he's been there.

"I really hate confrontation," I say, my voice suddenly shaky.

Jonah laughs, his shaggy blond hair falling in front of his eyes. "Well, Pia, I'm no expert, but I'd say you're exceptional at it."

I meet his eyes. "I'm screwed when Angelo finds out. He has to fire me for that. Heck, *I'd* fire me for that."

"So would I. And you owe me a tip for losing my table," says Bianca on her way past.

"Oh, God," I murmur.

"Who cares," says Jonah, all reassuring Texan charm. "I'm guessing this wasn't your ultimate dream job?"

"No, but I need it. I have a cash-flow problem."

"Join the club. I'm only doing this to fund acting classes."

"Actor, huh?" Every bartender in New York is an actor. What, they couldn't find a plane going to L.A.?

"I dance, too!" he says, doing the soft-shoe shuffle.

Then Angelo taps me on the shoulder.

"Pia, we need to talk. I'm sorry, but I'm gonna have to let you go."

"C'mon, are you serious?" says Jonah. "You can't fire her for standing up for herself."

"I have no choice but to fire her, I need to keep their hotel happy to ensure repeat business. They send a lot of recommendations our way. . . ." Angelo clasps his hands together anxiously. He's really a nice guy. I can see he hates doing this. "I'll pay you for tonight, you can keep your tips. No hard feelings?"

I sigh deeply and close my eyes. I'm so tired.

"Uh . . . hey, Pia?" says a voice. I look up. It's the cool young mom from table three.

"Hey," I say, trying to smile. "How can I help? Oh, God—the check?"

"No, don't worry, we've left enough for the check. I wanted to give you this personally," she says, slipping some money in my hand. "I also wanted to tell you that we saw—and heard—the whole thing, and you were great. And *illegitimus non carborundum,* and all that."

"Thank you! 'Don't let the bastards get you down,' huh?" My father says the same bastardized Latin quote when he's feeling wild and wacky. It's one of our few family jokes.

"Exactly," she says, laughing. "I'm Lina, by the way."

"Pia."

"I know."

"Um, oh . . . yeah." She shakes my hand warmly.

"Okay, well, take care." Lina turns and heads to the door, where her husband and the two kids are standing and waiting.

"Bye, Pia!" screams the little girl, waving enthusiastically. I wave back, and when they've left, look at the money in my hand. Two hundred dollars! That plus my earnings and tips from the last three nights puts me in at almost seven hundred. Not bad. But not enough to cover rent this month. Or bills. Or, you know, life.

"Okay, princess, I have an idea," says Jonah. "Firstly, drink this." He hands over a glass. "It's a gimlet. My speciality." I take a slug and nearly choke: it's basically pure gin.

"And B, come with me to my Saturday jobs tomorrow, dude! You'll see there are loads of easy ways to make good cash in Brooklyn. I'll split my earnings with you, fifty-fifty."

He's flirting with me. Even through the hit of gin I can see it.

"What kind of jobs?"

"It's a surprise, princess," Jonah says. "I will tell you, however, that the first job is sweet and buzzy. Just get to Williamsburg by 6:00 A.M. C'mon! What have you got to lose?"

He's right. And he's cute. And I need the cash.

I shake his hand. "Done."

When I get home, it's still early. Coco, Madeleine, and Julia are in the kitchen, as usual. We've somehow adopted the kitchen as the Rookhaven hub. Dinners, cards, chatting: everything happens here.

"Hey guys." I nod at them, grab Coco's *Us* magazine, and perch myself up on the kitchen bench. Sometimes being in a group is comforting, even if you don't feel like talking.

Coco is carefully measuring flour into a pink bowl, and there's a saucepan of asparagus risotto on the stove. Julia and Madeleine are at the table, both still wearing their suits and drinking wine—which, by the way, I've never seen Jules drink before, it must be part of her I'm-an-adult-now thing. They look clean-cut, upwardly mobile, happy, and employed. Yins to my yang.

"Hey P-Dawg!" Julia continues her story. "And they were, like, we need it by end of play! And I was, like, okay, no one told me that, of course I can do it."

"And?"

"Nailed it."

They high-five excitedly, like something out of goddamn *Wall Street*.

"How was work, Peepee?" says Julia, turning to me. "They let you off early, huh?"

"Yup." I pretend to be deeply interested in the magazine.

Julia gets up and helps herself to another bowl of risotto, and looks over at Coco. "Cupcakes?"

"No, lemon chiffon cake. Angie said cupcakes were so effing over," says Coco.

"There are cool and uncool baked goods?" Julia laughs and chokes on some risotto.

"Chew your food, Jules," says Madeleine. "Slow down."

"Too starving. In fact, I have been starving all day. I've eaten every, like, two hours since I got to my desk at seven in the morning. I only get up to pee or go to the vending machine."

"Me too. I ate a salad sandwich at my desk, just like my boss, and got a killer sugar crash in the afternoon."

Eat more protein at lunch, I think. Cut down on simple carbs like white bread. I once read a magazine article that said that avoiding sugar crashes was the secret to staying slim, and from what I can tell, it's true.

I love food, but I go easy on the sugar. And I never think about my weight much, unless my jeans get tight, and then I just eat more meat and less carbs for a week or two. The only person I know who eats whatever she wants and never gains weight is Angie. As a result she has zero body issues. If I didn't love her so much, it would be kind of annoying.

"Argh, sugar crash! I buy mid-afternoon candy for my team. Sweetness means love," says Julia. "Right, Coco?"

We all look over at Coco who is stirring and humming happily, lost in her thoughts.

"I haven't really made friends at work yet," says Madeleine.

"Give it time, dude!" says Julia. "The first people you meet are usually losers, anyway. Remember when I was interning at Morgan Stanley, and made friends with that chick from Long Island? Oh yeah, we used to go to Century 21 together at lunch and everything. Then I realized she was boring and because I was hanging out with her, everyone thought I was really boring, too. Social death by association."

"Okay," says Madeleine obediently.

"Oh, no!" shrieks Coco. "We're out of butter." We all look over. She gets really worked up about baking. "It's okay! I'll improvise."

Julia frowns. "By the way, while I'm thinking of it, why am I the only person who seems to notice when we run out of toilet paper and house stuff? We're starting a kitty jar for essentials, and Coco, you need to stop making food for everyone unless they've chipped in for it, okay?"

"I don't mind," says Coco.

"That's not the point," says Julia. "We all live in Rookhaven and it needs to be fair. Okay?"

Angie saunters in on her way out for the evening, looking insanely cool in five-inch heels and a long, white silk dress covered in black paint splotches. The dress is obviously expensive, probably stolen from her socialite mother, and customized by Angie. It's the kind of thing she does.

"Hey, kittens," she says casually, digging in her handbag, presumably for cigarettes.

"How was your day?" asks Coco shyly.

"Aces, if you exclude the parts that included the Bitch. I never knew arranging food photoshoots could be so boring yet stressful. Boressful."

Angie props an unlit cigarette in the side of her mouth, then starts tying her hair back into a knot. The Bitch is, obviously, her boss. Apparently she's Dutch and very demanding. "I'll have the last laugh. Every time she sends me to Starbucks for a nonfat latte, I get full-fat instead." Madeleine gasps in shock.

Coco stirs the saucepan. "Would you like some risotto?"

"Ah, Miss Coco, you are the best," says Angie, leaning over and eating a spoonful straight from the saucepan. "Amaze. Maybe when I get home later, sugar-pants, I ate a lot of sashimi today."

"You eat so much raw fish, you're like a fucking dolphin," says Julia.

"And how can you afford it?" says Madeleine. "Good sushi is expensive."

"My boss orders in for herself but never eats it. Why let it go to waste?" Angie fixes herself a vodka on the rocks, adding a squeeze of lemon from Coco's cake ingredients. "Anyway, I survived on brownie batter and wine during final semester. I'm trying to restore the nutritional karma."

"That's nothing, one Spring Weekend I ate every single thing on the menu at Taco Bell," says Julia. "Twice over." God, she's competitive.

"Sounds wicked cool. Okay, I'm heading into Manhattan for drinks with Lord Hugh, if anyone wants to join me. Pia? Why the hell are you so quiet?"

I take a deep breath. "I can't go out tonight. I'm getting up at 5:30 tomorrow. I've got a job. Or a date. I can't tell what it is. And I was fired. Again."

There's a shocked silence.

"Bartolo's *fired* you? Oh, honey, are you okay?"

"You're working at 5:30 tomorrow morning? Who the fuck works at 5:30 on a Saturday morning?"

"Who the fuck *dates* at 5:30 on a Saturday morning?"

"Tell us everything, now."

CHAPTER 5

It's dawn. Jonah and I are on a rooftop in Williamsburg, for our job-slash-date. He met me outside this building with two takeout coffees, beamed a big sleepy smile at me, and wouldn't tell me what we were about to do.

The thought crossed my mind that he could have nefarious plans for me. Then I saw that he was wearing a Care Bears T-shirt and pale pink canvas shorts tied with a piece of rope, and realized that any man who dresses like a Huckleberry Finn hipster cannot possibly be evil.

And now, as I sip my coffee—God, I love coffee—I can't stop looking over the river at Manhattan. It's so beautiful in the early morning sunlight, it looks practically CGI.

I can't leave Rookhaven, I can't leave New York. I want my life here too much, and more than that, I'm . . . I'm *hungry* for whatever it is that's waiting for me.

I just don't know what that is.

"Beautiful, huh?" says Jonah, joining me as I gaze out over the city.

"It's amazing," I say.

"I read somewhere that the philosopher Descartes says that a great city should be 'an inventory of the possible,'" says Jonah. "A place where anything can happen. Where you never know what's coming next."

"I love that," I say.

"Turn around, and say hi to the girls."

The girls?

Suddenly I see three hip-height blocks in the corner of the rooftop. I squint into the dawn sunlight and squeal. "Watch out! Bees!" I almost leap into Jonah's arms.

"Relax, pussycat." He pulls a mesh-covered safari hat out of his bag. "You're not scared of bees, are you? If you're going to be a wuss about it, wear the wuss hat."

I ignore the wuss hat, though, actually, I *am* scared of bees. "No, no, I'm fine. So . . . what are we doing?"

"We're beekeeping."

I nod, trying to look cool. Of course we are. We're in New York City. Why wouldn't we be beekeeping?

"I look after the hives for my buddy Ray," says Jonah, picking up a metal watering can contraption. "He runs a restaurant downtown. Nail it today, you can take over this job."

Pia Keller, beekeeper? "So, we're going to . . . milk the hive?"

Jonah lets out a loud laugh. "Are you serious?"

"No," I add quickly. I hate it when I say stupid shit. "I mean . . . so what are we doing?"

"We're going to check the supers," he says, igniting the metal watering can. "This is a smoker. The smoke makes them sort of stoned, so they don't mind when we check out their living quarters. Just be slow and quiet."

Then a bee lands on my arm and I run to the other side of the rooftop, squealing.

"Dude! Seriously!" says Jonah. "You'll scare them!"

"Sorry!"

"Just do what I tell you to do," says Jonah. Our eyes meet for a second, and he arches an eyebrow. Flirty McFlirterson. This *is* a date. But do I like Jonah like that? I don't think I do.

Suddenly I think of the guy I saw on Court Street, the Prince Charming wannabe with the ridiculously nice eyebrows and the loud British girlfriend. . . . Ugh! Why am I even thinking about him? After all, he's taken, and I'll never see him again. And I don't do relationships.

Why?

Well, his name was Eddie. And he was my first love. (Cringe, I know. There's no other way to say it.) I was sixteen, and had arrived at my third boarding school shell-shocked and miserable after being kicked out of my previous two schools, not to mention the ensuing parental hellstorm. Then I met Eddie. When we were together, I felt calm for the first time in my life. We just, I don't know, clicked. And he helped me study, stopped me from partying, got my life back on track. More than that, he made me feel happy, safe, understood . . . I felt *rescued*. He told me I rescued him, too—from the cookie-cutter New England girls he'd grown up with, from never laughing till he cried, from the suffocation of being popular yet lonely as hell. It was all bullshit, of course. The only person who you can ever rescue is yourself.

Anyway.

Just as we were about to meet up for the first time all summer before heading off to college (him to Berkeley, me to Brown), he broke up with me. Over the phone! His exact words: "Pia, let's face it. You're a flight risk, it's never gonna work. I'm just doing this before you do."

Even now, just thinking about it, I feel like I've been slapped. He dumped me because I was too fickle, too irresponsible, too untrustworthy. He dumped me because of who I am . . . or who he thought I was, anyway, and since he knew me better than anyone, it's the same thing, right?

I'd never known I could feel pain like that. Even remembering it now makes my throat ache with a big, painful tear-lump. You know that feeling?

I was staying with Angie in Boston at the time and had the biggest anxiety attack of my life. I thought I was dying. I couldn't breathe, my heart was racing, everything was spinning, and all I could think was *it's over it's over.* . . . Angie ran in minutes later, though it felt like hours. She told me later she'd heard a strange moaning sound I don't even remember making.

The next few weeks were . . . indescribable. I think that when a relationship ends, it's a little bit like a death, and I was beside myself with grief.

Angie doesn't really do heart-to-hearts, but God, she was amazing during that time. . . . She listened while I boozed and ranted. She held my hair back when I puked and stockpiled Kleenex for my tears. She reprogrammed my iPod so I didn't have to listen to songs that reminded me of Eddie. She picked me up at the end of each night, carried me home, and put me to bed. She was, quite simply, the perfect best friend.

Then I started college, and decided to never talk about it again. It was the only way to contain my misery and act like Little Miss Happy Party Girl.

So that's the Eddie story. That's why I'm always single and only have casual flings. Why would I ever want to go through heartbreak again?

Urgh. I hate it when I think about Eddie. My brain goes back to him, over and over again, like when you're eight and you have a tooth that's about to fall out and you just wiggle it constantly.

But unlike a tooth, Eddie never falls out of my head.

My reverie is interrupted by Jonah walking up to me and tweaking my nose. "You want to see the honeybees, princess?"

Wearing woolen gloves, Jonah takes the lid off a hive and pulls up a wooden tray. It's thick with honeycomb and crawling with drowsy stoned bees.

"I guess you gave them a buzz," I say, slapping my thigh with delight at my own joke.

"You are hil—wait for it—arious. Okay, check it out," he says. "This one is full of honey. It kind of blows my mind. Give bees a home, and in return they create the sweetest thing in the world."

"What kind of flowers do they eat?" I ask, trying not to flinch every time a bee buzzes near me. "Have sex with. Whatever. Pollinize. Pollinate. You know what I mean."

"Any flower, really, or fruit trees, berry bushes," he says. "They fly up to four miles for their pollen, so that could get them to Central Park. And there's the Brooklyn Botanic Gardens for the lazy bee, of course."

I watch a fat little bee do two perfect figures of eight around the crowd, rubbing its fuzzy, chubby little body against its neighbors in a kind of soft-shoe shuffle.

"They're so beautiful up close," I say softly. "So busy and happy. They're sort of comforting, you know?"

I stop myself, realizing that I've probably said something stupid again. I catch Jonah's eye, but he's not laughing. Instead, he leans in to kiss me, then at the last moment, something inside me says *nope* and I pull away.

Thank God, Jonah takes it like a man. "I love the smell of rejection in the morning!"

I laugh. "Sorry, dude. I'm just not . . ."

"Nothing to apologize for," he interrupts. "Easy come, easy go, sailor. Let's get to work."

A couple of hours of honey-milking later, I've decided beekeeping is definitely not for me. It's too dangerous (or I'm too wussy, whatever). I spent most of the time running back and forth over the rooftop whenever bees landed on me. Now we're in Jonah's beat-up old car, the sun is shining, and I've got a basket of hand-labeled Kings County honey jars on my lap.

"Baby, you're a *fiyaaawork*!" sings Jonah along to Katy Perry on the radio.

"I feel so awake! It's so much fun to *do* something!" I say. "I love it!"

"What's life usually like for you, princess?" asks Jonah, laughing. "You just sit back and let slaves feed you grapes, or what?"

"Ah, bite me. This car is disgusting, by the way." It's filled with empty food wrappers and smells like feet.

"This? This is nothing. You should see my apartment. I share it with five other dudes, it's like a petri dish of disease. The other guys are always getting sick, but not me!" He grins proudly. "Constitution of a Texas buffalo."

Ew. Guys our age are so happy to live like pigs. I don't get it.

"So, how do you fit in all these jobs around your acting career?"

"Dude, I wouldn't call it an 'acting career.' I've been here six years and nothing's really happening. Still, I'm having fun. Sometimes I help out my friend's band, Little Ted. I take acting classes sometimes, the rest of the time I just mess around."

"Cool," I say, though actually, six years of just messing around sounds kind of depressing. "What was your last acting job?"

"Diesel ad campaign." He's trying to sound cool and failing.

"A TV commercial?"

"Uh, no. Web."

"A Web site campaign? Isn't that modeling?"

"No, it was moving image. It was acting."

I'm doubtful about this (my motivation in this scene is *denim*!), but never mind.

At that moment, my phone rings.

I stare at the screen for a second, then press silent. It's my parents. I haven't spoken to them since the post-party phone-call disaster, and I don't want to start now.

A minute later, my phone beeps. A message. May as well get it over and done with.

My dad starts speaking first. "Ah, Pia, it's . . . 2:45 P.M. in Zurich, which makes it 8:45 A.M. in New York, you're probably still in bed"—No, I'm not, I'm *working,* I think defiantly—"We're calling to tell you that we'll be in New York in October."

My mother interrupts him from the extension. "And unless you have a job, a real job, you are coming back to Zurich with us where we can look after you!"

Then my father interrupts her again. "We will call you tomorrow. Try to be awake and sober."

Click.

I press "delete," hang up, and sigh.

Now, I know thousands of girls my age are totally independent from their parents, they'd just tell them to back off and cut all ties. . . . I don't want to do that. Part of me still hopes that maybe, one day, the weird estrangement of the past few years will end. After all, they're the only parents I've got. I really want them to be proud of me. Most of the time, I don't even think they like me.

I look out the window, lost in thought. Suddenly the sunshine looks kind of bleak. Who am I kidding? I can't make a career out of goddamn bee-milking. I need a job, a real job . . . and fast.

"Today is a special day for lucky guys and gals," says Jonah in a radio announcer voice. "It's Food Truck Festival at the Brooklyn Flea! And that's where you, Pia Keller, will be working! Do you know the Brooklyn Flea?"

"Of course!"

Actually, I only went to the Brooklyn Flea for the first time a couple of weeks ago, with Angie and Coco in tow. It's a gigantic collection of tented stalls selling everything from vintage stuff to design stuff to art stuff to, well, there's just a lot of stuff.

Then I pause. "Wait, what's a Food Truck Festival?"

"Jeez, you really are new here, aren't you?" he says. "Food trucks are trucks that drive around the city selling—wait for it—food."

"Well, duh," I say, blushing. "Like ice-cream trucks."

"Think bigger," says Jonah, pulling into a parking space.

"Kebab trucks," I say as we get out of the car. "Oh, I think I saw a cupcake truck once in SoHo."

"Bigger."

We walk down the street, toward a sign saying BROOKLYN FLEA FOOD TRUCK FESTIVAL, and now I know what he means by bigger. Lined up, one after the other, like gigantic colorful shiny toys: food trucks of every possible description.

Gobble Cobblers, Mac'N'Cheese, Schnitzeldog, Lang Kwai Fried Dumplings, The Spelthouse, Mexineasy, The Artisan Cheesemakers, Everyone Hates Offal (with the strapline "Fry Me a Liver!"), The Queen's English Trifle Guild, Screamfer Ice Cream, Mash and Stew in It, Simple Simon the Pieman, Macaroonatics. . . .

"Punny," I comment. "How do they make all that food in the back of the truck?"

"They have elves," says Jonah.

"I'm getting hungry," I add, looking up at him.

"Just you wait, sugar."

People are already waiting patiently in line to get their food before a long day at the market. Wow, people will do anything for a good meal in this city. These trucks must be raking in the cash.

Jonah stops outside a dark green food truck with A MEAL GROWS IN BROOKLYN painted on the side in white block letters. The side awning is up, revealing a short, handwritten chalkboard menu.

BREAKFAST

French Toast with Raisin Bread (DUMBO)

Bacon (Mill Basin) with Fried Eggs (Brooklyn Heights)
on Buttered Sourdough (DUMBO)

Buttermilk Cake Donuts (DUMBO)

And it's ALL local, sustainable, seasonal, grass-fed,
hand-reared, and organic whenever possible!

"This is Ray's brother Phil's truck. The specialty is bread, but almost everything is made, grown, killed, or cured in the borough. Get it? A Meal Grows in Brooklyn."

"Actually, the raisins are from California," says a red-headed guy coming out from behind the truck. He's one of those aggressively ironic early-thirties Brooklynites who has a handlebar mustache and wears vintage cowboy shirts. Phil and Jonah do a little man handshake-hug combo, and Jonah introduces me. Apparently Phil runs an organic bakery-slash-café in DUMBO, and has the truck on the weekends for fun.

"Everything is grown right here in Brooklyn?" I ask skeptically.

"Brooklyn is full of food, *ma petite.*" Phil peers into the basket. "Dang, those bees are acing it! I love it when my brother has a good idea. Of course, that's also probably why Ray is richer and more successful."

"He can't grow a 'stache like you, though," says Jonah. "Do you miss the beard?"

"Not so much," says Phil, twirling his scarlet mo. "Anyway! Let's see . . . ricotta cheese and honey flame-toasted sourdough?" He raises his voice. "Lara? Sweetie? Do we have that ricotta?"

"Yep," says Phil's wife, a pretty woman with messy hair, strolling out from the back of the truck.

"Sourdough from our organic bakery in DUMBO, handmade ricotta from a friend of mine in Fort Greene, honey from Williamsburg. Brooklyn food. Get it?"

"Got it." I nod smartly.

"How's the eggs and bacon coming along, honey?"

"Small problem." Lara gets the giggles. "We forgot the eggs." I get the feeling this isn't the first time they've forgotten something.

"Plain bacon sandwiches?" says Phil doubtfully. "Yawn. Any ideas, guys?"

"Bacon . . . um . . . and bacon?" says Jonah.

"What about bacon sandwiches with chili jam?" I say. It's a favorite of mine. Eddie used to make it when we were hungover on vacations, using sweet chili sauce from a bottle. "Breakfast of champions, Keller," he'd say, pulling me onto his lap to eat it with him, one bite each at a time. Then we'd go out for gingerbread lattes, which are actually disgusting, I swear to God. Eddie said they tasted like the holidays. Urgh, stop thinking about him.

"Yes! I love creative thinkers! Okay, go explore, you two. I'll need you at noon."

So Jonah and I wander around the Brooklyn Flea, munching on the ricotta and honey sandwiches.

"So where are you from, princess?" says Jonah, his mouth full of food. "Ricky and Vinnie told me all about you, said you were European, but I thought you were Indian or Pakistani or something."

Or something? "Uh, I was born in the States. We moved countries a lot, if that's what you mean," I say, as we pass a stall selling antique mirrors that would look really cute in the hallway at Rookhaven. I should come back when I have money. If I ever have money.

"Oh, yeah? That's gotta be weird."

I roll out the usual responses. "School is school, no matter where you are. Study hall, after-school clubs, homework. . . ."

"You never went to school in the States?"

"Yes, I did. From twelve onward I went to boarding school here . . . three, actually." I pick up some jewelry made from old typewriter parts. "Cool, look at this stuff!"

"Three? Dude, that is seriously weird! Where are your parents from?"

Weird. Again. How can I possibly ever feel like I belong anywhere when people always point out that I'm different? "My mother is from

India. My dad's from Switzerland, but he lived in the States for, like, thirty years. He's a lot older than my mother."

"Is that why your eyes are green? From your dad?"

"I guess." My eyes are a funny jade color; when I was growing up everyone thought they were contacts and I'd have to practically poke my eye out to prove they weren't.

"So you speak, like, three languages?"

"Not really."

"So, like, where is home?"

I fight the urge to groan. "Wherever I lay my hat, baby." It's one of my standard responses to that unanswerable question. I don't know where home is. Why does everyone care about home so much? Because once they know where your home is, they think they know who you are?

"Man, your life is freaky."

"Mmmhmmm." I start looking through vintage fur coats. I can never explain what it is like to be me. Only Eddie ever really understood me, and he rejected me.

God, this conversation is depressing me.

"You must miss your parents a lot."

"Uh, yeah . . ." I never miss anyone, I'm just used to saying good-bye. But people think you're so cold and hard when you say that.

"And I bet you were one of the popular girls at all your schools."

"Yeah. I was a total Heather."

Okay, so I sort of hung out with the popular crowd, but I was never really one of them. How could I be? Those girls had been wearing the same clothes, getting the same highlights, taking the same vacations to the Hamptons and Martha's Vineyard since they were born. I just didn't fit in: the color of my skin was different, my clothes were different, everything. The only way to survive was to float above the fray, without being an outcast, and that meant always looking like I was happy, no matter what. And then I met calm, steady Eddie, and real happiness was easy. For a while.

Jonah picks up a pith helmet and tries it on. Nice biceps. For a second I imagine licking his arms, imagine him on top of me in bed . . . I wonder if it is normal to fantasize about sex with dudes I'm not romantically interested in. Julia would say no. Angie would say yes.

"I'm hungry again," says Jonah. "Wanna split a hot dog? Double ketchup! I once drank a gallon of ketchup for a bet. I won!"

And *phloof*! My Jonah sex fantasy is gone. Just then I see Angie about twenty-five feet away, in a tiny blue tea dress, holding the arm of an older Euro-trashy guy I've never seen before. Probably French, from the looks of his slightly too-short jeans.

Just as I'm about to shout to get her attention, Angie slaps him across the cheek. He pushes her hand away sharply and says something dismissive. Then she shoves him away from her so hard that he takes a step back. I can't hear what she's saying, but the last three words are very clear because she's shouting them at the top of her lungs. *Go fuck yourself.*

Everyone is staring now. "What a sweetheart," comments Jonah. Then Angie turns around and runs away. The guy flicks his floppy bangs a few times, and disappears into the crowd.

"She's my best friend," I murmur. Why hasn't Angie mentioned a new guy to me? I thought she was into Hugh, that English lord. Who the hell is this dude? I take out my phone.

"Yeah, you should probably call her," says Jonah.

"No . . ." God, men are stupid sometimes. If Angie wanted me to know about that guy, she'd have told me. She obviously didn't, and I have to respect that. But I can make it easier if she wants to tell me now.

I write Angie a quick text. *Hey, ladybitch. What up? Wanna hang out later?*

A second later I get a response. *Maybe. I'm out. Let's drink tonight.*

Typical Angie, I think as Jonah and I keep walking.

If I saw Julia having a fight with a mystery man I could just be direct with her. Not that it'd ever happen, of course. Mystery isn't her thing. Last time Jules hooked up with a guy she texted me while it was happening. Literally.

Not Angie. Once when we were on vacation in Thailand with my parents when we were fourteen, Angie told me that she was going to bed early. So I snuck out barhopping with a couple of the bartenders from the hotel. Come midnight, I went to the ladies' room in some dive, heard sobbing, and saw Angie's shoes under the cubicle door. I sat outside the stall for an hour, begging her to talk. She refused, and kept telling me she didn't need me, that she wanted to be alone. Eventually I left, and the next morning she'd checked out of the hotel and gone home to her parents.

I never found out what happened, and she didn't talk to me for almost a year after that.

That was the same year I got kicked out of my first boarding school, come to think of it.

Then the following summer she acted like everything was fine between us, so I just went along with it. Sometimes friendships are more complicated than any relationships.

"Penny for your thoughts," says Jonah.

I look at him and frown. "Sorry. They're worth more than that."

CHAPTER 6

It's nearly lunchtime at the Brooklyn Flea, and while Jonah lines up for a caramel-and-sea-salt ice cream, I lean against a beat-up old truck at the side of the market, people-watching. Is it compulsory for men aged between thirty and forty in Brooklyn to grow a beard, or what? Every male vendor has statement facial upholstery. And they all look so happy.

That's what I need: I need a job that'll make me smile.

Who am I kidding? I just need a job.

"Hey, watch it," says a gruff voice. It's an older woman with long silvery hair curled around the top of her head in a chignon.

I look back at the truck behind me with alarm. It's a food truck, I now realize, painted pale pink and older than I am. I didn't think it'd damage that easily. "I'm sorry, I—"

"I'm kidding." She grins at me. "This is Toto."

"Toto the truck? As in the song, 'Africa'?"

"It was that, or Orchestral Manoeuvres in the Dark," she says. "Toto seemed easier. I'm Francie."

"Pia." I lean over to shake her hand. Very firm handshake, I notice.

"You taking a break?" she asks.

I'm thrilled that she thinks I might actually work here. "Not exactly . . . I'm waiting for a friend. I love this place, though. Everyone seems so happy. Especially the food truck people."

"They should be, those upstart trucks are making a damn fortune," she says, checking her iPhone. Impressive. My mother confuses the remote control and the cordless phone. An iPhone would induce a total meltdown.

"Really?" I say. "Do you work here, too?"

"Nope. I'm trying to sell her. No luck," Francie says, sighing and patting the truck, as though it—I mean she—was a dog.

"Why not?"

"She's old." Francie shrugs. "She's fully equipped—she used to sell ice cream at Coney Island—but she doesn't have all the modern bells and whistles they want. And her engine ain't great."

"Poor Toto," I say sympathetically, giving the truck a pat. Her paint feels sort of warm and grainy, rather than the high-shine gloss of all the other food trucks. And I like her shape, too. I know nothing about food trucks, or any kind of motor vehicle for that matter, but Toto's kind of . . . cuddly.

"How much is she?" I ask.

"She's nine thousand dollars, give or take a hundred. My problem is I don't want to sell her to someone who won't love her."

I could love that truck, I think suddenly. Can't you picture me driving her? Selling food out of the back? I could do that; I know I could . . . if only I could cook.

Damn.

"Okay, gotta go, honey. I've got a date at Battersby at five."

She opens the truck door, jumps nimbly in, and drives away with a salute.

Deep in thought, I turn around and almost knock over Jonah and Bianca, that bitchy punk-headed waitress from Bartolo's.

"Look who I ran into!" says Jonah happily, his face full of ice cream. He leans over conspiratorially. "Bianca's hungover."

"I was celebrating never having to visit that freaking pawnshop on Pitkin again," says Bianca. She's talking exclusively to Jonah. Classic mean-girl stuff. "Cosmo gave me my money and my truck is on the way!"

"He's a loan shark. It's his money," says Jonah.

"Whatever! It's mine now!" Bianca goes into peals of seriously annoying laughter.

"What a surprise, running into you," I say in my sweetest voice. I bet she knew Jonah would be here.

Ignoring me, Bianca leans over and sticks her tongue right into Jonah's ice cream. It's a gesture of ownership so transparent I fight the urge to salute her. Whatever, sister. He's all yours.

"I really dig the whole food truck *concept,* you know?" says Bianca as we walk back toward A Meal Grows in Brooklyn. She's on Jonah's other side, talking just low enough that it's hard for me to hear her. "I love how we're teaching the huddled masses the intrinsic value of food that truly nourishes, body and soul. . . . It feels so right that I'm finally starting my own artisan caketruckery."

Huddled masses? Artisan caketruckery?

"Dude, you're gonna rock!" says Jonah.

"Seriously, J. Maybe food trucks are the beginning of something bigger, and the drones in Manhattan will stop poisoning Mother Earth now, and realize that we're here to make the world a better place for our children's children."

I snort with laughter. Is this chick for real? I go to exchange a glance with Jonah—sorry, "J"—but I see he's nodding. "I see your point. It's all about education, about educating people that what they eat really makes a difference."

"That's what food trucks are all about!" shouts Bianca. "We need to harness the Zeitgeist, influence pop culture, establish grass roots that can grow into trees!"

"I thought food trucks simply made life easier for people who can't afford the time or money to sit in a damn restaurant every lunch break," I mutter, half to myself. "And since when does grass grow into trees?"

There's a pause. "I'm sorry, what?" says Bianca.

I clear my throat. "My friends who work in Manhattan always say they don't get time for lunch. A food truck should make their lives easier, right? It's fast, cheap, good food."

"Well, that's true, too," says Jonah.

"I bet you have a lot of friends in *Manhattan*," Bianca says snarkily.

"Oh, I do." I flash a fake smile. Wow. She is such a skank-face.

We reach A Meal Grows in Brooklyn, and Phil leans his head out of the truck. "We need your help! We've almost run out of our lunch food already!" he calls, and starts laughing, slightly hysterically. "It's not even noon!"

Lara hurries toward us. "Jonah, can you please drive me back to the bakery to get more supplies? We didn't plan this very well."

"Okay, and I'll call Ray," says Jonah, frowning in that Boy-Scout-I-can-fix-it way that nice guys always do. Eddie had a frown like that. "He'll be sure to have something we can use. Buffalo mozzarella, maybe, or some of that awesome local sausage—" He pulls out his phone.

"I'll come with you, too," adds Bianca insistently, linking an arm through his and smiling at me as she pulls him away. "So are you working at Bartolo's tonight? My friend is playing this gig in Red Hook—"

Jonah pulls away from her. "Pia! Dude, you coming with us?"

"And desert a food truck emergency? No way!" I say, and shout at Phil: "Hey! You need some help in that kitchen?"

"Hell, yeah!" he says. "Come on in!"

Okay, I mostly wanted to get away from Bianca's annoying whine, but four hours later, I don't think I've ever had so much fun with something not involving booze and/or a bed. I *love* working in a food truck!

It's everything I loved most about Bartolo's—talking to people and seeing them enjoying great food—without the annoying bits, like running around, getting the bill, and picking up dirty dishes.

"Why don't we make a topless sandwich, you know, with just the bottom half of the bread?" I say to Phil, noticing a lot of people, especially women, immediately discard half the bread and scrape off the more calorific ingredients, like sour cream, or fried onions. "Or a salad? Or make the heavy stuff like sour cream optional?"

"That's not what people want, Pia."

I guess the sustainable food movement doesn't include sustaining the size of your ass.

By 4:00 P.M., we close up, open some ice-cold drinks, and lean against the truck, talking about the day. I love feeling part of the team, even though the team includes skank-face Bianca. She and Jonah spent the afternoon handing out A Meal Grows in Brooklyn flyers and tasters.

Phil gives me a hundred dollars and a jar of Kings County honey.

"Wow, thanks, are you sure?" I say. "I only worked for a few hours!"

"Honey, you earned it," says Lara. "Take the money and run."

Jonah and Phil are talking about sourcing local pears, and Lara and Bianca are talking about what to name Bianca's new business (sorry, "caketruckery"). So I zone out. Today was fun and all, but let's remember the big issue: I need a real job. A sour feeling fills the center of my chest as I think about how broke I am, how I don't know how I'm going to pay rent next month, let alone eat.

My thoughts are interrupted by Phil banging on the truck to emphasize his point.

"What's really amazing is that the food truck movement has—literally—covered all bases in a matter of years," Phil is saying. "There's something for everyone."

I don't want to argue, but . . . that's just not true.

"There are some ethnic food groups underrepresented, I guess," muses Lara. "It's hard to do *churrascaria* from a truck."

"Someone should do a Texan food truck," says Jonah dreamily. "Iced tea, chicken-fried steak, white gravy, fried oysters . . ."

"Why don't you do it?" says Phil.

"Because it sounds like a lot of work." Jonah starts laughing good-naturedly at himself.

"There's room for more artisan cake," says Bianca insistently.

I roll my eyes and stifle a snort.

"What do you think, Pia?" says Phil. Shit. I didn't think anyone was paying attention to me.

"What do I know?" I say. "I'm not a food . . . specialist. I mean a cook, uh, chef. Whatever."

"Your opinion is valid," says Lara. "Sometimes it takes an outsider to see things clearly."

"And your bacon chili jam sandwich was the most popular item on the breakfast menu today," says Phil.

"Come on, don't make me get the wuss hat again," says Jonah.

"Fine." I try to sound confident. "I think there's nothing in these trucks for people who don't want a fatty, salt-laden carb-overload. Like, if I'm working in an office and I'm going to take a lunch break, I don't want to eat a Mexineasy sweet-n-sour burrito with sour cream and cheese, or a Charter pie, whatever the hell that is."

"Chicken and leek in a cream tarragon sauce topped with pastry," interjects Phil.

"Exactly! Cream *and* pastry! I mean, come on!" I can feel a rant coming on, and I don't want to stop. "I love food, I love to eat, but I don't want something fattening, and I don't want a sandwich that will send me into a carb coma or grease that will make me burp garlic oil all afternoon. On the other hand, I don't want some ancient anemic salad from a deli, because it'll only fill me up for twenty minutes and then I'll be hungry again."

"Chicks burp?" says Jonah.

"I'm serious! I want a big fresh crunchy salad with loads of protein, like tuna, or poached chicken, or boiled eggs, and I want lots of flavors, like ginger and garlic and, um, chili lime marinade." I trail off; trying to talk food the way the guys have been all afternoon is tough. "And endives and almonds and radishes and, um, avocado, and reduced-fat cheese, and just enough fat in the dressing to taste good. . . ."

"Well, good luck finding it," interrupts Phil. "Try a salad bar. Or go to a restaurant."

"Most girls my age can't afford to eat in a restaurant every day, and there aren't enough salad bars. We want a food truck with fresh food that tastes good, and isn't loaded with fat and calories." I pause for a second, as my little idea seed suddenly bursts into flower. "We want SkinnyWheels."

"Well, hon, girls your age are a tiny subsection of the population," says Phil.

I'm thinking aloud now. "Actually, it's got nothing to do with age. There are thousands, no, millions of women like me. Guys, too, I'd bet. I love to eat, but I have to make smart choices. It's about a balance, don't you see? Between food that tastes good and food that's good for the size of my ass?"

Phil and Jonah shrug. Lara is nodding thoughtfully. Bianca is looking at her nails.

And then I make a decision that might just change the rest of my life.

I jump down from the front of the truck.

"Where are you going?" says Jonah as I march away.

Without breaking my stride, I shout over my shoulder, "I'm going to buy myself a goddamn food truck."

CHAPTER 7

"I'm here to see Cosmo. I'm, uh, a friend of Bianca's."

I've never been in a pawnshop before. I came straight from the Brooklyn Flea to Pitkin Avenue, and it's every cliché in the book. Greasy windows, bad lighting: the modern-day last-chance saloon. Right now, this is my only option. Plus, if it worked for Bianca, it'll work for me, right?

The pawnshop guy—straight out of central casting with a perma-toothpick and everything—picks up his phone and dials. "Cosmo? Business for you. Nah, you'll like this one."

I'm nervous as hell, so I try to look like hanging out in pawnshops is something I do every day by playing Pretend Shopping with the sad little engagement rings lined up like orphans. A few minutes later, Cosmo arrives.

He's wearing well-cut pants and a perfectly pressed shirt, and his head is freshly shaved. Not good-looking, but kind of suave. He could be anywhere between thirty and fifty. He gives me a sturdy handshake as he looks me right in the eye and smiles, showing perfectly white teeth and very pink, healthy gums.

"Cosmo Ferris."

"Pia Keller."

"A pleasure to meet you. Shall we go out back and talk?" He's well-spoken, with a soft Brooklyn accent.

"Let's go to the diner instead." Cosmo seems legit, but I don't think stories that start "So she went to the private room behind the pawn-shop" tend to end well, do you?

We head to the diner next door, and both order bottles of still water. I try to look as professional as possible considering I'm wearing cutoff jean shorts and probably smell like A Meal Grows in Brooklyn. This is a business meeting.

"I really need to hydrate," says Cosmo. "I love Smartwater, have you tried it?"

"Oh, yeah, it's the best," I say. Julia was obsessed with Smartwater last year.

"It's all I drink now. I compete in triathlons, and my trainer put me on to it. It really gives the body all the electrolytes it needs."

Wow, a triathlete moneylender. The unsettled feeling in my stomach eases a bit. I kind of like this guy.

As our drinks arrive, Cosmo nods at a few people in the diner: he's clearly a well-established local. This is a good sign. He's not some under-world kingpin, or whatever. Not that I'd recognize an underworld king-pin if I fell over him.

"I'm glad Bianca told you about me." Cosmo smiles genially. "Great kid. So, here's my deal. I'm a Brooklyn boy, born and bred. I run a suc-cessful security firm, that's my primary business and source of income, and these days, knock wood, it mostly takes care of itself. I've been a professional moneylender for about four years, since I had trouble, my-self, getting a loan from a bank, and realized that sometimes good, hon-est people just need a little helping hand."

"Right," I say, nodding. He makes sentences far more complicated than they need to be. I wonder if he thinks it makes him sound smart. Some people just talk that way, I guess.

"I make the loan, you pay it back in weekly installments, with a lump sum at the end of an agreed period, plus a reasonable rate of ten-percent interest, of course, as you'd probably expect. My interest rates are comparable to or lower than any of the major banks, as I'm sure a smart girl like you can see. It's all very straightforward."

"Uh-huh." Convoluted syntax or not, it makes sense. And his rates *are* lower than a bank.

"So how much do you need?"

"Just nine thousand dollars," I say. "I'm starting a business. I'll have profits immediately, so paying you back won't be a problem."

Food trucks are cash businesses, which means immediate profits, right? A Meal Grows in Brooklyn made thousands today. And there's no rent, no overhead aside from the food and a commissary to park it at night. This is the only way that I can build a business and a career, make money and impress my parents. It's a short-term loan for a long-term solution. Suddenly my heart is beating faster with excitement. I'm really going to make this happen.

"Let's make it a nice even ten thousand," says Cosmo.

"Okay."

He takes out a tiny ledger book and starts writing.

"Let's see . . . ten thousand, at a weekly interest rate of ten percent, makes it a one-thousand weekly repayment, then, in six weeks, you'll just owe me the original ten thousand. It's very simple."

"Great!" I say. That seems like a hefty interest rate, but then again, once I'm making thousands every day, it'll be nothing. This is business.

He starts talking about loan extensions and how the rates will change. If I don't make the ten thousand back in time, I'll just sell the truck before the end of the loan period and pay him that way.

"So, I'll transfer you the money every week?"

"No, no, let's make it easier," he says. "I'll come over to your place and pick it up in cash every Sunday at 7:00 P.M., okay?"

"Okay," I say. "So . . . what happens now?"

"I take down your details, you read and sign the contract, I give you the cash, and you're all set." And it really is that easy.

Two hours and a quick visit to Francie later, I'm the proud owner of Toto the truck.

Toto and I hit Union Street just as the sun is going down, and I'm in such a good mood. She doesn't have any air conditioning, and her radio hops around any station broadcast within a half mile. Somehow, with perfect timing, "Happy Together" by the Turtles comes on. I'm singing along at the top of my lungs.

"Imagine me and you, I do . . ."

A delicious sense of calm and well-being comes over me as I drive up Union Street. The acrid-sweet smell of barbecue is drifting in the air, kids on bikes are shouting in that slightly hysterical way kids do, and two little girls are actually playing hopscotch. It's ridiculously idyllic, spoiled only slightly by Toto's engine, which coughs like a chain-smoking coal miner.

With great difficulty, I reverse park just outside Rookhaven, and look over and see Julia, Madeleine, and Coco on our stoop, chatting happily with beers and a bowl of Doritos between them. I lean out the window, pull my aviators down to the end of my nose, and shout, "Well, howdy!"

Julia looks up at me, gasps, and drops her beer. It rolls down the front steps, spurting foam and clunking all the way. I jump out of the truck, slamming the door behind me, and pick up the beer.

"Why—how—the hell—do you have a truck?" says Julia.

"I bought her." I feel elated. "Her name is Toto!" We all turn to look at her. Toto is even bigger and rustier than she looked at the Brooklyn Flea earlier today, and her pale pink color is a cross between Pepto-Bismol and a piglet. "Don't you just love her?"

Francie was so excited that I wanted to buy her that she didn't even mind that I'd stalked her to her date at Battersby. She took me to her place just around the corner to give me the keys and all the papers right away.

"Where'd you get the money?" says Julia, handing me a PBR. I don't normally drink beer, but this evening, it's exactly what I want.

"Pawned some jewelry." I don't really want to hear Madeleine's snarky comments about going to a moneylender.

"She's like a big metal zit," says Madeleine, right on cue.

"Don't talk about Toto that way," I snap. But even Madeleine can't put me in a bad mood. "Guess what! I'm starting a food truck business called SkinnyWheels!"

Julia's jaw drops open. "You fucking what?"

I quickly tell them all about my day and my idea. "I'm starting small—just two salads, with lots of protein. All I need to do is make the food every evening, and start driving and selling during the day! I did it all day today, it's so easy! What do you think?"

"Mega-awesome!" says Coco. "That is the coolest thing I've ever heard!"

"Where are you going to buy the food?" says Julia. "And you don't cook."

"The market, or Trader Joe's, duh," I say breezily. "And I can bake chicken and arrange a salad, you know, I'm not a moron. How hard can it be? Salads aren't even real cooking! I might need Coco's help as I was thinking about trying to make a low-sugar dessert."

I smile hopefully at Coco, who claps her hands excitedly. "I'd *love* to!"

"What's the expected ROI?" says Madeleine. I ignore her and make a mental note to look up ROI later.

"Don't you need a license, or something?" says Julia. "And to register the vehicle?"

I wave a hand. "Easy. I have to send in some paperwork with my name on it, blah blah blah. The truck is already licensed as Toto's Ice Creamery. I'll paint 'SkinnyWheels' over the top. It's just a name, and I'm leasing the permit from the owner since everyone does that." Francie talked me through it all. There seems to be a lot of slight-of-hand about the food truck vendor permit system in New York, which suits me just fine.

"Where are you going to make the food?"

"In our kitchen till I get enough cash to go to one of the proper kitchen commissary thingies," I say. This part is, I'm aware, bending the rules a bit. "We've got that big spare fridge in the laundry with, like, nothing in it. And I'll make sure it's all sanitary. You know, gloves, clean knives, that sort of thing. If that's, um, okay with you guys?"

"Of course it is," says Julia. "It's just . . . *you*? A food truck?"

"This is the most ridiculous idea I've ever heard. Who would buy food from *you*?" says Madeleine.

For a second, my heart sinks. She's right. What the hell am I thinking?

"I would!" says Coco. I clink beers with her and smile gratefully.

"You know what, I would, too," says Julia slowly. "It's crazy, but I would. Will you park near my office first?"

"I'm showering." Madeleine stomps up the steps and bangs the front door shut behind her.

"Dude, she showers like three times a day, it's really weird," I say. Julia gives me a shut-up look. "It is!"

"Well, if it isn't the Rookhaven rookies!"

We all look up to see Vic and his sister, Marie, ambling along the sidewalk. Marie looks a bit like Vic, the same big pointy ears and a face crumpled like an old love letter, with pale pink fluffy hair. It suits her. She looks like a very old pixie.

"Hi, Uncle Vic! Hi, Aunty Marie!" chorus Julia and Coco, sounding about five years old.

"Look at that!" says Vic. "A pink truck!" They're both eating lemon ices.

"The truck is mine," I say proudly. "Her name is Toto! I'm starting a business! A food truck business!"

"You don't say," says Marie. "Looks like one that used to sell lemon ice at Coney Island."

"It's the same truck!" I exclaim. "Well, it could be. Maybe. It was an ice-cream truck."

"That's a great pedigree, sweetie," she says. "Oh, we loved Coney Island when we were younger. Do you remember, Vittorio? On a day like today, we'd go to Ravenhall! Now that was a swimming pool! Vic would swim the entire length, holding his breath, just to impress Eleanor." Vic doesn't react to this story, just keeps eating his ice cream. Was Eleanor his wife? The one he gave the rosebush to, the one who died? Marie continues, barely drawing breath. "Oh, and then we'd stop at Williams Candy. The caramel corn was to die for. You know, I think it's still there. Vittorio, we should go."

"Caramel corn and dentures, now there's a great idea," says Vic. Then he looks over at me. "So, I heard you made a little scene down at Bartolo's last night."

Was that really only last night? It seems like so long ago.

"Oh, God, yes, um, oh, Vic, I really enjoyed the job, and I love the restaurant," I say honestly. "I am so sorry, I guess it reflects badly on you—"

"I heard the full story from Ricky and Vinnie at the club today."

"Angelo is too uptight," interrupts Marie. "Always was. He was an uptight kid. His mother, now, there was an uptight woman. Tense! I'm surprised she managed to push him out—"

"Marie," interrupts Vic warningly. She rolls her eyes with a little grin, and goes back to eating her ice cream. He turns to me and says, surprisingly: "Well, good for you for standing up for yourself. So now you've got another job, huh? Think you can stick it out this time?"

"I will," I say. "I promise."

"How are you, Aunty Marie?" asks Julia. "How's the hip?"

"Oh, can't complain. Coco, honey, would you help me down the stairs? I'm gonna lie down. Vittorio, it's time for you to rest up, too, you hear me?"

"Who died and made you boss?"

As Coco helps Marie, Julia offers Vic a beer, but he refuses. He seems happy to just lean against the stoop in the early evening sun.

"You look just like your Aunt Jo, you know," he says to Julia. "And Coco looks just like your mother."

"I know," says Julia. "The older Coco gets, the more she reminds me of her. I don't think she knows."

Coco bursts back out of the garden-level apartment, leaps up the stoop two steps at a time, and runs into our house, banging the front door behind her, and comes out a few seconds later with a basket of homemade blueberry scones.

"Marie's favorite," she says, skipping down the stairs back into Vic and Marie's house.

"Yep, just like your mother, always baking and helping," says Vic.

"She was the best," says Julia. There's a pause, and no one says anything.

"Well, I better go look into this blueberry scone phenomenon," says Vic. "Can't have my sister eating them all by herself. I'll be back out here a little later."

"Some of my earliest memories are sitting out here with Vic and

Marie and my mom on summer evenings, watching the world go by," says Julia, half to herself.

"I really like them," I say.

"Me too. It makes me feel so safe, knowing they're here. It's like Rookhaven really belongs to them. Or they belong to Rookhaven."

"Does he have any kids of his own?" I ask.

She shakes her head. "No kids. My mom's family moved in during the sixties, I think. Vic moved straight downstairs, and Marie moved in when her husband passed away. They're like family." She meets my eye and smiles, but her eyes are sad.

I hold my beer up to hers. "To friends who are like family."

We clink, and drink.

An hour later, Coco's back sitting on the stoop with us, and I've got a thoroughly giggly beer buzz. I have a truck! I'm starting a business! I've got a new career!

We're talking about men. Or as Coco calls them, *booooyyysss*.

I tell the girls all about Jonah. "Verdict: not my type. Not even for a fling."

"You want to fall in love." Coco nods knowingly.

"No fucking way!" I say. "However, I'd be happy to *like* someone for a prolonged period of time. And have the sex."

"Please. I have not had anyone near my sugar in, like, fourteen months." Julia casts sad kitten eyes at us.

"I wish you wouldn't call it your sugar," I say.

"Why, because I should call it my hoohoo, the way you used to?"

"Hey. Don't insult my hoohoo. My hoohoo has never let me down." I pause. "Actually, my hoohoo constantly lets me down, the little bitch."

Coco clears her throat. "I'm thinking about joining a club or taking a class to meet more guys. Have you heard of Brooklyn Brainery? And there's bocce ball at Union Hall."

"Men playing bocce ball are either Vic's age, or the worst kind of hipsters," says Julia.

"I think we should go for older men," I say. "Guys our age need more time in the oven or something."

"Yeah," says Julia. "And I think guys think I'm weird for being, you know, ambitious and caring about my career and stuff." She frowns, pulling away some of her beer bottle label.

"All you really need is someone kind, hot, and smart," I say. "It seems like guys are only ever two out of the three."

"And he has to be funny," says Julia.

"And he has to laugh," I say. "Not just say 'that's funny' when I'm being funny."

"Affirmative. And he can't be skinnier than me and he has to have a college degree."

Coco is watching Julia and I make out this list of attributes like a kid at a tennis match.

"Where are we going to find dudes who are older, single, kind, smart, educated, funny, and hot?" says Julia.

"What about your office?" I imagine Julia's workplace is a combination of *Wall Street 2* and *American Psycho*. "Come on. All those buff men in suits . . ."

"No," says Julia. "None of the guys that I sit near, anyway. They're all the worst kind of frat boys. And none of the older ones even talk to me. It's like I don't exist."

"It's probably against some kind of policy," suggests Coco. "You know, because of sexual harassment."

"I don't think so, most of them are banging their assistants," she says, sighing. "They're disgusting, anyway. I wouldn't want an office fling, I just hate being ignored. How am I ever supposed to meet anyone?"

"There's a salsa class place on Smith!" says Coco.

"Salsa class? No goddamn way," I say. "It's simple. Go to a bar. Men will be there. Make eye contact. Give it twenty minutes. Voilà."

"Yeah, like it's that easy," Julia says, rolling her eyes. "Anyway, what kind of quality control is that? He could be a total cockmonkey!"

"The world is full of cockmonkeys." I nod. "The question is how hot they are."

Coco giggles and Julia rolls her eyes.

"Ladybitches!" says a voice. It's Angie, hiccupping and wavering slightly on the stoop. "I've been at Spring Lounge in SoHo all afternoon with Lord Hugh. The drinks were sta-*rong*."

"Things getting serious with the good lord?" I am dying to ask about the fight with the Brooklyn Flea guy, but I know she'll never tell me in front of the others. She probably wouldn't tell me even if we were alone.

"Ah, Hugh . . . my lord and savior," she says, then squints up at the sky. "Sorry, God. You know I'm only kidd— Whoa!" She falls off the step. "Oopsh! No, never mind, all good, nothing to see here, move along. . . ."

"Dude, she's shitfaced," says Julia.

Duh.

"I wanna go out!" Angie shouts. "Let's get ready to rumble!" She starts shadowboxing, her purse whipping back and forth. "Ow, ow, owww. Bag boob bang."

I stand up and take one of her arms to take her upstairs. Julia gets up and takes the other one. "Come on, drunky. Upstairs."

"I'm not that kind of girl, goddamnit. . . ." Angie starts walking up the stairs slowly, mumbling to herself. "Blow jobs are a privilege, not a right."

"What?" say Julia and I in unison, and start laughing hysterically.

"I'll make her some toast and hot tea," says Coco, hurrying behind us.

"I am fucking starving," Angie enunciates clearly. "Carb me up, Scottie!"

An hour and seven pieces of buttery toast later, Angie passes out. I need to keep an eye on her. There's that whiff of self-destruction about her. I know it well. I had it after Eddie.

Coco and I are in the kitchen talking about baking while Julia and Madeleine watch some Nicholas Sparks movie (I just cannot handle that shit, why would I *want* to cry? And by the way, why are they staying in on a Saturday night when Jules was just complaining about never meeting men? I'm staying in because I'm working. That's totally different. And, let's face it, hilarious.).

Coco really knows her stuff when it comes to low-fat baking. Like using canned pumpkin or applesauce to make cakes, instead of oil or butter. We agree to avoid high-fructose corn syrup at all costs, and fake sugars (most of them bloat me like a starlet in rehab). Coco suggests organic cane sugar, agave syrup, or even maple syrup.

"Sounds perfect. I'll spend tomorrow making just two simple salads,"

I say, planning out loud. "Then all I have to do is paint the truck and get on the road first thing Monday morning. Easy!"

"Easy," echoes Coco happily.

I make a list of things to buy at Trader Joe's tomorrow. I'm glad I have that extra thousand dollars leftover from buying the truck: I think I'll need it.

"This is so exciting!" Coco is such a positive person to be around, I'm sometimes not sure if she's actually being sarcastic. "I really think your truck idea is totally super-awesome." She plays with the spine of the book she's been reading, *Rilla of Ingleside* by L. M. Montgomery, then flips it open to the first page, absently stroking the name written there. *Kim Lucalli*. Her mom. Lucalli was her maiden name.

"Thanks, Coco," I say. "I think your low-fat baking ideas are totally super-awesome, too."

"You're not scared at all, it's like . . . wow," she says, blinking her big blue eyes at me.

"I do get scared sometimes," I admit. "I'm trying to ignore it in the hope the fear goes away. And I'm kind of excited, too. I saw a hundred people doing this food-truck thing today. If they can do it, I can, too." This really is how I feel . . . and whenever I think it, I feel my heart give a little elated jump. SkinnyWheels! Yeah!

"So how about you, kitten-pants? How's work?" Coco shrugs. She never talks about the preschool where she works. I try another subject. "Seeing anybody? Interested in anyone?"

"Yes! Um, I've been"—a deep sigh—"in love with my best friend, Eric, for like, four years? I know we'll end up together someday, we get along so well. . . ."

"Really?" I say. In my experience, girls who say "I know we'll end up together" tend to be a short stroll from psychotown.

"He lived on our street in high school, and I drove him to school every day when he totaled his car and we just talked for hours. The only problem is that he sees me as a friend and I'm not great at, you know, flirting. And since we left high school it's been hard to keep in touch." She sighs again. "He slept with Emily, my *former* best friend, at prom."

"No," I say. "What a bitch."

"A hellbitch," agrees Coco. "It wasn't his fault. He was drunk and she totally took advantage of him."

"He tripped and landed in her vagina, huh?"

Coco giggles despite herself. "No! I wish he hadn't done it, but he didn't know how much I like him . . . and I can't help it, I like him anyway." She's a bit further from pyschotown than I thought. That's a relief. "Have you ever been in love?"

"No," I say automatically. "Well, yes, but . . . it doesn't matter. Where's Eric tonight? Maybe we can go and see him."

"Oh, no, he's at Yale," she says importantly. "How do I make the transition from text friends to text flirting?"

"Be sarcastic. Be a smart-ass. Guys love a surprising text. It's like . . . a little mental rough-and-tumble."

Coco casts an anguished look at me, drumming *Rilla of Ingleside* with her fingertips. "What do you mean?"

"Flirting is just a game. It's easy, it's nothing. Look, I'll show you."

I pick up my phone and start casing through the numbers. Who can I practice on? Thompson I'm ignoring, not that he seems to be noticing, Dave, no, Jonah, hell no, Matt H., no, Matt W., no . . . Mike.

Mike! Perfect. He's called and texted like sixteen times in the past two weeks, I've just been too busy and stressed-out to reply. I owe him.

"Okay, so this is what I'd text to get his attention. . . ." I say, tapping.

From me: *Hell of a week. Rewarding myself with Doritos and beers. Am I turning into a middle-aged man?*

"Oh! That's funny," says Coco. "Mike who?"

"And now we wait for a response." I get up for a glass of water and ignore her question. Halfway through filling up the glass, a response comes.

"What a keen bean!" Coco's far more excited than I am.

I raise my eyebrow as I read it out loud.

From Mike: *Hmm, evidence inconclusive. Have you recently invested in a Porsche and/or hair plugs?*

I raise my eyebrows to myself. Cute text. I wouldn't have expected that from him.

"Tell him you bought a truck!" squeals Coco. "Ask him if he knows anything about driving stick."

"I think that might push the entendre the wrong way, sugar-nuts. Okay, I wouldn't usually respond to his text straightaway, but for the sake of this lesson, I will. How about this?"

From me: *Actually, I just bought a pink truck. I think it brings out my eyes.*

From Mike: *You're kidding me. This I have to see . . .*

From me: *Play your cards right, and maybe, just maybe, I'll let you sit in the passenger seat one day.*

From Mike: *Wow. Would bribery work? How about a drink? When are you free?*

"See?" I say to Coco, putting the phone down. "Easy. Now it's your turn."

"It's easy for you. He obviously already liked you," says Coco glumly.

"No, he didn't," I say firmly. He couldn't, right? It was just a one-night thing. "So. What was your last text to Eric?"

"Um, I asked him about whether his mom liked poinsettias at Christmas," she says, biting her bottom lip. "I hadn't heard from him in days, so I just wanted to send a little hi, you know, like a wave."

"There is no such thing as 'just waving' when it comes to flirt texts," I say. "And Coco, questions in text tend to be obvious demands for attention, and that one is no different."

"I sort of thought maybe that would make it seem legitimate. Like, maybe my dad had some poinsettias he needed to sell, you know?"

"Christmas is months away. . . . Never mind. What did he reply?"

She shows me the text. *I'm not sure. You'd probably have to ask my sister.*

"Wow," I say. "Man of few words."

"I'm still trying to figure out what to say."

"How about: *Wow, you must be going for Son of the Year. Nice work, tiger.*"

"I can't text 'tiger!'" she squeals.

"What have you got to lose?"

Making a little *eek* sound, Coco taps out the text and turns to me, smiling gleefully. She really is so pretty, especially when she smiles. Such lovely eyes and natural blond hair. She just needs to wear a tiny bit of makeup. And maybe pluck her eyebrows. And stop dressing like she's four sizes larger than she is. Coco has a gorgeous figure, all boobs and curves, but was much bigger in high school, when I first met her. I think she's stuck in that mentality.

Her phone buzzes. *What are you, the Parent Police?*

"I should say 'Yeah, spread 'em!'" says Coco, laughing at her own daring.

"Try . . . *I might be. I might not be. I guess we'll never know.*"

Eric responds right away. *How's life in the big city anyway, Miss Coco?*

"Now you ignore him," I say firmly.

"What?" says Coco. "But he asked me a question! Finally! He never asks text questions. I always have to ask the text questions."

"No, you wait till tomorrow, then say, *The big city is giving me terrible hangovers. At least, I'm blaming the city. It can't be the booze.* It alludes to the fact that you're out and busy on a Saturday night."

"I'm not. I have no plans."

"That's not the point. As far as he's concerned, he's just one of the many men you could be texting. So wait till tomorrow, and he'll be thinking about you all night."

"Ahh . . ." says Coco, realization dawning on her face. "God, this is so cool! I always imagine us falling in love after years of best friendship. It would be so romantic. My mom and dad were best friends for years, did you know that? Then they fell in love." She sighs happily. "That's what I want."

"I hate romance," I say. "And love doesn't last."

"Love does last!" She's scandalized. "You have to fight for love. You do!"

"You shouldn't have to fight for anything."

Then my phone buzzes again. It's a text from Angie.

PARRRTEEHHHHHJJKt887

"I thought Angie was still upstairs. . . ." I murmur.

"Angie?" says Coco. "No, I saw her leaving when I went to the bathroom earlier."

"Shit."

If she can't even text clearly, she's not in good shape.

I text back. *Are you okay?*

She replies. *HELLZYAH! Four coldy flu tablets and a Dr Peppetfw with tequillll. In cab to Lwer Eas tSde, Ludlow/Grand u comin?*

I'm not an overprotective friend, I'm really not. But I have a feeling something is very wrong.

So I run upstairs to change into a nonfood-marked dress and heels. Part of me is delighted to have an excuse to dress up, is that shallow? Oh well.

"You know what, Coco?" I say, poking my head in the kitchen before I leave. She's sitting at the kitchen table with a hot chocolate, reading her book. "Maybe there is one thing you should fight for. Your friends."

CHAPTER 8

I get out of the cab on the corner of Ludlow and Grand, and I can already hear the raucous, semi-scream-filled sound of a great night in action.

There's music throbbing from the top of a three-story building and people are spilling out onto the balcony and fire escape. I think I've found my party.

The noise gets louder as I walk up to the third floor, stepping over couples making out and past a guy on the phone screaming, "I said to bring the corn dogs!" Then I get into the apartment. The lights are dim and when my eyes adjust, I can make out a packed room full of people dancing and screaming and drinking.

But no Angie.

The apartment is tiny, smoky, and very crowded with what I'd guess is a music-Euro-fash crowd (lots of skinny guys with deep-V shirts and pissed-off-looking girls with chronic eyeliner habits). She's not in the kitchen, not in the first bedroom. . . .

Finally, I reach a room filled with people speaking French. A guy is photographing two girls about my age making out on the bed (ew) and a group of guys next to the far wall are doing coke off a glass picture frame.

And then I see them—Angie's shoes, her favorite YSL heels that she stole from her mother, are poking out from the other side of the bed. I push my way over. She's passed out cold on the floor, a layer of white powder caked around one nostril. *Merde!*

"Angie! Angie, can you hear me?" She's breathing, at least. I try to get her to sit up, but she flops back to the floor.

"Is she with you? We don't know her," says one of the dudes, in a drawly uptown accent. "She seems real fun, though."

"Yeah, she's with me, fuck-face," I snap. "And we're leaving."

Angie stirs slightly.

"Peeeeyaaaaa . . ." Her voice is croaky. "My favorite girl . . ."

"That's me, sugar-lips," I say, half-carrying and half-dragging her out of the room. We reach the front door and head down the stairs.

"I feel funky," she says. "My heart is racing."

"Yep, coke will do that to a girl."

By the time we're at the bottom of the stairs, she's walking almost entirely by herself again, until she's almost knocked over by a couple hurrying in the door.

And Angie and I gasp in unison.

It's the floppy-haired French guy. The one I saw her fighting with at the Brooklyn Flea earlier today. And he's with a beautiful dark-haired woman.

"Excuse us," says the man politely, with a slight European accent, his eyes flickering over us without a hint of recognition.

"Fuckpuppet," says Angie under her breath. She pushes my supporting arm away and angrily watches them walk up the stairs. "I'm talking to you! Ya fuckpuppet!" The woman puts her hand (with an enormous, sparkly, diamond-clad ring finger) on his back and follows him up the stairs.

He's . . . married?

Outside on the street, Angie pushes my arm away, crouches by the gutter, leans to one side, pulls her long white hair entirely over the other shoulder, and starts throwing up. Practical Puking 101.

I quickly sit on her nonpuke side and start rubbing her back. She shudders, tears rolling down her face.

"It's okay . . . it's okay . . ." I keep saying, like some kind of wind-up best-friend doll.

"It's not," she whispers under her breath, before reverse-chewing another mouthful. "It's really not okay."

At midnight on Saturday on the crowded Lower East Side, no one bats an eyelash to see a crying girl throwing up in the gutter. I try to remember the last time I threw up from booze. It's been a long time, now that I think about it. Not since I stopped drinking those alcoholic caffeinated sodas. Yay for me.

Ten minutes later, Angie stands up to hail a cab. "I'm fine," she says. "Thanks for rescuing me."

"Anytime."

After we get in a cab Angie stares out the window and refuses to say anything. So I gaze out my window, too, thinking about the party. What was she *thinking*?

Then we stop in traffic on the Brooklyn Bridge.

And Angie opens her door and steps out of the cab.

"What the hell are you doing?" I gasp, grabbing her arm. She pulls away from me—sheesh, she's strong, particularly for a drunk girl—and slams the cab door. I grab my bag and jump out after her, ignoring the shouting cab driver.

"Angie!" I yell.

She's treading the line between two lanes, arms out like a tightrope walker. Cars beep furiously as the traffic in our lane starts to move.

"Look at me!" she shouts. "Look at meeee!"

"Angie! Stop! Come the fuck back here!" I shout.

Ignoring me, Angie runs in front of a Prius. The driver screeches to a halt. I run after her, giving the deeply disapproving Mr. and Mrs. Prius a thumbs-up and mouthing "thank you."

The traffic stops again. Angie is half-walking, half-running away from me. Then she disappears.

"Angie!" I yell. *"Angie!"*

A trucker leans out his window and starts singing "Angie" by the Rolling Stones. *"Oh, Angie, don't you weep . . ."*

I cannot believe I'm dodging cars on the Brooklyn fucking Bridge at midnight.

Then I see Angie. She's climbed on top of a Hummer that's headed right toward me. Her hair is blowing in the wind and she's doing a Rose-from-*Titanic* pose.

"Angie!" I shout as she passes me. "Get the fuck down!"

Like a miracle, the traffic stops again. Angie is about thirty feet in front of me.

Still on the roof of the Hummer, she bows to the traffic behind and in front of her, and does a perfect handstand.

For about two seconds.

Then she crashes into a crumpled heap on the Hummer roof. The driver jumps out and starts screaming at her. I run as fast as I can, pull Angie off the top of the truck, ignoring the hysterical driver, and drag her to the side of the bridge to a little alcove where we can shelter. Angie is weeping silently, her eyes wide and staring at nothing.

"What the hell, Angie? Have you got a fucking death wish?"

Angie blinks and looks at me for one long second, and then closes her eyes. I look around, trying to figure out how we're going to get off the bridge. Horns are wailing as cars speed past. We're exactly one careless driver away from being smithereened against the wall.

A cab pulls over, but the light isn't on. I glance at it, confused, and wave it past.

"Need a ride?" says a British accent.

I glance at the cab, ready to say "No."

But I can't.

Because it's the guy. The Prince Charming guy. Who handed me my shoe just a few days ago.

For a second I forget to breathe.

Then I remember where I am, who I'm with, and the problem at hand.

"Um, a ride, yes, please," I say quickly. "My friend is a little out of it. I just want to get her back to our house."

"No problem, hop in."

I pause for a split second. Is it safe? I don't even know him. He could be a psycho.

He reads my mind. "I swear I'm not a psycho."

I quickly get in next to him, pulling Angie after me. She's doing her mute staring-into-space trick again.

I'm pressed up against the guy's body and, no word of a lie: I start tingling. I wonder if he remembers me. Don't be stupid, Pia, of course he doesn't.

"Corner of Court and Union," I say.

"I gotta report this," says the driver.

"Does fifty dollars change that?" says the British guy.

The driver steps on the accelerator.

"Thanks," I whisper. "I'll pay."

"Don't worry about it," the guy whispers back. "Bribery is a hobby of mine."

Our eyes meet, and yet again, I forget to breathe. I just gaze at him. Who *is* this dude? I notice the tiny scar on the bottom of his lip, and wonder what he'd be like to kiss, and think again how nice his eyebrows are but actually I don't think he does wax them or thread them or whatever because they're just sort of naturally perfect but it feels like these are things I've seen many times before, like I *know* him. . . .

Then I realize I'm staring and grinning like a total moron. Self-consciousness overwhelms me. Of course I don't know him. Like, seriously, what is *wrong* with me? And where the hell is his girlfriend? Why isn't he with her at midnight on a Saturday, rather than playing knight-in-shining-yellow-cab? He's too cocky, too confident. Clearly a player. A cockmonkey fuckpuppet bastard, the kind of guy I should avoid at all costs.

But God, he's hot.

The cab is so quiet. I can hear him breathing. I wonder if he can hear me breathing. Oh God, now I'm not breathing at all. I might pass out.

"Um, thanks for stopping," I say finally.

"I caught the end of your adventure," the British guy replies. "I have friends who used to taxi surf across the Williamsburg Bridge."

"By 'friend' you mean 'you,' right?" I say, raising an eyebrow.

"Dash it, you broke my code. What are you, some kind of enigma machine?"

"Did you just say 'dash it?'"

He grins. "I'm Aidan."

"Pia."

We shake hands in an awkward-yet-flirty way, and I can feel my heart or maybe my entire torso beat *thumpetythumpthump*. Aidan looks like he wants to laugh, like he knows how I'm feeling and what I'm thinking, oh, God, my stomach is tingling. . . .

"So . . . you live in Brooklyn?"

"Yeah. Actually, I'm on my way to meet a mate for a nightcap at Minibar. It's sort of my local."

"I've heard of it," I say. (I totally haven't.)

"My dog prefers Bar Great Harry. Probably because they let him in."

I'm fighting the urge to ask exactly where he lives, what kind of dog he has, where his girlfriend from the other day is, and if he'd ever consider dumping her to date me instead. Thankfully, before I can start frothing at the mouth, the cab driver interrupts.

"You're from London?"

"More or less," says Aidan.

"You been here long?" the cabbie asks him.

Angie stirs, and I look over at her and make a slight are-you-okay face, and she shrugs. She's clearly tired, and sad, but fine. But who was the French guy? And what the hell is going on with her?

I tune back into the conversation.

"About six years ago," Aidan's saying. He's got a very deep, self-assured voice. Sexy.

"What do you do?" asks the cabbie.

"Uh, boring financial stuff," he says, then glances at me. "But I am totally hip and groovy in every other way, obviously."

"I went to London once," says the cabbie. "The food, man! I don't know how you guys survive over there."

I cringe inwardly. Never criticize a stranger's country unless you have lived there.

"It's a miracle," says Aidan. "Frankly, I'm surprised any of us are still alive."

I turn to him and grin, trying to make up for the cabbie's rudeness, and he winks at me, his eyes crinkling with a secret smile. I wink back and I feel that hot tingling again, so I quickly drop my gaze. *Ohplease-askmeoutohpleaseaskmeoutohpleaseaskmeout—*

Then, too quickly, we reach Union Street. Angie somehow rouses herself and staggers out of the cab. "Thank you so much, for, um, being our knight in shining armor," I say. "Here, this is for the cab fare, or the tip, or whatever—" I try to put a twenty in his hand.

"No, no. Consider this karma. Pay it forward. Or whatever that awful movie was called."

Aidan puts his hand on mine and I swear to God, electric sparks shoot through my hand and up my arm. I flinch from shock and snatch my hand away.

His sexy-cocky smile fades. "You okay?"

"Yes . . . No. I mean, yes."

Our eyes meet again. There's a pause. Suddenly the world is totally silent.

For a second I'm overwhelmed with the urge—no, not to kiss him (though that would be, you know, just fine). I want to talk to him more. I want to close the cab door and just keep going, wherever he's going. It feels like it would be the right thing to do.

Stupid, I know.

And impossible. I can't ask for his number out of the blue, it's just not my MO, and he hasn't asked for mine, and anyway, he has a girl-friend. She's tall and glamorous and loud and sexy. I saw her on the damn street. Jesus, Pia. Get a grip.

So I get out and slam the door without looking back.

CHAPTER 9

I never used to like waking up alone. Even if I woke up next to the wrong guy, it was better than being by myself. Just two weeks ago today I was lying here next to Mike, yet to deal with the chaos of my post-party life. I wish I hadn't slept with him, by the way. Massive oopsh. The first guy I ever slept with was Eddie. We waited three months, and finally did the deed at Thanksgiving, at his parents' house, during the first snow of the year. It was so—oh, God, why am I thinking about this? I'll just get upset and I have a big day ahead.

It's time to get the SkinnyWheels show on the road!

First: Angie. I need to figure out what's going on with her. When we got in last night, she just came upstairs and went right to sleep.

I knock on her door. A moan tells me she's awake.

"Good morning, ladybitch."

Her room smells as bad as it looks: there are more clothes on the floor than in the closet, and there are so many paintings and sketches pinned up you can hardly see the wallpaper.

"I need sustenance," she moans. "My kingdom for a French fry."

"You have a kingdom?"

I look down at her, sprawled on the bed, hair a wild mess, eyeliner even more messy-cool than usual.

"Let's talk about you, my kamikaze friend. Talk about crash and burn: you were a total mess yesterday."

Angie shrugs. "I got afternoon drunk, came home, carbed up, and passed out. What's the big deal?"

"Umm . . ." Shit, I hate telling people what they did when they don't remember. It usually seems kinder to pretend it never happened. But I think Angie needs to know.

"You had a bit of an oopsh, ladybitch."

"I did?"

So I tell her about the "coldy flu" text, the party, the coke, and finally the gymnastic-surfing-on-a-Hummer journey over the Brooklyn Bridge.

When I'm done, she puts her pillow over her face and screams into it.

"I don't remember any of that! This is the oopsh to end all oopshes!"

"What is going on with you? I know it's not your style but really, maybe we should talk about it," I say, as gently as I can. "And there's something else. I saw you at the Brooklyn Flea yesterday. Having a fight with some French guy."

"Oh. Him."

"Yeah, him. And I guess you don't remember this either, but we saw him at the party."

"Did I do anything?" Angie clutches my arm.

"No . . ." I say. "Well, you called him a fuckpuppet. He pretended he didn't know you." I pause. "He was with another woman."

Angie lies back, puts her pillow back over her face, and screams again. I lean forward and grab it off her.

"Talk. Now," I say. "Everything."

She sighs, grabs a cigarette from the pack on her nightstand, and puts it, unlit, in the corner of her mouth. "His name is Marc. We met in

Cannes last year, but he lives in SoHo. Remember when I told you I was skiing in Vail with my UCLA friends?"

I nod.

"I lied. I spent the week with him, skiing in Megève. He told me then that he was married, but separated, and that we might have to cool off while he got a divorce, blah blah blah." She sighs. "Then . . . anyway, I went to Cannes again this summer with Annabel, remember?" Angie always calls her mother by her first name. "She wanted some mother-daughter bonding time or some shit like that. I saw him there with his wife. I confronted him, he confirmed it, but said that they were having a trial separation and were together for a family gathering and he only loved me. . . . God, I hate him, he's just like my fucking father, just lying all the time. It's my fault. I'm a gullible cliché."

"It is *not* your fault! And he's a total cockmonkey!" I exclaim.

Angie stares at the ceiling, lost in thought.

"And so . . . then what? How did you get from there to slapping him at the Brooklyn Flea?"

Angie turns to face me, propping the still-unlit cigarette in the side of her mouth. "On Friday night I met up with Lord Hugh and his friends, remember? But Hugh ignored me, so I texted Marc just to boost my ego—or compound the rejection, whatever. He replied, and then later on, when I was drunk enough, I went to his place."

"Well, sex is just sex," I say, trying to make her feel better.

"I'm starting to think sex is never just sex. . . . Anyway, I'm surfing the crimson wave, and he's not into that. I think I dislocated my jaw from blow jobs, actually." She rubs her face, frowning. I laugh, and she hits me with a pillow.

"Then what happened?"

"Well, I made him take me to the Brooklyn Flea yesterday to force him to act like a boyfriend, I guess. And that's when he told me he really was back with his French bitch wife and he had to go pick her up from the airport, like, immediately. And he thought it was best if we never saw each other again." Angie's voice is whispery with tears. "I guess he thought I wouldn't make a scene in public."

"How dare some ancient Euro-trash piece of *merde* treat you like that!" I feel hot with anger. God, I *hate* it when my friends get mistreated. "Do you want to get revenge? We could egg his house, or something."

"He's not worth it. I knew about that party last night because I stalked him on Facebook yesterday when I got back from the Flea. I guess that, later on, drunk me decided I'd surprise him. That's pathetic, right? After the way I made you stop Eddie-stalking that summer. . . ."

"No, no, it's totally understandable." And I don't want to think about Eddie. Or that summer. "Is that all?" I say. "I mean, is that all that happened with Marc?"

A pause. Angie closes her eyes again. A signal that the conversation is over.

"Okay, you don't have to talk about it. . . . Tell me about the Spring Lounge instead."

"It was a birthday thing for someone from Penn. It sucked. I got kicked out for smoking a joint at the bar. . . . Screw it, I don't care. I'm leaving soon, you can come and visit me in L.A. and have lots of crazy sex with hot actors."

"Sounds great." I'd hoped that Rookhaven was growing on her, the way it is on me. That she was starting to feel like it was, I don't know. Home. Guess not. Time to change the subject.

"I bought a food truck."

"What the what?"

I tell her the whole story, omitting the Cosmo details.

"I love it," she says. "Sounds like a surefire hit. Maybe you can employ me. Get me away from the Bitch."

"I can't afford to employ anyone. And I don't think you should call your boss the Bitch."

"Why not? She's a total dog. It's the correct terminology."

"Funny. Want to help me go food shopping and then make the salads?"

"Can I watch and make sarcastic comments instead?" Angie climbs out of bed, still wearing her clothes from last night.

"If you shower first and change out of that thing, you can do anything you like."

"Oh, wow." Angie sits back down on the bed. "Holy shit, I am hungover."

When I get back to my room, there are two missed calls from my parents. No message. For a second, I consider calling them back. But I can't. And not because I don't want that whole we're-coming-to-New-York-to-force-you-to-leave-Brooklyn conversation. But because I have a job to do. I have a business to start.

Step one: ingredients.

What I thought would be a straightforward shopping expedition turns into a scavenger hunt for the right ingredients, disposable salad boxes and knives and forks and tiny salad dressing things, and then paint for the truck. Angie's so hungover that she only sticks around for an hour, then bails to go get a restorative mani-pedi.

By the time I get back to Rookhaven, it's 3:00 P.M. and I've spent every penny I had leftover after buying Toto. The idea of ten thousand dollars gone in just twenty-four hours is petrifying. It gives me a sort of giddy sick feeling . . . like financial vertigo.

But you have to spend money to make money, right? And this is business. I get back to Rookhaven and find Coco, Julia, and Madeleine draped over the sofas in the living room, watching a Kardashian marathon.

"Okay! Let the food trucking begin!" I say.

They don't move.

I wash my hands, put the chicken breasts in the oven, and write my menu. I've decided to do it elementary-school style.

Salad 1 = chicken + avocado + snow peas + beets + cherry
          tomato + reduced-fat feta + baby greens

Salad 2 = turkey + watercress + almonds + apple + celery +
          reduced-fat cheddar + baby greens

Dessert 1 = brownie (– fat)

I would eat those salads. I think.

And low-fat string cheese was on special at Trader Joe's, so I bought eight packs of them, too. I'll charge twenty-five cents more than I paid and make a profit. (I am pretty proud of myself for thinking of that.)

I called Lara and Phil as I was driving around Brooklyn to ask how to book Toto into the food-truck-commissary thing. They're hooking me up with their contact. There are commercial kitchens, too, so I'll prepare all my food there. Cooking in Rookhaven is a teeny tiny sanitation violation. Even though I'm, like, totally clean.

"Why don't you add sunflower seeds? Or candied walnuts?" says Coco, standing at the doorway, holding *Daddy-Long-Legs* by Jean Webster open against her chest. I think she's been reading on the stoop. "Or raisins, or cranberries?"

"Calories," I say. "I mean, you're right, they're delicious. But this is SkinnyWheels. I gotta deliver what I promise, the only high-fat items are the almonds and the avocado, which are so good for you, it's like eating Crème de la Mer. . . ." I'm rambling.

I look at the salad menu and frown. "Sheesh, I wish I knew more about cooking. I seriously have no idea if these are okay, you know?"

"They look great," says Coco reassuringly.

I Googled a few low-fat salad dressing recipes on my cell as I was shopping, and purchased extra-virgin olive oil, avocado oil, red wine vinegar, cider vinegar, raspberry vinegar, Worcester sauce, whole-grain mustard, Dijon mustard, freshly squeezed lemon juice, and natural fat-free plain yogurt.

I figure I'll improvise something.

Hmm.

"Avocado oil and cider vinegar," says Julia from the doorway. I look around: Coco's gone. I didn't even notice. I've been kind of preoccupied.

"It has to be reduced fat." I make an anguished face. "I mean, you need some fat for taste, and if you don't eat a bit of fat you never feel full, but. . . ."

"So try one part oil to two parts vinegar," she says. "And one part lemon juice. And salt and pepper. Use a screw-top jar, like an old peanut butter jar, so you can just shake to mix. My Aunt Jo had loads of them. They're in the side cupboard over there."

I mix it. I shake it. We taste it.

"That is *excellent*," I say in surprise. "But you never cook!"

"I'm very good at dressings," she says, grinning at me. "My mom showed me. It was our thing."

"Then we'll call it Kim's Dressing," I suggest.

"Call that one Julia. I have another one we can call Kim," she says. "Olive oil, red wine vinegar, whole-grain mustard, salt, pepper. That was her favorite."

"So good!"

Sitting at the kitchen table, Julia at the head with me on her right (I always have this seat, it's where my ass belongs), we sample each dressing, sipping from spoons like medicine.

Then I try my own dressing: lemon, Dijon, yogurt, olive oil, and vinegar.

"Amazing! Fivie!" says Julia, holding her hands up for a high five.

"No fivies. Fivie ban, Jules."

Back when Maddy and I were still close, we once banned Julia from saying or doing "fivies" for a fortnight. We had no choice. Jules fivied for goddamn everything, it was out of control.

For a second I feel sad. I wish Madeleine and I were still friends sometimes.

Then Julia grabs my hand and forces me to high-five her.

"Hah. Suck it."

"Thanks for this," I say. "I don't have a clue what I'm doing."

"Does anyone?" says Julia. "So, how much are you charging?"

"I think six dollars per salad," I say. "Who can say no to a six-dollar salad, right?"

"Not me! Will you come to my office first tomorrow?" she says. "I really want to be your first customer."

"Hell yeah, sister!" I say, grinning. This is really going to work! I'm going to drive a food truck!

"What's that smell?" says Madeleine, coming into the kitchen.

"*Merde!* The chicken breasts!" I run over to the smoking oven, and open it to reveal charred, perfectly lined up chicken breasts. Smoke billows out and engulfs the kitchen. I grab the oven mitt and take them out. "That's like a hundred bucks worth of goddamn chicken!"

"I'll get you more chicken, relax," says Julia, opening the windows. "Make your salads. I'll be back in half an hour."

"You'll never get a parking space for that shit-bomb in Manhattan," says Madeleine, leaning against the doorframe.

"Thanks for the hot tip," I reply, not turning around. Did I say I wish we were still friends? Yeah, well, I take that back.

By the time Julia returns with thirty raw chicken breasts, I'm sweating and swearing, and suddenly plagued by the feeling that I've bitten off more than I can chew. Every inch of the kitchen bench, table, and floor is covered in tablecloths (sanitation!) and open salad boxes. It looks like a picnic on steroids. I'm trying to share the chopped vegetables evenly between all of them, while wearing sanitary gloves one size too big. And completely freaking out.

"Thank you! Don't come in here!" I shout to Jules in the doorway. "This is a sterile environment! I need to cook the chicken!"

"How are you going to cook the chicken when you can't get to the oven?" asks Julia.

We stare at each other across a sea of salad boxes. A long pause.

"Throw the chicken to me," I say, taking off my gloves.

Julia looks like she's trying not to laugh, and throws me the chicken breast packets one at a time. I drop them in the sink, wash my hands, put the gloves back on, open the packets, take the chicken out, season with a little salt and pepper, arrange on the trays, remove the gloves, wash my hands again, move the salad boxes and tablecloths out of my way one at a time, make it to the oven, put the chicken in, edge carefully back, and wash my hands again.

"Easy," I say out loud. "See? Piece of goddamn cake."

Finally, the chicken breasts are perfectly cooked, cubed, distributed evenly, and every salad box is closed, one by one.

One by one, they all flip open again.

So I scream.

"What? What is it?" Angie and Coco come running in.

"The boxes won't stay shut," I say miserably. "Look." I close one of the plastic salad boxes, using the little plastic notch thing. It pings straight open again. I could cry. But that really wouldn't help.

"I can't do this," I say. "What was I thinking?"

"Rubber band?" suggests Coco. "Scotch tape?"

"No, stickers!" says Angie, and runs upstairs, returning a moment later with dozens of sheets of large heart stickers.

"What the—"

"Stationery cupboard at work. They're cute."

"You stole from your place of employment."

"Stationery doesn't count. It's like other people's cereal."

"You've been eating my cereal?"

The heart stickers are the perfect salad box solution and totally goddamn adorable. I feel almost positive again. This might just work out.

"You forgot the feta cheese," says Angie, reading my menu.

I let out a scream of anguish.

Carefully opening every box again, I put exactly seven squares of low-fat feta cheese in each one.

"Now, it's time for the second salad!" I say, trying to sound positive and gung ho. I can do this. I can. So it hasn't been the best first day ever, so what. *Illegitimus non carborundum*, just like that nice woman at Bartolo's said.

"Umm, Pia?" says Coco. "Can we use the kitchen to make dinner?"

I look at the clock in dismay. How did it get to be seven o'clock? "Oh, God! I'm sorry. Order pizza. I'll pay. Or sushi. Whatever."

"Sushi! Arigato!" says Angie.

"I'll call Bartolo's!" says Coco. "Oh, sugar, I have to ask the others what they want." She runs out of the kitchen.

"Here," I say, handing Angie a wad of cash. "Pay for the pizza and sushi with this."

"You must be running out of cash, ladybitch, seriously," says Angie doubtfully.

I wave my hand with all the blasé confidence I don't feel. "Doesn't matter. I'll make it all back in no time."

The second salad is easier, thanks to help from Coco and Angie. Then I decant the dressings into the tiny dressing containers and write "Kim," "Julia," or "Pia" on top in a big laundry marker, while the girls close the boxes.

"You should add baked sweet potato," says Angie. "And artichoke hearts."

"And sprouts," says Coco. "And beans! Beans are super-awesome." Then the doorbell rings. "Dinner!"

Feeling much more cheerful, I place all the salad boxes into the second refrigerator in the laundry. They look so beautiful and neat, all stacked up one on top of the other.

Now all I have to do is make low-fat brownies! Coco gave me her mom's foolproof recipe. I use my phone to multiply it by three, and substitute canned pumpkin for oil, as she suggested.

I am going to make a damn fortune from this. I can feel it. And I'll pay back Cosmo in time and be really successful and my parents will see it for themselves and life will be perfect.

Three hours and four brownie batches (one burnt, one didn't cook properly, one dropped on the floor, one perfect) later, I'm nearly finished. I cut all the brownies up into generous squares, put them in the salad boxes—they look pretty pathetic marooned in the salad boxes, I need to get something to individually wrap them instead—and stack them to the side with the salads.

Then I look around.

Our cozy little kitchen looks worse than it did after the party. The burnt-chicken smell hasn't left, somehow, and there is brownie batter on Coco's goddamn herb garden. And how are there little bits of feta all the way over underneath the kitchen table? And, oh, my God, is that brownie on the ceiling? I feel guilty. Like I should be reprimanded for kitchen abuse.

"Sorry, Rookhaven," I mutter. "I'll look after you, I swear."

I spray and scrub and sweep every inch of the kitchen. I even mop the floor, something I don't think I've ever done in my life. When I'm done, I look around at how clean and perfect it is and feel a bizarre, exhausted sense of satisfaction.

It's almost midnight. Everyone else has already gone to bed.

Starving, I eat one cold, congealed slice of salami pizza and the leftover end of a dragon roll maki on the way upstairs.

At my bedroom door I find three little notes:

The first note covers a stack of printouts: *I did some research. Here are the menus to all the best salad places in New York. For inspiration. Coco xxx*

The second note says: *Good luck tomorrow. Go get 'em tiger. Jumanji x*

The third note is covering a stack of cash that looks suspiciously like the money I gave Angie earlier: *Your money. Sorry ladybitch. A. PS: For you . . .* And underneath it is a cartoon of Toto, with a little cartoon Pia leaning out the driver's window. The words "SkinnyWheels" are written in a fat black cursive script on Toto's flank. The overall effect is sort of '70s and scratchy, with big red hearts dotted all over the truck, and a big red lipsticked mouth on the front grill. Underneath it, Angie wrote, *We're not in Kansas anymore, Toto!*

I know Angie is giving me this as a good luck card, but as a truck design, it's perfect. Silly and charming and cool—the ideal antidote to the hyper-glamorous logos of all the food trucks I saw at the Brooklyn Flea.

She's so talented. I wish she still took art seriously.

Then I see my phone. I left it on my bed all day, which is completely unlike me. I have three texts.

From Jonah: *Hey, princess, wanna come join us at Seersucker? Bianca and I are here!*

Urgh.

From Mike: *How's your weekend treated you? How's that pink truck? How about that drink? x*

Double urgh.

From a mystery number: *Hey. I'll be over at 7 pm next Sunday night for the first collection. Look forward to catching up! Cosmo.*

Isn't Cosmo friendly! Imagine if I end up buddies with my money-lender, how about that?

I don't have the energy to shower, or brush my teeth, or anything. I have never, ever been this tired but I still need to paint Toto with the new SkinnyWheels name and heart designs.

Mentally counting backward I figure I probably need to be on the road by 9:30 A.M. in order to find a good spot, so I need the paint job to be done and drying by 8:30 A.M., and I need to load the truck, and I really need to shower because I don't think I did today though I can't even remember, and that means forty minutes to blow-dry my hair, and I haven't done any laundry, and I don't have any clean panties, and I need to pick up napkins and maybe some bottled water and diet soda, and I need to get change for the cash register, and oh, damnit, I don't even have a cash register so I need to leave Rookhaven by 8:00 A.M.

I set my alarm for 5:30. And then fall—no, crash—to sleep.

CHAPTER 10

"Would you buy a low-fat, low-carb, high-protein salad from a pink truck called Toto?" I shout through the truck window at eight the next morning.

"I *so* would!" calls Coco, waving at me from the front stoop. "Good luck!"

"Go, ladybitch, go!" shouts Angie, lighting a cigarette. "Give me a woo!"

"Uh . . . woo!" I shout, trying to put Toto in gear. She grumbles for a few extra seconds, and for a moment I worry my career is over before it's even started, then coughs to life.

"*Woo!*" I say again, more authoritatively this time, throwing a fist punch out the window as I drive down Union Street. It's Monday morning, and I am ready to *work*!

Toto looks *great*. I wrote "SkinnyWheels" on her sides in bright red paint, and dotted her with hearts just like Angie's drawing. She looks girly and funny, but not schmaltzy. Sort of dilapidated and effortlessly cool. How Brooklyn.

The radio kicks on, and finds one of my favorite songs, "Here It Goes Again" by OK Go. I kind of like not being able to tune Toto's radio: it's like leaving my musical choices in the hands of fate. Or maybe Toto chooses for me.

I've missed driving. Julia taught me at Brown (a serious test of our friendship) and then let me borrow her car. She had a little brown VW Beetle we called the Poomeister. It died, tragically, in a confusing diesel-versus-unleaded accident last year. (Hey. It could have happened to anyone.) Anyway, I can't wait to sell my salads and—

Bang!

What the hell was that? I screech to a halt. That was a damn loud bang, it sounded like a gunshot. I think. Like I would know.

"Did you hear that, Toto?"

Everything is silent.

I start driving again. What's that whiffle-whiffle sound? It sounds like—

"You blew a tire!" shouts a voice.

I slam on the brakes again. On the sidewalk is a woman walking with a little girl and boy. The little boy is crying, probably because of that banging sound. I wonder what it was.

"Your back tire is blown!" she shouts again. I look closer. I know them!

"Lina!" I say. "Hi!" I get out of the car and cross over to them. "Hi, Pia! Hi, Gabe!" Lina is the woman who tipped me that two hundred dollars at the restaurant! It seems like forever since I met them at Bartolo's, but it was only Friday.

"You're moonlighting as a food trucker now?" she says, laughing. "Look guys! It's Pia from our pizza place!"

"Is there a gun?" The boy is still crying. Pia is shyly hiding behind her mom, peeking out at me. I wink at her as Lina comforts Gabe.

"No, honey, it was the tire on the truck! It popped, like a really big balloon."

Finally, it sinks in. "Sh . . . ish kebabs! My tire!" I say, remembering the kids. "I don't know how to change a tire!"

"There's probably a spare in the truck, right?" says Lina. I make an anguished search-me face, and she laughs. We all walk to the back of the truck, and I remember something Francie, the former owner, mentioned: everything "else" is in a trapdoor underneath the floor of the food truck.

"I'll help you," Lina says ten minutes later, when we have the tire and jack lying next to the truck on the road. "It can't be that hard."

"Oh, don't worry, I'm sure you have better things to do."

"Hey, I'm free all day. I'm taking a Mommy Day from work," she says cheerfully. "Kids, you want to help Pia with her truck for a little while?"

"Yeaaah!"

Lina seems to be the kind of mom who can say anything in an excited voice and her kids will squeal with enthusiasm.

For a second, I stare at the bedraggled blown tire, and the huge spare one (seriously, what do those things weigh? A hundred pounds?) next to it. The jack looks like a torture contraption. I have no idea what to do.

Then, a lightbulb moment. I take out my phone, go to YouTube, type in "how to change a truck tire," and watch the video. It's pretty straightforward. Hubcaps, lug nuts (heehee), jack . . .

"I would never have thought of that," Lina says, gesturing to the phone. "Seriously, that's impressive work."

I can't help laughing. Nothing I've ever done has *ever* been called "impressive work."

"So, why are you driving a food truck, anyway?"

As I change the tire, I tell her about my food truck idea, leaving out the fired-for-naked-table-dancing-with-Captain-Morgan and borrowing-money-from-a-guy-in-a-pawnshop bits. I say, instead, that I wanted to do it because I can't get a job as I'm only a graduate.

"Ah, the no experience, no job/no job, no experience catch-twenty-two," she says. "I remember that."

"Yeah, it seems bananas that after four years at college, I'm not even qualified to do Starbucks runs . . . but there you have it."

"I remember that stage," she says. "It's really hard. Starting adult life is tough, but everyone tells you it's going to be so easy after college."

"Exactly!" I say. She's being so nice to me that I want to cry. Typical.

"SkinnyWheels. It's a great idea, killer USP."

I have no idea what a USP is. "Thanks!"

"So, you must be passionate about food, huh?"

"Not really," I say. "I mean, I love to eat and I love going to restaurants and everything, but cooking has never been my thing. But I'm passionate about this idea, because it's mine, and no one else is doing it. And I think people want it."

"Spoken like a true entrepreneur."

Once the tire is changed, I offer them each a free pumpkin brownie, on the house (uh . . . truck). Pia and Gabe have been singing made-up songs to us for the past half hour, which is pretty damn adorable.

"Listen," says Lina as I climb back into the truck. "If you need anything, you should call me. I mean it." She hands over her business card. "Good luck today. I have a feeling you'll be a big success. And if you happen to be outside my office one day, text me. I'll make sure everyone in my building knows about it."

"I will, thank you!" I say. I'm elated. "And thank you, again, for the amazing tip last week."

She smiles and shakes her head. "Anytime."

This is it, I think, as I cruise over the Brooklyn Bridge. Me. Going to Manhattan with my food truck. I'm too excited to even be nervous about driving in the city. *My* city. I see girls my age walking to work, all carrying coffees and gym bags, all of us starting our adult lives with an adult job. . . . It's kind of funny to think that we were all babies at the same time, we all went through the childhood stages of Elmo and American Girl and *American Idol* and training bras and *Twilight* and first kisses and first waxes, and now we're all finally hitting adulthood.

Go us.

I text Julia on the way to Manhattan and reach her midtown office by 12:30. After I park down the street with surprisingly little difficulty (Ha! Suck it, Madeleine), Julia bounds over, shouting at the top of her lungs.

"Oh, golly! SkinnyWheels! This is the best food truck in the whole world!"

Glaring at her, I put the hand brake on, and head around the back of the truck to open up.

"Line up!" Julia is bossing someone. "Behind me. Go! Go!"

I place ten of each salad on one side of the counter, stack the dressings next to them and the brownies on the other side, and then open up the serving window.

Julia reaches up and helps me arrange the knives and forks, keeping up her running commentary the whole time.

"I can't believe I'm helping SkinnyWheels set up for the day! This is the coolest thing I've ever done! I am so psyched! Someone high-five me!"

I try to smile, but I'm suddenly so nervous, I can hardly breathe. I have no idea what I'm doing. I can't run a food truck. What if this doesn't work? What next? And how the hell will I pay back ten thousand dollars plus another thousand every Sunday for the next six weeks?

"May I take your order, ma'am?" I ask Julia, my voice tiny and high. I look behind her and see a line of two people patiently waiting. A line? Customers!

I can do this.

"I'll have one chicken salad with Julia dressing because it looks uh-mazing, and a low-fat brownie, please!" Julia is practically shouting. God, she's a bad actress. "Wow! This is gonna be the best lunch, ever!"

"That'll be six dollars for the salad, fifty cents for the dressing, and two dollars for the brownie, making a total of"—I pause, silently counting as fast as I can, yes, I know it's pathetic but I'm shit at math—"eight fifty, ma'am."

Julia hands me a twenty dollar bill. "Keep the change."

"No, I can't do that," I say firmly. "You need change."

"Thank you!" she says, sashaying away before I can force the money on her. I hear her shouting at the top of her voice again, "A salad from SkinnyWheels! Holy moly! This is super-awesome!"

"Hey," I say to the next guy in line, a spectacled geek. "What can I get you?"

"I'll have the turkey salad, the Kim dressing, and three string cheeses," he says.

I see two other people join the line, and stifle the urge to punch the air.

"What's the calorie count on the chicken salad?" asks a pinched-looking woman with frizzy hair.

"Uh, I, um—I'm getting them tonight. I'll have them this time to-morrow."

"Then I'll come back tomorrow."

The next person asks for a chicken salad and a low-fat brownie. Then I sell a turkey salad. Then two brownies and a turkey. Suddenly, the line is five people long.

"What's the fat count in the dressing?"

"What's your Twitter account?"

"Are you on Facebook?"

"What's your Web site?"

"Do you take requests?"

"Can I get a salad with no cheese?"

"Why is this brown?" says one large redheaded woman, pointing at something in her salad box.

I peer in. "It's avocado."

"You should put lemon juice on it. Then it won't go brown. That's disgusting."

"Okay . . ." (Rude!) "Would you like to swap it?"

"No. This is still a better value than the deli across the street."

"Thank you, ma'am!" I say. "Next customer!"

"Where is the nearest Chop't?"

"Seriously?" I say to the guy who asked that. He's a banker in a suit, mid-twenties, an ex-jock I'd guess, the kind who stopped playing sports in sophomore year of college and put on fifty pounds and now tries to keep his weight down by eating "clean." I know his type.

"Yeah," he says, smirking at me.

"I don't know that. And if I did, I wouldn't tell you. Their salad dress-ings are loaded with hidden fats and calories and sugar, anyway."

"They are?"

I have no idea. "Yes."

"Your salads are kind of boring."

"Well, they dance if you ask nicely."

"How do you make the low-fat brownies?"

"That's a secret." He raises an eyebrow. "Okay. It's made with pump-kin."

"Seriously? Explain to me how pumpkin can possibly substitute for good old-fashioned butter." Is he flirting with me? I don't have time for this. "Where are you from?"

"I'm from Brooklyn. If you're not going to order anything, step aside, hungry customers are waiting."

"Feisty." The guy smirks and ambles away. My words are echoing in my head. *I'm from Brooklyn.* Well, I am.

By 2:20, I've sold thirty chicken salads, thirty turkey salads, forty-eight brownies (well, forty-five, if you don't include the three I gave to Lina and her kids), and sixty-four string cheeses. I forgot to get water and diet soda, but I'll have it tomorrow. And I've taken requests for vegetarian salads, and more kinds of low-fat desserts, and I'll get a URL and start a Facebook page and Twitter account tonight. Easy.

Best of all, I've got six hundred dollars in cash in my cash register (okay, it's an old Barbie lunchbox that I found in the kitchen in Rookhaven).

That night, inspired by my successes of the day, I write a little something for the Facebook page to explain to customers why SkinnyWheels is so special.

WELCOME TO SKINNYWHEELS

Everything we make is baked, never fried. We try not to add sugar, we never add sweeteners, and we would not touch corn syrup with a ten-foot pole. We also don't add salt unless absolutely necessary, and we avoid gluten. So when you eat our salads and snacks, you know you're getting just what you ordered.

The bottom line? We love food. But we also love our bodies. And we don't want to choose between them.

And lastly, I have to do the calorie counts. It seems like every damn person in Manhattan counts calories. So I am going to weigh and measure all the salad ingredients for tomorrow, estimate the calories with the help of good ol' Google, and then add them all up.

The only problem is that I can't do it.

My numbers aren't working out. Only 78 calories for the chicken salad, though awesome to imagine, just can't be right.

I do the numbers again. This time I get 743 calories. That can't be right, either. . . . That would have to be a deep-fried chicken breast, stuffed with lard and then rolled in chocolate.

I place my forehead on the kitchen table and make a moaning sound for a few seconds. Then I bang my forehead against the table.

This kind of cheers me up, so I do it again.

And then one more time for luck.

"Well, that looks normal," says a voice. I look up. It's Madeleine. "What's going on?"

"I can't do math," I say quietly.

"Well, we knew *that*," she says, grabbing some leftover chicken and broccoli stir-fry from the fridge. I sigh. Typical bitchy Madeleine comment. "Why don't I do it for you? Math is my thing."

I'm stunned. "Are you sure? It's calorie counting."

"Oh, that's totally my thing." Madeleine sits opposite me, doling out the stir-fry into two bowls, and hands me a fork with the kind of easy familiarity that people have when they're, you know, friends. "I calorie count whenever I'm bored."

"That sounds . . . fun?" I'm dubious. Not to mention stunned that she's talking to me. "I'm trying to work out the chicken salad."

"Four ounces of chicken breast? A hundred and twenty calories. No skin, baked, right?"

"Right."

"That's one-twenty. . . ."

"Okay . . ." I start scribbling it down.

"The vegetables, plus the reduced-fat feta, plus . . . okay, that's one-ninety-four."

I'm staring at her, openmouthed. "How do you know all this?"

"I don't know. . . . I learned them in high school. It's like riding a bike, you never forget."

"But you never diet."

She pauses. "I guess my mom—our home life—is a bit, uh, dramatic. When I was a kid I did times tables in my head to keep myself calm. Calories were just a step up. Counting is calming."

"I can honestly say I have never thought that," I say. Madeleine looks at me and cracks up, and I start laughing, too. This is the first time we've laughed together since freshman year. Since the night of I Hate You, Pia.

"Okay, okay, enough messing around. Hand me the next salad," she says, forking some broccoli into her mouth.

By the time we've finished, I'm almost tearful with gratitude.

"This would have taken me all night. Thank you so, so much," I say.

"No problem," she says. "I actually came in here to see if you needed help with your numbers. Profits and losses and all that. It's not hard, but there's a knack to it."

"Can you figure out a way for me to make more money without cloning myself and Toto?"

Madeleine thinks for a second. "Put your prices up by a dollar. Charge seven dollars for the salads, one dollar for the dressing, and three dollars for the desserts. And make the sides three dollars, too."

"But what if people who bought from me today come back tomorrow?"

"Launch special. It's time to get serious." She shrugs. "People can put up or shut up."

I write everything down as we finish the stir-fry.

"Why are you being so nice to me?" The words are out before I can stop myself. "You're never nice to me. Not since . . ."

Madeleine jumps up and rinses out our bowls, and my words trail off. A really long silence follows. I'm staring at Madeleine and she's staring into the sink.

"I'm sorry about that night," she says finally, without turning around. "I was embarrassed about it, and then I was angry at myself. I guess I just took it out on you, and then it was just sort of the way things were."

"But why . . . why did you say that stuff?" I ask. "I thought we were friends."

Another long silence.

"Everything is—or was—always easy for you," she mumbles finally.

"What?" I say. Did I just hear her right?

Madeleine turns around, chewing her bottom lip.

"You always seemed to have everything so easy. At college. Your parents are rich, you're thin, your skin is perfect, you make friends easily, you always look just right. You've never had a problem in your life."

My jaw drops open. "That's why we haven't spoken in years? Because you think everything is easy for me? That's not even true!"

"Whatever," she says. "And that night when I said that stuff, I'd heard the, um, guy I liked talking about you. He was crazy about you and you were totally oblivious. I was, I don't know—"

"Jealous?" I say. "Who was the guy?" I don't remember Madeleine liking anyone in freshman year, she was all about studying.

Madeleine sits down and picks up the pack of cards, shuffling them awkwardly. "Does it matter? I guess I just thought, it's not fair. Nothing ever goes wrong for you. You're always at the center of everything. People always automatically like you. When you say something, everyone listens. It's like you have . . . a sense of social entitlement or something."

"Social *entitlement*?" I don't know whether to laugh or cry. Or slap her. "But—but I just try to be friendly. This is hilarious. I've spent my entire life trying to look like I belong and never feeling it, and it worked so well that you hate me!"

"But you never look nervous. Or awkward."

"Just because I act like that doesn't mean I'm not a total mess on the inside, dude," I say. "And everything has *not* been easy for me. I was kicked out of two boarding schools, okay?"

"You were? Why?"

"I don't want to talk about it right now," I say, my voice shaking. These are the hot, shameful memories I try to bury deep inside of me. Deeper than my Eddie memories, deeper than anything else. The memories that make me hate myself.

Madeleine still won't let it go. "But I bet you were popular."

"Popularity is a myth," I say. "And I never fit in anywhere, not really. I don't keep in touch with anyone from any of my boarding schools. I had panic attacks. . . . I still do, sometimes. After I was expelled the second time, my mother told me she was ashamed to have me for a daughter." I close my eyes, willing the memory to go away. Even thinking about that makes me feel sick. It was the worst fight ever. "Things between my mother and me have never been the same."

"Your parents love you. They call you all the time. My dad hasn't called me since my thirteenth birthday. And my mother prefers my stepbrothers to me. It's like a family joke, it's so obvious."

"Maddy, this is ridiculous. Are we competing over whose life is the shittiest? I don't know what it's like to be you, you don't know what it's like to be me, so how can you judge?" I feel tears coming on. Oh, God, no, please don't let me cry. "I'm just trying my best, Madeleine. Jesus!"

"Okay, I'm so sorry," she says. "I was wrong. I'm sorry, please don't cry!"

Tears are escaping out of my eyes and running down my face. "I hate crying, it's so *itchy*. And I wasn't even sad."

"Sometimes crying just feels good," says Madeleine, and we both laugh through our tears, sorry to sound like an episode of fucking *Gilmore Girls,* but it's true. "I didn't mean to upset you. I'm fucked up." She pauses, staring into space. "I'm totally fucked up."

"Everyone is fucked up in different ways!" I say. "That's what makes us special."

Madeleine laughs.

This is nice. Slightly awkward, but nice.

"So . . . what's with you and my brother?"

For a second, I'm too shocked to reply.

"Um . . . nothing."

"What, do you think I'm blind? I saw you making out at the party! And he told me you guys have been flirting over text!"

We have? Oh. *Merde.* That textual healing tutorial for Coco.

"Well, Mads, you know, um, I think your brother is an incredibly nice guy, and really funny and good-looking, but . . ."

"You just hate those nice, funny, good-looking ones, huh?"

"Ha," I say, thinking about that Aidan guy from the cab the other night. He was perfect. But I'll never see him again. And there is no such thing as perfect.

Madeleine sighs. "Just promise me you won't break Mike's heart. He's only had one girlfriend."

"I won't," I say. As if I could break his heart! Jesus, we only kissed once. Okay, we had sex. Whatever. "I promise."

Madeleine jumps up again, looking through her herbal tea collection. With all the serious stuff out of the way, I can't think of anything to say. How do you start chatting normally after so many years of ignoring each other?

"I love living here," she says finally, looking around the kitchen. "I feel like it's the only thing in my life that works right now."

"You don't love your job?" I'm surprised.

"I wouldn't say *love* . . . I mean, it's fine. I just feel stressed about how much I have to do sometimes."

"Yeah, you work really long hours."

"No . . . I mean, like, how much I have to prove. I need to get on the fast track for promotions at work, and that means impressing the right people, and I need to find a boyfriend and then a husband, and get married and have children, all by thirty."

"That's, like, eight years away," I say. I never think about being thirty. Hell, I never think about being twenty-five.

"But that's a lot to do. And I'm the only person who can do it. No one is going to do it for me. What if I fail?" She's staring into space, chewing her lip. "Sometimes I feel like getting through school and college and landing my first job was this long, exhausting marathon, and now someone's said, okay, whatever, now you have another marathon right away. I'm right back at the starting line. It's like everything I've done so far doesn't count."

"Everything will work out just the way you want it to," I say. "At least you know what you want."

Madeleine laughs. "I do not! I just know what I'm supposed to want! And what if it doesn't work out? What if I'm the person who ends up unemployed and single and living at home with my mother, watching *Jeopardy*?"

"Then . . . you'll probably be totally happy with that decision."

"I don't want to be happy with that decision! I don't want it!" Madeleine slams her hands on the table.

"Okay, Maddy, calm down. . . ." Then I say the four words I never believe when I say them to myself. "Everything will be fine."

Madeleine looks over at me. "I hope you're right."

CHAPTER 11

It's Sunday afternoon. Cosmo's coming over in a couple of hours for his first thousand-dollar interest payment. I'm looking forward to catching up with him.

Once I pay him, I'll only have three hundred left in my Barbie lunchbox. I admit, I was kind of expecting to earn a bit more, or for the ingredients to cost a bit less, you know?

But it was only my first week. I had a lot of unexpected expenses. And you need to spend money to make money, right? It's weird for me to be so work-focused, but I love it. I still have ages before I have to repay the entire loan (and before my parents arrive), and by then, I'll be rolling in the Benjamins, as they say. (Yeah, they totally say that.)

Want to hear something shocking? Maddy and I are definitely friends again! It's making life at Rookhaven so much easier. Take yesterday afternoon, for example: we hung out in the kitchen as I was experimenting with low-fat banana bread recipes, and then Angie, Julia, and Coco tested them with us and then—this is the real kicker—we all played cards around the kitchen table. It was Angie's idea; she's a poker fiend from way back. Talk about good clean fun: it was like something out of a goddamn Norman Rockwell painting. If, uh, Norman Rockwell characters played poker for matchsticks and drank beer.

And from what I can tell, Angie's recovering from her meltdown. She's currently at some all-day boozy brunch in Manhattan. Julia's gone to a kickboxing class, dragging a reluctant Coco along with her. I think Madeleine is upstairs. And I'm eating leftover ham and pea soup that Coco made last night and writing out tomorrow's menu.

Salad 1 = chicken + avocado + snow peas + beets + cherry
       tomato + reduced-fat feta + baby greens

Salad 2 = turkey + watercress + almonds + apple + celery +
       reduced-fat cheddar + baby greens

Salad 3 = (tuna + low-fat mayo) + boiled egg + sweet corn +
       cannellini beans + iceberg

Salad 4 = avocado + cherry tomato + sweet potato + spinach

Salad 5 = cottage cheese + apple + ham + almonds + baby
       greens

Dessert 1 = brownie (– fat)

Dessert 2 = banana bread (– fat)

It's not exactly the most exciting salad menu ever, I know. But it's getting there.

I take a moment to send a tweet. *11am tomorrow: 23rd and Park. Savor your food and save your ass with SkinnyWheels x PS first 10 to RT get a free brownie.*

I've also expanded the dressings. There's a tzatziki one called Angie, a ginger-miso one called Coco, and a low-fat ranch dressing after Madeleine. Ranch has never been my favorite, but it's growing on me. Ha.

At that moment, my phone rings. Mike.

Again? He's called almost every night this week. And texted, and Facebooked.

I contemplate ignoring it—he'll get the message, right?—and then I remember Madeleine's request. I really don't want to ruin this new dé-tente we're enjoying.

Apparently I need to make my feelings clear. Simply ignoring him in the weeks since we hooked up clearly wasn't enough.

So I make my voice super-chilled and calm.

"Why, hello."

"You're alive! Okay, I've gotta go, there are some Saint Bernards pa-trolling the streets right now looking for you. . . ."

I can't help laughing. "I've been a busy girl, Michael."

"Michael! Wow. Nobody's called me that since I was seven and stole an Oh Henry! bar from a grocery store in Maryland."

"You stole an Oh Henry! bar? Does anyone even eat them?"

"I love them," Mike says, sounding hurt. "Seriously. They're the best candy bar ever."

I laugh, but I'm waiting for him to get to the point. C'mon, dude. I have to get up early tomorrow.

"Well"—he clears his throat—"I was wondering if you'd like to have a playdate next weekend. You know . . . go to the park, play on the swings, feed the ducks. . . ."

"Dude, that'd be great, but I've started this business. I'm experi-menting with low-fat cookie and cheesecake recipes."

"You bake?" he says, barely containing his amusement.

"Affirmative," I say, trying not to sound annoyed. Why does every-one find it so hilarious that I bake now? It's not rocket science. Julia came into the kitchen this morning and saw me wearing Aunt Jo's frilly apron and oven mitts, and laughed so hard she fell over and hit her head on the doorframe.

"I'll help you," he says. "I know a guy who keeps chickens in Red Hook. I'll get you some eggs."

"Are you kidding?"

"Nope," he says. "Best eggs you ever tasted in your life."

At that moment the doorbell rings. Cosmo!

"Aces," I say quickly. "That would be awesome. Can you bring them over? Maybe next Saturday?"

There's a pause. "I'm your egg delivery boy now?"

"Uh, I didn't mean it like that," I say, walking out of the kitchen toward the front door. Why is Mike so damn touchy? Sheesh. Just like Madeleine. "How about we grab a drink or something on Friday night instead and you can give them to me then."

"Friday night, eight o'clock? Brooklyn Social? It's a date!"

"It's a drink," I say firmly as the doorbell rings again. "I gotta go." I hang up, reaching for the door. "Cosmo!"

But it's not Cosmo.

It's a giant. A Transformer-shaped giant in a tight black T-shirt and black jeans with huge beefed-up shoulders and no ass. The kind of guy who thinks he's buff because he takes steroids and pumps iron, though the reality is acne-studded fat city. *So* not my bag.

"I'm Nicky," he says in an unexpectedly high voice. "Cosmo is in the car."

I look behind him and see a Prius double-parked next to Toto.

"Cosmo drives a Prius?"

"He's highly evolved," says Nicky. I grin at him, thinking he's being funny. He's not. "I'm here for the money."

"Sure, I've got it upstairs, why don't you come in and have a seat?" I say.

"No, I'll wait here."

Nicky folds his arms and a sudden realization washes over me: Nicky is a heavy. He's the brawn, the muscle, the bad guy.

And all of a sudden, I'm scared.

"I'll . . . just . . . get it now."

I leave the front door open, because closing it on his face feels kind of rude, and run upstairs. Then I run back, as fast as I can, a clutching fear in my stomach, and hand over the envelope.

"It's there, the full thousand, you don't have to count it."

"If it's all the same to you, I will anyway," says Nicky. I nod, and watch as he meticulously counts the money twice over, then nods. "Next week, have it ready," he says. "Cosmo doesn't like waiting."

Nicky walks slowly down the stoop, back to the Prius, and gets in the passenger side. Cosmo turns to talk to him, then looks out the window and up at me in the open doorway for a second.

Then he drives away.

At that moment, I hear Vic coughing from his customary early-evening position on the bench outside his apartment.

I lean over the stoop. "Good evening, Vic!" God, I hope he didn't hear any of that.

"You fraternizing with those guys in the Prius?" he asks.

"They're just friends."

"Friends like those," he mutters. "You watch yourself, Pia, you hear me?"

"I will, I promise," I say, trying to sound lighthearted. "Don't worry about me."

Vic doesn't reply, so before the silence can get awkward, I say, "Night!" and head inside.

CHAPTER 12

But by the end of the week, I've decided that the whole Nicky-Cosmo thing is fine. Totally fine.

Nicky can't help being a roid-droid. Well, he can, obviously, but whatever. Maybe he's insecure. Maybe he was a skinny, helpless little teenager who got picked on by the bigger kids. Judge not lest ye be judged, and all that shit.

Anyway, I've had another awesome week on the SkinnyWheels trail. I've easily made enough money to pay Cosmo back this week and everything. I'll have no problems making it all back, I know it.

I think Toto is in a good mood, too: her radio magically tuned into a local station's Village People hour when I parked in Washington Square, and I've been singing along to "In the Navy" and "Milkshake" all morning.

And that's when I see her.

Skank-face Bianca.

Driving a brand-new, glossy black food truck with "Let Them Eat Cake" painted in red letters on the side.

That truck is brand-new! It looks like Darth Vader! It must have cost tens of thousands! Did she borrow that from Cosmo? She's blasting "Low Rider" by War over loudspeakers, so everyone turns to look at her.

When Bianca is no more than ten feet away, her truck slows down to a crawl. She smiles at me smugly as our eyes meet.

Her slogan reads, "Salads and cakes with all of the taste and none of the calories."

Oh, my God.

That bitch stole my idea!

My fists clench and my face grows hot. I am so angry it is actually *painful*.

Next to her shiny behemoth, my darling Toto looks like an old toy missing half its fur. No one loves an old toy except the owner. Everyone loves the shiny new toy.

I must calm down. Work first. Anger later.

I plaster a big smile across my face, get back in the truck, and start serving. When my day is over, I start Toto, head for home, and e-mail all the girls from my cell.

That skank-face waitress copied my idea. Pleeeeeease check out @letthemeatcake or the FB page and if she's anywhere near you, go buy something. I need details. Then I need revenge.

Just think: all that time I was giving my little speech at the Brooklyn Flea, she was making fun of me—but secretly noting it all down so she could start an identical business, too!

"Cockmonkey!" I scream as I drive down Houston. Even swearing doesn't make me feel better, and you know swearing when driving is emotionally restorative. The radio creeps stations, as it does whenever I'm driving, from "Macho Man" by the Village People to "I Hate You So Much Right Now." "Damn straight, Toto!" I yell.

By the time I get back to Brooklyn, I have e-mail replies:

From Angie: *Want me to cut the bitch?*

From Coco: *Oh no!!!!! That is SO UNFAIR!!!!! I'm doing afterschool activities will be home soon to talk!!!! xxxxxx*

From Julia: *M and I checked it out. Very similar salads, low-fat cookies etc. Bought one of everything. Taste-test tonight. We can deal with this.*

From Madeleine: *Don't worry, her truck looks like Darth Vader. And I stuck gum to the window when she wasn't looking. Mx*

I love this new supportive Madeleine.

But skank-face Bianca has put me in a foul mood. It's Friday night! I should be focused on finding a decent happy hour, getting drunk, and hooking up, like every other twenty-two-year-old in the world. Not fuming and worrying.

I get back to the commissary and clean the truck, my brain going at a hundred miles an hour. I can't offer a truck as big, shiny, and pretty as skank-face's, but if I work hard enough, maybe I can come up with more ways to impress customers. If they like the food, they'll tell a friend the next day, right? All I have to do is work harder.

I'll start doing breakfasts on Monday, I decide, walking back to Rookhaven. Maybe that would give me the edge over Bianca's stupid Let Them Eat Cake truck. I could make egg-white omelets, maybe, or do low-fat pancakes. The profits on pancakes must be insane. And what about a SkinnyWheels loyalty card? A tell-a-friend campaign? Yes! I could print up postcards with the SkinnyWheels logo on them; they're cute and people might send them to their friends, and then when their friends bring the postcards to the truck, they get 50 percent off their first order! Yes! Yes! I punch the air with joy, garnering a strange look from a woman walking past.

It's still only 4:00 P.M., so I head upstairs for a very long bath in the second floor bathroom (there's only a shower on my floor). It's very old school: pale pink, with a claw-footed bathtub that you can practically swim in. I do a full de-stress treatment: face mask, hair mask, leg shave, body scrub, the lot. But my brain still won't stop. Bianca copied me. I'm only barely making enough money to pay Cosmo back. How am I going to pay Cosmo back? What if I can't do it? And what about my parents?

I'm working myself up into a frenzy. A might-have-a-panic-attack frenzy.

Breathe, I tell myself. *You're fine. Everything will be fine.*

And for once, I actually listen.

When I get out of the bath, feeling slightly calmer, I notice some words just visible in the misty mirror. Someone obviously wrote them on the mirror in steam this morning and forgot to rub them out, so the fresh steam brought them up again.

UGLY UGLY UGLY.

Holy *merde.*

Who would write that? The most likely culprits are obvious: Madeleine or Coco. They're the ones who use this bathroom, along with Angie, but Angie showers at night. And Jules and I use the shower on our floor.

The heaven and hell of shared living: there are no secrets. If one girl at boarding school is bulimic, everyone knows about it. Ditto if she's fighting with her sister, or crying over a guy, or her parents are getting a divorce. I learned early how to protect my privacy. Not writing anything private down, ever, is the most important rule. Including on mirrors.

Maybe whoever wrote it was just having a bad morning. Maybe it's not a big deal. Who knows.

That's it, I want a drink.

I put on my motorcycle boots, because I feel like kicking some bitchy skank-face ass, and my backless black dress. I take the book I've been reading, *The Best of Everything,* as it's pure escapism. Purse, gloss, keys, done.

As I walk down Union Street, my mind wanders to Aidan. My knight in shining yellow cab.

Odds are, in a borough of 2.5 million people, I won't run into him again . . . and yet I can't stop secretly thinking about him. I tingle at the idea, a funny squirmy buzz that sort of makes me feel sick. I wonder where he is right now.

The flipside of Aidan though, is the memory of Eddie and all the reasons I can't get involved with Aidan, even if I have the chance. *Flight risk.* I never want to go through a breakup like that again. Ever. If someone as kind, strong, smart, and steadfast as Eddie looked into my soul and saw that I just wasn't good enough, that I wasn't—let's face it—worth loving, how could any other half-decent guy act differently?

Exactly.

I'm staying single.

Usually, I turn right at Court Street, but it makes me think of driving into Manhattan for work. So today I turn left, and walk past Carroll Park, past people out enjoying the last of the summer sun . . . till I find myself outside Minibar.

Where Aidan likes to drink.

There's no harm in checking it out, is there?

(I believe they call this stalking lite.)

Minibar is exactly the *bijou* little drinking den that the name implies. Exposed brick, tin ceilings, wood floors. I order a vodka on the rocks and take a seat at the booth next to the window.

This place is sort of cool, but dignified. It's not trying too hard to impress you, but it's not unfriendly, either. It's just right. No wonder he likes it.

I text all the girls to join me as soon as they can. Only Angie replies.

Worst day ever. FUCKING EDAMAME PHOTOSHOOT. In a drink. Having bars. Join? Think tonight is gonna get wiiiiiiiild.

Ah, great, kamikaze Angie is back.

I've never been the type to worry about my friends, but I'm starting to wonder if everyone is actually a total mess. It's like we're all pretending to be fantastic but secretly freaking out, all the time. I wish college had warned us.

I sigh deeply.

"Long day, baby?" calls the bartender.

He's cute, but for once in my life I'm not in the mood to flirt, so I just smile/grimace at him and stare out the window. God, it's nice to sit in silence. After the go-go-go of the past few weeks, I can look out the window and just . . . be.

After a few minutes, however, "just being" gets pretty boring. So I pick up *The Best of Everything* and start reading.

> *He'll never call me, Barbara thought, so I can think what I want about him. It's perfectly safe to have fantasies. . . . It's just a crush, but I feel it.*

God, that's just how I feel. I wonder where Aidan is right now. He has to be somewhere. Sometimes living in New York seems like an endless version of that movie *Serendipity*. You could almost-but-not-quite run into the same people, the same potential friends or enemies or lovers, for years. How many times have I come close to bumping into Aidan in the past few weeks? What if I almost-but-not-quite run into him forever?

At that moment the phone in the bar rings, and the bartender answers it.

"Aidan! Dude, yeah, I've still got it. . . ."

Aidan! Aidan, Aidan? My Aidan, Aidan? I mean, he's not *my* Aidan, Aidan, obviously, but—

"Well, if you're gonna let your dog sleep in my bar all night, I'm gonna hang on to his stupid chew toy, you know." I hear a squeaking sound, and look over. The bartender is holding up a giant rubber bone, the kind that dogs carry around with them sometimes, like a canine security blanket. "Yeah, yeah, I'll make sure no one else takes it. It'll be safe. Have a good weekend, mate."

And he hangs up. The way he said mate was the way you might talk to a British person to make fun of their accent. *May-t. May-t.*

"Hi!" exclaims a voice, and I look up. It's Coco. "This is awesome! I didn't even know this bar existed!"

"Sit down, Coco, I'll get you a drink. What'll it be?"

"Oh! Um . . . okay. Oh, God!" Coco gazes at the menu. "I don't know. . . . What are you having?"

"I'm having vodka on the rocks," I say.

She makes a face. "I'll have a glass of wine. White. No, red. No, white."

I go to the bar to order Coco a glass of chenin blanc.

"Is she twenty-one?" the bartender asks.

"She sure is," I say, with my widest smile. Actually, she's twenty, but she can handle it. The rest of the civilized world lets you drink at eighteen, for Pete's sake. I'm trying to figure out how to ask him about Aidan. I can't, I realize. Not without looking like a crazy stalker. And worse, he'd probably tell Aidan about me. I'm annoyingly easy to describe.

Merde.

"Tell me all about this biyatch who's copying you!" says Coco when I get back.

Yes. Think about work. Not Aidan. "Well, it's skank-face Bianca, the waitress from Bartolo's, the one who was flirting with Jonah at the Brooklyn Flea," I say. "Anyway, she listened to everything I said about SkinnyWheels, then went and copied me."

"Why would she do that?"

I look at Coco, confused. Why would Bianca copy me? Because that's how some people work. Because she's the kind of competitive girl who just wants to succeed at all costs. Because something about me annoyed her. Who knows? Who cares?

Instead of saying all that, though, I shrug.

"Let's talk about something else till Julia gets here."

"I have so much to tell you," says Coco. "Remember the texts we sent to Eric the other weekend? Well, he totally replied. Let me show you."

We go through all of Eric's texts, one by one, and I offer the best analysis I can. Actually, the dude sounds like a dumb jock to me, but who am I to judge? I've been that soldier. I've fought that battle.

"And he's in New York! Tonight! I think he might want to see me!"

She shows me his last text. *Pre-gaming from 3pm. The blackout express is on its way to party town.* Urgh.

"I'm going to play it cool," says Coco. "Can you help me plan what to say? Do you think he likes me?"

Coco and I spend the best part of the next half hour planning her text reply. She's so nervous, you'd think she's never been on a date, never had a boyfriend, never had se—

Oh, my God. I bet she's never had sex. She's held a torch for this guy for, what, six years? She hasn't had a boyfriend in the time I've known her, she's certainly not the barhopping social-animal type, she's never mentioned another guy. . . .

I don't know anyone my age who's never had sex, except for, you know, the Bible thumpers at college. And most of them were probably doing it in secret; one of them dropped out to have a baby (I don't get it—do they think if there's no condom, it doesn't really count?).

I look at Coco thoughtfully. She's brushing her blond fringe out of her eyes, like a little kid. She looks so damn vulnerable. I just want to protect her and make life better for her. She seems like she needs it.

"I am sure Eric likes you," I say. "It's impossible he's never wondered what might happen between you guys. You're far too gorgeous."

"No! You mean that?" says Coco, blushing pink with pleasure. "I . . . oh, wowsers, let's just send this text."

In the end, we settle on *Have a blast. Let me know if you need any tips, big guy.* Coco is almost sweating with nerves as she sends it.

"Hands up if your day sucked ass," says a voice. I put my hand up and turn around. It's Julia. "I'm getting a beer. And a tequila."

"We've been working on this deal," she explains, once she sits down. "I did my one tiny part perfectly, and everyone was happy with me. But then I corrected my boss in front of everyone and—actually, he's not my boss, he's just more senior in my team—and anyway, he literally screamed at me to, and I quote: 'shut the fuck up and fuck the fuck off.' "

Coco and I gasp. "Are you serious?"

"That's nothing," she says. "My work is so aggressive. It's kill or be killed, it's like the fucking *Hunger Games*. It makes me feel sick. I actually have"—she lowers her voice—"diarrhea from nerves sometimes."

"Ew," I say. Julia's never been so honest about her job before. Most of the time she paints it perfect, in her determined little type A way.

Julia rubs her eyes. Only girls who don't wear mascara or eyeliner can do that. If I even touch my face, I become a giant inkblot.

Jules sighs. "I didn't think it would be like this. I thought I'd finally fit in somewhere . . . but I don't. I never do."

"You don't?" I'm surprised. Jules always seems so confident. Captain of everything, so smart and loud and sure of herself . . .

"I just can't imagine doing this for, like, the next forty years." Julia suddenly looks like she's trying not to cry, and I'm overwhelmed with the desire to protect her at all costs, too. She deserves to be happy.

"Maybe you shouldn't think in terms of forty years. Think about short-term goals," I suggest, trying to be practical and helpful, the way she would for me. "Like, from now till Christmas."

"But I'm a long-term goal person. I've reached my first long-term goal—a banking job—but I don't feel like I thought I would." She pauses, and hiccups a waft of booze. "I don't . . . I don't . . . feel like me."

"Maybe just relax and try to enjoy it," I say. "Life is meant to be fun, otherwise, what's the point?"

"Spoken like a true hedonist," she says, rolling her eyes. Ouch. I've been working really hard lately, damnit.

"Well, you don't have to be a banker," I point out. "There are other careers in the world."

"Yeah, maybe I'll quit. Go back to college, do an MBA, or travel or something," she says.

"What?" I'm stunned. The idea of Julia leaving Rookhaven just feels wrong.

And Coco looks like a kid who's just discovered Santa doesn't exist.

"You'd leave me again? It was bad enough when you went to college—"

"No! Of course not!" says Julia quickly. "And it's great, really, I mean, it's amazing, totally my dream job." She smiles brightly at us. "It's what I've always wanted. I just need to get through the first year and it'll be so much easier. And the money is great, and the bonus should sweeten it, right?"

She takes a long swig of her beer without looking at us.

"I think we all just have to do our best," I say. "We're all in the same boat. We're all starting out."

"Let's all have another shot," says Julia, slamming her empty bottle down on the table. "And I have skank-face's food."

Ten minutes later, we're halfway through the wares from Let Them Eat Cake. The salads aren't very good—one chicken, one tuna, uninspiring vegetables and brown curling lettuce—but the cakes are exceptional.

"*Merde,* these are good." I despair, chewing another bite of a blondie.

"Wowsers. These are not low-fat or low-sugar," says Coco, eating an oatmeal cookie. "Trust me. I can tell. My heart only beats this fast when I eat a lot of sugar."

"I know, I can actually taste the butter and cream." Julia is simultaneously enjoying a key lime pie and a red velvet cupcake.

"How can we find out?" I throw my utterly delicious peanut butter blondie down in disgust, and then pick it up and have another bite.

"Wasn't there some kind of fat and carb experiment in chem class?" says Julia excitedly. "With like, a Bunsen burner, and—oh."

We all sit back, dejected. We're never going to get our hands on a Bunsen burner.

Another round of tequila it is.

"I thought you didn't do shots," I say to Julia. "I thought they were the reason the housewarming party got so out of control."

"Yeah, well, maybe I'm tired of being in control." Lick, sip, suck. "Madeleine is on three dates tonight," Julia adds.

"What?" say Coco and I in unison.

"She decided it's time to get a boyfriend, so she's been Internet dating. She's got them lined up for super-efficient forty-five-minute drink-dates after work tonight, one-two-three, like dominos." Julia pauses. "Shit, don't tell her I told you. I think it might be a secret."

"Sheesh, she is organized," I say. "Why doesn't she just do what we did at college: get drunk in a bar and see what happens?"

"She never did that," Julia reminds me. "She dated Sebastian, and that was it."

"Oh, yeah." Sebastian. Math major. I don't think I ever even heard him say anything.

I get another round in, and Julia goes to the bathroom. Coco is still staring obsessively at her phone, so I gaze out the window, wondering where Aidan is, and why I have a crush so strong that I'm thinking about him this much, days later. . . .

And that's when I get a text from Angie.

Just ran into Eddie at Brinkley's. What are the fucking odds?

I blink a few times. Did I read that right? Eddie? Maybe it's an auto-correct mistake.

I reply: *Eddie? My Eddie?*

Angie replies: *Mr. Flight Risk himself.*

I reply: *Are you sure?*

Angie replies: *Ladybitch, we all went skiing together, remember? I know your ex when I see him.*

CHAPTER 13

"I'm having a cigarette," I mutter to Coco, and run outside the bar.

I lean against the wall, trying to breathe and think at the same time. It shouldn't be hard, but it is. Eddie's here? He's in New York? Walking the same streets at me? Part of me wants to text back "did he ask about me? How did he look? What was he wearing? Was he with a girl? What was she wearing?" and about a million other questions.

But I also don't want to know. I don't want to know anything that would make him part of my present rather than my past. Wait, maybe I do. . . . No, no, I don't, I don't want anything to do with him. He broke my heart. I trusted him and loved him and it was the stupidest thing I ever did.

A second later, another text arrives. Thank God Angie can read my mind.

No chitchat. We just said hi. He was on his way in, I was on my way out . . . He looks just the same as ever. Wasn't with a girl.

It seems almost strange he exists, ridiculous that for the past four years he's been walking around eating breakfast and studying and living a life, when I've been effectively mourning him. Is that weird?

I put a cigarette in my mouth and light it with shaky hands. Why is my heart pounding like this? How can just *hearing* about Eddie still have this effect on me?

Another text from Angie.

Dude, are you there? Should I not have told you? Do you want to meet me?

Shit, I better reply. I need to make her think I'm fine. Act natural.

Yes, no, of course, thanks for telling me, small world! Talk tomorrow!

Yeah. Real natural.

I stub out my cigarette and head back inside. Julia is ordering more shots. Yes. Drinking. Drinking is good.

"More shots!" I shout. "And whiskey!"

It's a good thing that Julia and Coco don't know anything about Eddie, because I don't want to explain why, years later, hearing he's now living in New York has spun me into a quasi-meltdown.

Instead, I want to talk about why love sucks ass.

"There is no point," I say, slamming down my third whiskey sour. "No point in any of it. Either you'll reject him or he'll reject you."

"Any of what?" says Julia, hiccupping slightly. "And who is rejecting who?"

"Men, love, the men thing," I say. "Better to be single and just have, y'know, buck fuddies. I mean fuck buddies."

Julia laughs so hard at "buck fuddies" that she nearly falls off her chair.

"Yes there is! Soul mates!" says Coco, devastated I'd even consider saying otherwise.

I shake my head. "Soul mates don't exist. Love is just hormones and good timing."

I look around. The bar is full of beautiful Brooklynites starting their evenings, and I'm hungry.

"Starving," I say, a full sentence suddenly seeming like a lot of effort. "Need food."

Julia punches the air. "Yesh! Where?"

"Bartolo's!" I say, instantly cheered at the thought. Yay! Lovely Bartolo's, with lovely pretty Jonah. Thank hell we're just friends. I'm never going to have any boyfriends again. And I'm going to stop thinking about stupid Eddie, and for that matter, stupid Aidan, and I'm going to stop crushing on him immediately, too. Love sucks. Yeah.

We roll out of the bar onto Court Street. Everything is a bit fuzzy and warm, and I keep tripping over my own feet.

Holding hands with Jules and Coco, I skip into Bartolo's, straight up to the bar, where Jonah, lovely beekeeping Jonah, is opening a bottle of wine. I am delighted to see him.

"*Jonah!*" I say, landing with a skippy thud. "How the sweet hell are you, my little cowboy? Your hair looks nice. Be honest: is it highlighted?"

"Dude, have you been drinking?" says Jonah, laughing. I introduce the girls. Coco high-fives him and Julia leans over to give him a kiss on both cheeks, and I realize, they're hammered. Am I hammered?

"We are just *so hungry*," I say in a library whisper, seeing a tray of cheesy lasagne go past. "So, is skank-face still working any shifts? I mean Bianca?"

"No, she quit," says Jonah, looking confused by the "skank-face" comment. "Hey, guess what? I'm starting my own business! I'm gonna be a bee-babysitter! So many people are into the urban bee thing now, you know? But they don't always have the time or know-how to look after their bees. So I'm gonna be, like, the bee dude."

"The Bee Whisperer," I say.

"Yeah! Bee Whisperer! Great name! You are good at this stuff, can you give me some advice on the whole start-up thing?"

"Of course!" I say, though really, isn't it just common sense? Find customers, give them what they want, make money. "Anytime!" Suddenly I get the hiccups, and I quickly press my fingers in my ears and start swallowing (it works, I swear). Julia notices and laughs uncontrollably.

"Hey, why don't I take you guys out to the kitchen? Vinnie and Ricky will look after you."

"This is so *Goodfellas*," says Julia.

"Can we get something nonalcoholic to drink?" says Coco. "I don't feel very well."

"You just need food," I say. "My boys! Vincent! Richard!"

Vinnie and Ricky are surprisingly delighted to see us, but perhaps they get drunk people storming the kitchen every night of the week. We sit at a tiny table in the corner, and little taster plates start arriving: courgette fries, eggplant rollatini, garlic knots, buffalo mozzarella salad, chicken romano, spaghetti carbonara, baked ziti, linguine in white clam sauce, tiny pizzas of every variety. . . . Every bite is delicious, and we stuff and scarf with drunken delight.

"I am going to learn how to cook like this, I swear it," says Coco.

"So good," I say through a mouthful of spinach and ricotta pizza. "So, so good." The moment I began eating, I sobered up. Funny how that happens sometimes. I still can't believe Angie saw Eddie. I wonder where he's living, or what he's doing. . . . No, no, think about something else.

"Woman cannot live on salad alone," says Julia. "Stick that in your truck and smoke it."

"That doesn't make any sense. And I never said you could live on salad. SkinnyWheels is about balance. Remember? Balance."

"Yeah, yeah, balance, you keep telling me. Can I have more of these garlic thingies?"

I turn to Vinnie and Ricky, who are hard at work chopping, grilling, and serving. "I've started a food truck business, guys."

"Yeah? What kind of food truck?"

"Salads with loads of protein and low-sugar, low-fat desserts . . ."

Ricky and Vinnie look over at me uncomprehendingly. They have probably never used the words "low-carb, low-sugar, low-fat" in their lives.

"Anyway, you know sk—I mean, Bianca? She totally copied my idea! She's selling salads and low-fat desserts all over Manhattan in some big shiny Darth Vader truck!"

Vinnie and Ricky exchange a look.

"You can't trust that Bianca," says Vinnie. "She messed up orders and always blamed the kitchen."

"Skank-face!" Julia hiccups.

Ricky comes over to me. "So you're making all the salads, every day, all by yourself? And doing all the baking? That's a lot of work, Pia!"

"Coco helped with the baking," I say. Coco grins proudly. "It's hard work. I have total respect for real chefs like you." I flutter my eyelashes at them and Vinnie throws a piece of pepperoni at me.

Ricky points to a cardboard box in the corner. "Take a look. We were about to throw out a big food processor and an old deli meat cutter. You can use it to cut vegetables real thin."

"Ooh, wow, really?" I could double my dessert batches, and make paper-thin carrots and radishes and celery, oh my. "You sure you don't want them?"

"Just take them," says Vinnie. "And, Pia, if you're buying your meat and veggies at the market, you're getting ripped off."

"Yeah, totally," agrees Ricky. "Let us order for you. We pay, like, half price what normal people do. Just text us what you want by four o'clock every night and pick it up in the morning."

"That would be amazing!" I say. I quickly tap their numbers into my cell. "Would Angelo mind?"

They both shrug. "He shouldn't have fired you. We're not talking to him."

Oooh. Power play at Bartolo's.

Julia is leaning back, head against the wall in a food coma. "Wow, that was, like, the most intense food experience of my life."

"Oh, my God!" Coco squeaks, nearly falling off her chair. "He *texted* me! Eric! He wants to meet up! I have to go! I need to go to . . ." She looks at her phone, one eye squinted closed. "He's at a house party at Windsor Court on Thirty-first and Third."

"Oh, that's Murray Hill," I say. "Want me to come with you?"

"No, no, I can handle this by myself. I'll get the train," she says. "I'm a grown-up. . . ." She burps like a trucker, then covers her mouth in giggly shock.

"Pia, guess who!" says Jonah, coming from the hallway.

Holy shit, it's Bianca, half-shaved punk-hipster-hybrid Bianca, sauntering into the kitchen at Bartolo's like she owns it. I'm so stunned, I can't speak.

"Hey, guys," she says casually, as Jonah, looking absurdly delighted with himself—is he really *that* clueless?—heads back out to the bar.

"I saw your truck today," I finally stammer.

"Thanks," she says, picking up a piece of pizza from the tasting plate and sniffing it.

Suddenly, I'm bursting with anger. "How dare you steal my idea? And how *dare* you stand here like you've got nothing to be embarrassed about after your little drive-by this afternoon? You're nothing but a— a— a copycat!"

"A copycat?" she echoes, laughing. "What is this, grade school? What exactly do you think I did, princess?"

"Have a fight with a chainsaw?" says Jules under her breath.

"Don't play cute! You know just what you did!" I probably look and sound a lot like my mom right now. "You totally took my idea—"

"I've been thinking about it for a long time, Pia. Low-fat? Low-sugar? It's what the people want!"

"Screw you!" From now on, I hate anyone who uses the term "the people."

"Your desserts are full of fat and sugar." Coco's voice is quivering with the stress of confrontation. "I can *prove* it."

Bianca rolls her eyes. "I'd like to see you try, sunshine. Vinnie, Ricky, I need your help. Can you add my daily food needs to the restaurant's order so I don't have to pay the markup?"

The guys shake their heads sorrowfully.

"It's against the rules," says Vinnie.

"No can do, sister," agrees Ricky.

"Gee, that's too bad," I say, smiling as smugly as I can.

"Shut up, you brat," she says, finally losing her temper.

"You think I'm just a brat?" I raise my voice. "By the time I'm done with you, you're going to wish you'd never met me!"

"Are you threatening me?"

"I'm warning you!"

We're both shouting now.

"Why don't you go back to your rich parents? You don't belong here!"

"I do belong here! This is my home!"

Jonah runs in, a look of shock on his face. "What the hell is going on? The entire restaurant can hear you!"

"She's a fuckin' fruitcake, J," says Bianca, all innocence. "She's totally insane."

"Your bitch needs a muzzle," I snarl. Bianca turns around and, I swear to God, is about to charge me, when Jonah grabs her by both arms and pulls her out of the kitchen.

Wow! The adrenaline rush of battle. "I want to kill her!" I exclaim.

"That was awesome!" says Ricky. He and Vinnie seem to be delighted with the evening's drama. "The bitch who needs a muzzle! Ha! Classic."

"But you better get out of here before Angelo comes back," says Vinnie.

We slip out the back door and into the alleyway behind Bartolo's.

I light a cigarette. I haven't been smoking recently, mostly because I don't want to smell when I'm working. And there's this rumor going around that it's bad for you. But it is kind of nice after a fight.

Wow. Bianca. What the hell is her damage?

"Oh, my *God*! I am so nervous about meeting Eric!" hisses Coco at my side. "Feel my palms!"

"You'll be totally fine! Just be yourself."

"What if myself isn't good enough? Don't you just wish you could be someone else sometimes? God, I do."

Coco heads for the subway entrance. "Coco, why don't you get a cab instead? It's safer."

"I, um, oh, I didn't get enough cash out." Coco suddenly looks incredibly young. I have never felt so protective of someone in my life. This guy had better be nice.

"A cab's much easier, honey," I say, thrusting fifty dollars into her hand. "That's enough to get home, too. Call me if you get lost or anything, okay? Remember, have fun, be safe, and . . . yeah, uh, that's it." I'm not so great with the motherly lectures.

"Where's she going?" says Julia in a surprised voice. "Cuckoo? Where are you going?"

"She's going to meet some friends, and you and I are calling it a night," I say, frog-marching her up Smith Street.

"I don't want to go to school on Monday," she mumbles.

"You mean work," I say.

"Same difference. Except that I loved school and I hate work. I'm about to turn twenty-two years old, Pia. Twenty-two! I'm ancient."

"You're not! You're just starting life!"

"I'm tired of starting life. I miss college. Don't you wish we could just go back?"

No way, I think. I love my life right now. I love walking in the door at Rookhaven, I get this *mmm* feeling, sort of safe-and-comfortable, that I've never felt anywhere I've lived before. I love being surrounded by my best friends at all times. And I love driving Toto around, and talking to new people every day, and thinking of ways to make SkinnyWheels a success. It just fits me. And life has never fit me before.

But I don't say that, as the contrast between my attitude and hers might upset her.

"College would get boring," I say. "Remember the showers? And the food? Come on. Grown-up, I mean adult, life is way better."

Julia mumbles something unintelligible, stumbling slightly over a tiny crack in the sidewalk.

"What?"

"Adult life can kiss my heart-shaped ass."

"Who told you your ass was heart-shaped?"

I'm still laughing as we walk past Brooklyn Social, and then I remember.

Mike!

I check my phone. Four missed calls from him at eight o'clock . . . It's past ten.

"Shit," I say. I keep walking, one arm holding up Julia, and dial his number. It rings seven times before he answers.

"Hello?"

"Dude! Mike? Hello?"

"I waited for an hour," he says eventually. His voice sounds very far away, like he can hardly bear to speak into the phone.

"Oh, God, I'm really sorry."

"I had a basket of eggs. I looked like the fucking Easter Bunny."

I burst out laughing, until I realize he's seriously pissed. He does not like to look silly. "Mike, I'm sorry. I totally forgot. I was with Julia and Coco, and then we went to eat and I just . . . I have no excuse. Forgive me?"

There's a pause. "So are you still out?"

"Nope. Heading back to Rookhaven." I pause as Julia drops her purse, staggers trying to pick it up, and falls over. "Jules is trashed."

"Want me to come over?"

"Oh, Jesus, no—" I say, without thinking, as I hook my phone between my shoulder and my ear and try to pull Julia up at the same time. "I mean, um, I'm just . . . I'm really tired. I'm sorry. Maybe . . ."

"No problem," he interrupts. "I gotta go. Bye."

And just like that, he hangs up.

Whatever. I'm not going to waste any more time thinking about him.

Jules is now pretending to do the running man up Union Street.

"Jules, you are one cheap drunk."

"You're a drunk," she says.

"Great comeback."

Just as we reach our stoop, Julia turns to face me, a pleading look in her eyes. "Tell me everything will work out."

"Everything will work out," I say, putting both my hands on her shoulders. "I promise. One way or another."

I wish I believed it.

Julia stares drunkenly at me, then heads up the stoop. "Pia, one last thing about that Bianca girl," she says over her shoulder.

"What's that, kitten-pants?" I say, helping her up the steps.

"Let's nail the bitch."

CHAPTER 14

Since last night's showdown in the kitchen at Bartolo's, I've been watching Bianca's Twitter and Facebook accounts. *The original and the best!* She keeps saying. *Hands up if you hate SkinnyWheels! Skinny-Wheels is a rip-off! Try my real food that tastes great with none of the calories!* And so on. All day long I was furious, but then, I realized that Julia was right.

And revenge, like vodka, is best served straight up and extra cold.

So I rang Jonah this afternoon, on the pretense of apologizing.

"I just feel really bad about arguing with Bianca," I lied. "Can you give me her address? I'd like to apologize."

"That's so sweet of you, she'd really appreciate that," he replied. I stifled a snort of disbelief. How can he still not see through her? Or is he just one of those annoying people who likes everyone?

Now, we're all in the kitchen, dressed in black, and we're about to execute Operation Karma Is a Bitch.

We look like female ninjas. Well, female ninjas of varying degrees of fitness and enthusiasm.

Julia is lying on the floor, complaining about feeling bloated and applying black camouflage makeup in horizontal stripes across her cheeks from a tin of shoe polish. Coco is washing up the tray of macaroni and cheese she made for dinner. Madeleine is slicing and eating a pear very slowly. And Angie's hungover and still wearing sunglasses. I haven't asked her about Eddie, thanks to a superhuman self-control I didn't know I possessed.

"Okay team, let's go over the plan again," I say.

"We know what we're doing! Jeez, when did you become such a control freak?" says Julia, trying to zip up her pants. "I am seriously retaining water. And I think my jeans are shrinking. And my bras."

Coco beams at me. "I'm so excited! Scared! But excited!" Of course, Coco would be psyched if I said we were going to drown kittens. Apparently Eric was hammered last night, but "so, so nice," and at the end of the night he put her in a cab and kissed her on the lips good-bye. She is taking it as one small step away from a declaration of love and a marriage proposal.

"Me too," says Madeleine, narrowing her eyes in concentration as she cuts another sliver of pear.

"I'm psyched." Angie's tone suggests otherwise.

"Game faces, you guys," I say. "Let's roll."

We all walk out of Rookhaven together. Angie and I are leading. Angie offers me a cigarette, but I'm too keyed up to smoke. She lights her own, then holds it between thumb and forefinger, as though she's in a prison yard. "Do I look tough? I'm trying to look tough."

Julia is singing. "Hit the road, bitch, and doncha come back, no more, no more, no more, no more. . . ."

"I'm pretty sure that's meant to be 'jack' not 'bitch,' " says Madeleine.

"I'm improvising."

"I'm getting nervous!" says Madeleine, skipping up to us and hooking her arms through ours. Gosh, she's really thawing lately.

As we approach Gowanus, the genteel, cozy brownstones of Carroll

Gardens disappear and everything looks dilapidated. Shuttered storefronts, peeling signs, and a graffiti'd train overpass that seems to go on forever.

"This is totally where we'd be murdered if this was a movie," says Julia.

Angie frowns. "I think I went to a club around here once."

At the next block, Team A (Coco, Jules, and I) stops and turns right. Team B (Angie and Madeleine) continues walking to the next block.

With our best nonchalant "Who me, officer?" stroll, Team A approaches Bianca's home at number 144, a blue clapboard house set back from the street. The Let Them Eat Cake truck is parked outside. All the lights in the front of 144 appear to be off, but that doesn't mean she's not there.

Suddenly my heart is hammering in my throat.

I text Team B. *All clear, proceed with caution.*

The street is completely deserted, and the only sound is a dog barking from a few blocks away. I am walking as slowly and silently as I can. Just like a real ninja.

I lift up my hand and give a double-fingers-pump "forward" signal, like I've seen in action films.

Julia makes an exploding sound and shakes with suppressed laughter.

"Shut it!" I hiss. "It's go time. Coco, keep watch."

Julia takes off her backpack, pulls out the spray paints, and we execute the final step of Karma Is a Bitch.

Julia starts snickering again.

"Julia Russotti!" I whisper. "Shut the hell up!"

She really has the giggles. "I can't help it! This is so funny!"

"Julia. Hush. Now," Coco manages to snap while whispering. Wow. They must teach that intense-but-scary whisper to all teachers.

Within a few minutes, we're done, and have regrouped on the corner of Third Avenue.

I text Madeleine and Angie. *Team A is clear. Team B confirm status.*

No response. Coco, Jules, and I look at one another anxiously.

I wait for sixty very long seconds, then text again. *Team B. Confirm status, urgent.*

Nothing.

"They've been busted!" whispers Julia.

"No way, they're too clever for that," replies Coco in an even tinier whisper.

"You don't have to whisper, guys, we're forty feet from her damn house."

I text one last time. *Confirm status or we're coming to get you.*

We wait for another minute, and then look at one another. Can you get arrested for creeping around a backyard dressed as a ninja? Instinct says yes.

"Jules, stay here and keep watch," I say. "Coco and I will go find them."

"I don't want to stay here by myself!" she says. "This area is creeping me out."

Then I hear a scream.

"Go! Go!"

A split second later, Madeleine and Angie hurtle out of the darkness toward us.

"Run!" I shout.

I'm leading the sprint, and I can hear the girls behind me, all panting and giggling.

"This is ridiculous." I hear Angie gasp.

Then I hear a police siren.

"The cops!" yells Julia.

I speed up, sprinting as fast as I can through the Brooklyn streets, the girls hot on my tail.

"Turn left! They're tailing us!" shouts Angie, and we all squeal with fright.

I turn left, my arms slicing the air, the sidewalk disappearing under my hurtling legs. I'm running so fast that I can hear the wind whooshing past my ears. The girls are still right behind me, our feet hitting the sidewalk in unison as we turn onto Second Avenue. I'm really hitting my stride now, I feel so strong and awesome, I've never run so fast in my life. This is amazing! I'm going to run more often, I'm going to join a jogging club, I'm—

"This is a dead end!" shouts Madeleine. "You're running toward a *dead end*!"

She's right. It is. I laugh uncontrollably and promptly fall over. Then

Julia trips over me and we all fall into one another, *bang-bang-bang*, like a freeway pileup.

"Ow," I say, laughing so hard my stomach hurts. "I think I skinned my elbow."

"Oh, my God, that was close," says Madeleine. "I could feel the cop car closing in on us!"

"I don't think the cops were really after us, sugar-nuts," says Angie.

"My knees hurt, I think it's my old soccer injury," says Julia. "I could totally have run all the way home."

Now that I've stopped running—and laughing—my chest feels like it might burst. I take back what I said about jogging. I have a cramp. My face is on fire. I really need to quit smoking.

Coco finally catches her breath. "What happened? Why were you guys running?"

"We climbed onto the garage and into the yard, just like we planned on Google Maps," says Angie.

I nod approvingly.

"Then we scaled the fence, and saw a light on the third floor," adds Madeleine.

"So we climbed onto the first floor deck, moved some furniture, climbed to the balcony on the next floor, and then I stood on Madeleine's shoulders to get a look in the window."

Madeleine nods, rubbing her right shoulder awkwardly. "We played rock-paper-scissors for it. I lost."

"And?"

"And . . . she was baking. And those baked goods are *not* low-fat."

"I got photos of giant buckets of oil and corn syrup and instant egg!" says Angie.

"*Yay!*" we all start cheering. Julia high-fives herself.

"Even better? She's using generic no-name cake mix! None of this is artisan local organic sustainable, whatever the hell that means—"

"Awesome!" Julia jumps up and down with excitement, then suddenly flops to the ground. "Ow, my knee, ow."

"Okay," I say, thinking aloud. "I could e-mail this to all the food truck blogs and Web sites tomorrow morning, really expose her, make a scandal out of it. . . . Is that going too far?"

"Hell no!" Angie yells, at the same time that Madeleine says, "No way," and Coco exclaims, "She stole your idea and lied! She deserves everything she gets."

After we get home, Coco and Julia start watching *Marley & Me,* Angie and Madeleine disappear to their rooms, and I feel inspired to research more salad recipes. I need to get the edge on every other salad vendor in New York and make SkinnyWheels the best. I've never felt so committed in my entire life. I think my parents would be proud. For once. Maybe.

Then, at about 11:00 P.M. there's a knock at my door. It's Julia.

"What's up, pussycat?"

"Pia, I've decided it's time for me to meet a man."

"Okay," I say, sitting up straighter, as clearly this is a serious discussion for Jules.

"Here's my rationale. My job sucks, but I can't do much about that, right? And I know I could do like a photography course or a cooking course in my spare time, but you know, I'm really not arty or . . . uh . . . culinary."

"Right," I say.

"So, what's missing is a dude."

"Got it," I say, trying to sound as serious as Jules clearly wants me to. "So . . . Internet dating?"

She shakes her head. "No way. Too intense. I just want to do what you do. Pick up guys in bars."

I crack up. "Yeah, because that always works out." Then I realize she's not joking. "Okay, well, you just . . ."

"I know, I know. The eye contact thing you always talk about. It doesn't work for me, Pia. I don't look like you."

"You don't dress like me," I correct her. "The right clothes, hair, and makeup will give you confidence. Confidence equals charisma, and charisma equals attention from guys. That'll make you feel good, so you'll be more relaxed, funnier, and all that good stuff. You'll be yourself but, you know, the best possible version of yourself."

"So what now? A fucking makeover montage like a chick flick?"

I grin. "Yes. Before the next time we all go out, you will have your very own makeover montage."

"Sweet," she says. "Thanks, P-Dawg. Knew you'd know what to do."

She disappears. I'm thrilled: Julia has always resisted my attempts to give her a makeover before. She has gorgeous hair, but it's permanently in a ponytail, and she has great boobs, but she smushes them by always wearing sports bras (I know, I know). And she dresses like she sets herself a timer in JCPenney once a year and goes on a spree, which, for all I know, she does.

Yikes, I hope my advice pays off. I have always hated telling people what they should do, because it makes me responsible for their happiness. And what if things went wrong? Then they might hate me. But maybe that's stupid. I'm starting to realize that a lot of things I think are kind of stupid.

Restless, I put on my favorite Elmo slippers and grab *The Best of Everything* and head downstairs to get a bowl of cereal. On the way into the kitchen I run into Madeleine. She's dressed up in . . . running gear?

"You're going for a jog now? Madeleine, it's the middle of the night!"

"There's a midnight running club in Brooklyn Heights," she says, putting her headphones in her ears.

"Why would you want to go jogging at midnight?"

"It helps me clear my head," she says, and with a swish of her ponytail, heads out the door.

She's already jogged today. And gone to yoga. And had three showers. That's weird, right? I keep thinking about that *UGLY UGLY UGLY* writing on the mirror. I wonder if it was her. And if it was, what do I do about it? Tell Julia? How do you confront someone about something that they may have just written when they were in a mood or having a bad hair day or something? We all have bad thoughts sometimes, after all. You just have to hope that the good thoughts outnumber the bad ones.

As I pour milk onto Kashi Honey Puffs mixed with Cheerios, I hear a clink from the deck, and peer out. It's Angie, drinking and smoking by herself. I open the door and shuffle out. She looks gorgeous, in a tiny green dress I've never seen before.

"Is that Marc Jacobs?"

"Affirmative."

"How the hell are you buying new Marc Jacobs outfits when your parents pay your rent and you steal sushi from your boss?"

She shrugs, and takes a deep drag. "A gift. You like?"

"I love," I say, chomping my cereal.

Then I notice she's not smoking a cigarette. It's a joint. And the drink is pure vodka with a slice of cucumber for garnish.

"Angie. Seriously. I know I'm not the poster child for the anti-drugs brigade, but Julia sure as hell is. And it's her house. Couldn't you have waited till you were, like, somewhere else?"

"And get arrested? I think not."

She won't meet my eye. Something's wrong, I realize suddenly. Something's really wrong. Should I say something? Maybe she'll talk, like she did the other morning, maybe she won't do her fly-trap act.

"Are you okay? Has something—"

"Hold this," she says, standing up. She takes a pair of scissors out of her bag, leans over, and cuts the bottom eight inches off her dress.

"What the—"

"That's better," she says, letting the fabric fall down to her heels and scooping it up with the toe of her shoe. "Okay. I'm heading to a bar in Tribeca. Wanna join?"

"Nah," I say. "Angie—"

"Your loss." She shrugs, interrupting me again, and drains the rest of her drink slightly unsteadily.

"Listen, Angie, do you wanna talk? Is it Marc?"

"Do you wanna talk about Eddie?" she counters.

Ouch.

And five seconds later, she's gone.

Then, on my way back to my room, I run into Coco. Oh, Jesus, she's been crying.

"What? What's wrong? Coco?"

"Marley dies," she says, taking a deep shuddering breath.

"Oh, yeah, well . . . he's a dog. In. A. Movie."

"And Eric hasn't texted me back," she adds, tearing up. "We kissed and now . . . nothing. I've sent him two texts tonight, but nothing! He's totally ignoring me!" Ah, so *that's* the real reason.

"Okay, just ignore him," I say. "Indifference is like catnip to men."

"But what if I ignore him and he ignores me and that's it? What if I could have made something happen, just by making a little extra effort? It can't be over!"

I know that desperate panic thought-spiral. Thinking like that can make you crazy. "That's not how it works. Trust me. He's probably just hungover, or having a quiet night studying back at college. . . ."

She shakes her head. "He's still in Manhattan, at a party on Seventy-first and Lexington. He said so! On Facebook! Why wouldn't he invite me along?"

"Maybe it's not the kind of party you can bring guests to," I say. Though, obviously, if a guy wants to see you, a little thing like not having a plus-one invitation won't stand in his way.

"No, it's because. . . . Oh, forget it. It's just like high school," she says, and runs up the stairs.

"Coco!" I call. "You want to talk about it?"

"No!" she calls back, her voice sounding unnaturally high. "I'm fine, honest!"

Then she slams her door.

I thought I was the only fuck-up, that everyone else was happy and making life happen, just the way they always wanted.

Guess I was wrong.

Maybe we just have to figure out what we want our lives to be, and how we're going to do it. And we need to help one another. We're all in this together—this house, this period of life, this strange predicament of being adult and not knowing what the hell that means.

Suddenly, what I want is totally clear. And it's not SkinnyWheels. It's not making the money. It's not impressing my parents.

I want to be *better* at being me. If that makes any sense at all. I want my life to be all about hard work and good friends. Not meaningless sex and free handouts and Eddie-induced kamikaze partying. And not doing and taking whatever I want with no thought for the consequences. I want to be the best possible version of myself. A new, improved Pia.

And I'm the only person who can make it happen.

The first step? Delete all the photos from the Bianca raid tonight. A prank is one thing. Sabotaging her entire business is another.

Anyway, we've renamed Bianca's truck with the spray paint, and maybe that's revenge enough.

She'll find it tough to sell from a food truck that's now called Let Them Eat Cock.

CHAPTER **15**

Pancakes are an amazing invention. They cost six cents to make, cook in about a minute, and everyone loves them. So as the first (and only) item on my breakfast menu, they're perfect. In just one day I've doubled my usual profits.

So, obviously, I'm in a great mood as Toto and I drive through Manhattan this sunny Tuesday morning. I'm singing along loudly to Toto's magically changing radio, which has found "Let's Get Loud" by Jennifer Lopez, a song that Angie and I made up a totally sick dance to when we were ten. That was probably the last time Angie was uncool. (Of course, making up dances is extremely cool when you're ten.)

And I texted Lina, that nice mom, earlier to give her a heads-up that SkinnyWheels will be outside her building today. Her card says she's VP of Strategy for Carus International, whatever that means.

Humming happily to myself, I park, tweet my location, set up, and start shouting, "Pancakes! Breakfast pancakes, gluten-free pancakes!" (Yeah, it's totally lame, but it works.) Once a line forms, I can stop yelling. For a food truck, the single best advertising is happy customers stuffing their faces.

Angie helped me brainstorm new salad ideas last night. I've added five new, much more sophisticated salads to the roster this week, all high in crunch and taste and some with a little extra low-gluten carby goodness in the form of quinoa and brown rice, and some with skin-nourishing omega fats, like almonds and avocado. I'm getting more inventive with herbs, too: dill, rosemary, basil, mint . . . they can really gussy up a salad. And yes, I just used the phrase "gussy up a salad."

Just like yesterday, the line for pancakes is five people long within minutes.

"You should get fat-free Cool Whip!" yells one overly skinny woman.

"I think Cool Whip is pretty high in chemicals," I say in my best polite voice. "This truck is real food only."

"But it's fat-free!" she shrieks, scurrying off on spindly little legs. Anorexics don't visit SkinnyWheels much, probably because they don't trust my calorie-counting skills, and they prefer to eat sugar-free Jell-O to real food. There were so many ana girls at my second boarding school, it was practically a trend, like Tory Burch shoes or getting your bath towels monogrammed in a not-really-ironic-at-all way.

By the time the pancakes have sold out it's 11:00 A.M., and time to prep for lunch. I put the serving hatch down and am cleaning up when there's suddenly a loud knocking at the back of the truck.

I open the back door and look out. "Hi, can I help you?"

It's a guy, early thirties, maybe Vietnamese descent, wearing a Knicks cap and a furious expression.

"You're in my spot."

"Huh?"

He points over his shoulder, and I see a food truck double-parked. It's called Banh Mi Up.

"You're in my spot. I park here. Every Monday through Friday. From eleven till four. So move it."

I try to reply, but my voice has disappeared. Oh, no, not again. I'll just move, I hate fighting, it would be easier to just back down, right?

Then I think about the new, improved Pia. I can handle this. I have a right to be here, too.

I take a deep breath, and, thank God, my voice turns up. "I don't see your name on the sidewalk."

"I beg your pardon? Look, little girl, I've been parking here every Monday through Friday for three years. I *am* the food truck movement."

I get down from the truck, stand right in front of him, and try to look arrogant. "What is your problem?"

He narrows his eyes. "You're my problem. Get in your pathetic little truck and drive away, princess, or I'll call the cops."

"So call the cops! What are they gonna do? The one thing I know about food trucks is they stop wherever the hell they want. You want to serve food in the same spot every day, buy a fucking restaurant!"

"You have no idea who you're dealing with!"

"Neither do you!"

Flipping me the double bird (seriously?), Banh Mi Up jumps in his truck and speeds away with a screech of tires.

I give Toto a loving pat. How dare he call her pathetic?

"Nice work," says a voice. I turn around. It's Lina.

"Thanks," I say. "Jeez, the food truck world is pretty brutal, huh?"

"Deeply brutal," Lina agrees. "Try the hotel and restaurant world. It's like a Roman gladiator battle."

I laugh. "Having a good day?"

"I'm on my way to a focus group run by market researchers trying to prove why anything innovative and new just won't work. . . ."

"Fun," I say. "I always wondered what 'market research' really meant."

"It means 'to destroy creativity.' So, I'm going to send an e-mail to my whole company about SkinnyWheels, okay?"

"Tell them to use the code word Lina for a dollar off the desserts," I say.

She laughs. "Right on, but let's not use my name, they all think I'm an egomaniac as it is. The code word should be something else . . . *Brooklyn!*"

Lina must have some serious pull in her office, because from twelve on the dot, the line snakes almost to the end of the block. One guy likes the low-fat brownie so much, he comes back and lines up all over again for three more, which kind of defeats the purpose of eating low-fat, but whatever. Within two hours, I'm just about out of food, which is when a pretty girl about my age comes up, followed by a guy with a beard and a tiny digital camcorder.

"I'm Becca, and I'm from *Grub Street, New York* magazine's food and restaurant blog. Can we interview you for a piece about the latest food trucks?"

I don't even need to think about it. "Hell, yes."

"There's been a lot of buzz about your truck on Twitter and the food truck blogs. How did you come up with the concept?"

"It just seemed obvious to me. People need good, fast food that won't give them a sugar crash or carb cravings. New Yorkers shouldn't have to choose between a full stomach and a great ass. You can eat well, and cheaply, from a food truck—as long as it's my food truck."

Becca grins. "Nice."

Suddenly I hear screams of laughter.

Becca looks around. "Oh . . . my . . . God . . ."

There's another pounding at the door. Not again! That Banh Mi Up guy is nuts!

I slam the serving hatch closed, run to the back of the truck.

"What do you want now?" I shout, swinging open the back doors.

But it's not him.

It's Bianca. Looking as aggressively punkster, half-shaved-head, blind-person-dressed-me as ever.

And behind her is her big black truck, now spray-painted with the words "Let Them Eat Cock."

I can't help it: I start laughing uncontrollably.

"You did this, didn't you?" she screams. "I didn't even notice till lunch when someone asked me how much it would cost to see me eat cock!"

I laugh so hard, I have to hold myself up on one of the doors.

"Admit it! Admit it!" she screams.

"Are you the owner of that truck?" interrupts Becca.

"I am," says Bianca. "Who the fuck are you?"

"Charming," says Becca, arching an eyebrow. "I'm from *Grub Street*. And may I say, inspired marketing idea."

It's like the sun just came out in Bianca's face. "Well, hi! I'm Bianca, this is my food truck. I'm dedicated to artisan cakes that nourish you, body and soul!"

Grinning broadly, I get back in Toto, applauding myself. Operation Karma Is a Bitch was a success.

CHAPTER 16

If a stranger is just a friend you haven't met yet, then a stranger in a karaoke bar is just a rock diva you haven't yet high-fived after her solo of "Bohemian Rhapsody." I'm discovering this as we celebrate Julia's twenty-third birthday in an insanely noisy and welcoming SoHo karaoke bar called Baby Grand.

But no one seems to be in a party mood except me.

We started the night with a few drinks at home, then on to dinner in Chinatown. I kept getting the giggles about the name of the restaurant (Big Wong King, ha!), Angie is drinking hard and talking little, Coco is staring at her phone obsessively (Eric hasn't been in touch), Madeleine is nervous about the dude she's asked to join us later (one of her Internet dates we're not supposed to know about), and Julia is jaw-grindingly tense. It's like we're all locked in our private worlds of worry. *Come on,* I want to yell, *it's Saturday night!* I've never had so many quiet weekends as I have since moving to New York!

The old me would have left to find myself some fun, but I don't want to do that tonight. I genuinely want the girls to have a good time. Particularly Julia, since I know she always thinks about her mom on her birthday and feels sad. She deserves—no, she *needs*—a fantastic birthday. But right now we're all just passively watching other people sing. We're not even talking to one another.

"That's it!" I say, when a husky-voiced woman finishes "Careless Whisper" by Wham! "We're having shots!"

Everyone looks over at me. No one says yes, no one says no.

I head to the bar. "Christ, if this party were a patient, I'd order a defibrillator," I mutter.

"Coming right up," says the bartender. Huh?

Two minutes later, I'm carrying five glasses of Defibrillator back to the group. It's a tumbler three-inches deep with champagne, vodka, tequila, and lemon juice.

"Okay, compadres," I say. "Down in one."

The girls obediently pick up their drinks and sink them. Then everyone shrieks and coughs and does the usual strong-drink routine. Except Angie, who nods appreciatively.

"Fivies!" screams Jules, high-fiving everyone.

We decide to do a karaoke chain (everyone picks the song for the person to their right—but can't tell them what it is), as a guy with perfect eyeliner sings a rendition of "It's in His Kiss" that the crowd goes wild for.

"I hate karaoke," says Angie.

"Everyone hates karaoke," I hiss. "It's Julia's choice. Suck it up."

Angie makes a face and salutes me, and I turn to the others.

"Ready?"

Julia is lunging, as though stretching before a big game. "I was born ready."

The eyeliner guy on stage finishes with a booty shake.

"Remember everyone," he shouts, "let them eat cock!"

What?

"Did he just say . . ." says Coco.

I stop Eyeliner as he barges past me. "Did you just say 'let them eat cock?'"

"Yeah!" he says. "It's this food truck! I saw it on *The Early Show* today! It's so amazing!"

"*The Early Show* . . . on CBS?"

"It was in the *Post* yesterday, too! It sells cakes, but they're like, totally good for you," explains his friend, a tall blond guy wearing a leather choker. "And my friend Bobby's friend Dodie's drag bar is buying advertising on the side of the truck!"

"There's a Christian parents group who are, like, totally angry about it, it's hilarious," says Eyeliner.

"I heard you can even buy Let Them Eat Cock T-shirts! And it does parties for a five-hundred-dollar booking fee, plus the cost of the cakes!" says Choker. "I'm getting it for my bar mitzvah."

"Uh . . . you're thirty-two," says Eyeliner.

"Shut it, bitch!"

They carry on to the bar, leaving us open-mouthed in shock.

"It's true," says Angie, looking at her iPhone. "I just Googled her. Let Them Eat Cock is all over the news."

"She'll be a huge success," I moan. "Goddamnit!"

"Karma really is a bitch." Julia burps. "Oopsh. 'Scuse me. My round!"

"Don't think about it tonight, Pia," says Madeleine. "There's nothing you can do about it."

I sigh. "Well, if there's one thing I'm good at, it's ignoring my problems."

"Atta girl."

Then "Coco Russotti!" comes out over the loudspeaker.

"Me? First? Oh, no—" Coco looks so petrified that I stop thinking about Let Them Eat Cock for a second. "I can't, I can't—"

"You can do it, Coco," I say firmly. "I believe in you."

Coco walks haltingly to the microphone, as we all scream in delight. She looks like she's about to face a firing squad, but she's got nothing to worry about: Angie chose her song, and it's "Baby, I Love You" by the Ramones. The crowd sings along, and she ends with a standing ovation.

"Go, Coco!" screams the guy beside me. "Yeah! Fuckin'ay!"

Angie and I exchange a look, and then I realize: this must be Eric.

Who else could it be? He's cute, in a not-tall-enough-mild-acne-yet-still-arrogant-jock kind of way.

"Eric!" Coco hurries over. "I didn't know that you were . . ."

"We were at Tonic East, got your text, thought we'd come down!"

Coco smiles at him adoringly, and Eric introduces his friends Tad and Wilcox. Tad is cute, but a classic attention seeker, wearing tennis sweatbands on his wrist and head. And Wilcox is a yuppie in the making (polo shirt, collar popped), either very shy or very drunk, because he can't make eye contact.

"I'm hitting the bar," announces Tad.

"It's my round!" says Julia, and pushes her way next to Tad. "It's my birthday," she says, chewing her straw and looking up at him from under her eyelashes. Go Julia!

"Thanks, I got it," he says, turning away from her without smiling. What a jerk. I fight the urge to smack my palm on his forehead.

Trying not to look hurt, Julia turns around, and her gaze lands on Angie. "I can't believe you're actually wearing black frickin' leather shorts."

Angie looks down at her outfit—leather shorts and a very tight top, her hair tied back tightly, and twice the amount of eyeliner as usual—and shrugs. "I can't believe you were going to wear sequined wedge flip-flops till Pia and I gave you a frickin' makeover."

"Okay, kids, play nice," I say. Damn, I thought those two were getting along after Julia's makeover montage (complete with '80s songs, natch).

Julia looks great, by the way: tight jeans and an amazing jacket that Angie found at the Brooklyn Flea and customized, and she's wearing her hair down for once in her life, blow-dried perfectly by Coco, makeup by *moi*. I hope she gets to flirt with guys tonight. Sometimes male attention is practically medicinal.

It's getting even more crowded in here and our group is jammed against one another in a messy little knot, but the conversation still isn't flowing. I turn to Wilcox.

"So, Wilcox, are you and Tad at college with Eric in Connecticut, too?"

"Yale," he says loudly, nodding. "Yale."

Oh, God.

"Coming through! Defibrillators all around!" Tad pushes Julia and Wilcox out of the way to stand next to me and Angie, and hands out the drinks. "What was your name again? Angie? Listen, you wanna come jeans shopping with me tomorrow?"

"No."

Unabashed, Tad monologues about karaoke experiences at college ("'Don't Stop Believing,' man! Best *ever*!").

I check my phone, and see a text from Mike. Urgh. I thought he wasn't talking to me.

Got your voice warmed up?

A pointless attention-seeking text letting me know he's forgiven me for the Easter Bunny incident. I automatically go to delete it, then remember Madeleine's plea to be nice.

So I reply something smart-mouthed but meaningless: *I was born warmed up.*

A second later he responds.

Ain't that the truth.

Double urgh. Delete.

Then Angie's name is called.

"Woo! Angie!" yells Coco, and Julia, Madeleine, and I all join in, cheering wildly in unison. Angie looks at us in surprise, and a big smile flashes across her face. Then she sees the song I picked out for her, and chokes out a surprised laugh.

She looks out at us. "This one's for Pia, Julia, Madeleine, and Coco."

It's "You Belong With Me" by Taylor Swift. Angie is dressed like a dominatrix model, and she has to sing her heart out like an American Pie country music sweetheart.

So she undoes her chignon so it cascades down in ringlets, vintage Taylor-style, grabs the microphone, and smiles with such wicked sweetness that everyone sits up a little straighter. And then she belts out the song, with total enthusiasm, horrifically off-key. That's all it takes: the crowd joins in, and roars with approval when she's finished.

"And now everyone should sing Happy Birthday to my friend Julia! She's twenty-three tomorrow!" she shouts at the end of the song. "I know it's lame, okay? Just do it anyway!"

"That's me!" shouts Julia. "I'm the birthday girl!" The entire bar turns and serenades her with the birthday song. Julia is beaming at the attention, practically giddy with birthday joy. *Thank you, Angie,* I think. *You just turned the night around.*

"That was the best birthday present, *ever!*" says Julia, laughing and reaching out for a high five when Angie returns.

Angie high-fives her, and then offers a birthday hug. Yes! Julia and Angie! Friends!

At this moment, I know the night's going to be absolutely great.

"You big marshmallow, you," I say when Angie sits back down next to me.

"I guess you dorks are rubbing off on me," Angie says. "Julia and I didn't get off to the best start, but I really like her. I like everyone, and most of all, I like the five of us together. . . . That Let Them Eat Cock thing was the most fun I've had in ages."

I grin. "Me too."

"I've never felt . . . I don't know," Angie trails off. "It's like we fit together, you know? The five of us. We don't fit, but we fit anyway."

"Don't move to L.A.," I say suddenly. "Don't leave Rookhaven. Stay here with us. Please, I don't want you to go."

She looks over at me and smiles. "I thought you'd never ask."

Next, Julia sings "It's Gonna Be Me" by 'N Sync, the song Coco chose for her. After a couple of bars, she begins automatically doing the dance she learned for it in junior high. She's at that perfect stage of drinking to be confident but not sloppy: fist pumps, leg rolls, heart taps, 180 jumps, turns, and swivels—it's a complete boy-band routine.

She gets a standing ovation and on the way back to us, a very hot guy stops her, but she just grins coyly at him and comes back to us.

"Playing hard to get?" I say, seeing the guy staring after her.

"I'm not playing, I *am* hard to get," she retorts. "Let's get another drink!"

Next a guy with the deepest voice I've ever heard is singing "Stay" by Lisa Loeb, and the night gets a little shot-tastic. Julia is making everyone high-five her and saying, "Woo!" Coco and Eric are about an inch from kissing. Tad and Wilcox are doing some made-up dance involving the running man and tap dancing. Then some of Angie's friends, Sirvan and Mani, arrive: two handsome, polite, and conspicuously wealthy Iranian playboys.

While they're getting drinks, Angie and I head outside for a cigarette.

"Where'd you pick them up?" I say.

"London." She shrugs. "They're sweet. And rich. What more is there?"

"Right on," I say.

"Man, I feel good," she adds, exhaling smoke rings.

"Margaritas will do that to a girl."

"It's not the booze. It's the Adderall. Wilcox has it."

Wow, she just met him and has already scored prescription drugs. Kind of impressive. Last time I combined Adderall and booze I woke up naked next to a professor of American literature. (No, I didn't take American literature, but that's not the point.)

"Take it easy, Angie, would you? I'm not in the mood for another bridge performance."

"Narc."

A couple of drinks or so later, I run into Madeleine in the bathroom. Her eyes are red and swollen.

"Are you okay?" I say.

"Yeah, fine, nothing," she mumbles. She's very drunk, I suddenly realize. Slurring. "You know how I invited this guy I met, uh, Andrew? He's not coming."

"Oh . . ." I say. "Bummer. Well, Angie's friends are surprisingly sweet considering their Patek Philippes cost more than our house, or take your pick of Tad or Wilcox—"

Madeleine looks up and rolls her eyes. "I'm not interested, Pia! Jesus!" She staggers on the spot slightly. "Why are you forcing everyone to have fun?"

"Nice attitude," I retort, and slam the stall door as she leaves. How rude. God, I hate it when people just take their bad moods out on you! I was just trying to make the evening work! Besides, if she's not going to mingle, how the hell does she expect to ever meet anyone? The Internet can only do so much, you know?

I wash my hands, reapply my bronzer, and leave just in time to hear the opening notes to "Feeling Good," the Nina Simone song. "Birds flying high, you know how I feel . . ."

Damn, the singer has a beautiful voice: deep, sultry, sad . . .

Then I see the stage and my jaw drops.

It's Madeleine.

She's so mesmerizing that the entire crowd is silent for the first time all evening. She sounds sad and soulful, earthy and honest. I've never heard anything like it.

And I never realized how gorgeous Madeleine is until now. She's in an understated long-sleeved black dress that makes everyone else in the bar look pathetically overdressed, but really, it's not the dress. It's her. Madeleine is radiant.

When she finishes, the entire bar is silent for a few seconds. Then it rains, no, it *thunders* applause.

"Moomoo! I never knew you could sing like that!" exclaims Julia. "I chose that song because I thought we'd all join in with you!"

"Um . . ." Madeleine is smiling so much, she can hardly talk. "I took classes in junior high, but then in high school it clashed with mathletes, so . . ." She shrugs and hiccups. "Can I have another shot?"

The host comes on. "Next up . . . Pia Keller!"

Merde.

CHAPTER 17

I can't do it. I can't stand up in front of everyone. My voice will disappear. I'm going to have a panic attack and/or crash and/or burn and/or collapse in a hysterical pool of sweat and vomit. I can't do it, I can't. . . .

"Go, *Pia*!" shouts Julia, pushing me through the crowd.

I somehow make it to the stage, painfully aware of how tiny the room is, how piercing the lights, how silent the crowd, and how hot and claustrophobic I suddenly feel. There's a bilious fear-lump in my throat—or is it puke? Oh, crap . . . I glance down at the karaoke screen and can just make out the words "99 Red Balloons," but the lyrics are swimming in front of my eyes. *You and I in a little toy shop / Buy a bag of balloons with the money we've got . . .*

My vision is too blurred to read it, but I can't get down off the stage. I can't back out now. I can't—I won't—fail.

I can do this.

The music begins. I still can't read the words, but somehow, I open my mouth, remember the lyrics, and start singing. The first few lines come out as squeaky whispers, but gradually, I get louder and louder.

The crowd gasps and a split second later, I realize I'm singing the original lyrics . . . in German.

My father loved "99 Luftballons." He played it constantly, from a German *Best of the '80s* compilation CD. I couldn't translate it, but I can sing it. I just need to hang on and get to the end of the song.

"Hast du etwas Zeit für mich . . ." I feel like my voice is coming from another person altogether, someone tiny and shaky. But when I dare to look up, people are smiling. I grin back, and then at the end of the first verse, the electro-rock kicks in and I start clapping along, the crowd joins in, and then I start singing again, more confidently this time.

"Ninety-nine Luftballons . . ."

The moment I finish the song, I'm covered in a light sheen of fear-sweat, but there's no fear left. Only exhilaration. I feel euphoric, invincible, ecstatic! Karaoke: free MDMA!

I can't stop smiling. It feels like the entire bar is roaring approval and I can hear Julia above everyone else. I do a little curtsey-bow, and then jump down and run over to the girls.

Before I can get to them, though, I'm picked up and twirled around.

By Mike. What the hell is he doing here?

"Put me down!" I'm wearing a tiny gold dress. Why do guys always want to pick you up when you're not dressed for it?

"Pia! That was so amazing!" Mike looks less cute tonight than I've ever seen him: he's had a bad haircut and his blue shirt billows in the wrong places.

"Thanks," I say, edging away from him. Out of the corner of my eye, I see Coco and Eric making out at the bar. Yes! I fight the urge to punch the air. Good for her!

"You are so gorgeous when you smile, you know that? I got your text and I was, like, hell yeah, that's my girl—"

I frown. My girl? "Mike . . . seriously, don't."

"Don't what?" he says, putting his hand up to stroke my face and I realize he's hammered. "You look worried, honey."

Honey? "Okay, we need to talk," I say, jerking my head away from his hand. "Come outside."

He follows me out to the street, and I light a cigarette to buy some thinking time. How do you break up with someone you're not dating?

"God, you smell good. What is that?"

"Oh! Thanks, it's Kiehl's Original Musk— Wait. Listen. I don't know what you think is, um, going on between us? But I don't want anything like that."

"You have intimacy issues, I get it. Just friends. Friends with benefits, right?"

"Intimacy issues?" I can't help laughing. "No, Mike. No benefits. I don't like you like that. I didn't mean for, um, us to happen."

"You didn't mean for us to *happen*?" He laughs, but there's a hard edge to it. "Madeleine's right, you're an arrogant bitch. You just fuck with people and walk away. . . ."

They've been talking about me? I thought Madeleine and I were friends now! Suddenly I don't want to be part of this conversation. "Are we done here?"

"No!" shouts Mike. "We are not fucking done here!"

"Mike, you're drunk. This is a stupid conversation. There is nothing going on between us, and there never will be. Deal with it." He grabs my arm, but I pull away, throw my cigarette down, and push past him back into the bar. What a cockmonkey!

Is he overreacting? Am I arrogant? And a bitch? I can't tell anymore. I don't care. I just want to forget the whole thing. Actually, I want to ask Madeleine what the hell she's doing bitching about me to her brother when I thought we were friends again, but I can't tonight. Not on Julia's birthday.

I stop next to Angie and grab my drink. Then Mike strides in, whispers to Madeleine, and a second later they both head outside. At the door, she turns and gives me the biggest death stare I've ever had in my life.

Shit.

I drain my glass in one gulp as Jules bounces over. She's hammered. "That guy just asked for my number! His name is Mason! But let's get pizza! I am starving! Because, well, I just puked. But I'm good, I'm good. A well-timed puke can make the night, you know?"

"Where were you the night of the housewarming?" says Angie. "That Julia wasn't any fun at all."

"I was being responsible," enunciates Julia loudly. "And being responsible sucks cock. Am I right?"

"Amen to that," says Angie.

Julia mimes riding a horse. "Yeee-haw"

Angie turns to me. "Seriously. I fucking love this chick."

"I have some friends over at Cipriani Downtown," says Mani. "Shall we?"

"Bring it on," says Angie, hopping off her barstool.

"No! I want something dirty and New York!" shouts Julia. "Pizza! Where's my sister?"

"We're going for a drink uptown," says Coco, sidling over with Eric, with a cat-that-got-the-cream look on her face.

"Wooooooo!" exclaims Julia. "Luh-vers! C'mon, Peepee! You and me!"

So Julia and I walk up to Spring Street as Coco and Eric jump in a cab, and Angie heads off with Mani and Sirvan. A month ago I would have been with them: drinking champagne, dancing on tables, probably starting an unsatisfying short-term dalliance or two with someone inappropriate.

Now it seems more appealing to grab a slice with Jules and go home so I can sleep and get up early to do SkinnyWheels prep. Tomorrow's Cosmo repayment day. I hope it's as easy with Nicky as it was last Sunday. The less chitchat with that man-mountain, the better.

"Thanks for making tonight awesome," says Julia, slurring slightly. "I had so much fun. A guy asked for my number and I didn't even cry once, and I always cry on my birthday."

"That's awesome. See? Told you a makeover would work."

"I feel like I can count on you. I never used to feel like that."

"You can," I say, trying to take it as a compliment. "You can always count on me, Jules."

As we're standing outside Pomodoro, waiting for our slices to cool down, we run into Tad and Wilcox.

"After-party, ladies?" says Tad smoothly, leaning over to take a massive chomp out of Julia's pizza. She giggles and pulls away. "I know a secret all-night bar in the East Village."

Everyone knows a secret all-night bar in the East Village.

"Can't do," I say. "Heading back to Brooklyn."

"Screw that! I'm game!" says Julia. "Where are we headed?"

Wilcox is standing very close to me, staring at me.

"Down, boy," I say. His eyes betray a gnarly drug-booze cocktail. Maybe Klonopin or Xanax to calm him after all the Adderall.

"Wilcox! Dial down the stalker shit, man," says Tad.

"Yeah, c'mon, Wilcox," says Julia. Tad takes another bite out of her pizza and she squeals and slaps his arm, looking delighted. Is that how I act when I'm drunk? Probably.

"Take my pizza, Tad," I say. "You guys have fun. I'm getting a cab back to Brooklyn. Jules, will you be okay?"

"Yeppers!"

I head toward Broadway, through the usual Saturday night party crowds. Funny: if I was alone on a deserted country road at this exact moment in time, I'd be petrified. Nature, silence, shadows . . . creepy. But in a big city, I feel safe.

Finally, I see a free cab half a block down. I sprint toward it, and just as I open the door, some guy gets in the other side.

"Mine!" I shout, in my best ballsy I'm-a-New-Yorker voice. "This cab is mine!"

"I saw it first!"

"Get out! Out!" I yell.

Then I have to stop myself from gasping, because with a stabbing feeling of recognition so strong that it almost hurts, I realize it's him.

It's Aidan.

The guy from the street. The guy from the Brooklyn Bridge. The guy that New York is clearly throwing across my path, as though trying to tell me something.

I think my heart has stopped beating.

I may die.

But that's okay.

"You!"

"You!"

Aidan grins widely (perfectly, gorgeously, warmly, urgh, every-thingly) and my chest does a strange pucker of excitement/fear.

"What are the odds?"

"Slim to nonexistent."

"Heading to Brooklyn?"

"The one and only."

"I'll have him stop on the Brooklyn Bridge so you can jump on the roof."

"Deal."

Aidan leans forward to direct the driver while I frantically search through my bag for a breath mint. I bet I smell like pizza and cigarettes. Goddamnit. My chest has seized with a sort of fright, like when you slam your finger in a drawer. Aidan! Again! Oh, my God!

Aidan winds down his window, and looks over at me with a grin. Long legs in dark jeans and a dark shirt, no jacket, hair is messier than I remember, but in a good way, not in a uses-more-product-than-me way, am I gushing? Yah, I'm gushing. Sorry. What should I say? My stupid brain is empty. Oh, sheesh, I've never felt this nervous in my life.

"So," he says. "You're stalking me, clearly."

"Clearly," I say. I wonder how old he is. Late twenties? I quickly rearrange my legs so that there's no chance of taxi-seat-induced cellulite (yes, it's a totally normal thing to do).

"It just underlines my theory that New York is a village," he says. "Sooner or later, you meet everyone."

"That's pretty deep."

"I'm a very deep person. Profound."

"Yeah, I can see that. You're like a little philosopher in an Aubin & Wills shirt. How original of you, by the way. Do they hand them out with British passports, or what?"

"You hate the shirt? The shirt was a present from my sister. The shirt never did anything to you."

"Yeah, but it's planning something. I can tell."

We lapse into silence. This flirty repartee is nerve-racking! I'm sweating, I can't quite catch my breath, and my brain is jitterbugging from topic to topic. I wonder where his shouty girlfriend is, I wonder if he's been thinking about me, I wonder where he lives, I wonder if my deodorant is still working, I wonder—

Suddenly, Aidan turns to me and grins, that little scar on his lip lit by the lights of the city outside, and all I can do is smile.

"So, talk me through your night."

"Um, it was my friend's birthday. Karaoke bar. I sang '99 Luftballons.'"

"'Luftballons'? You mean you sang it in German?"

"Yes," I say, laughing at the look on his face. "It was an accident. It's my dad's favorite song. He's from Zurich and they speak Swiss-German there. . . ."

"I know. I'm smarter than I look."

"Well, that's a blessing," I say. "Sorry. I'm just used to explaining it as part of the whole where-are-you-from thing."

"I get it. My mother's Argentinian. My dad's Irish. We lived in L.A., B.A., D.C., and finally London, a city without an acronym, when I started high school."

"I bet people think that sounds complicated."

"Yeah, but it's not. Not when you're the one doing it."

"Exactly!" I exclaim. Whoa, calm down, Pia. "I seem to have spent my whole life telling people that moving countries six times before you turn seventeen is really boring."

"My sister and I have a saying: everything is normal when it's normal to you."

That's the perfect way of putting it, I think to myself. He gets it, he really gets it.

Glancing out the window, I'm dismayed to see that we're already on the Brooklyn Bridge. The journey is practically over. I wonder if I can jump on him and start kissing him between here and Rookhaven without looking like a psychoslut. Probably not.

I glance over at Aidan and catch his eye. For a second, I think he's about to come out with another smart-ass remark, but instead, he just smirks at me, his eyes warm and steady and kind, and now I can feel my heart beating and my stomach squirming, oh, God, I can't talk, this is agony. . . .

As we turn off the bridge, he clears his throat. "Are you hungry?"

"Almost always."

"Okay, we're making a pit stop." He leans forward and talks politely to the driver. "Sorry, sir, change of plans—we're headed to Park Slope, Fifth Avenue and Ninth Street, please."

"Park Slope?" I repeat. "Seriously?"

"Daisy's Diner," he says, grinning at me.

I want to lick his teeth.

"They serve disco fries."

"Disco fries?"

"Fries with cheese and gravy. I always get that, plus a grilled cheese sandwich and a banana and strawberry milkshake with double banana."

"Double banana?" I love the way he says banana. *Boh-nuh-nuh.*

"A plain banana and strawberry milkshake isn't bananary enough for me, so I ask them to put two bananas in." He pauses for a second. "Or double the ersatz banana flavoring. Whatever it is."

"Sounds totally disgusting. I'm in."

"Are you one of those girls who eats only sushi? Please say no."

"No, I'm one of those girls who pretends to eat like a man in order to impress one."

"I'm one of those girls, too!"

"I guess you and I are going to be BFFs."

"I guess so," he says, and for a second our eyes meet and my chest goes *thumpetythumpthump.*

I'm just about to open my mouth, to say God knows what, when his phone rings. He looks at it and answers immediately.

"Em?"

I freeze, a ball of fear slamming into my stomach. A girl! The same girl from the street? The girlfriend? Ex-girlfriend? Wife? Ex-wife? I check quickly. He's not wearing a wedding ring, but—

"Okay, Emma, calm down, sweetheart."

Oh, God, he *does* have a girlfriend. . . . I can hear a woman's slightly hysterical voice on the other end of the line.

"Right, fine, I'll come now," he says. He looks out the window. We're almost at Park Slope. "Yes, yes, I'll come now. Right now. I'll be there in ten minutes. Yes, yes, yes, I love you, too."

Aidan hangs up and leans forward to the driver. "Would you mind pulling over? It's an emergency. . . ." He turns to me. "I'm so sorry, you must think I'm very rude."

No I don't, I think you're gorgeous and taken and out of my league and not interested in me at all, I have never felt this right about someone before, and I don't know what to do, I think numbly. But I don't say that. Obviously.

Instead, I try to look calm, and say: "I understand. Another bridge-surfer, huh?"

He grins, then immediately looks distracted again.

"Please take her to Union Street, mate," he says, quickly jumping out and closing the door after him. I slide over to the window, staring out at him as he quickly texts on his phone.

Is that it? Isn't he going to ask for my number? Should I ask for his? For a split second I contemplate the fact that he's about to disappear from my life again and a feeling of utter dread clutches at my stomach.

But he has a girlfriend. I need to get a grip!

Aidan leans in and hands the driver a twenty.

"No, no, I can pay!" I protest.

Aidan shakes his head. "Not a chance, Pia. This is my shot to make up for bailing on you . . . but what are you doing next Thursday?"

"I—" What do I say? He's going to meet another girl but he's asking me out on a date? That's the first time he's said my name. It sounds so lovely.

"Meet me at Minibar at eight," he says. "Please."

"Um . . ."

"C'mon. You owe me for two cab rides now!"

"Um, let me think about it, give me your number."

"No. No numbers, no e-mails, no texts, no excruciating pre-date Googling and Facebook repartee. Just . . . show up. And see what happens."

We meet eyes. And I know there's only one answer.

"I'd love to."

Then the cab takes off, and he's gone. Again.

Did I really just make a plan to meet up with a guy who's currently on his way to see another woman? That's like Stupid Chick 101! Okay, so I was paralyzed by nerves and excitement and good old-fashioned sexual attraction. But that's no excuse. . . . Is he just some cockmonkey who thought I'd be happy to have a cheap and meaningless hookup over disco fries? It didn't feel like that.

Then again, I bet it never feels like that. I bet every girl who acciden-
tally becomes the other woman to a cockmonkey says it didn't feel
cheap and meaningless. I should ask Angie. She has the most experience
in that kind of thing (I'm not insulting her, but you know, she kinda
does).

Do I meet up with him next Thursday at Minibar or not? The idea of
seeing him again in a formal date scenario makes me feel unbearably
squirmy, my stomach buckling in . . . what? Excitement? Fear? Both. It
almost makes me want to run away.

Flight risk.

Eddie.

But I'm *not* a flight risk. I can stick things out. And I am a new, improved Pia, so goddamnit, shouldn't that mean that I should explore
this thing with Aidan when it feels so different than anything I've ever
had before?

Oh, God, I don't know. Sometimes I think I can convince myself of
anything if I try hard enough.

I turn and walk toward Rookhaven. I can't help but smile at little
Toto parked so happily in the darkness outside. I usually park her in the
commissary on Saturday nights, but I'm painting SkinnyWheels Twitter and Facebook details on her sides tomorrow morning, so thought I'd
keep her out.

Then I notice it: something's wrong.

She's not pink anymore. Blood-red paint is slashed across her sides,
her tires are slashed, her headlights destroyed, her windows broken, her
windshield wipers ripped off at the base.

My poor darling Toto has been battered to a bloody pulp.

CHAPTER 18

The next day begins unexpectedly early, when Coco knocks on my door.

"Pia? Pia? Pia? Are you awake?"

"Yes . . . No. Yes."

"I need your help. I . . . need to get that pill."

"Advil? Look on my shelf in the bathroom," I mumble. What was I dreaming about? Aidan. Lying in bed with Aidan, giggling, and I felt so warm and honeyish and happy . . . but something bad happened last night. Oh, God, my truck. Toto. Someone has destroyed Toto. It must be Bianca, right? Or the Banh Mi Up dude? Or Madeleine and Mike? Why does it seem like so many people have a reason to hurt me? And oh, God, Aidan asked me out! He's so delicious, but—

Then Coco pipes up again.

"No . . . the other pill. The one for sex. Unprotected sex."

My eyes open. "What? Get in here."

Coco creeps in, still wearing her clothes from karaoke last night, and has the telltale signs of a good night being bad: chapped lips and a red, raw chin.

"You couldn't ask him to shave?"

"I'm so sorry," she says, her voice all high and wavy. "I don't know who else to turn to, Julia would never understand, and—"

"It's fine, it's fine!" I say. Oh, God, poor Coco. "Tell me everything. I am completely, one hundred percent awake."

Coco laughs, but it comes out as a choked cry. "I feel so awful. I was so drunk, I don't even remember how it started, but then I sort of sobered up really fast. He didn't even look at me during, um, it. Not once. Then I just lay there while he passed out and then I got dressed. I saw his eyes open in the reflection in the mirror, but when I turned around, he pretended to be asleep."

"What a cockmonkey," I say, shuffling over on my bed so there's a spare pillow next to me. "Come here."

She lies down next to me and stares at the ceiling. "And I had to leave, and I didn't know where I was, and—"

"Whose apartment was it?" I say.

She shrugs. "I don't know, he said it was a friend's who was out of town. I can't believe we did that in a stranger's bed. I mean the sheets weren't even clean, there wasn't any toilet paper or soap in the bathroom, it was such a—a—a fucking dump. . . ." Tears are falling down her cheeks. I don't think I've ever heard Coco swear before.

"Oh, honey, I am so sorry." I lean over, grab a box of tissues, and hand her one. "Okay, well, was it nice, at least? I mean, the sex?" I ask. Yes. Try to focus on the positives.

"I haven't—" she starts, then corrects herself. "Well it was, up to a point, it was very, uh, nice, and then it wasn't." She takes a deep, shaky breath. "He didn't even treat me like . . . I don't know, I thought we were friends. I know that's stupid. Oh, Pia, I have never felt so sick, I have a pain in my stomach—" Silent tears run down her cheeks.

"It's okay, this stuff happens all the time and it's nothing to get upset about," I say, trying to sound experienced and reassuring. "We all hook up with the wrong person and wake up wishing we hadn't, it's a horrible feeling but it doesn't matter. In the end, it just doesn't matter."

"But he . . . he came inside me," says Coco, looking like she might throw up. "He didn't even look me in the eyes and I was trying to imagine how I should be feeling and instead just felt—oh, God, I can't bear it, I want to be sick. . . ."

"Shhh," I say, stroking her hair. "You don't need to feel bad. He's your friend, you liked him for so long, you had no way of knowing that it wouldn't be like you wanted. You did nothing wrong. He's an idiot, Coco."

"What if I get AIDS? Or one of the other ones?"

"You don't have AIDS." And I doubt he's getting enough action to be unknowingly carrying an STD around.

Coco is crying too hard to respond. I lie next to her, stroking her hair as she cries the remnants of her makeup into my pillow.

Eric turned up last night for one reason: to get laid.

What a cockmonkey.

I look over at sweet, trusting Coco weeping silently next to me, and suddenly feel so furious that I want to track Eric down and scream at him. Maybe slap him a few times. It is just not acceptable to take advantage of someone who can't protect themselves.

But all I can do is help Coco.

"And I didn't have any money for a cab, so I had to get the subway home, and we were in Washington Heights, so it took forever, and everyone was looking at me, and there was this lady with dogs who just kept muttering *slut* . . ."

"Okay," I say, cutting her off before she can start crying again. "What time is it?"

"It's, like, nine," she says, looking at her watch. "I can't handle this feeling, Pia. I can't—"

"Coco, stop torturing yourself," I say. "Right this second. Everything is going to be fine." Kind but firm is the only way to handle this. "Go shower. Put this on afterward." I hand her my Lancôme Hydra-Intense mask. "It was invented specifically for morning-after-stubble-rash issues. And then we'll go and get breakfast and talk about it. Everything will be fine."

"And get that pill thing," she adds.

"And get that pill thing." I nod. "Remember, this feeling won't last forever. We all feel bad sometimes, but it goes away. It always goes away. Just tough it out and you'll be a better and stronger person because of it."

"But I really . . . I thought I loved him."

"This isn't love," I say to her. "Love is easy. If it's hard, you're not doing it right."

Do I believe that? What the hell do I know? The only man I've ever loved dumped me and told me I should have expected it, that it was practically my fault, in fact. Oh, God, don't think about Eddie right now.

"I know." Coco is finally calming down. "Okay. I'll go shower."

"And remember, you have to kiss a lot of frogs before you find your prince. And Coco, there have been a lot of frogs in my life."

Giggling, Coco hurries out of my room, and I lie back on the pillow. Poor Coco.

And poor Toto. I really need to fix my battered truck today. Who would do that to her? I need time to figure it out.

But Coco needs me, too.

Okay: Toto can wait. After I've helped Coco, I'll call one of the body shops on the other end of Union Street, and see if they can fix Toto.

I wonder who did it? The Banh Mi Up dude doesn't know where I live. Madeleine and Mike couldn't have had the time. (Urgh, I am *so* not looking forward to seeing Madeleine after last night's not-quite showdown.) And that leaves Bianca.

Hmm.

Coco and I are on our way to CVS on Court Street within an hour. It's unusually warm, and I'm wearing a short, flippy coral skirt, my favorite white shirt with the sleeves rolled up, and some tan leather sandals I bought in Greece a few years ago. I'm telling you this because in contrast, Coco is wearing jeans and several layers of long-sleeved tops that she's pulled over her hands, as though trying to hide from the world.

"I'm so nervous. How do I ask for it? What will they think?"

"I guarantee eighteen girls have already bought it this morning, sweetie," I say. "It's not a big deal, okay? It's fine."

But as we near the CVS, Coco is actually shaking. "I can't ask for it. I can't."

"No problem," I say. "I'll do it. Just wait here and I'll be back in five minutes. Okay, honey?"

I am so damn motherly today, huh?

I remember the first time I got the morning-after pill. The condom broke. Condoms often break when the guy doesn't know what he's doing. A little tip from me to you. Not because their penis is too damn big, whatever the guy might like to think.

Flashing my most confident smile at the pharmacist, I ask, "Can I get Plan B, please?"

He hands it over without batting an eyelid. Thank God. One time Angie bought Plan B from a pharmacist wearing a Jesus fish pin, who then started an abstinence lecture, so Angie accidentally-on-purpose knocked over a jar of lip balms.

After paying, I head back outside to Coco, hiding in a doorway down the street.

"Hey, presto," I say.

"You're so brave!" She takes the bag like it contains a bomb. "I bet nothing ever scares you."

"Let's get breakfast. You shouldn't take this on an empty stomach."

"Will it make me throw up?"

I think back to the first time I took it, and the ensuing foamy vomiting storm. The boarding mistress, an evil bitch named Mrs. Ellis, thought I was bulimic or on drugs. She would have really freaked had she known the truth. "Maybe."

"Oh, God, smell that. . . . I haven't had one in years," she says longingly as we walk past a Dunkin' Donuts. "So fattening."

I grab her arm and we march in. "You can do whatever you want today."

"Isn't this against the rules of SkinnyWheels, or something?"

"Everything is fine in moderation. The point of SkinnyWheels is not to be extreme in any direction," I remind her. "It's about choice, and balance, and— Hi! I'll have two large caramel Coolattas and one of those pink frosted doughnuts for me, please, and—Miss Coco?"

"A Bavarian kreme," she says instantly.

"And we'll also get . . . you know what, I'll get a mixed dozen to go, and then five of those chocolate chip cookies." I turn to Coco. "A little birthday hangover surprise for Jules."

"She has such a sweet tooth, just like me," says Coco.

"Sweetness means love, isn't that what you guys always say?"

"That was our mom's saying." Coco shrugs.

As we leave Dunkin' Donuts, Coco has something on her mind. She keeps clearing her throat as if to say something, then makes little "mmm" sounds instead. Finally, she spits it out: "When did you take the morning-after pill?"

"Uh, at college, twice. Just after one-night things . . . And once at boarding school."

"You went to a lot of high schools, right?"

"I did," I say. Suddenly, for the first time in my entire life, I feel like talking about it. Maybe hearing about someone else's poor decision-making skills will make Coco feel better. "I was expelled twice. The first time was for cheating. I was too scared to go home to my parents with a bad report card, so I cheated on a math final and was caught. And the second time I was kicked out for, um, for coke."

Coco is shocked. "You were a drug addict?"

I almost laugh. "No! I was stupid, that's all. I was hanging out with seniors, my boyfriend Jack was kind of wild, you know, and everyone was doing it. . . . So I agreed to keep all the coke in my dorm room. He said since I was younger and new, they'd never search my room . . . but they did. And that was that."

"That's so unfair."

"It was my fault. Wasn't thinking about consequences." I pause, lost in thought. "I hate the girl who did those things. Hate her."

"Was Jack the guy you got the morning-after pill with? Was he your first?"

"My first what? Oh! No, that was Eddie. He went to my last boarding school. Eddie was my first—only—serious boyfriend. Jack was just using me for a bit of fun."

"What happened with Eddie?"

"Dumped me." I can't bear to tell her all the details.

"Men are such cockmonkeys."

"They can be." Suddenly, I think about Mike. I slept with him and then basically ignored him. Just like Eric did to Coco. What does that make me?

"I don't think you should have been expelled," says Coco, linking her arm through mine. "You're such a good person. One of the best people I know. I always feel better about things when I'm with you. They should have been proud to have you at their schools."

I smile at her, my vision suddenly blurring. Goddamnit, the someone's-being-nice-to-me tears strike again.

We pass Carroll Park. "Let's go in here and sit down."

"Okay!"

I have the feeling that no matter what I suggest, she'll say "Okay!" in that cheery little voice.

"Well, all riiiiight," says a Texan voice I recognize. Jonah! Sprawled out on the ground next to his bike and a Dunkin' Donuts bag, wearing hot pink Crocs.

"Are you wearing those ironically?" I ask. "Because it's not obvious enough."

"They make my feet happy, princess," he says, grinning up at me.

"You remember Coco, right?" I say.

"I sure do," he says. "Miss Coco, you sit down here and let's talk about doughnuts."

Coco immediately drops to the ground next to him. Everyone seems to feel instantly at ease with Jonah. I wonder if it's the Texan accent.

"Vanilla kreme with frosting?" He holds out his bag to Coco.

"I've got a Bavarian kreme," she says happily. "I used to like vanilla kreme, too, but then . . ."

And off they go, chatting away about fillings and frostings. Closing my eyes, I turn my face up to feel the sun's warmth. It's shining so brightly, it feels like it could be midsummer instead of fall.

I finish my doughnut and tune back into the conversation. ". . . and then we went to karaoke, and then Pia came home and found someone trashed Toto!"

"No way," Jonah says. "Man, that bites. Who would do that to you?"

"Yeah, who knows . . ." I say. I'm pretty sure it's Bianca skank-face wreaking revenge for my revenge, but I'm not about to say that until I'm sure.

"One of my buddies has a pal who works in a body shop. I'll call him, we can fix this."

"It's okay, I'm on it," I say. "Just because I'm twenty-two and a girl doesn't make me an idiot."

"Really?" he says doubtfully. "I'm not so sure about that." I throw a piece of doughnut at him and he catches it in his mouth. "Dude, I can take care of it for you."

"Thanks, but I can take care of it for myself," I say. "My business, my problem."

"Hey! I'm still totally into that Bee Whisperer idea. You know, starting my own business, being my own boss. . . . When can you help me?"

"Anytime," I say. "What have you done for it so far?"

"Uh . . . nothin'," he says, laughing. "You know me, baby. I'm a laid-back kinda guy."

"I think you have to be a little bit obsessive about starting your own business, Jonah," I say. "No one's going to make your dreams come true except you."

Wow, that was pretty deep of me.

"That sounds like hard work," says Jonah.

That's exactly what I would have thought a few months ago. But I've been consumed with SkinnyWheels for weeks now. If I hadn't been, it would never have gotten off the ground. And I've loved every minute. "It doesn't feel like hard work when it's your passion."

Suddenly, and for maybe the first time ever, Jonah looks serious. "Well, the only passion I have is acting, dude."

"Then that should be your focus. Okay, stick a fork in me, I'm done," I say, standing up and brushing doughnut crumbs off my body. "Toto ain't gonna fix herself."

Jonah grins at me, and winks at Coco. "Later, alligators."

Coco grabs my arm with glee as we leave Carroll Park. "He's *cuuuute!*"

CHAPTER 19

"Morning, kids," says Angie, walking into the living room.

"It's three o'clock in the afternoon," says Julia. "You're wearing sunglasses inside."

"I know. I didn't get home till six this morning. Oooh, doughnuts. Any double chocolate left?"

It's Sunday afternoon and Coco, Julia, and I have been watching *E! News,* or as Coco simply calls it, "The News."

"Look at that woman's arms. *She* needs a fucking doughnut."

"She looks like a praying mantis," says Angie, her mouth full.

Jules shouts with laughter. "She does!"

"Shh, you guys," says Coco. I'm trying not to think about Nicky coming over in a few hours, or how much Toto's afternoon at the body shop cost, or Bianca trashing my truck, or Madeleine being annoyed at me again. But at least I've done all my prep for tomorrow's Skinny-Wheels work and updated my Facebook and Twitter accounts.

Instead, I'm thinking about Aidan, and last night's cab ride. And Aidan's smile, and his thighs, and his mouth, and his eyes, and his voice and hands and accent and the way he smirked when we flirted and—

Shut *up*, Pia. It doesn't matter if Aidan liked me. He has a girlfriend. He's out-of-bounds. Never fall for a guy who is taken. I make a lot of mistakes in life, but I never make that one. . . . To me, it's the law. Well, a general rule, anyway. Guideline. Memo. Whatever. It's a bad idea.

So why am I considering meeting him for that drink on Thursday?

My head keeps saying "stupid move" but my heart says "what has your head ever done for you, sweetie?" Anyway, is it your head or your heart you're meant to trust? I can never remember.

The presenter is dramatically intoning about some starlet's drug problem. "Is she headed for a complete meltdown?"

Coco turns to us, her eyes wide with excited importance. "She totally is!" Coco seems to be over her Plan B/Eric crisis from this morning, or maybe she's just good at ignoring things she doesn't want to think about, too.

"Oh, shit, I keep meaning to tell you guys. You have to pay rent today," says Julia.

"Rent?" I repeat.

"Yeah, rent," says Julia. Her voice is husky: she stayed out with Wilcox and Tad pretty late. No hookup, but she's in a good mood anyway. I told you male attention has restorative qualities. "Dad says you and Angie didn't transfer the money last week. But to make it easier, he suggested you could give me the eight fifty and I'll give it to him tonight at my birthday dinner."

"Uh . . ." How could I have forgotten something as important as rent?

"Just write a check." She shrugs.

My stomach crunches with that all-too-familiar money fear. I can't write a check, there isn't that much in my account.

And I can't pay rent as well as pay Cosmo.

Yesterday I had three thousand in cash in my hands! But then, after who even knows how many rounds of shots at the karaoke bar, a little personal celebratory beautification, one present for Julia, and one hugely expensive body shop visit for beat-up Toto later, and I only have thirteen hundred dollars left.

Rent is eight fifty.

And Cosmo's payment is one thousand.

If I pay rent, I'll only have four fifty left for Cosmo. If I pay Cosmo, I'll only have three hundred for rent. I have to choose between paying Julia and paying my loan shark.

Merde.

Angie takes nine hundred-dollar bills out of her purse and hands them to Julia.

"Just give me the change another time. Sorry I forgot to do the automatic-transfer thing. Can I pay in cash every month instead?"

"You carry nine hundred bucks around in cash? What are you, some kind of mafia don?" says Julia. "And I think my dad would rather we just paid automatically so he didn't have to worry about it." She frowns, scratching her boob. "Shit, I think there's frosting in my bra."

"I thought you owned Rookhaven," says Angie.

"It's in a trust for us. Dad takes care of the overheads and mortgage payments," says Julia. "We inherit Rookhaven fifty-fifty when Coco turns twenty-one. Ow, you guys, I'm serious. My boob is really itchy."

"Does it have to be tonight?" I say.

"Yes," says Julia, one hand deep in her bra. "Dad's taking Coco and me out for dinner for my birthday in a couple of hours."

"Can I pay it later in the week?"

"Dude, it was due like ten days ago. You'll have to pay it again in a few weeks, why not just get it out of the way?"

"Yeah, P, you must be loaded by now," says Angie. "I've seen how much you make every day."

"Most of that goes to buying produce and gas and stuff, um, but yeah, of course I am," I say quickly. "One sec."

I run upstairs, pull my cash shoebox out from under my bed, and take out eight fifty. Cosmo was a nice guy, I remind myself. He knows I'm good for it. I'll just pay more next week. I can't let Julia down.

For a second, I picture Nicky's roid-charged arms and humorless shark eyes.

I feel dizzy.

Calm down, Pia. What's he gonna do, beat me up? I mean, seriously! This is Brooklyn, not . . . wherever it is people get beaten up for overdue loans. Right?

I head back downstairs, give Jules the rent money, and then keep watching E!, mindlessly letting the shows wash over me like waves in the ocean. All I can think about is Nicky's face when I tell him I'm not paying the full amount this week. Oh, God, on top of Toto, and Bianca's revenge . . . everything is going wrong. Just when I thought I had it all figured out . . .

It's fine! It's fine. It'll be fine. Probably. Right?

I hope the girls leave before Nicky comes over. I really don't want them around when I'm talking to him, as the truth would have to come out, and borrowing ten thousand dollars from a loan shark just doesn't look good. Though it honestly seemed like a logical choice—my only choice—at the time.

"So . . . what time are you meeting your dad?" I ask casually, flicking Coco's hair to get her attention.

"We're leaving in about twenty minutes," she says.

I turn to Angie. "What are you doing tonight, ladybitch?"

"Heading to one of those brunchy party things in the Meatpacking. I was meant to meet some people at midday but you know, I was feeling all cozy here."

"You're six hours late for brunch?"

She shrugs. "They'll still be there."

"You better hurry," I say, looking at my cell. It's nearly ten past six. Cosmo's henchman will be here in less than an hour.

"Since when are you my social secretary?" says Angie. "Why do you want me out of the house so badly?"

"I don't. I'm, um, going upstairs." I hate it when I'm obvious.

I head up to lie on my bed, sick with nerves. I try deep breathing to calm myself down. It doesn't work.

Wait a minute!

Lightbulb-above-my-head moment!

I can sell Toto! For exactly what I paid for her! If I can do it today, I'll pay all the money back tonight, I'll have Cosmo off my back, and I'll only have my parents to deal with!

My mind is racing. Al, the mechanic who runs the body shop where Toto's currently being patched up, told me he just sold a food truck for $45,000. He buys them cheap, does them up, and sells them on.

I grab my cell.

"Al's Auto."

"Hey, it's Pia? From earlier today? Uh, I was wondering . . . how much would you pay for Toto, I mean, for my truck?"

"About three thousand," he says immediately. "Maybe."

"What?" I'm shocked. "But I paid nine thousand for her!"

"You were ripped off," he says. I can hear him chewing something sloppy. Ew. "The engine needs a total overhaul, there's rust everywhere, the tires are shot. . . . Four thousand, max."

"Good to know," I say numbly. "Thanks, Al."

I hang up, feeling sicker than ever. Francie ripped me off. So much for cool old ladies. She must have seen me coming a mile off.

I lie back down on my bed again and stare at the ceiling.

I'm so fucked.

The front door opens and closes a few times. Angie, Jules, and Coco have all left. Thank God. I check the time on my cell. 6:40 P.M. I just want to get this over and done with now.

6:42 P.M. I can't stop looking at the time.

6:43 P.M. It's like an addiction.

6:48 P.M. Like, seriously.

Dingdongdingdongdingdong.

I grab the money, run downstairs, my heart hammering in my chest, and open the door with the biggest smile I can muster. A muscle is twitching in the side of my cheek.

"Nicky!"

"Hey," he says. He's looking at his cell, not at me. I take in his huge bulk again, his gargantuan shoulders and tiny chicken legs, and feel intimidated. Just as he intends, I'm sure.

"Here," I say. I try to open my mouth to explain that I'm a little short, but I can't say anything. I just hand him the cash and watch miserably as he counts.

"You're short," he says.

"I know," I say quickly. "I'll pay it back next week, with extra interest if you want, but I had to pay rent this week so—"

"You need to give me five hundred and fifty dollars, now," he says. He crosses his arms and looks at me. "You don't wanna piss Cosmo off, do you?"

"Cosmo will understand. . . ." Ah, my squeaky mouse voice is back.

Nicky shakes his head. "I'm not leaving without the full thousand. Trust me. You don't want to deal with the consequences."

"But I don't . . ." I look out to Cosmo's car. I can see his arm through the window. "If I could just talk to him—"

Nicky sighs impatiently, opens his jacket, reaches into the inside pocket, and pulls out . . . brass knuckles?

I gasp. "You're gonna hit me?"

"Do you have the money?"

"Yes—but next week—I can't—"

Nicky shrugs, and puts on the brass knuckles, pulls a leather glove on over it, and pushes past me into Rookhaven.

"No, no, no, please." I turn and follow him. "Nicky, I don't— please don't come in, I promise—"

He walks straight through to the kitchen.

I scamper after him, begging desperately. "Please, please, please don't, I promise that next week—" Nicky looks so out of place, so wrong in our lovely serene kitchen. He pauses in front of the sink, looking at Coco's herb garden on the sill.

"Nice décor. Very homey."

Then he punches the window. The sound of breaking glass is so loud that I actually make a little crying sound. He's going to destroy Rookhaven, one window at a time, to teach me a lesson? Then what? It's just me and him, alone in the house!

Suddenly, I feel sick with fear.

"Do you have the five hundred and fifty you owe me?"

"No, I don't, but please—"

"I have it," says a voice. I turn around.

It's Coco, standing at the doorway, her outstretched hand clutching the cash. She's shaking slightly, and she is very pale. But she's holding his gaze.

Nicky looks at me, then at her, and shrugs. "Fine. Trust me, it's better this way. You get the rest of Cosmo's guys involved, with nice little girls like you, you've got a whole other situation."

"Get out of my house." Coco looks and sounds tough as nails. Wow. We follow him back to the front door.

"Next week, have the full thousand, or you won't like what happens," says Nicky over his shoulder, skipping down the stoop two steps at a time.

As Coco closes the front door and double bolts it, I sink to my knees and lean over. Oh, God, I can't see properly and my breath is all uneven and shallow again, and I'm making a funny wheezing sound. No, please, not a panic attack, not again. . . .

"I can't— I can't— I can't—"

Suddenly a brown paper bag is thrust into my hands, but I'm shaking so hard I drop it, so Coco holds it over my mouth. For what feels like hours, I breathe in and out, with no sound but the crinkling of the paper. I feel like I'm watching myself from a distance: a trembling, shaking mess, heart racing uncontrollably, brain short-circuiting.

What have I brought into our home?

My stomach clenches, and I curl up into a ball on the hallway carpet, Coco by my side, stroking my clammy forehead. It's so comforting, almost motherly. I looked after her this morning and now she's looking after me. Like family.

"I'm so sorry. . . ." My voice is croaky. "This is all my fault."

"Are you okay? Should I call a doctor?"

"Why . . . how are you here?"

"I felt sick from the Plan B just before Dad came over, so Julia went alone. I'm fine now, but are you going to be okay?"

"Oh, God, I'm so sorry! That's my fault, too! The Plan B is my fault! Everything is my fault! No matter what I do, I fuck everything up!"

"Calm down. You're hyperventilating. Everything is not your fault."

An hour later, the kitchen window patched up with newspaper and duct tape, we're sitting at the kitchen table, and I've calmed down and told the entire story. Coco nodded the whole time and never made a wow-you-are-an-idiot face, which I really appreciate. Because I feel like a complete moron.

"I'm so sorry, I'll pay you back, I'll—"

"Don't worry about it," says Coco. "It was emergency money. And that was definitely an emergency."

"The thing is, I really thought I could do it," I say, numbly. "The first two weeks were so easy. But buying food costs so much, and the commissary, and gas, and rent, and bills, and I had to fix the truck, and now Bianca's Let Them Eat Cock is like, the flavor of the month, which will inevitably affect my customer numbers, you know?" Everything is just pouring out now. "And I still have to pay ten thousand, plus the one thousand interest payment every Sunday, and I now owe you money, too. How could I have been so stupid? How could I have taken so many risks?"

"I can see how it seemed, um, rational. . . ." says Coco.

I shake my head. "It wasn't. It was reckless and idiotic. I'm so scared. I think that guy Nicky is petrified of Cosmo. How bad must Cosmo be if a thug like that is scared of him? Seriously, what will he do to me if I can't pay it back? Beat me up?"

"I don't know. But I don't think we want to find out."

"And my parents are coming to get me in three weeks. I wanted to prove to them that I could make it on my own. What if I can't? I'll have to ask them to pay it for me, and they'll make me move in with them!"

"I'm going to make you some hot chocolate," says Coco. "It's what my mom always made when we had bad dreams. I still make it whenever I can't sleep in the middle of the night."

"Your mom sounds so nice," I say.

"She was," Coco says. "She was the best."

I'd never describe my mom as the best. But . . . I know she loves me. I do. She always seems annoyed at me, but I know it's because she only wants what's best for me. She just doesn't understand me.

But, considering I was kicked out of school twice, cheated, took drugs, never took anything seriously, maxed out every credit card they ever gave me, and have always done whatever the sweet hell I wanted, that's not exactly surprising. If I was my kid, I wouldn't understand me, either.

And now I'm in debt to a loan shark.

My parents will be so disappointed.

Or, maybe it's just the kind of thing they expect me to do, because I've always let them down. So they won't be disappointed. They won't even be surprised. And that's even worse.

Coco puts a big mug of thick hot chocolate in front of me, and a bowl of marshmallows next to it.

"Keep adding marshmallows as you go along, so you don't have to worry about running out."

Then she takes both my hands in hers, a gesture of affection so sweet, I want to weep.

I sigh. "I have to tell the girls, don't I?"

I hear footsteps in the hallway, and then Julia's voice. "Tell us what?"

An emergency house meeting is called to order an hour later.

"Before we start, it's time to pay the kitty," says Julia, presiding over the meeting like a judge, in her usual seat at the head of the table. I'm on her right, Coco's on her left, Angie's next to me, and Madeleine's next to Coco. "Thirty each."

"You wrote down an agenda for the emergency house meeting?" Angie stares at her in disbelief. Julia ignores her. "Also, a cleaning roster. At the moment Coco and I are doing everything, and it's not fair. I'm going to write a list of chores and put it on the refrigerator with a week-by-week name roster."

Angie is playing with the deck of cards we keep on the kitchen table. "I can't believe I bailed on Mani for this shit. Can't we pay someone else to clean?"

"No. Okay, Pia, over to you."

Great.

"Why are we here?" Madeleine hasn't even looked at me since she got home. "I have Bikram at nine."

I take a deep breath. "I borrowed ten thousand dollars from a loan shark to buy Toto and start SkinnyWheels. I thought he was nice, but um, I'm starting to realize, I mean, I have realized, um, that he's not nice. He's dangerous. And I am so sorry that I brought this into Rookhaven."

"A loan shark? And what do you mean, 'into Rookhaven?'" snaps Madeleine. Then she looks behind me, at the patched-up window. "Are you telling me he *broke* our *window*?"

Coco jumps up and puts the kettle on. Sheesh, she hates confrontation even more than I do.

I nod. "Well, not him. His, um, assistant."

"His assistant?"

"Tell the whole story," says Julia. "From the very beginning."

Telling the story takes about twenty minutes, thanks to Madeleine repeating, incredulously, half of the things I say. Just to really hammer it home how ridiculously stupid I am.

"You found out about a loan shark from that crazy bitch and you thought that was like a *recommendation*?"

"You liked him because he drank *Smartwater*?"

"You told him where we *live*?"

"He has a thug who does his *dirty work*?"

"He came into *Rookhaven*?"

"You now have two and a half weeks to make *thirteen thousand dollars*?"

When I'm finished, there's a moment of silence.

"I was trying to make a life for myself, to prove to my parents—and to me—that I can do something, that I can work. . . ." I say, stumbling slightly over the words. "I am so sorry that I did this. I understand why you're angry."

"You understand why I'm *angry*?"

"Okay, Maddy, that's enough," says Julia. "I get why you're pissed, too, but really, you're not helping."

"How can I help, Julia?" snaps Madeleine. "There is a loan shark who knows where we live and will do God knows what to Pia or any of us if she doesn't pay." She turns to me. "You're a fucking idiot."

I flinch. But she's right.

"It's true. I am a fucking idiot. But I swear, I swear I'll make it better. I'll make the money. I'll work harder. Toto will be fixed by the morning, and I'll sell the best salads you've ever seen in your life. Nothing will stop me, nothing. You have nothing to worry about."

Madeleine raises an eyebrow.

"I believe you can do it," says Julia supportively. Whether she means it or not, I appreciate the sentiment, and smile at her gratefully.

Angie has been by far the least perturbed by my actions. It would take a lot to shock her. "And if not, we'll just help you. I can ask the parentals—"

"We can ask our dad, too," says Julia.

"No way," I say quickly. "I don't know how or why it came to this, but this debt represents everything that I need to change about myself and my life. And I need to fix it myself, without help from my parents, or your parents," I say forcefully, looking each of them in the eye. "It's really important to me. I'm going to work every minute of every day and make the money back. It's the only way."

"Okay," says Julia immediately. "I understand."

"But I'm here if you need me," says Angie. "I mean," she adds quickly, looking around at the other girls, smiling tentatively, "We're here. We are all in this together."

"Always," says Coco.

"Absolutely," says Julia.

Madeleine isn't agreeing, but she's not disagreeing, either.

As I look around at the faces of my best friends, I realize I've never felt this safe and secure before. My parents, though I know they love me, never seemed to forgive me—let alone forget—my mistakes. But this is love without conditions attached. Understanding without judgment. I know this sounds melodramatic, but it makes me feel like I really can make my life what I want. Like I'm invincible.

This is what it must feel like to come from a perfect family.

And Angie was right.

We're all in this together.

Then I look around, and realize Madeleine has just walked out.

Not entirely perfect, then.

"That chick is so fucking uptight," says Angie, shuffling the deck of cards like a Vegas dealer. "Has anyone ever seen her wear something sleeveless? She even jogs in long sleeves when it's seventy degrees out. I think she has fake arms. They're made of, like, wood, or something."

"She doesn't have wooden arms," says Julia.

Angie continues shuffling. "You know what she needs? A good fuck."

"Stop that," snaps Julia. "Deal the damn cards. Pia, you need to go talk to Maddy. One on one."

She's right.

I stand up and walk out to the hallway, where Madeleine is going through the mail.

I clear my throat. "Madeleine?" She refuses to look at me, but doesn't walk away. I take it as encouragement.

"Madeleine . . . I'm really sorry about Nicky coming here, and, um, I hope you can forgive me one day . . . and I'm really sorry about the thing with your brother, too. I thought Mike felt the same way I did. It was just . . . casual."

"Well, he's a much nicer person than you are," she says. "And much less slutty."

Ouch. "Well, that's true. I'm not proud of how I treated him, and I'm going to call him to apologize." I think for a second. "Look, I'm not going to fall in love with him and get married and have babies. I can't help it. I didn't feel that thing . . . that thing you're meant to feel, and I can't pretend I do." Madeleine finally looks at me, her face unreadable.

"I don't know why you're telling me," she says. "I don't give a shit."

Suddenly I feel very tired.

"Madeleine, at some point, you're going to have to decide if you like me or not. And if you do, we need to be unconditional friends," I say wearily. "I would never try to hurt you. I would never judge you for anything you do. But I expect the same from you. We are on the same side."

Before she can respond, I turn around and walk out of the house.

Even though it's past eight and it's late enough in the year that the leaves are starting to turn, the stoop is comfortingly warm against my butt. I gaze at all the lit windows framing Union Street, with all the families and people and lives behind them, and sigh.

No matter how deep I breathe, my chest still feels tight, like there's some air I just can't quite exhale.

Secretly, in my heart of hearts, I'm not anywhere near as confident about making the money back as I said I was. I'm tired. And scared. And juggling so many worries that it's like a carnival ride of thoughts in my head, round and round and round: Cosmo, my parents, Nicky, Madeleine, Coco, Bianca, Eddie, and let's not forget I'm supposed to have a date with Aidan on Thursday night.

I wonder if I should go or not.

I can't even tell what's a good idea anymore.

"Everything is *merde*," I mumble.

"Hey, girlie," says a voice. I look down over the stoop and see Marie coming out of her house, holding a glass of something sparkling, and taking a seat on the bench.

"Oh, hi, Marie," I say. "It's me, Pia. . . ."

"Ah, the truck driver," she says. "Come on down here so I can see you."

I skip down the stairs and sit down next to Marie.

"You wanna tell me what you're cursing in French about? You're young, you're beautiful. . . ."

"I don't feel young or beautiful," I say. "I feel tired."

Marie laughs: a surprisingly youthful cackle. "You can sleep when you're old, and everyone you know is dead."

"That's so cheerful, Marie, thanks," I say.

She cackles again. "Okay, okay. Sorry, everyone's problems are serious when they're theirs. Tell me more. What's wrong with your life?"

"Um, it's complicated. . . . Money. And my job . . . you know, the truck. And people are never what I expect them to be. And I seem to make mistakes no matter how hard I try to do the right thing."

"Well, making mistakes is what makes you human. And like it or not, life *is* complicated. My mother always said life is like the Hydra."

"The what?"

"The Hydra. A many-headed monster killed by Hercules. Every time he lopped off a head, a new one grew in its place. . . . Life is like that. Every challenge that you overcome will be replaced by a new challenge." She pauses, thinking. "And that's the way it should be. The only way to find success and happiness in life is to take a risk sometimes."

"Is life ever easy?"

"Not if you're doing it right. But it will be interesting. And fun. And filled with joy."

I suddenly want to lean my head against her shoulder. Both my grandmothers died before I was born. I wonder if they were like her.

"I'll try my best. But what's going to happen next? How can I survive?"

"You survive with laughter . . . and with the support of people who you love," she says gently. "Your family. Your friends."

"I love my friends. But I haven't spoken to my parents in weeks," I say, a lump in my throat. "They think I'm a child."

"Of course they think you're a child, they're your parents. They saw you screaming, naked and covered in blood, when you were one minute old. They'll never see you as an adult," she says, sounding almost cross. "But they'll always love you. And they want what's best for you. Maybe they think leaving Brooklyn is what's best."

I nod. "They definitely do."

"Well, try to see it from their point of view. So much garbage is talked about parents and children and—what's that stupid phrase?—emotional neglect. Jeez! They love you, but they won't be your best friends. They shouldn't be. They're your parents. You can't change them and they can't change you. All they have to do is love you. And all you have to do is let them love you, and love them back."

She makes everything sound so simple.

"Walk me inside, honey," she says. "I'm getting cold."

I help Marie up. "My hips," she explains when it takes her several seconds per step down to their apartment. Inside, it's warm, well-worn, and comforting. Sort of like Marie.

Vic's sitting back on one of the La-Z-Boys, watching some old black-and-white movie and eating candy corn.

"*The Philadelphia Story*, Vittorio? Again? And that sugar will rot your teeth."

"It happened to be on," he retorts. "And I'm seventy-eight years old, Marie. If my teeth were gonna rot, they'd have done it by now." He looks at me. "Hey, girlie."

"Looks like a great movie," I say.

"It is," he says.

We all watch Katharine Hepburn in silence.

"She's beautiful," I say.

"And so like Eleanor," says Marie. "Real class, with a sassy mouth."

My ears perk up. Eleanor! Vic's wife?

Vic turns to look at Marie and smiles, but his eyes look shiny and sad. "I was just thinking the same thing."

I want to ask them to tell me more about Eleanor, and what happened to her, but I already feel like I'm intruding. Vic changes the channel abruptly and hands the remote to Marie.

"Go on. I know you want to watch your show."

"What's your show?" I ask, expecting her to say *Jeopardy,* or *America's Got Talent.*

"*True Blood,*" she says. "My grandson bought me the box set. I like that Eric Northman. He's got something."

Vic rolls his eyes at me and grins.

I pause at the front door and turn.

"Thanks for your advice, Marie."

"Anytime, girlie. Remember, life is about taking risks."

On the way up to the house, I reach into my pocket, pull out a quarter.

Heads I go on the date with Aidan. Tails I stay home and work on SkinnyWheels.

I flip it, catch it, and slap it down on the back of my hand. I take a deep breath, and look down.

Merde.

CHAPTER **20**

"Which one of you hellbitches stole my hair serum?" I yell.

Silence.

It's Thursday night. Seven o'clock. I'm in my bedroom in panties and a bra, my hair wrapped in a towel, my body greasy from the moisturizer I've just slathered on. I got back twenty minutes ago from another unbelievably busy SkinnyWheels day and now have exactly an hour before I'm due to meet Aidan at Minibar. And I'm already running late on the beauty schedule.

"My hair is air-drying and soon it will be beyond human control all night and it will be all your fault!" I yell. Goddamnit! Why don't I live with boys? I would not have this missing-beauty-item problem if I lived with boys.

"Dude, do you really think Coco, Maddy, or I would know what the hell to do with hair serum?" Julia is pausing at my doorway, eating a banana.

I pause. "Good point." I march upstairs to Angie's bedroom and open her door. Typical: it looks like it was just hit by a sartorial tsunami, leaving a high tide of fashion detritus on every surface. I spy my hair serum propped against a stack of photos and sketches, and make my way through the orgy of belts, bags, and bras on the floor to grab it.

"Why would she even need this? She's got silky fairy hair!" I mutter.

"Why are you so tense?" says Julia, leaning against the doorway. "You've had a million dates."

"I . . . uh, I don't know," I say, hurrying past her and back downstairs.

"Can you please put some clothes on?" she calls after me. "I really don't need to see you in your underwear."

"You're such a prude!"

"You're so European!"

"Ha!"

I apply the product, section my hair in butterfly clips, pick up my hair dryer and brush, and start blow-drying. It is so unfair that I have this much hair. So unfair.

There's a tentative knock at the door. "Can I help?" says a voice. "I'm good at blow-outs." I look up and see Madeleine.

"Really?" I say. "God, yes, please."

We've barely spoken since the showdown the other night. Is this a sign that we're friends again? Properly friends?

Madeleine sits down behind me, her sleeves pulled down low over her hands as usual, and picks up the brush and hair dryer.

"Are you nervous?"

"No," I say automatically, then meet her eyes. "Okay, yes. I'm so nervous that my tummy is itching on the inside."

"I hate that!"

Perched on the floor in front of my mirrored closets, with Madeleine expertly drying my hair, I quickly apply makeup: a natural blend of foundation and illuminator to make me look glowy but flawless, and me-but-better blush, eyes, and lips. My hands are shaking so much I mess up my eyeliner, so I just smudge it and hope it looks a bit punk.

I realize that in the scheme of things to feel nervous about in my life right now, a date with Aidan should rank somewhere behind "making $13,000 to pay a loan shark" and "figure out a way to escape parental pressure to leave New York." But for some reason, it's not. I've convinced myself—yet again—that I'll make the money through sheer hard work: I worked from 4:30 A.M. until 10:00 P.M. every day this week, and made over $4,500. If I can keep it up, and not fuck up again, I'm not going to have a problem paying back the money in full and then I'll have a working business to impress my parents with. Right? Right. (See how good I am at putting thoughts out of my head? It's a gift, it really is.)

Now. WhatthefuckamIgonnawear?

The problem with a meet-me-at-a-bar date is that I want to look as great as possible, without looking like I've made too much effort. Dresses feel too dressy, skirts too girly, tanks too booby, shirts too worky, and then of course we have the whole shoes issue. Lastly, let's not forget I'm in Brooklyn, not Manhattan, and Brooklyn requires a kind of knowing nonchalance. I can't look like I've made too much effort.

Usually, focusing on what to wear helps me to control my nerves. Not tonight.

I'm about to see Aidan again.

"*Merde!*" I shout.

"You okay?" says Madeleine, putting the hair dryer down.

"Fine, good, fine, fine . . . wow! You're done already? That's perfect! Thank you!"

"Pre-date snack!" says Coco, coming into the room bearing a tray. "Toasted cheese sandwiches. You need to line your stomach."

I'm too nervous to eat, but I take one and smile at her. "Thanks, Cuckoo."

Coco beams. "So, what are you gonna wear?"

"Okay!" I stand in front of my open closet, Madeleine and Coco sitting on my bed like an audience. "Let's start with these boots."

They both nod seriously.

"And let's pair them with something low-key, but surprising. Like this little white dress."

"Nice!" says Coco.

"But . . . what if that's too much?" I say. "Or too plain. Or what if I spill something? I don't even know if we're eating."

"What about shorts?" says Madeleine.

"Good idea," I say, nodding quickly. "Like this?" Black shorts, skinny knit black top.

"Yes! Cool but not too cool, dressy but not too dressy. . . ."

"And tie my hair in a loose side-braid," I say. "I don't do legs and hair at the same time."

"Right," says Madeleine. "This isn't the Real Housewives of Brooklyn."

"Oh, my God! That would be so awesome if it was," says Coco.

"God, I feel like I've just finished an exam. Dating is so exhausting."

I spray on my perfume, look at my phone. I'm going to see Aidan in twenty minutes.

Suddenly, I've got that shaky breathless feeling that is almost like— Oh, *merde*.

I drop to the floor and lie flat on my back.

"Are you okay?" says Coco. "Do you want a paper bag?"

I stare at the ceiling. Oh God, oh God, oh God—

"Ignore her, she's being a drama queen," says Angie, sauntering into my room with a tall glass of ice water and a blue clutch. She hands them both to me. I sit up, take a slug of the drink, and choke: it's pure vodka, not water.

"Jesus, Angie."

"For courage. And borrow my clutch. Mani gave it to me. Alexander Wang."

"Wow, seriously? Thanks!"

"Remember, find out if that chick is his girlfriend," says Julia, standing at the doorway. "That is question numero uno! And if she is, throw a drink in his face."

"And don't let him pay for everything," adds Madeleine.

"And take gum for fresh-breath emergencies," says Coco.

"And if you decide to bail, just fake a cramp," says Angie. "Like, a menstrual one."

"Okay, that's enough moral support, thank you," I say, charging out the door. There is just too much estrogen in this house sometimes.

"Good luck!" shouts Julia as I head downstairs. "And remember question numero uno!"

"Oh, my God, it's just a stupid date," I mumble as I close the door after me.

I reach the bottom of the stoop, close my eyes, and take another slow, deep breath.

"You'll be fine, honey-nuts." It's Angie. She bends over for a second to do up the straps on her heels, then takes out two cigarettes, lights them both, and saunters down the steps, holding one out for me. "I'm walking you to Minibar. Then I'm heading into SoHo to meet Mani."

"You're spending a lot of time with that dude," I say as I take the cigarette. "I smell a crush."

"Actually, it's Chanel Bois des Iles, but you can call it a crush if you want." Angie swings her bag over one shoulder and we head down Union Street. She's wearing a new gray dress with hot pink heels and looks, as usual, like she just stepped out of a high fashion magazine, one of those edgy ones with the girl on the cover snarling instead of pouting. I feel impossibly low-key in comparison, but I'm comfortable. And I feel like me.

"Really," I say doubtfully.

"Okay, I admit it. He's so nice, we talk and talk. . . . He's not all Cipriani's and Per Se. On Tuesday we had dinner at this little hole-in-the-wall noodle place in the East Village. It was so awesome. And he sends me the sweetest texts." She sighs happily, and though I can also smell the booze on her breath, suddenly I realize: Angie is a closet romantic.

"I'm so happy for you," I say, smiling, and linking my arm through hers. Maybe tonight will be okay. If Angie has found a good guy, that proves it's not impossible.

I can do this.

Aidan is sitting at the bar when I walk in. Our eyes meet, and when his face lights up, a hot squirmy thrill races through my body.

Oh, *merde,* this isn't going to be easy at all.

He stands up to greet me (tall! Very tall!), and I smile, nervously flicking my eyes up to meet his again.

"Pia."

"Aidan," I croak. I clear my throat and say it again. "Aidan."

He leans over to kiss me on the cheek and I try not to flinch with nerves. His skin is warm but not too warm, and he just shaved. A sandalwoody aftershave: warm and earthy. "What can I get you? Champagne, I assume?"

"Beer is fine," I say, sitting in the chair he's pulled out for me. My heart is beating painfully fast again.

"Girl of the people," he says, ordering me an Amstel. I glance up at him. He's real. He's really real. "So, are you a vegetarian?"

"No." I reach for a smart-ass comment, and thank God, one arrives. "I'm very committed to eating dead animals."

"Good. So am I. I've put our name down for a table at Frankies across the street. It's a meat place."

"Aces."

Pause.

Where has the old I'm-so-experienced-at-dating Pia gone? I can't think of what to say. I can't think of what to do. I can't think of anything, in fact.

Merde.

What would my friends do? Julia would talk about work. Madeleine would stay silent like the Sphinx. Coco would babble and giggle. And Angie would sit back, smirk, arch her brow, and act in control.

That seems like the winner, don't you think?

So I sit back and take a sip of my beer, then swivel my eyes up to look at him.

He's doing just the same thing to me.

Come on, Aidan. Take control of the conversation, please, I think as forcefully as I can.

Instead, he just looks over at me and gives a tiny grin.

A challenge.

Well, I'm not speaking first.

I take another sip of beer, still looking at him. To help calm my nerves, I find myself focusing on the little scar on the bottom of his lip. I bet girls always ask him where that scar is from. I will not do what other girls do. If he is a cockmonkey—and his calm self-confidence makes me wonder if he might be—then I will not fall for his act.

Then I remember: Julia's question numero uno. "Do you have a girl-friend?"

"Excuse me?"

"You heard me."

"No, I don't, but thank you for inquiring," he says. "And do you have a boyfriend?"

"No. Why would you ask me that?"

"Well, why would *you* ask *me* that?"

"Because you bailed the other night to see a woman," I say. "Emma. Or Emily. Or, um, whatever her name was."

I don't mention seeing them on the street together all those weeks ago. Too stalkery.

"Oh, you mean Emma. My sister," says Aidan. "I'm so sorry about that, you must have thought me very rude. Her boyfriend had just dumped her, for the third and final time." He holds up his phone. "Look, here's a photo of us on Christmas Day with our parents last year. See? Brother. Sister. Same nose. Sadly for her."

"I believe you." I glance at the phone quickly, just to be sure: it's the stylish British woman I saw him with on the street that day. His sister. They do look alike. Damn. Now I seem like a jealous psycho. That's even worse than a stalker. "Good. Just, uh, a routine background check."

"Hey, I totally get it."

"There are a lot of cockmonkeys out there."

"Cockmonkeys?"

"Players . . . you know, one of those guys who cheats and lies to get what he wants."

"Oh, you mean a cad. A scoundrel. A total bounder. I can assure you that I am not any of these things." He pauses. "I'm really bloody boring, now that I think about it."

I start giggling nervously. God, I love his accent.

Aidan's cell beeps. "Well, what do you know. Our table is ready."

Frankies 457 Spuntino looks just the way you'd want a modern Brooklyn restaurant to look: quirky but grown-up, with a dilapidated serenity that is almost but not quite unaffected. But it's the backyard that really makes me gasp: a little fairyland, with flowers, vines, and candles strewn everywhere. It's magical. I pause on the stairs leading out of the restaurant, just to gaze.

"I know," Aidan says, pausing next to me. "It's a real dump."

My nerves make me giggle a little too loudly at this. I quickly try to shut myself up, but I have a chronic giggling fit. Oh, God. By the time we get to our table, I still haven't stopped.

"Still laughing, huh? I didn't think it was that funny," says Aidan. "I mean, really. I can be much funnier than that."

I erupt into giggles again, oh, God. This is like giggling Tourette's. With concerted effort, I press my lips together, my chest still hiccupping with squashed nervous laughter.

"Would we like a prosecco to start?" asks the waitress.

Aidan turns to me. "Would we?"

I manage to nod. Then we're silent again. So far I've grilled him about a mythical girlfriend and then giggled like an Ewok on laughing gas. Nice.

"We should just play twenty questions, and get it over with," says Aidan.

I can do that. "Okay. Shoot."

"Brothers? Sisters?"

"Only child. And is it just you and, um, your sister Emma?"

"Emma and three brothers."

"Older or younger?"

"All older. Emma's eleven months older than me. I was a surprise."

"The spoiled baby . . ."

"Neglected youngest, more like. What's your relationship with your parents like?"

"Uh, distant. My father is kind of old, he's not exactly a talker, and my mother is insanely achievement-oriented. You know how stereotypical Indian mothers just want their daughters to get married? Mine just wants me to have a work ethic and stop getting into trouble."

Aidan grins. "You? Trouble?"

The waitress delivers our prosecco. "Ready to order?"

"Umm . . ." I say, looking at the menu in my lap. I seem to have forgotten how to read.

"How would you feel about ordering lots of wine and antipasti and cheeses and breads, and just having a seven-course picnic meal?" says Aidan.

"I would feel very comfortable with that."

We order, and as the waitress leaves, we clink our glasses lightly. I meet his eyes, and we both smile. I suddenly feel every part of me relax. I'd forgotten what it felt like to be with him. This warm, sure, *right* feeling.

"My turn for questions," I say. "Why did you move from London to New York?"

"I guess I feel at home here. I don't really feel that way anywhere else."

"Neither do I," I say. It's true. I really do feel at home here. I belong. I think of New York and Brooklyn and Union Street and Rookhaven, and I think, *mine*. "I'm Swiss-Indian, you know, but I really feel like I'm not defined by my nationality. I didn't choose it, there's nothing I can do about it. . . . I hate being judged by something I have no control over."

"I understand exactly what you mean." Aidan grins at me. "Everyone can belong in New York. Okay, my turn. Favorite ice cream?"

"Strawberry," I say.

"That's so uncool. I thought you'd say raw cocoa with chili cardamom, or something totally fly."

"Fly? Nice word. You're so hip. Well, I have always liked pink food. Probably because I'm a girl. You?"

"Choc chip mint."

"Oh, come on, *that* is uncool," I say. "What are you, six?"

"I'm twenty-nine. And you?"

"I'm twenty-two," I say. "Dude, you are old."

"And you are . . . far younger than I thought," he says, laughing in apparent shock. "Christ! I thought you were mid-twenties at least."

"Are you saying it's time for me to get Botox?"

We finish the glasses of prosecco so quickly that Aidan orders us a bottle while we keep playing Twenty Questions.

He finds out about the places I grew up, and Rookhaven, and the girls, and SkinnyWheels, and how I love Toto more than anyone has ever loved a truck, ever.

In turn, I discover that he works for a venture capital company (whatever the hell that is; he gives me his business card to prove that he's not making it up: *Aidan Carr, Senior Associate*); loves his dog, Ziggy, whom he adopted when a friend got a divorce ("Zig was traumatized, but we got through it"); spent a year after college working in Australia; and has fourteen nieces and nephews thanks to his elder brothers.

"Fourteen!" I'm shocked. "That's kind of excessive, isn't it?"

"We're lapsed Catholics, but old habits die hard," he says.

Twenty Questions was an inspired idea. And every tiny piece of minutia I discover about him makes me feel confident that my initial instinct to like him and trust him—the same instinct I've been doubting ever since—was right.

"Are you glad you moved around so much? Growing up, I mean."

"Definitely," says Aidan. "I think being an expat brat means you can adjust to new situations easily, make friends quickly, all that sort of thing."

I grin. "Expat brat, huh. I like that. But most expat brats I know are, um—"

"Fucked up?" he suggests.

"Yeah," I say. "I guess so. You seem kind of unfucked up."

"Here's what I think." Aidan lowers his voice like he's sharing a secret. "There is no unfucked up. People think there is, but there's not. We're all fucked up in different ways. It's simply a question of making your fuck-ups work for you."

"What a beautiful sentiment. You should put that on a Hallmark card."

"Maybe I will."

We grin at each other as our crostini arrive.

"I like your eyebrows," I say.

"I like your thumbs," he replies.

"My thumbs?"

"They're very long and elegant. Look." He picks up my hand. The touch of his fingers on mine makes me shiver. It feels so intimate. And scary.

I pull away and concentrate on my crostini. "I bet you say that to all the girls you meet in cabs."

"Well, yes, but usually I'm lying."

"Oh, charming."

"I am, aren't I?"

Our eyes meet, and I'm flooded with that warm feeling again.

Aidan pauses for a second. "Right, I've been thinking about it, and we should just get the first kiss out of the way."

"Before we even finish eating?" A kiss? Now? The idea has my heart beating in my throat with excitement.

"God, yes. Do you know how much garlic is in some of these dishes? This is just smart planning. Trust me."

"Smooth, Aidan. Smoooooooth."

He pauses. "Smooth like charming and debonair, or smooth like— what was the term? A total cockmonkey?"

"Charming, I think," I say, frowning as though deep in thought. "Debonair."

"I knew I should have brought some character references," he says. "Okay, fine. In the interest of making it clear I'm not a cockmonkey, let's not kiss tonight. Let's say that the kiss has to be saved for the next time we meet."

"It does?" I say with a stab of disappointment.

"Yes," he says. "And now, let's eat. Because bubbles make me giddy as a schoolgirl."

I giggle again and realize that I'm a little drunk.

"Tell me more about your food truck."

"Um, I'm thinking about hiring a helper this weekend, actually. I know this actor who seems to spend his life doing odd jobs for people around Brooklyn."

"Thank God actors are useful for something. Oh, try this. Chicken liver with pistachio. Don't look at me like that, it's amazing."

I bite into the chicken liver skeptically. But he's right: it really is amazing. "All these things that you always think are horrible are actually so delicious, isn't it incredible?"

"Incredible. Next time we should go to The Spotted Pig and have fried pig ear, it's recockulous."

"You're a real food person, huh?"

"No, just greedy. Okay, keep talking."

"That's all there is to tell," I say. Not entirely true, but "and I owe a loan shark thousands" isn't first-date conversation material. "I had an idea, I bought a truck, I'm trying to make it work."

"You're so grown-up," he says, shaking his head and grinning.

"Oh, my God, I am *so* not," I say in shock. "I'm a complete mess, I promise."

"But you've got everything figured out," he says. "It took me years to find out what I wanted to do with my life."

"Years?"

"Well, I was a trainee in an investment bank, hated it, got a job at Google that I thought was the answer to everything, hated it, then went back to investment banking and still hated it. I felt like such a loser . . . but eventually I figured out what would make me happy. And now here I am."

"Taking over the venture capital world?" I say.

He laughs. "Something like that." He glances up at me and grins. "It's interesting and fun. I'm happy."

"Interesting and fun is what it's all about," I say.

"I'll drink to that."

We pause for a second and raise our glasses to each other, my heart goes *thumpetythump*.

"I don't think I've got everything figured out." I feel so comfortable confiding in him, it's bizarre. Like we could just talk all night and it would be this easy. "And I don't know if I'm meant to be a food trucker forever. Or even work in the restaurant industry. I'm not particularly gifted in the culinary arts." He grins. "I don't know what I'm meant to do with my life, actually, but I'm trying as hard as I can to work it out." I pause. "And I guess that's okay."

"Okay? It's incredible," says Aidan. "You're twenty-two and you're out there, making it happen for you."

"Thanks, but God, I'm so far from making it happen." I sigh, gazing into my glass. "I just want to prove to my parents that I'm not a total princess, that I can do something with my life beyond spending their money. And that I'm not the disappointment they think I am." I blush. "Um . . . anyway, sorry, I'm being boring."

"No, you're not," he says. He reaches out and grabs my hand. "I love talking to you. You're perfect."

His hand feels so right on mine, his skin is so warm and smooth and, yes, that's exactly the word, *perfect,* and our conversation is honestly the most relaxing yet stimulating and enjoyable that I think I've ever had, that all of a sudden I feel like all the pent-up worry and tension is finally leaving my body. I feel clear and calm for the first time in weeks.

I look at Aidan's face, and feel . . . *certain*. This is right. It just is.

And that's when I see it, out of the corner of my eye, the outline of a person so familiar that I instantly turn to stare: very tall, dark-haired, well-cut suit and shirt, no tie. . . .

I breathe in sharply and snatch my hand away from Aidan.

"What?" says Aidan.

I turn back to him, but I can't speak.

Because just twenty feet away from us is the first guy I fell in love with. My high school boyfriend who wooed me, won me, dumped me, and told me I deserved it and should have seen it coming.

Eddie.

CHAPTER 21

I grab my glass of prosecco and drain it.

Then I pour myself another and drain that, too.

"Where is that waitress? Do they have any vodka?"

"Are you okay?" says Aidan, frowning.

"I'm fine. Can I get another drink?"

"Of course, I was going to order some wine. . . . Are you sure you're okay? You don't look—"

"I'm fine!" I interrupt him. "Let's just get some more drinks!"

For the next twenty minutes, I focus on watching Aidan's lips move, nodding when he pauses, and laughing when he smiles. But slowly he stops smiling.

"Look, is there something you want to tell me?" he says. "Did I say something, or—"

I drain my third glass of wine. "Nope! Chillax, hahaha . . . No, no, everything's fine." I quickly stand up, nudging the table slightly as I go. Everything wobbles, but nothing falls. "Phew!" I say. "Now, if you'll excuse me, I'm going to the . . . thing."

Aidan stands up to see me out—such good manners—but I can't even acknowledge him.

All I can think is: Eddie. Oh, my God, Eddie.

Even though it's been forever since I last saw him, the moment I clocked his profile against the back wall of the restaurant, I knew him. How can you remember someone so well—his walk, his voice, his mannerisms, the way he pulls his chair in, *everything*—after so long apart? And why, why, why am I freaking out this much? I am over him! I am completely over him.

I weave my way through the backyard, trying not to ricochet off tables as I go. Eddie's table is right next to the restaurant wall. As I'm heading up the outside steps, I glance down at them. He's got his back to me but it's Eddie, it's definitely Eddie. He's with a slim girl with perfect honey-colored hair, and sitting across from them is a sophisticated-looking older couple. Her parents, I guess. I pause at the top of the stairs, just as Eddie says something and they all laugh loudly.

I walk blindly into the restaurant, almost knocking over a waitress as I go.

"Ladies' room? Please, where tell me?" I say. Apparently I am unable to structure a proper sentence.

She points me to a door opposite the kitchen, and I skip-run toward it. Once in, I use my foot to knock the toilet seat closed and sit down, my breath coming out in heavy, uneven gasps.

Eddie.

We were together for almost two years. It's not just my brain that remembers him, it's my body. I know exactly what his jaw feels like against my lips, what his fingers feel like entwined in mine. I know what his voice sounds like when he growls "Keller" first thing in the morning. I know that he's secretly still scared of the Count in *Sesame Street* and can recite *Toy Story* from start to finish. I know that despite being one of the most popular guys at boarding school, he hated it until he met me. I know it all.

I know that when he told me I was perfect and he loved me, he lied.

And that, apparently, I should have seen it coming.

I look down at my hands. They're shaking.

I didn't bring the clutch to the bathroom, so I don't have my phone. I can't even text anyone. Angie would know what to do . . . or maybe even Julia. And Coco would offer moral support. Madeleine . . . ah, who knows what the hell she'd do.

I wash my hands in the sink, and stare at myself in the mirror, trying to breathe. I will *not* have a panic attack. I will *not* allow that to happen.

"Pull yourself together, Pia." I try to sound as stern as I can. "Stop being such a fucking loser."

Good pep talk.

I exit the bathroom and walk back through the restaurant toward the garden.

Then, as I turn to walk down the stairs, there he is. Eddie. Standing right in front of me.

I try to speak, but nothing comes out. My voice is gone.

Eddie's mouth falls open in shock. "Pia!"

I lean against the rail for support, attempting to fake the cool serenity I don't feel, and arrange my face into a happy, surprised smile. But my heart just skipped about four beats, my hands are trembling so badly I have to hide them behind my back, and I feel like I'm suffocating. Oh, God, it's going to happen, a panic attack—

"What are you doing here?" he says. "You, in Brooklyn, of all places?"

"I'm . . . dinner—" I manage to say, the sound of the sea roaring in my ears. "You?"

"Uh, dinner with Josephina, my . . . and her parents."

"G-g-g-great," I say. I can feel a tiny muscle pulling in my cheek as I smile, making my lip flicker. I see his face suddenly change, dropping the all-American-boy bravado.

"God, Keller . . ." he says, coming up the steps toward me and reaching his hand out to touch my arm.

I instinctively flinch, pulling away before we can make contact, and push past him down the steps.

Just as I reach the bottom, I turn around and look back up. Eddie is paralyzed, staring at me, but I can't read his face. He looks—upset? Confused?

"Good to see ... running into you," I mumble, nodding frantically in an attempt to get the words out.

Before he can say anything back, I turn and hurry back to Aidan.

I pick up my wineglass before I've even sat down and start gulping frantically. Fucking hell, that was a nightmare.

Aidan is looking at me with a mixture of amusement and concern.

"You wanna tell me what's going on?"

"No," I say. "Let's get really drunk."

"Let's not," says Aidan. "Let's just go back to having a good time."

The conversation limps along. I drink as fast as I can and can't think of anything to say. This is too hard, I realize, looking at Aidan's face. I can't do it. I don't want to try. I don't want to take any more risks.

"Pia, what's wrong?" says Aidan, a few minutes later. "I thought we were having a good time—"

"Yeah? Well, so did I, but I'm always wrong, about everything," I say, waving my glass wildly. "You seem like a nice guy, but you're probably not. You're here because you're bored, or because you think I'm someone I'm not, because you want an easy fuck and I look like I might provide it."

"That's a ridiculous thing to say," snaps Aidan, his face darkening.

"Is it?" I say. "It's the truth. That's what people do. That's life."

"That's life? I think—"

"I don't care what you think. We're done here," I snap.

"Fine," he retorts.

Aidan calls for the check and we wait for it in silence while I drink the rest of the wine. When it finally arrives, he won't let me pay, so I just throw half the bill down in cash and storm out of the restaurant, ignoring Eddie's table, ignoring everything.

I reach the street and take a deep breath of fresh air. I didn't melt down. I am still in control.

"So that's it?" shouts a voice. I turn, and Aidan's behind me. "I see you on Court Street and think about you for days." He remembers seeing me that day? I didn't think he'd remember that.... "Then fate throws us together in the back of a cab—twice!—we have half of a perfect dinner, and then you decide it's not worth your fucking time to see what happens next? Nice one, Pia."

"Don't you dare shout at me!"

"Why not? You're shouting at me!"

"You don't know me! You can't talk to me like that!"

"I do know you," he says, his face creased in anger. "You feel out of place everywhere, but make friends easily. You love travel but never feel at home. You love feeling part of something, but want to be independent."

"Stop analyzing me!" I scream.

"I know you because you're just like me, you idiot!" he shouts back.

Fortuitously, a cab is going past the moment we hit the sidewalk, so I immediately yell "Taxi!" and it screeches to a halt. I get in and slam the door before Aidan can stop me.

"Where to?" asks the cabby.

"Manhattan," I say, not looking around to see Aidan, who I can sense is just standing still, staring at me from the sidewalk.

"Anywhere in particular?"

"I'll tell you on the way. Just get me the hell away from Brooklyn."

I text Angie frantically. *HelphelphelpEDDIE*

She calls immediately.

"What the fuck?"

"He was at the restaurant, I freaked," I say.

"Where's the British dude?"

"I ran away."

"Come and meet us," she says. "I'll have a vodka the size of Maine waiting for you."

"Address?"

"We're in the West Village. Go to Grove and Bleecker and then call me."

"Done."

We're not even on the Brooklyn Bridge yet. I close my eyes, willing the cab to hurry up. I want champagne, vodka, tequila, a cigarette, a smoke, in fact for the first time since being kicked out of boarding school I want a line. . . . Anything to make these feelings go away.

I'm tired of working. I'm tired of worrying. I'm tired of taking risks. Nothing will ever work out for me. I don't even want to be me anymore, and obliteration is the only answer.

CHAPTER 22

Next thing I know, it's three in the morning.

"Pia! We're leaving!" shouts Angie above the music.

"You're *boring*!" I shout back.

The guy next to me—Stef? Stan? Something like that, anyway—throws his head back and cackles, and then high-fives me. He's hot, in that long-haired, over-privileged, trust fund way, and I have a feeling I'll be hooking up with him later. I kissed some other guy at the bar an hour or so ago. I wonder what happened to him. Whatever. Right now I just want to have fun!

"Don't you have a truck to drive in like, three hours?" Angie says. She and Mani have been canoodling all night, she's hardly partied at all. "Come on, I'll take you home."

"Fuck the truck!" I say, with all the brazen, heady confidence of half a gram of coke and a bucketload of champagne. "Fuck it!"

"Pia, seriously." Angie gives me the listen-to-me face.

"Angie, *seriously*," I mimic. I do not want to listen to anyone. I feel great!

"What about SkinnyWheels tomorrow?"

"Fuck tomorrow!"

Soon after that, she and Mani leave. I don't know where they're going, or where we are. We've been barhopping since eleven. Now we're in some place with no closing time and loud music. There are just four of us left: me, Stan/Stef, and a couple who've been wrapped around each other like vines for the past two hours, Veronique and Charles.

"Where to, Stef?" says Charles. Ah, good. At least I know Stef's name now.

"Party at my place," says Stef.

Charles looks at me, then winks at Stef. Does he think I'm blind or stupid? "Let's do it. Ready to roll, ladies?"

"You're with me," says Stef, linking his fingers through mine. His cool fingers feel wrong linked around mine. But I erase that thought by necking another glass of champagne. "It's an impressive talent, drinking champagne that fast."

"I have no gag reflex," I say, swiveling my eyes up at him.

"Whoa!" he says, laughing in shock. "Babe, you are awesome!"

Next thing I know, we're at Stef's place, a spacious all-white apartment on Columbus Circle with only a flat-screen TV that takes up an entire wall and freezing-cold, white leather sofas.

"When did you move in?" I say, turning to him. We're on one sofa; Charles and Veronique are on another.

"Two years ago," says Stef.

"You can't afford a decorator?" I say. "Wow, times are tough."

"I've been busy."

"You work?"

"Hell no, baby, I just have a good time." Stef leans over and kisses me, pushes me back on the sofa, and my brain gets lost in the kissing. The next thing I know, we're alone.

"Let's have another line and get naked," suggests Stef, kissing the spot behind my earlobe that makes me shiver all over.

"Um . . ." The lights in the room have been switched off, and I can hardly see Stef's face in the dim light from the hallway. Suddenly I can't remember what he looks like. But he kisses me some more, then rolls over on the sofa so I'm underneath him, grinding into me.

"Ow," I say. "Belt."

"I'll take it off," he says.

A little voice in my head whispers, *you shouldn't be here*.

I close my eyes and ignore it. Just keep kissing him, ignore thoughts of Eddie, Aidan, SkinnyWheels, and everything else . . .

"You're making me so hard," whispers Stef, and grabs my hand to show me.

No.

I snatch my hand away and sit up. "I don't want this."

"Sure you do," says Stef.

He holds my arms down and shifts quickly down the sofa, kissing and licking the inside of my thighs, edging the hem of my shorts up with his tongue. Coco helped me pick out these shorts. Was that just a few hours ago? It feels like years. What the hell am I doing in an empty apartment with some strange guy licking my thighs? God knows where his tongue has been.

"No," I say, pushing him off me, and pulling my legs up to make a barrier between us. "I don't . . . I don't want to be here."

Stef sits back and quickly arranges his hair. Always the cool guy, clearly. "No problem. Where do you wanna go, babe? I'm heading to the Bahamas on Friday, why don't you come with me?"

"No," I say, climbing unsteadily off the sofa. Where are my boots? "I want to go home."

"Fine," he says, flicking a switch that takes him from caressing to cold. Spoiled brat guys do that, I've noticed, when you tell them you're not going to sleep with them. They think it'll make you feel bad and immediately yearn for approval and kindness again by dropping your panties. Sadly for him, I've played that game too many times. He gets off the sofa. "I'll take a leak, and we'll talk about it."

The moment Stef is in the bathroom, I leave the apartment. It's past 5:00 A.M. I was awake and working this time yesterday. God, that feels so wrong. I should be at work now. I should be picking Toto up from the commissary, making her salads, driving to Manhattan.

I've really fucked up.

The Manhattan streets are gray, windy, and freezing, and by the time I find a cab and get back to Rookhaven, the sun is up. Oh, God, I meant to work today. I need to work every minute I can to earn enough to pay Cosmo back. How can I have not even have thought about that once all night?

Shivering, I tiptoe into Rookhaven.

Shit. Voices in the kitchen. Madeleine and Julia, I'd guess. I try to sneak up the stairs without being heard, but then—

"Pia? Wow, looks like it was a good date!"

I turn around. Madeleine and Julia, both in jogging gear, ready to hit the streets in their perfect and capable way, and then go to their jobs that they're perfect and capable at and come home to their perfect and capable lives.

"No," I say. "It wasn't. I fucked the date up, and he'll never talk to me again, then I went drinking, things got crazy, I did drugs and went home with some random dude, and now I'm missing a day of Skinny-Wheels, so Cosmo will probably just slice off my toes one by one or something. Hey, if you're going to ruin your life, do it properly, right?" They are both staring at me, open-mouthed with shock. I can just imagine what they're thinking. "Yes. I'm a fucking loser, okay?"

Before they can reply, I turn around and march upstairs to my room. Somehow I get the energy to shower and wash the stickiness of the night away and then—finally—I climb into bed.

The confident coke buzz is long gone, leaving me exhausted, but my brain is still racing in that jittery, anxious, cokey way, not settling on any one thought for long, just spiraling ever-downward. Aidan, Eddie, Toto, Mike, Jonah, Bianca, Julia, Angie, Madeleine, Coco, Cosmo, Nicky, my parents . . . I can't find a single thought to comfort me. Everything is too complicated, too hard.

My mind continues to jump unhappily from thought to thought until, sometime around 7:00 A.M., I edge into a dreamless sleep.

CHAPTER **23**

It's early evening, and I haven't gotten out of bed yet. I've been awake for an hour. Maybe two or three. I can't tell. All I know is that the light was coming in the window when I woke, and now it's not. I can't bring myself to move.

There's a knock at my door.

"Pia?" It's Julia. "Emergency house meeting. Kitchen. Now."

I open my mouth to talk, but nothing comes out.

"Pia? Are you awake?"

"Yes!" I finally get the words out. "Just getting dressed."

That confirms it. A house meeting in my honor. I fucked up.

Again.

I haven't exactly been a stranger to feeling bad over the past few weeks. Just about all of it self-inflicted and avoidable. But nothing compares to this. It's a mixture of self-pity, regret, self-flagellation, and good old-fashioned misery, with a dash of hangover for added spice.

Without thinking, I pick up *The Best of Everything* from my nightstand and open it.

> *"Whenever you're miserable," Sidney said, "it seems as though you've always been unhappy and you remember all the bad and disappointing things that have happened to you. And whenever things are going wonderfully well it suddenly seems as though life has never been so bad."*

Goddamnit. This book keeps reading my damn mind.

I get up and pull on jeans and a frayed men's Prada shirt that I think Angie stole from an ex-boyfriend. Oh God, last night. Oh God, today. Oh God, my past and my future are a mess.

I'm on the edge of an abyss, staring down, about to fall in, and I'll never find my way back, ever, ever again.

Jules probably wants to kick me out. I bet that's what the house meeting is about. I wouldn't blame her.

Sighing, I head downstairs. Everyone is sitting soberly around the kitchen table, staring at me.

"Pia . . ." starts Julia.

"Is this an intervention? I swear I don't need one," I say. No one laughs.

"We just wanted . . . we wanted to talk to you," says Julia gently.

"I'm sorry I was rude this morning. I wasn't, um, myself."

"We're worried about you. We feel like you're having . . ." Jules bites her lip.

"A breakdown," says Madeleine.

I close my eyes and sigh. "It's not a breakdown. It's just . . . I fucked up. Again."

Coco hands me a chocolate chip cookie still warm from the oven. Sweetness means love, I think, and smile at her. She smiles back.

"Thank you. I thought I was a new, improved Pia, but I'm not. Everything I touch turns to *merde*." I sigh. "I'm just gonna call my parents. I can't do it. I can't make the money back."

"Why do you think that now? You were so positive all week!" says Coco.

"I don't know." I stare into space, thinking. "I guess seeing Eddie reminded me of how I felt when he rejected me. . . ."

"Who the hell is Eddie?" asks Julia.

"Just a guy. A guy I went out with a long time ago. A mistake. Just like going on a date with Aidan was a mistake, and the loan was a mistake, and SkinnyWheels was a big giant fucking mistake," I say. "You wanna hear something funny? Eddie dumped me on August 26, which is why I always get as drunk as I can on the anniversary. That was the night of the housewarming, which was why I was dancing on a table while deep-throating a bottle of Captain Morgan, which got me fired, which got me the job at Bartolo's, which got me to the Brooklyn Flea, which was why I ended up buying Toto and getting into debt with a loan shark. It's like a chain reaction from hell. Mourning Eddie on August 26 is why I'm in this whole entire mess."

"I think you're wrong," says Angie quietly.

"What?"

"You're wrong. I don't think you mourn August 26. You celebrate it. You just don't realize it, because it suits you, in some fucked-up way, to pretend Eddie was the perfect guy who looked into your soul, or whatever the hell you think he did, and saw that you were undeserving of love. But it's not true." She pauses. "He was an uptight control freak, Pia."

"What? No he wasn't!"

"He made you a study timetable and updated it every night."

"He was helping me be a better student!"

"He kept you away from me that entire ski holiday."

"He didn't like drinking!"

"He chose what you wore, he made you check every decision with him first, he tried to control everything you did! If you ask me, the only reason he broke up with you was because he knew it would be too hard to monitor everything you did when he was at Berkeley and you were at Brown. He was a fucking pain in the ass, Pia. And he didn't know you. Because anyone who really knows you can't help loving you just the way you are."

Silence. And suddenly, I don't know what to say. Because she's right. He did do all those things. And yet . . .

"I was a mess." I sound as uncertain as I feel. "I was a total mess, and he fixed me, I was a fuck-up, I was—"

"You were a normal kid, Pia. A teenager doing her best to survive her reality, that's all." Angie's voice is shaking with intensity. I've never seen her like this. "You know what I think makes you act like this? Your secret belief that you're not worthy of happiness. You've gotta forgive yourself for the coke and the cheating and all that shit, Pia. You bury it so deep that I bet you never even really let yourself think about it, and yet that guilt influences everything you do. No one cares what you did when you were fourteen."

"My parents do," I say in a tiny voice.

Angie sighs. "They care more about what you're going to do with the rest of your life."

Julia clears her throat. "Uh . . . excuse me? What coke?"

"What cheating?" asks Madeleine.

"And exactly what happened with Eddie?" says Coco.

Two hours later, I'm all talked out. And, for the first time in years, I feel light.

"It won't happen again," I say. "No more drugs. Ever. I promise." Suddenly, what I've done really sinks in. "But I can't believe I missed another day of SkinnyWheels. I've only got two weeks to make thirteen thousand dollars." I let out a hysterical laugh. "Let's face it. It's not gonna happen. I can't do it."

"Of course you can!" says Coco.

I shake my head. "I'm gonna call my parents. Get them to bail me out. Pay off the loan. Go work as a PA or whatever the hell they want me to do. This food truck thing was just a really stupid idea."

"That's it! I am so fucking over your attitude!" exclaims Angie, standing up so fast her chair knocks over.

"What?"

"I've known you for twenty-two fucking years, Pia, and I've never seen you as happy as you've been the past few weeks. So excuse me if I don't want to sit here, listening to you make pathetic excuses and accepting failure as inevitable because you don't want to try. You're the master of your own downfall, Pia, you always have been, and you are again."

I want to say something, but I can't talk. I just stare at her, helplessly.

Angie walks to the doorway, turns, and looks at me. "Call me if you decide to stop feeling sorry for yourself. I'd love to help. In the meantime, I'm out of here."

She disappears, and a few seconds later I hear the front door slamming. Julia, Coco, and Madeleine look as shell-shocked as I feel.

"She's right," I finally say. "She's totally right."

Julia looks at me. "You should . . ."

I nod. "Yeah. I know."

When I get to the front door, Angie's already at the bottom of the stoop, lighting a cigarette.

"Angie!" I shout, running down the steps. "Angie, you're right. I know you are. I'm going to try. I promise."

Angie takes a drag of her cigarette, without looking at me. "Sorry I lost it in there. It's so not me."

"No, it was the right thing to do."

Angie grins wryly. "That's why it's so not me."

"Thank you," I say.

"Do we have to hug now, or some shit like that?"

"Yes," I say. "We do."

Angie rolls her eyes, but we lean in and hug each other tightly. Angie's so much slighter than I am. I always think she's taller and bigger because of her personality, but she's so thin I can feel her ribs and shoulder blades. Suddenly I feel protective of her.

"Can we talk about you now? And you can tell me what's been going on with you?"

"Fuck, no," she says. "Everything's fine now, anyway. I'm meeting up with Mani in half an hour. I'll see you later." She hoists her bag over her shoulder and strides off down Union Street.

I'm walking back up the stoop when I hear a voice behind me.

"Pia!"

I turn quickly. It's . . . skank-face Bianca?

What does she want?

"You're okay," she says in relief. "When your Twitter went silent today, I thought maybe . . ."

Suddenly I see that she's a mess: pale, jumpy, with mascara smeared around her eyes.

Looking over her shoulder, she runs up the stoop and pushes me into the house, closing the door behind us.

"Cosmo," she says. "Cosmo told me you borrowed from him, too, and I'm so sorry you found him through me, Pia, I really am."

"What?"

"I'm leaving," she says, her voice shaking. "I borrowed over eighty thousand to start Let Them Eat Cake. Originally I was just going to make artisan cakes, I swear, but then I heard your low-carb high-protein idea and I knew it would work, so I copied you, too. Anyway, I've already missed an interest payment, and I can't . . . I can't face him again. I'm not making money as fast as I thought I would, he's already increased the amount I owe, and then he . . . I'll never . . ." She swallows anxiously, unable to get the words out.

"He hurt you?" I finally say. "Nicky? Was it Nicky?"

"Nicky? Nicky's the nice one," she says, taking a packet of cigarettes out of her satchel with trembling hands.

Bianca's not just upset, she's terrified.

"Where are you going?" I ask.

She shakes her head. "I just wanted to tell you to watch out. Don't miss a payment, don't let him get anything on you, and most of all don't let him into your house. Okay?"

"Okay," I say.

"Promise me!" she says. "He's not what he seems. Just pay Nicky and get it over with and get away from him."

"I promise!" I say. "I'm sorry, but why are you telling me all this? Last time I saw you, you weren't exactly my biggest fan." I pause. "And I'm pretty sure you destroyed my truck the other night."

Bianca sighs. "I don't have a lot of, uh, women friends. That's just the way it is. And yeah, the red paint thing was me. I'm not sorry. It was revenge for Let Them Eat Cock. But being responsible for bringing . . . *that* into your life . . ." She shudders. "I had to warn you."

And with that, she opens the front door, runs down the steps two at a time, and jumps into a waiting cab.

Now I know what I have to do.

I have to work harder than anyone has ever worked before.

CHAPTER **24**

This is it.

My last day of working under the shadow of my debt.

The last two Sunday payments were flawless: I opened the door with all the girls standing behind me, handed Nicky the envelope, watched him count it, and watched him leave. Without saying a word.

I've worked twelve hours a day, every day, with Jonah (my new employee) by my side.

And the girls are helping me. Julia meets me to clean up Toto every night, Madeleine helps me prepare every morning, Coco is constantly inventing amazing new low-fat baked goods, and Angie is secretly using her boss's connections to offer special deals to every food magazine and Web site in New York, resulting in a deluge of the who's who of the Manhattan food world, a mention in *The New York Times* last Sunday, and Page Six on Wednesday. Cha-ching!

And now it's the last Friday before the big payment is due to Cosmo, and I've got the ten thousand dollars.

All of it.

Every last penny.

I've been worried about Rookhaven getting robbed and having to earn ten thousand from scratch, so I sleep with it under my pillow and carry it everywhere with me. Right now it's safely under the carpet on the passenger side of Toto. You can't even tell it's under there.

Everything else is great, too—well, mostly. Coco seems to have bounced back from her morning-after-pill/Eric trauma. Julia went on a date with that guy she met in the karaoke bar, Mason, and is happier than she's been since we graduated. Angie is still with Mani, and has also spent a surprising number of nights at Rookhaven, just hanging out with us. Even Madeleine seems happy. You know, for Madeleine.

Now as I drive Toto toward Manhattan, just as I hit the midpoint of the Brooklyn Bridge, the sun reflects off the Midtown skyscrapers one by one, making the whole city sparkle. It's my Manhattan now, my Brooklyn, my New York. For the first time ever, I feel like I belong . . . like maybe, if I'm lucky, I'll get the life I want.

I suddenly remember a line from *The Best of Everything*.

It was all like a dream in which you could have anything you wanted, if you were very, very careful.

That's exactly how I feel.

For the first time in more than seven weeks—maybe ever—I feel invincible. Like nothing can stop me.

Two weeks ago I spoke to my parents and assured them I was working hard "in the hospitality industry" and making good money. They clearly didn't believe me, but they're landing in New York City on Tuesday, so I can show them how hard I'm working, that I am finally doing something good with my life. I hope they'll be proud.

I park outside Lina's workplace again, since she texted last night saying her colleagues were begging her to convince me to return. I prep the pancakes; I always have a few ready in advance, so they're quick but hot off the griddle.

"Pancakes! Breakfast pancakes, low-fat, gluten-free pancakes!"

The breakfast line soon stretches down the block, and at the front of the line is Lina, holding hands with her little boy, Gabe.

"Gabe!" I say, leaning out the window so he can see me. "You've got a job already? That's good, little man. You've gotta earn your keep."

Gabe launches into hysterical giggles. "I don't have a job. I'm *four!*"

"Our nanny is sick, so I've got Gabe till lunch," says Lina. "We've really missed you around here. You're by far the most popular food truck."

"Pancakes!" Gabe is squealing with excitement.

"Well, then your office must have exceptionally good taste and trim waistlines," I say. I give them an extra pancake in each order, and throw in three extra agave syrups and fat-free Greek yogurts.

"Thank you, Grown-Up Pia!" shouts Gabe.

Lina and I both get the giggles at this. "That's what we call you at home so everyone knows you're not little Pia," explains Lina.

"No one's ever called me a grown-up before," I say. "I like it."

I'm so busy this morning that I hardly look up, though I could swear—I mean really, really swear—I see Aidan walk past at one point. My heart jumps into my throat and I do a textbook double take, but he—if it was even him—immediately disappears. That's the fiftieth time that's happened since I went full psycho and ran away from our date.

I shake my head to clear my thoughts of Aidan, and serve the next customer, a girl about my age shouting on the phone. "Hell no, I'm not returning his calls! That was the worst date ever! My life is hard enough right now, right? Okay, honey, call me later, bye."

She hangs up, and looks up at me.

"My date last night phoned his mom at ten to give her a good-night kiss. He's twenty-nine years old. I said, do you need me to change your diaper? He said, no, I wipe my own butt now. And he was *proud*."

I laugh so hard I almost can't give her the order. God, I love people. And yes, I know I sound like a total loser by saying that. But they're just so funny and nice. I'd hate a job where I didn't get to interact with people all day. Working in a cubicle? Only corresponding with the outside world by e-mail? Forget it. I was born to do this!

"Let me in!" shouts a voice. It's Jonah. He jumps in and immediately assumes his usual easygoing I'm-here-to-help-y'all attitude that customers just love.

"Does he come with the dessert?" asks the dump-date woman.

"I sure do," he says, flashing his best I'm-a-good-ol'-boy smile at her. "But I'm full of sugar."

"Oh, I think that'd be just fine." She's practically meowing. She reluctantly takes her food and leaves.

"Great line, Jonah," I say. "Okay, more working, less flirting."

"Yes, bossman," he says. "Hello, sir! How may I help you?" He turns to the next guy in line.

"I was hoping *she* would serve me," says the guy, one of my regulars: a chubby accountant type, cheap suit and a light sweat.

"She's busy, but she sends her best regards," says Jonah smoothly.

The accountant ignores him. "I just wanted to tell you that I've lost ten pounds since I started eating your lunches three weeks ago!" he says triumphantly. I lean over and high-five him.

"Dude! That's incredible, well done! Thank you for telling me!"

"No, thank *you*! I've tried every diet there is!"

Smiling, I turn to the customer behind him. It's the *Grub Street* video blogger, Becca.

"Hi there!" she says. "Can you give me a sound bite about how you feel about being nominated for a Vendy Award?"

"Wow! I was? Who would nominate me? I mean—I was?"

Becca grins. "It's kind of a big deal, you know. It's the Oscars of the street food vendor world. Okay, I'll start filming now. . . . Speak up, there's a lot of traffic noise. In fact, shout if you can."

"Oh, yikes, thinking on my feet isn't my strong point," I say, but before I even have time to panic and get that acid public-speaking stomach and inevitable panic-driven muteness, the little red recording light comes on.

So I open my mouth and somehow, the words just come out. "I'm Pia from SkinnyWheels, and I'm honored and delighted to be nominated for a Vendy Award. It shows that New Yorkers want a food truck that cares as much about their asses as their taste buds! Go Skinny-Wheels!"

I must have been shouting much louder than I think, because the entire line erupts into cheers and wolf whistles. I blush. Oops. Wow.

I've never even been nominated for anything in my life. Even if I don't win, this is a sign. Everything is going to be fine.

We run out of pancakes around 10:30 A.M., as usual, close the window, and put out the CLOSED TO PREPARE FOR YOUR SKINNYLUNCH!

sign that Jonah made. (It's a little perky for me; I might remove the exclamation point.) We clean up from breakfast and prep for lunch. God, it's so much easier with two people.

"Hey, guess what. A Meal Grows in Brooklyn is no more. They ran out of money."

"No kidding," I say. "Poor Phil and Lara! Are they okay?"

"They're fine, they're pretty easy come, easy go, you know?"

"Yeah," I say. "I guess so." But all I can think is: what a shame. A Meal Grows in Brooklyn was such a great idea. But it failed anyway. A good idea isn't enough. You need to work as hard as you can, too. You need to be dedicated. You need to give it everything you've got. . . .

"Hey, Jonah . . . would you consider working for me full-time, once I can, you know, pay you more?" I say. He's working for a criminally low wage at the moment.

"Can I have time off to go to auditions?" he asks.

"Of course! Since when do you have auditions?"

"Since I got an agent last week," he says modestly.

"Dude! That's incredible, congratulations!" I say.

"Pia, it's all thanks to you. Remember that Sunday in Carroll Gardens, how you said that the only person who can make my life happen the way I want is me?" he says. "It really shook me up. I've been sittin' around all these years, waiting for something to drop into my lap. . . . Well, screw that!"

"Damn straight! Dude, I'm so happy for you, well done! And if you have an audition, you just head right off."

"Cool," he says. "Uh, so I can leave early this afternoon? They're casting a part for this lawyer show—I mean, it's totally a long shot—"

"Yes! Which one? The one with that woman who was in the thing with that guy? I am obsessed with her eyebrows."

We talk and prep the food, enjoy an unusually busy lunch period, then Jonah heads off to his audition, and I keep serving.

Sometime after 3:00 P.M., the line dwindles.

And that's when it happens, just as I'm handing over a salad to one of my regulars, a geek in a button-down shirt.

A huge *bang*. Toto shakes and lurches beneath my feet, reverberating with a crunch of metal and breaking glass.

The geek and I freeze and look at each other.

"Did you hear that?" I say.

His eyes are wide with fear. "It sounded like Godzilla hitting your truck!"

I quickly open the back doors: it's a skinny bald guy I've never seen before. He's wearing a hooded sweatshirt and basketball shorts, has an unhinged, ultra-focused look in his eye . . . and he's attacking my truck with a baseball bat. He's already taken out one rear brake light, and the moment I get out of the truck, he slams the bat into the other.

"Are you fucking crazy?" I scream. "Get the hell away from my truck!"

"I wouldn't talk like that if I were you," he says in a singsong voice, swinging the bat above his head like a professional ballplayer. I suddenly notice that he's sweating, and one eyebrow is twitching uncontrollably. Shit, he *is* crazy.

"Please stop hitting my truck with that baseball bat," I say, trying to sound calm.

He ignores me, still swinging the bat above his head. "This is just a taster."

"A taster of what?"

He swings the bat again and slams it into the door, denting it, my truck, my darling Toto.

And suddenly, I feel a little crazy myself.

"That's it! I'm calling the cops! You fucking lunatic! You're out of your fucking mind! You can't destroy someone else's property!"

Then he reaches into his pocket, pulls out a ringing cell phone, and hands it to me. "It's for you, Pia."

He knows my name?

I grab the phone.

"Hello?"

"Hello, Pia my darling," says a familiar voice. "Cosmo here."

A chill runs through my body. "Cosmo."

"I wanted you to meet Nolan. When Nicky can't do something, Nolan does it."

"Oh . . ." I say, eyeing up Nolan. He's sniffing and chewing and dipping his head up and down to nonexistent music. He's not nuts, I suddenly realize. He's on meth or crack or something. He's a junkie. And another one of Cosmo's henchmen.

Cosmo sounds like he's smiling. "How are you, sweetheart? How's business?"

"Why did you do this? I've got all the money, I wasn't going to. . . ." I can't quite get my thoughts in order with a hopped-up addict just inches away from me. "Why beat up my truck?"

"I thought it might be nice to remind you that I'm a serious business-man. In case that little punk-headed bitch told you otherwise. Get it?"

Bianca. He knows about Bianca coming to warn me about him. And now he's pissed. How could he know that?

"Got it," I say quietly.

"I'll be at your home in person on Sunday night, seven o'clock."

"I'll be there." My voice is a tiny whisper.

"Good. Oh, and I liked that little outfit with the shorts you wore out with that guy. Will you wear it on Sunday for me?"

I gasp. My date with Aidan. He's been watching me. Suddenly I feel like throwing up.

"Gotta go, Pia! Look out for Nolan. He's a bit of a live wire."

Cosmo hangs up and I hand the phone back to Nolan, who is still swinging the bat in big circles over his head.

"Please get away from my truck," I say in what I hope is a controlled, super-confident voice.

"I've called the cops!" shouts a voice.

"You better leave," I say to Nolan, trying to stare him down. "If the cops find you, you're fucked."

Nolan sneers. "Stupid move, bitch. I was gonna break your truck windows and leave it at that. But instead, I'm going to your yuppie fuckin' brownstone and I'm gonna break every fuckin' window one by one. Just to teach you a lesson."

I gasp. "You wouldn't—"

"I hope that little blond girl with the big tits is home. I like her."

Holy shit! Coco? "Don't you touch her, you junkie piece of—"

Nolan lets out an ear-splitting Tarzan yell, shaking the baseball bat in my face while jumping up and down. Then he runs around Toto, taking wild swings. The entire truck shakes with the sound of crunching metal. The customers and passersby who have been rubbernecking our fight from a safe distance scatter. I hear more breaking-glass sounds, but I can't move. I feel paralyzed by shock, or fear, or something. Like one of those dreams where you're trying to scream, but you can't even squeak.

Then he runs up the street to a little red car, jumps in the driver's side, and speeds away.

Oh, my God.

He's heading for Rookhaven. He's going to break every window and do who knows what to Coco, who is due home from work at any moment. And Vic and Marie are probably home, what if they hear something and come out? What would he do to them?

I don't have time to think, I don't have time to do anything. I just have to get home and stop him from destroying my house and hurting my friends. So I slam Toto's back doors and shout "Sorry! Next time!" to the few remaining would-be customers gawking from a safe distance, then run to the driver's seat and get in.

For a second, Toto won't start. "Come on, Toto, come on . . ." I mutter. She coughs and splutters, but the phlegm clears and she roars to life. I swing out to the street, do a totally illegal U-turn, put my aviators on, and head for the Brooklyn Bridge. I haven't packed away everything in the back. It's going to be a bloodbath of salad back there, but I don't care.

From Midtown all the way down through the East Village, I speed down every shortcut, side route, and secret alley I know, taking corners on two wheels, cutting in front of people and swearing at cabs that pull in front of me.

I feel like I'm in a movie. If it wasn't for the sick fear churning in my stomach, I'd almost be enjoying this.

Then, just as I'm about to cross Houston, I get a red light.

I'm usually careful, but I know from experience that these are some of the slowest red lights in Lower Manhattan, and this is an emergency, damnit.

So I race it, at about ninety miles an hour.

The next thing I hear is the sound of a car crashing, but it's not me, I'm fine, but—

Then the wail of a police siren, *merde*, there's a cop car right behind me! I need to stop, I know I need to stop, but I'm on some kind of "fight or flee" autopilot, and instead I slam my foot on the accelerator again. The cop's right behind me, of course, why didn't I stop, holy shit is this happening? Somehow I control myself, and pull over, my heart hammering painfully.

In a hyper-daze, I pull on the hand brake, take off my sunglasses, and try to smile as I see the policeman walking up to my window.

Stay calm, Pia. Calm.

"What seems to be the problem, officer?"

CHAPTER 25

Defective brake lights.

Running a red light.

Reckless driving.

Leaving the scene of an accident.

Unlicensed operation.

"I am really sorry, sir, the license belongs to the former owner and I'm just doing the paperwork now, and the brake light was just broken like five minutes ago, um, about that, there's this guy, he's crazy, I think he's on drugs, he's driving a red car, and he's going to my home at Union Street, in Brooklyn." I'm babbling now, but I can't help it. "He's going to break all the windows and maybe attack my roommate—"

The police officer seems pretty pleased with himself. I guess it was a lucky break for him: he was following the other car, because the woman driving it was drunk or something, and so when I ran the red and caused a collision, he got us both. The drunk driver is fine, hammered but unhurt, thank God.

"That may be, ma'am, but we're going to have to impound your vehicle," he says.

"What? Are you nuts? No way! I have to go home!"

"Ma'am, please calm down."

"But you can't do this! You can't— I can't—" I look around at Toto, beautiful pink Toto blinded by her broken headlights. "Just let me go home and I promise I'll come by the police station later and we'll figure it all out. I promise."

"Ma'am, calm down."

"I am calm!" I say, sounding more and more hysterical with every word. "Let me go! I mean it!"

"Ma'am, please lower your voice, and hand over the keys to your truck."

Hand over Toto? Hand over the keys to the only thing standing between me, a loan shark, and my parents? Where ten thousand dollars is hidden in an envelope underneath the seat? No. Never.

Then I make the biggest mistake of my—let's be honest—mistake-filled life.

I put my hands up and push him, just lightly, away from me.

Twenty minutes later, I'm in the back of a cop car, in handcuffs, speeding through Manhattan.

It turns out that arguing with a police officer, pushing him, and trying to run away is kind of the same thing as resisting arrest.

Or, um, exactly the same thing.

The next few hours pass in a blur. I'm searched, relieved of all my possessions, and then they read me all the charges against me, my mug shot is taken, someone asks me if I'm sick or on any drugs. I can barely listen to most of it, words simply float past me now and again, some of them mean something, some of them don't. "Central Booking" and "arraignment in the morning" stand out.

And that's how I ended up spending the night in a bullpen holding cell in Manhattan Central Booking in downtown Manhattan.

I'm so beside myself with worry about Nolan and Cosmo and Coco and the girls that at first, I barely think about the ten thousand dollars hidden under Toto's carpet. Then I remember again, and my brain darts back and forth between the two worries like a ping-pong ball. I can't mention either worry to the police officers, as it looks so sketchy. I was threatened by a loan shark's junkie henchman? I mean, is borrowing from a loan shark even legal? And what would they think about ten thousand dollars hidden under the carpet of my truck? They'd think I was a drug dealer or something.

What the hell kind of idiot gets herself into a mess like this?

Don't answer that.

But being in police custody is probably the safest place for ten thousand dollars, right? Who's gonna steal from the police? No one. Exactly. So as I finally arrive in the windowless cell where I'll be apparently spending the night, I decide all I have to worry about is Nolan. And he's more than enough.

The jail cell isn't the dark, tiny dungeon I would have imagined. It's large, warm, and overlit with migraine-inducing white lights that do nothing for the anemic mildew-green walls, or the filth-encrusted toilet in the corner, or the pay phone that's missing a handset. Oh, and it reeks of stale bodies and booze and piss and shit and good old-fashioned fear-sweat.

There are a half-dozen other women in the cell already. Half are loudly drunk or high. The others are sitting quietly on the metal bench running along the walls of the room, eyes shut, in a bid for their own personal escape. I guess privacy can be found when you close your eyes, no matter where you are.

"Welcome to the Tombs, Bollywood!" shouts a voice. Bollywood. Guess that's me. How original.

I ignore her, and ignore the stab of fear that runs through me. I'm alone. In *jail*. I discover immediately that the pay phone is broken, so, though I really don't want to disturb the other women in the cell, I try to get the officer on duty's attention.

"Excuse me, ma'am?" I call tentatively. "I need a phone? Please! I need to make a call!"

Nothing. At all.

I try again.

"Excuse me? Ma'am? Officer? I need a phone! I need to warn someone about something!"

Nothing.

I clear my throat, and sort of whisper-shout as clearly as I can. "Helloooooooo—"

"Shut up!"

I spin around. There's a woman right behind me. She's gaunt and yellow, with a neck tattoo spelling out "Peaches."

"Sorry," I say in a small voice.

Peaches narrows her eyes at me. "What the fuck is your fucking problem?"

I start stammering. "I was just trying to warn somebody . . . because . . . there's a crazy guy, and—"

"There's always a crazy guy!" shouts a woman in the corner. "We've all got crazy guys!"

Every woman in the cell cracks up laughing, and my stomach churns with panic.

"But he . . . he is dangerous," I whisper. Peaches is staring me down. I smell cinnamon gum and bourbon.

"Dangerous?" repeats Peaches. "Well, someone let her out of here!"

They all collapse laughing again.

"I just need a phone, okay?" I say. "I need to make a call."

"Why? What's so important that it can't wait? And where are you from, anyway, Bollywood?"

That's it.

I look her right in the eye. "I'm from Brooklyn. I owe ten thousand dollars to a crazy loan shark who sent his thugs to beat up my truck, destroy my business, and threaten my best friends, and if I don't get a phone call, I will not stop screaming all night. Got it?"

Peaches turns toward the bars. "Officer! We need a fuckin' phone call here! Medical emergency!"

She seems to know how to get attention. As I walk out, she high-fives me. "Good luck, Bollywood!"

But as I stare at the grimy pay phone the officer marches me to, I can't remember my friends' numbers. At all. Does anyone know phone numbers these days? I can barely remember my own number half the time! How can the world be so über-connected but so easy to get lost in? In fact, the only number I know is my parents'.

I pick up the handset and dial.

"Operator."

"Can I please place a collect call to Julia Russotti, Union Street, Brooklyn?"

There's a pause.

"There's no one in Brooklyn under that name, ma'am."

Merde. The home phone isn't in her name. The bills are directed straight to Julia's dad; they're included in the rent. But the day we moved in, there was old mail under the door, still all addressed to Julia's aunt Jo . . . it was Jo . . . Jo . . .

"Try Jo Lucalli."

A moment later, the phone rings and a breathless-sounding Julia immediately accepts the charges.

"Pia! Oh, thank God, where the hell are you? We've been so worried!"

"Is the house okay? Is everyone okay?"

"Yes, fine, we're fine. Where are you?"

"I'm . . . I'm in jail. Is everyone safe? Nothing happened to Coco or Vic or Marie?"

"No, nothing, everyone's fine. . . . Sorry, where did you say you were?"

"I'm in jail, Julia."

A split second later, the insanity of this statement hits me and I start laughing uncontrollably. Pia Keller: brat, princess, party girl, Brown grad, failed PR agent, loan shark client, food truck owner, and now . . . jailbird.

It's hilarious.

Julia isn't laughing, however, and keeps saying, "What?"

Eventually I calm myself down long enough to talk properly.

"So can you please come in the morning and bring a checkbook? I'll need to pay a fine or bail or whatever, I'm so sorry, I'm good for it. I promise." Thank God my ten thousand dollars is safe under the carpet of Toto's front seat, somewhere in an impound lot under lock and key.

"Yes, of course. But you have to stay there all night? Can we do something now? Can we come and see you?"

"Well, no, you can't just swing by and say hi, I mean . . . I'm in jail," I say, and start laughing again. I seem to be slightly hysterical.

"Pia, what the hell happened?"

I tell Julia everything as quickly as I can. She's not alone; every now and again she relays the updates of my story in bullet points to Coco, Angie, and Madeleine. I can hear them in the background: "Oh, my God," "Fuck me," and "Tell her to wash her hands after using that phone."

"Well, he didn't come by Rookhaven," she says when I'm done. "We haven't seen him at all."

"Nothing? You're sure?"

"Totally sure."

"And everyone is okay?" I say again. Nolan didn't go to Rookhaven? What could have happened to him?

"Everyone is fine," she says. "We're all here. We're just glad you're okay."

"I miss you." Suddenly I realize there's nothing left to say. And now I have to sit in a jail cell with a bunch of scary women till morning. "Oh, God, I'd better go."

"Are you gonna be okay?" asks Julia.

"Yes!" But my voice comes out high and strangled. Tears well up in my eyes and overflow down my cheeks, the kind that just won't stop. "Thank you so much. You're the best. All of you . . . I don't know what I'd do without you. You guys are the best things in my life."

Julia sounds like she's about to cry. "Stay safe, okay? We love you, we'll be there first thing in the morning."

"Okay," I say. A painfully large lump fills my throat. "I love you all, too."

I hang up, and for a second there's nothing but silence. A silent hallway, in a silent police station, in the noisiest city in the world. Then the officer walks me back to my cell, as I frantically wipe my face on the way.

"What up, Bollywood? Your crazy guy okay?" calls Peaches.

"He disappeared," I say. "I don't know where he is."

"He'll turn up," she says. "They always do."

I sit down, alone, in the corner of the cell. I don't want anyone to talk to me. I will not cry. This will not break me.

And then I close my eyes and focus on Rookhaven.

I think about the peeling rosebud wallpaper and the creaky floorboards underneath the carpet. I think about the view from my bedroom over Union Street, and the way the sofa fabric feels against my cheeks when we all watch TV. I think about Vic and Marie living underneath us and watching over us. I think about the kitchen, and how it feels when we're sitting around the table together.

And suddenly I feel calm.

I can get through this.

CHAPTER 26

The arraignment takes approximately nine seconds, and, with that funny vague jet-lag feeling that comes from being awake all night and not brushing my teeth, when I finally come out and see Madeleine and pay the fines, it takes me a while to realize she's alone. But we don't talk till we're outside the building.

The moment we're on the street, Maddy and I turn to each other and hug tightly for about a minute.

"It's so good to see you! Did you sleep last night? Are you okay?" she says at the same moment that I say, "It's so good to see you! I'm so sorry, I'll pay you back as soon as I can, I promise. . . . Where are the girls?"

"Marie passed away last night," says Madeleine.

I gasp.

"So they're staying with Vic until the family arrives. Her kids are taking care of the details and we just . . . we didn't want him to be alone."

"Oh, of course . . ." I feel all hot and woolly. Marie *died*? "How, um, how—"

"In her sleep. Early this morning. She went peacefully. Pia, you've gone white, are you—"

I half-collapse, half-sit, right where I am, on the cold concrete sidewalk. Oh, God, poor Marie. Poor Vic. Poor Coco and Julia . . .

Madeleine crouches next to me, holding a bottle of water to my lips. "Pia? Just breathe, okay, drink. . . ."

I take a few sips, then prop my arms over my knees, and stare unseeingly at the freezing concrete step between my feet. It's rainy today for the first time in months, with a real October chill in the air, and I feel cold, inside and out. Oh, God, Marie and Vic . . .

Madeleine takes off her jacket and sweater. "Put these on." She pulls me up to standing. "I don't want you to get arrested for loitering."

"I don't feel great." My voice sounds all high and thin.

"You just need to eat." Madeleine frog-marches me to a food cart on the corner, where she gets a Coca-Cola and a peanut butter bagel.

I stand numbly next to her, my brain in overdrive. Poor Vic. Poor, lovely Vic. His wife Eleanor died, Julia's mom and aunt died, his sister died . . . he must feel so alone.

How terrible it must be to have no one left who remembers life as it was when you were young. To be the only person keeping all those memories.

In silence, we get the subway back to Brooklyn. We sit in silence on the half-empty subway car, both of us alone with our thoughts, as I consume the bagel and the Coca-Cola without even tasting them.

Then I glance over. Without her jacket and sweater, Madeleine's wearing nothing but a sleeveless tank, and absentmindedly stroking the inside of her wrists . . . which are covered in little tiny white scars. I've never seen her bare arms before.

"Do you cut yourself?"

"I don't," she says, quickly, folding her arms.

We lock eyes for several long seconds.

"Okay, I used to. A long time ago. But then I saw a therapist and now I don't."

"Do you—"

"No. I don't want to talk about it."

"Maddy—"

"Pia, I said *no*." She hesitates, and then looks me right in the eye. "I'm allowed to have my secrets, too."

"You might feel better if you talk about them," I say. "I did."

"Yeah, well, I'll take my chances." She looks up. "C'mon. It's our stop. Don't worry about me today, okay? I'm fine."

When we get home, it's nearly 11:00 A.M. Julia and Coco are sitting on either end of one sofa, Angie is curled up alone on the other, all silently watching a *Babar* cartoon.

I sit down between Julia and Coco and pull them both in for a hug. Coco immediately folds into me like a little kid, crying noisily, but Julia just turns the TV to mute and blinks furiously.

"I can't cry anymore," she says. "I can't . . . or I'll never stop."

"What happened?" I say softly.

"Vic rang the doorbell really early this morning." Julia is playing with the stitching on one of the cushions. "I opened the door and thought he was having a heart attack, he was so gray, he looked awful, but he couldn't say anything, he just grabbed my hand and took me downstairs."

"Oh, God, no." Julia had to confirm Marie was dead? That's not fair, not after everything with her mother, she shouldn't have had to do that.

"And then Angie came down."

"I heard the doorbell," says Angie. With no makeup on, not even her usual morning-after panda eyeliner, she looks about five.

"Angie called the ambulance, and they came and. . . . Anyway, Coco and I stayed with Vic and tried to make him eat, but he just stared out the window and ignored us. Marie's daughters turned up half an hour ago and he left with them."

"It was so awful." Coco is crying into my shoulder.

Madeleine gets blankets and covers us in them, and then sits down silently on the other sofa next to Angie. I stroke Coco's hair. She seems so fragile and young. Who is going to look after her? Who is going to look after Vic? Who's going to look after any of us?

"Do you want to talk about Marie?" I ask, but Julia shakes her head. "Is your dad coming down?"

"He's in California for work."

We all watch Babar toddle around the screen.

"You know, I don't know why I've been making myself so stressed about my job," says Julia. "I should just quit. I could die at any moment.

I should be traveling the world and sleeping with men and taking drugs and being wild."

"What?" Coco sits up in panic. "Don't do that!"

"Unless that's what you want," I say.

"It's not," she says, sighing. "But I want to be happy."

We all sit there for a few minutes. That's all any of us wants, really.

"So. Anyway. How was jail?" says Julia.

We meet eyes for a second. The entire living room is in total silence. A second later she giggles, and repeats "jail!" in a disbelieving tone. Then we all lose it.

I laugh so hard I feel like I might burst. We laugh with that hysterical edge you have when you can't cry anymore or you'll collapse, when right at that moment existence is so awful that the only option left is to throw your head back and cackle. Julia is laughing so hard she gets the hiccups, and Coco runs out of the room, gasping, "I peed my pants!"

"Do you have Vic's nieces' numbers?" I ask after we've calmed down. "We should coordinate with them to, I don't know, look after Vic—or clean the house, make sure there's food, stuff like that?"

"I was thinking the same thing," says Julia. "He's staying with them for the next week, I think, but I offered to fill the fridge before he gets home, and strip Marie's bed. . . ."

She gulps, closing her eyes.

"You don't have to do that," I say.

"I don't want her daughters to do it," she says quietly.

"Then I'll help," I say. "You can do the fridge, I'll do the bed. When is the funeral?"

Julia shrugs. "They don't know yet. End of the week, I'd guess."

I know I should shower, sleep, or think about how the hell I'm going to get to the vehicle impound place in Quees to collect poor Toto and my ten thousand dollars before Cosmo com over tomorrow night. But I can't bear to be alone, and I can't bear to leave the girls alone, either.

And you know what else? The money, and the debt, and everything else, just doesn't seem that important compared to this.

All I care about right now is being here.

So we turn *Babar* back up, watch it to the end, and then Coco makes popcorn with her traditional topping of salt and dark chocolate chips, and we put on *The Mighty Ducks,* Julia's favorite childhood movie.

Halfway through the movie Angie comes over and squishes herself between Coco and me. She curls up under my arm, with Coco cuddling into her. Then Madeleine grabs a cushion and props herself on the floor in front of Julia and me, leaning her head on our knees. The five of us sit there for the next hour, draped over one another like kittens, all staring unseeingly at the trials and tribulations of the Mighty Ducks.

We're lost in our own thoughts, but I've never felt like more of a unit than I do right now. The five of us, together, no matter what. We're all in this together.

Considering the situation, it's probably strange I feel happier than I ever have before. But I do. I feel quiet, and calm, but happy.

The movie ends and we all sit there, strewn with popcorn crumbs.

"I have a cramp in my leg," says Julia.

"Yeah, me too," says Madeleine, rolling herself flat on the floor and then pulling her knees up to stretch.

"I need to brush my teeth," says Coco.

"I need to get Toto," I say. "And then I need to get ready to see Cosmo tomorrow night."

"Tell us what we can do to help," says Angie. "We're in this together, remember?"

"Will you come to Queens with me to get my truck?"

"Goddamnit. I knew I shouldn't have offered."

Picking up Toto takes the subway-walking-GPS-iPhone-waiting-begging hell you'd expect, but by four o'clock we're on the way home.

Angie is with me, not that she's been much company: she's barely spoken.

When we reach Brooklyn Heights, she lights a cigarette. I hate people smoking in Toto. "Dude, seriously—"

"Mani broke up with me," she replies.

Smoking is suddenly not only understandable, but necessary. "*Merde*. I'm so sorry. Give me a drag of that."

"I saw him last night. He said he thought it was best if we stopped seeing each other." She says it almost without any emotion at all.

"What a cockmonkey," I say.

"He's a fucking asshole! We only slept together for the first time last fucking week! One orgasm! He didn't even look my vagina in the face!"

"Hang on. . . . You can get off during sex? Like the sex bit of sex?"

"Of course. Can't you?"

"No, oral only."

"I can't concentrate during oral. They never know what they're doing, and I start wondering what's going through their minds as they toil away, and then I start thinking about what I'm gonna wear tomorrow, and then— Wait. That's not the point, Pia. What's wrong with me? Why am I only attracted to fuckpuppets?"

"Nothing is wrong with you! Obviously Mani's just another cockmonkey," I suggest. "Plain and simple."

"Cockmonkey!" shouts Angie. She leans out the window and screams it at the top of her lungs all the way back to Rookhaven. Screw it, I think, and join in. All men are cockmonkeys. So what if I was the psycho date from hell with Aidan? He's probably just a cockmonkey anyway. I saved myself a lot of time and bother and unnecessary underwear purchases.

Cursing at the top of your lungs while driving is surprisingly therapeutic. The last twenty-four hours have been crazy, but tomorrow I'm paying off my loan once and for all, and crazy Cosmo will leave me alone, and I'll never see Nicky or Nolan again. I'll be free.

"Cockmonkeys!"

As soon as we park on Union Street, I reach under the passenger side carpet to get the envelope containing Cosmo's ten thousand dollars.

It's gone.

My whole body seizes up in shock. "No!"

"What?" says Angie.

"No!" I shout, ripping up the carpet entirely. "It can't be— It can't be—"

I throw myself over to my side of the truck and scrabble at the carpet there. Nothing. Then I check the glove box, under the seats, the carpet in the back. Nothing!

"It's gone. It's gone!" I yell.

"What? What's gone?" says Angie. "Fuck, you're a drama queen! Calm down!"

"My money—the money—the ten thousand dollars—they stole it— the impound people!"

I drop to the pavement and scream.

CHAPTER **27**

"Stop screaming, you're freaking me out!"

A deathly quiet and calm overtakes me. "It's over, Angie, everything is over. I'll call my parents and tell them everything so they can give me the money to give to Cosmo when he comes over tomorrow. And then I'll go back to Zurich with them and never come back. I'll never pay the money back any other way. It's over."

"There must be another way," says Angie.

"There's not." My mouth is dry with horror. "This is it. End of the road. It's over."

Two hours later, sitting at the kitchen table with the girls, I find myself saying it again.

"It's over. I made the money. It's now in the pocket of some impound dude in Queens. It's gone."

"It can't be," says Coco, for the sixteenth time.

"There must be another solution," says Julia.

"There isn't," I say. "I can't sell the truck, it's not worth what I paid for it. I don't have any other money. And as much as you guys might want to help, I know you don't have ten thousand dollars between you, and you can't ask your parents. You just can't." I look around. No one is arguing. "It's over. I want you all safely out of Rookhaven tomorrow afternoon. I'll deal with Cosmo, alone."

"No way," says Coco.

"We're here with you, no matter what," agrees Madeleine.

"Girl power." Angie gives a fist pump. "That was ironic. An ironic fist pump."

I smile at them all. It's what I'd do if I were them, too.

"Don't sell the truck," says Julia slowly.

"I just said that I couldn't. That Al guy said it was worth like, nothing."

"No, I mean, don't sell the truck . . . sell the business," says Julia.

I frown at her. Sell the business? "But it's only six weeks old."

"It's successful," she says. "It's a unique idea, you've completely cornered the market. Your profits are incredible, you've had loads of publicity, your followers on Twitter and Facebook are passionate advocates. You have created a small, successful business, Pia. You could sell the whole thing for ten, twenty, fifty times what the truck is worth." She pauses. "I mean, I have no idea how much the business would sell for. But it sure as hell would be more than the truck."

I stare into space, thinking. She's right. She's completely right. I could sell the business. Just like Vic said all those weeks ago. *Have an idea, make it work, sell it on. . . .*

"But how . . . how do I do that?" I say. "Who would buy it?"

"I don't know," says Julia. "I haven't gotten that far. What about a venture capitalist?"

"What the hell is a venture capitalist?" says Angie.

"VCs invest in start-up companies in return for an equity share," says Julia.

"What the hell is an equity share?" says Angie, in exactly the same tone of voice. I crack up despite myself.

"You guys, be serious," says Julia.

"We are being serious!" say Angie and I in unison.

"Venture capitalists give you money to run your company, and in return, they part-own the business," says Madeleine. "They look for original ideas, you know, things no one else is doing."

"Aidan works in venture capital," I say. It's the first time I've said his name aloud in days. "I have his card."

"Call him!" says Coco.

"No," I say, closing my eyes tight to try to force away the thought of him. "That is not an option, either."

"I know you've been thinking about him," says Julia. "You get that moony look on your face."

Ugh, I hate it when I'm easy to read.

"You do," agrees Angie. "I think you should call Aidan, too. The date was good until you saw Eddie, right?"

I think back. It *was* good. In fact, it was more than good. It was perfect.

"It doesn't matter," I repeat.

"Do you still have feelings for Eddie?" asks Coco. "Is that what it is?"

"No!" I say instantly. I haven't even thought about Eddie at all, only Aidan. Seeing Eddie at the restaurant that night was just the past coming up to slap me in the face. And that's where Eddie belongs. In the past. I should have dealt with it years ago, instead of letting his stupid flight-risk comments haunt me like that. He wasn't perfect. He didn't know me. But it just doesn't matter. I'm over it.

And I'll get over Aidan, too.

"I am not turning to a guy to fix my problems, goddamnit," I say. "And anyway, he probably wouldn't help me. He thinks I'm a total psycho." Because I acted like one. But never mind that now, either. "So what do I do next? Google 'venture capitalist?'"

"Probably not," admits Julia. "You need an introduction . . . contacts. Aidan would have them."

"I will *not* call Aidan . . . and I don't have any contacts. I'd have to make a list. Cold-call them. But none of them will be at work till Monday anyway, and Cosmo is coming over tomorrow night." I feel sick at the thought.

"Maybe you could call people who *should* own a food truck that sells low-fat, low-carb, high-protein food."

"Can we order in from Bartolo's?" asks Coco. "We need to eat."

As we wait for our pizza to arrive, we brainstorm who might want to buy SkinnyWheels.

"Jenny Craig?"

"Ew, come on . . ."

"A gym chain? Equinox?"

"Tracy Anderson? Gwyneth's trainer?"

"That Soul Cycle place? Seriously, everyone who goes there is cut like a fucking diamond."

"Condé Nast? So they can feed all the skinny bitches who work for *Vogue*?"

"A model agency? I bet a model agency would love it."

"One of those weight-loss reality TV shows?"

"*The Today Show*?"

"Why the hell would *The Today Show* want SkinnyWheels?"

"Oprah? Oprah would totally buy it."

"That Hungry Girl chick?"

"No way," I say. "Even if those people *should* use a food truck to promote themselves, it doesn't mean they will. I can't convince them. They have strategy people who decide what they should do, and before that they have, like, focus groups and market research."

"How do you know all that?" says Angie.

"Lina told me," I say, pouring myself another glass of wine. Then I pause, thinking aloud. "Lina . . . who is VP of strategy for some big hotel and restaurant group. Carus International! She might have advice for me! Or contacts! She might be able to help!" I look at the kitchen clock. "It's eight o'clock on a Saturday night. I can't call her, can I?"

"You can e-mail her," says Julia. "Or text her. She lives around here, right?"

I nod. "I think so. I mean, she must, I met her at Bartolo's. I saw her on the street with her kids."

"So text her. Offer to bribe her with coffee tomorrow in return for a little career advice. It's flattering. People love to give advice. I must have e-mailed a hundred people for advice over the years, then we meet up and I listen to them talk about themselves."

"Really? Okay! I will!" I grab my phone.

Then the pizza arrives, and as we all start scarfing, I draft a text.

Hi Lina. Pia here. I was wondering if there's any way that I could steal thirty minutes of your time tomorrow for coffee and a chat? I need career advice . . . apologies for the late notice; it's a (semi)emergency.

That's good, right? I'm underlining the importance of it without being melodramatic.

Ten minutes later, I get a response.

Of course! Chestnut, 11 am?

By eleven-thirty the next morning, I've told Lina everything. From being fired for the Captain Morgan Facebook incident, to the ten thousand dollar loan from Cosmo, to everything I did to build SkinnyWheels, to—finally—spending the night in jail. I keep it as brief as I can, and skim over the Cosmo-is-a-crazy-freak elements, but it still takes twenty minutes.

"I'm not particularly proud of the loan shark." I'm using my spoon to make little circles in my yogurt and granola. Then I realize it looks disgusting, so I stop. "Or jail."

"Jail happens. I was arrested for smoking a joint in Washington Square when I was eighteen. So looks like I'll never run for president. But the loan shark is a different story. You don't want to get involved with people like that. I'm kind of worried, I think we should call the police—"

"No, no, it's fine, don't worry about that," I lie quickly. "I've got the money. My parents transferred it to me. But now I, um, need to pay them back. Like urgently." Urgh, I'm terrible at lying.

She takes a bite of her pancake, chews, and frowns. "This is not as good as yours."

"Ha! Thanks, but I'm sure that's not true. . . . Anyway. My friend Julia suggested I sell SkinnyWheels. The whole business, you know, not just the truck. I know it won't happen overnight, but I was hoping—like, really hoping—that it might be an option," I say. "And I was hoping you might have some advice for me."

Lina nods. "Okay, well, I can't—"

Then she stops, and stares at the wall behind me, deep in thought.

After about a minute, she blinks, and looks at me again, and then rapid-fires questions at me.

"It's only been, what, six weeks since you started? How did you think of everything? How did you know where to go, what to do, how you'd tweet and Facebook, how did you know what people would want?"

I think for a few seconds. "Instinct, I guess? SkinnyWheels was just an idea because it seemed to me to be so obvious. That's why I'm not sure if it's even a business idea worth selling. Anyone could do it. It's not that special."

Lina stares at me, and nods, lost in thought.

As the seconds tick into minutes, I realize she's trying to figure out how to tell me to get a grip. Oh, God, how embarrassing, I'm such an idiot. I'll apologize for wasting her time, I'll just say, never mind—

Then she looks me right in the eye and starts talking again.

"The gourmet food truck movement has been gaining a lot of traction over the past four or five years. People adore them. It's a combination of the allure of a genuine passion for specialty or gourmet food, the personal touch of being served by the chef or owner, and the toy-like adorability of the trucks. Plus, it's the new mom 'n' pop store. It's so personal; the owner *is* the food truck: they drive, cook, serve, and sell. In this day and age, having something that feels so *real* is a draw in itself."

I nod uncertainly. I feel like she's giving a presentation, but I'm not sure why.

She keeps talking. "You know exactly what you're getting with a food truck. It's fast, but it's not dirty, like most fast-food chains. The prices are low, it's great value. You can follow them online, track them down via social media, which makes it feel like an achievement when you find them. . . . It's like a game."

I nod. Everything she's saying makes sense to me. "I think people also get emotionally attached to trucks," I say tentatively. "They're really passionate about it. It's like seeing a buddy out and about around the city. You feel like you own that truck. People actually wave at me when I'm driving!"

"That's amazing!" says Lina. "And now you have food trucks pairing up with brands. I was in San Francisco a few years ago and got a snow cone from a food truck advertising some ski resort. I mean, fantastic idea, right? So brands can use the truck as the medium. Or the truck can pair with brands for events and launches—turn up, give food out, it's more exciting than the ubiquitous caterers with goddamn cupcakes. Like that truck Treatery, they've really nailed it. They pair up with brands but they keep their own name. Every time a brand pays them to turn up somewhere, their name gets a little more cachet."

"Right," I say. I don't really know what she's talking about.

"You may think 'anyone' could think of this idea, Pia, but that's not true. Some people are creative and original thinkers, some people aren't. The people who are tend to believe that whatever they create seems like the most obvious thing in the world, like you do. I'm a strategist, and I'm not particularly creative, but I can recognize a great idea when I see it. And more important, I can explain why it works." She stares at me, nodding fervently. I don't know what to do, so I nod back. "Tell me more about how you thought of the idea."

"Um, my roommates kept saying how they were in carb comas at work; I saw all these trucks selling greasy, fatty foods, and I'm the kind of girl who likes to eat but also likes to fit into tight jeans, you know? When it comes down to it, SkinnyWheels is all about vanity, really. . . ." I grin, trying to make a joke, but Lina isn't smiling.

"Vanity is a huge part of every major new business success in the past century," she says seriously. "It's human nature. When you look great, you feel happy. No one should ever apologize for that. That's the reason the fitness industry has become a multibillion dollar industry in the past twenty years. Not to mention fashion, cosmetics . . ."

There's another pause. I take a sip of my coffee, nodding. I don't know anything about the fitness industry, or fashion, or cosmetics. I feel like I'm frantically paddling to keep up as Lina's brain races ahead.

Then she smiles at me. "I think food trucks are really interesting, Pia. And I particularly think your take on food trucks is really interesting."

"Thanks," I say.

"Do you have any other ideas? Like, food truck ideas?"

"Yeah . . . I have lots of ideas. Driving a food truck leaves you a lot of time to daydream."

"Dazzle me," she says, rolling her eyes slightly on the *dazzle*.

"Uh, I think that there should be an all-day healthy breakfast truck. People want gluten-free pancakes anytime, I get requests at three in the afternoon that I can't fulfill because I'm always out of batter. And it should offer waffles, too, and seasonal fruit salad with fat-free yogurt. . . . And there should be a truck specializing in eggs: omelets, egg-white omelets, scrambled eggs. I get requests for that all the time but I don't have the capacity to do it."

"Go on," says Lina. Her eyes are gleaming.

"And my friends had a truck called A Meal Grows in Brooklyn. All the food came from the Brooklyn area, right? Sustainable, local, organic, hand-reared, yada yada. Such a great idea, and so Brooklyn. But they've failed, they had to close the business. Someone should buy the idea from them or, uh, the equity in the business." I talk quickly, trying to cover up that I still don't really know what equity means. "You could launch a chain of trucks nationwide, with different regions getting their own local produce on the menu. A Meal Grows in Santa Barbara, A Meal Grows in Seattle, A Meal Grows in Dallas . . ."

"A Meal Grows in Detroit?" says Lina, smirking.

"Exactly," I say. "And there should be a packed-lunch truck in the mornings, for people like my friend Julia who hardly ever leave their desk. So you could buy a good packed lunch when you're walking from the subway to your office, with a midmorning snack and an afternoon snack. Like a little school lunchbox! With a salad, maybe celery stalks with almond butter, a sugar-free flapjack . . ."

"Right on!"

"And there should be a dinner-for-two truck, for when you're heading home from work and you just want to put something in the oven and have it with your boyfriend or husband or whatever." I'm gabbling now. "People are always buying two of my salads at the end of the day, to take home and have for dinner, but in winter they're not going to want that, you know? They're going to need something they can warm up at home. Like a gingery-honey poached chicken with steamed vegetables, or a tuna steak that's marinating in herbs and all you have to do is grill it quickly on each side. I mean, you can get that stuff at Whole Foods, but let's make it so people can just pick it up after work right outside their office, without going out of their way or spending a fortune, right? And there should be an organic Italian food truck that gives you take-home packs of organic and gluten-free lasagne or pasta."

"This is fantastic! Keep talking!"

"And there should be a soup truck, but like, a really genuinely low-fat, health-packed, low-salt soup truck with gluten-free bread rolls. Half the soup places in this town have more fat and sodium than a Big Mac. . . ."

"Pia, this is great stuff. Really, really great stuff." Lina is frowning at me intently.

I beam. Why do I feel like I just passed an exam?

She clears her throat. "Look, I work with someone you should talk to, and I've been working on some things that might . . . hmm. I shouldn't tell you more till I figure out if and how it's going to work. Can you come to my office at ten in the morning tomorrow? You may have to wait awhile, his schedule is crazy, but if I'm any good at my job he'll find time to see you."

"Yes . . ." I say. I'm confused. Who is "he"? What would a huge, glossy hotel and restaurant chain want with a measly little Skinny-Wheels food truck? But I just nod. There's something about her enthusiasm and focus that makes me desperate to impress her. "Thank you, Lina, thank you so much."

Lina's phone rings. "Hey, hon . . . Okay, no problem, I'm coming now." She hangs up. "I've gotta go, Pia. We've got an afternoon playdate with another family with kids the same age as Pia and Gabe."

"Sounds like a blast," I say.

"Oh, it is," she says, pulling on her jacket. "It's like double-dating, but more potential for sandbox fights and tears. So I'll see you at ten tomorrow?"

"Yes!" I exclaim. Sheesh, Pia, dial down the desperation. "I mean, yes. And thank you so much for meeting me, I really appreciate it. You go ahead, I think I'll have another cup of coffee here. And, uh, is there anything I can do to prepare for tomorrow?"

"Can you get some photos of your salads and the truck? Apart from that, nothing. You're perfect."

She takes some money out of her purse and tries to give it to me for the check.

"No, no!" I say. "I'll pay. Thank you so much, again, for meeting me."

As we say good-bye and she hurries back to her busy, seemingly per-fect grown-up mommy life, my mind is spinning.

What is she planning? Should I have opened my mouth and both-ered her for every detail instead of pretending to understand? I met her for advice—but now I'm even more confused!

Okay, okay, it's fine. I'll just prepare for whatever happens in the meeting tomorrow, just like she said.

And try not to think about the fact that Cosmo is coming over in a few hours.

CHAPTER **28**

So the first thing I do is call Angie, and we drive Toto and some freshly made SkinnyWheels salads straight to her workplace in Chelsea.

"You're *sure* this is okay?" I ask for the sixteenth time.

"The Bitch is in Miami this weekend. And it's a food photography studio, I mean, it's just sitting there! Now, listen, we're gonna drive the whole truck into the underground garage, we have an area where we do big shoots."

Two hours later, I've got thousands of incredible shots of Toto and my salads.

"You are so talented!" I exclaim, looking at the shots on my laptop. Angie is brandishing a state-of-the-art digital camera like a pro, and even set up all the lighting, all by herself. I just watched in awe.

"You have no idea how *not* talented I am," she says. "These shots would make the Bitch scream in pain." She grins, and lights a cigarette. "She would be like this. *Angelique? Angelique?*" Angie puts on a pretend high-pitched Dutch accent. "Fail, Angelique! Why is my latte so cold? Angelique? You are failing, Angelique! Why is my driver not outside? Angelique? Why am I such a total fucking bitch to you every single fucking day?" She jumps on the table and starts humping the air. "Angelique! Why does no one want to fuck me? Angelique!"

"Angelique?"

Another voice. From the door.

We both whirl around in shock. It's the Bitch. Tall. Tanned. And angry.

"Why are you smoking? In my studio? And using my camera? And my lights?"

Angie pauses, still standing on the table, mid-hump.

"Um . . ."

"You're fired."

"You can't fire me! *I quit!*"

Angie jumps down, puts the camera carefully on the table, and then turns to give the Bitch the finger from both hands. "See that? That's a big bag of *I quit* with your name on it!"

"Okay, Angie, let's go." I quickly close my laptop and start dragging her toward Toto.

"And you know what else? All those lattes I got you were *full-fat!*"

I can still hear the Bitch screaming from the street.

Angie cackles all the way home, and dismisses my apologies.

"That was my fault, I'm so sorry—"

"Are you kidding? I can't believe I lasted two months! Don't you worry about me. New York is a big city. I'll find another job." She pauses. "Or maybe I'll just start a food truck business."

"Ha!"

Then, as we drive over the Brooklyn Bridge, that niggling thought I've been pushing to the back of my brain for the last few hours returns with a thud. Tonight, Cosmo is coming over with his monkey boys, Nicky and Nolan, to get his ten thousand dollars. And I don't have it.

What did I think was going to happen? Did I think Lina would have ten thousand dollars to just hand over? Did I think she'd find someone to buy the entire business on a Sunday afternoon? I am an idiot.

I'm simply going to ask Cosmo—okay, beg him—to give me a forty-eight hour extension. I'll explain that my money was stolen—because of crazy Nolan!—that I need a little longer to get it together.

Then, if whatever Lina is planning tomorrow works out, I'll do that.

If it doesn't, then when my parents arrive on Tuesday I'll explain to them, in person, why I need the money. Maybe actually seeing Toto, and seeing how hard I've been working, will make a difference. Maybe they won't be so disappointed.

I'll leave Brooklyn with them, go to Zurich, get some boring desk job, and pay them back every last penny. Then I'll come back to New York, and start again.

And that's just how it has to be.

CHAPTER 29

Letting ourselves into Vic's house feels wrong, somehow. Like we're sneaking in illegally, even though we have a key.

Julia breathes in sharply as we enter, as if to steel herself against the inevitable grief.

"This time two days ago, Marie was sitting right here," she whispers. "Talking, eating, breathing. . . . How can it be possible that someone can be alive and then be gone so fast?"

I don't know what to say. My life hasn't been touched by death before, not really, not like Julia's has. Imagine your mother dying . . . I can't. I don't even want to imagine it. I don't know how you'd ever get over something like that.

I just want to make today easy for Julia. Cosmo coming over in three hours really isn't a problem compared to what she's going through. It's not fair for one person to have to say so many good-byes to people she loves.

So I reach out and give Julia another hug and for a second she is shaking, and I think she's going to cry. But instead, she mutters "boob-squash," and pushes me away.

"Let's get this over with."

"I'll do Marie's bed," I say. "You go make sure the kitchen is all in order."

Marie slept in a single bed with pink, rose-covered sheets, which gives me an immediate lump in my throat, though I don't really know why. All her knickknacks are still out on her dresser and bedside table: dozens of photos, her tiny wristwatch and a tiny travel alarm clock that looks like something from the set of *Mad Men,* a well-worn copy of *Mariana* by Monica Dickens open next to it.

Quickly, I strip the bed and bundle the sheets into the corner. Then I fold the quilt and stack the pillows on top of it. The mattress looks so tiny and helpless by itself.

Heading into Vic's room, I strip his bed, too, and put on fresh sheets. Then I open his curtains. The place is immaculate: not a speck of dust anywhere. He only has one photo: a black-and-white picture of a girl smiling happily, shielding her eyes from the sun. She looks like Katharine Hepburn, except with bigger eyes and a pointy little chin. It must be Eleanor. His wife.

Now I feel even more like I'm trespassing.

"Julia?" I shout. "You okay?"

There's no reply.

Picking up the bedding, I hurry into the kitchen. Julia has her head in the fridge, and is rearranging the food.

"We need to buy fresh milk, butter, and bread," she mutters. "And I'd like to get some kind of soup or casserole thing to put in here for Vic when he comes home tomorrow."

"I'll go to Esposito's. He likes the lasagne. . . . Jules, I'm going to wash this bedding upstairs, okay? Why don't you come up with me? The place is immaculate. You don't need to be here."

Julia nods. She's hardly even listening to me.

I take her hand and we head back upstairs. The leaves are falling, and

Union Street feels unusually empty. Depressing Sunday night back-to-school type weather.

I put the bedding in the wash, head up to my room, and lie on my bed.

Only a few more hours till Cosmo is here.

You know what's almost the worst about all this? I hate the idea of asking my parents to bail me out again. They're in Zurich right now. It's the city that sleeps all day Sunday: there's nothing to do, nowhere to go. My dad is probably planning their trip over here, or reading the *Zürcher Zeitung* and making *tsk tsk* sounds to himself. My mother is probably on the phone, rolling her eyes, talking to her sisters about how I'm spoiled, silly, and a deeply disappointing daughter.

In twenty-two years, I've never surprised them. . . . Well, not in a good way. And they've never, ever said they're proud of me. Not once.

It's like they thought saying they were proud of me might make me complacent. It backfired: I became detached, instead.

Now that I haven't spoken to them in so long, I can sort of see our relationship for what it is. How I've always been ostensibly obedient but figured out how to float around them and get what I wanted, whether that was more spending money or supervision-free vacations with Angie. And I'm about to do it again, by asking them to bail me out of a ten thousand dollar debt.

If I were them, I probably wouldn't be proud of me, either.

But I've changed. I really feel like for the last six weeks, I've had a purpose: SkinnyWheels. I feel sure of myself for the first time in years, like I know what I want and if I work hard enough and am just a teeny bit lucky, I can get it. I feel, for the first time, that I'm where I belong. I'm home.

I start tidying my room and putting away clothes. I have dozens of pairs of heels, yet I've worn the same pair of Converses every day for weeks. Ridiculous.

Oh, God, I love this room, I love this house, I love everything about it, from the peeling wallpaper to the creaky floorboards. I don't want to leave. I want to stay here and make this my home for good. I want to help my friends figure life out. And I want to talk to Aidan and apologize for everything.

I want it all. But I can't have any of it.

I head downstairs to the laundry to put the bedding in the dryer, and walk outside to the deck. It's cold and windy outside. Summer is definitely over.

Lying down flat on the wooden table, like a snow-free snow angel, I gaze up at the dull gray sky above my head. Closing my eyes, I begin to speak.

"Thank you for getting me this far."

My voice sounds clear and thin in the chilly afternoon air.

"In the past six weeks I've been fired, broke, threatened, drunk, high, and arrested. My ideas have been copied, my property has been vandalized, and my love life is MIA. And I'm still here. I can keep going, no matter what happens. I am stronger than anyone thinks, and I promise I will figure out what to do with my life next, and I'll do it. I'll be fine."

And as I say it, I realize it's true. I really will be fine.

"But I need you to help protect my friends tonight. It's my fault Cosmo is coming over, and it's my fault that I don't have his ten thousand dollars. And I'm sorry, from the bottom of my heart, that I ever thought it was a good idea. I've learned my lesson. I promise. I promise I won't make the same mistakes again. Just don't let anyone get hurt. Please give me a sign if you can hear me."

Opening my eyes, I take a deep breath.

"One sign. That's all I'm asking."

At that exact moment, it starts to rain.

Not *trickle-trickle-splash-splash* gradual rain, but a sudden angry torrent like the special effects people in the sky typed "downpour" into their magic weather machine, and the clouds obeyed.

My eyes close again as I smile up at the sky, feeling the drops splatter over my face and body. I'm wearing a big sweater and some scraggy old jeans, so I've got a while till I'm drenched through, then I'll go shower. But right now I just want to lie here and enjoy it, let the cool rain run over my face and down my hair and neck.

Two hours till Cosmo is here.

CHAPTER **30**

One hour before Cosmo-time, everyone is home and in the living room. I've asked them to leave me to deal with him alone, repeatedly. They've refused, repeatedly.

"We're all in this together," said Julia. Which pretty much made me want to cry and hug her at the same time.

We're ostensibly watching some reality program about bridesmaids gone wild, all locked in the torture of anticipation. Angie is shuffling cards nervously, Julia is tapping her foot, Coco is reading the same page of *Little Women* over and over again, and Madeleine is chewing her hair. And me? I'm just running through doomsday scenarios in my head.

Then the doorbell rings.

"I'll get it!" says Coco, leaping up off the couch. I hear the door open, then a second later, "Piiiaaaaaaa?"

Julia and I exchange a look and both run out of the living room.

It's Cosmo.

Early.

With Nolan and Nicky behind him.

"Pia! Honey!" says Cosmo, smiling so widely it looks like his face might burst.

I haven't seen Cosmo face-to-face since the day we met. He's wearing jeans and another perfectly pressed shirt; he's freshly shaved and smiling widely. He doesn't look suave, though, I suddenly realize. He looks creepy. Standing next to him is Nolan, his arm in a sling, looking less focused and even more dangerous than he did on Friday. And on the other side is Nicky, the man-mountain.

"You're early," I say, slightly redundantly.

"I've got dinner plans," Cosmo says, looking at me with cold, hard eyes. "And anyway, I've *missed* you, Pia. I wanted to catch up."

"Aren't you going to invite us in?" says Nolan.

"No," says Julia, by my side. "This is my house. You are not welcome."

Cosmo barely acknowledges her. His gaze is exclusively on me. "So give me my ten thousand, little Pia."

I clear my throat. "I was hoping, um, you might give me an extension. Just forty-eight hours, that's all I need."

"What a bad girl you are." Cosmo puts his head to one side and gazes at me, and then takes a few steps inside the door to the hallway. Automatically, Julia and Coco and I step back. "I thought this would happen."

"I'm good for it, in fact I had it all, but because of, uh, the incident with Nolan, I crashed my truck and then I was arrested and the money was stolen."

"That sounds unlikely. But maybe we can work something else out," he says, taking another step inside. Again, Julia and Coco and I step back.

In my panicked mind, I start planning exit strategies. We could run to the kitchen and out to the deck, but the five of us would never all make it before the three of them caught up. We could run upstairs to one of the rooms, but none of them have locks.

"Please, please leave, and come back for the money in two days," I say to Cosmo, my voice coming out far stronger than I thought it would.

"No one's going anywhere," says Cosmo.

"What happened to your arm, Nolan?" I ask, in an attempt to create a distraction.

"Car accident. Friday."

So that's why he never made it back here to break any windows or hurt anyone. He was so out of his mind that he crashed his car.

"Ah, the whole gang is here," says Cosmo. I glance behind me and see Angie and Madeleine are now standing in the hallway. "Let's do it, boys."

At that moment, Nolan grabs Coco by the neck, pushing her toward the living room. She makes a scared yelping sound and pulls away from him, twisting in panic.

"Get off her!" Julia immediately tries to grab Nolan's arm away from Coco, but Nicky steps in, and with one of his meat-hook hands, lifts both her wrists above her head.

Then hell breaks loose: Angie and Madeleine run toward us as I try to pull Nicky away from Julia. Everyone is shouting and screaming at once, and all I can think is *no no no no no no no*.

At that moment, I hear a clicking sound.

Cosmo's pointing a gun.

At me.

I hear all of us gasp at once. I hate guns, I hate them. There's a small, dull, silvery death, just sitting in Cosmo's hand. . . . Oh, my God, what have I done?

"Are we all paying attention now? Good," says Cosmo. "Now, everyone walk through to the living room and we'll work this out like friends."

Cosmo grabs the top of my arm and pulls me through the hallway, followed by Nolan with Coco, and then Nicky, who is somehow restraining Angie and Madeleine with one hand and Julia with the other.

"What's he gonna do to us?" hisses Madeleine as we reach the living room, and I hear Coco let out a sob. Oh God, oh God, oh God . . .

Then I hear another, much louder clicking sound behind me.

I look around.

It's Vic. With a sawed-off shotgun.

"Who the fuck are you?" says Cosmo.

"It's the neighbor, the old man," hisses Nolan. Of course: he's been spying on us, he knows exactly who everyone is.

"I'm only going to say this once. Let the girls go and get out." Vic doesn't even acknowledge us: he only has eyes for Cosmo.

"Get the fuck outta here, old man!" snaps Cosmo.

"No respect for your elders," Vic says, sighing. "Never did."

"You've got a Lapua?" says Nicky in awe. He's staring at the gun.

Vic has never looked so strong and tough. "Put the gun down, Antony Cosmolli."

"How the fuck do you know my name, old man?" mutters Cosmo, but he lowers the handgun so it's pointing at the floor.

"Screw this," mutters Nolan. I glance over just in time to see him whip a knife out of his pocket and turn to Coco, but a split second later, there's a deafening *bang* from Vic's shotgun, and the knife drops out of Nolan's hand. He's screaming, doubled over his bleeding hand in pain.

Nicky lets the girls go, quickly taking Nolan's other arm out of its sling, and using it to wrap his hand. Nolan is making a high-pitched keening sound. The rest of us are rooted to the spot in shock.

"Shut the fuck up, Nolan," snaps Cosmo. He hasn't taken his eyes off Vic.

"Here's your money," says Vic, taking an envelope out of his back pocket. "Take it and get out."

Cosmo grabs the envelope, and opens his mouth to say something, but then thinks better of it, and heads toward the front door. Nicky and Nolan follow immediately behind him, Nolan's slingless broken arm hanging down helplessly as he holds his other bleeding hand to his chest.

Vic follows, shotgun in hand, and I walk behind him. We stop at the front door and watch them hurry down the stoop.

"Don't come back here. Ever," says Vic. "Do you hear me?"

"Ever," I repeat.

Cosmo ignores us, unlocks his car door, they all get in and moments later are speeding down Union Street.

"I don't think you'll be seeing him again," says Vic.

I turn to him. "Thank you, Vic, thank you! I can never thank you enough. How did you know?"

"When you start talking to the heavens from the deck, check to make sure your neighbors aren't listening first, girlie," he says. He's got a glint of anger in his eye, but looks drawn and gray, and suddenly I remember.

"Oh . . . Vic. I am so sorry about Marie," I say.

"Me too," he says gruffly. "But it's her money that just paid that little idiot. After I got home, I saw the stripped bed, and I decided to air the mattress. She had a lot of cash stuffed under there. About ten thousand dollars, in fact. Stubborn, that one. Never trusted banks."

We head back to the living room, where the girls are sitting, paralyzed with shock. I feel high: adrenaline is pumping through my body. Fear, elation, relief, horror . . . everything, all at once.

"I'm so sorry, I'm so sorry," I say, running up to Julia and Coco, who are both still white with fear. "Are you okay? Is anyone hurt?"

"Everyone is fine," says Vic calmly. "None of you has anything to worry about. He won't be coming back."

"How do you know?" says Madeleine. "What if we just started a war with those thugs?"

"You haven't," says Vic. "He won't be back here."

"How do you know?" asks Coco.

"I'm friends with his uncle, I'll be calling him later today," says Vic. "And I know his type." And with that, the Cosmo conversation appears to be closed.

"Why do you have a shotgun?" asks Julia, her voice a tiny whisper.

"I've been minding it for a couple of friends since 1972," he says. "I'm kinda surprised it worked, frankly."

"You're like Clint Eastwood in *Gran Torino*," says Angie in awe.

"Are you all okay?" I say. "I'm sorry, I can't believe that happened, I'm so sorry."

Everyone is talking at once.

"I'm fine, I'm fine—"

"I think I'm gonna be sick, I have never been so scared—"

"Did that really just happen?"

"I swear to God, Pia, if you do something like this again—" That's Madeleine.

"I'm so sorry," I say, yet again. I feel like I'll be saying sorry forever. "I can't believe that I got you all into this, and I'll never do anything that stupid again, I promise."

"It's fine," says Angie calmly. "It was a situation you couldn't control. We all understand."

Julia, Madeleine, and Coco slowly nod, and I am overwhelmed with relief. They don't hate me.

"Oh, my God, look, there's his finger," says Coco, looking behind the blood-spattered sofa. She peers closely. "Dirty fingernail. Ew. We should put that on ice."

"Are you serious?" says Angie. "We should flush it down the fucking toilet."

"I got the whole thing?" says Vic. He sounds proud.

Julia walks over to the sofa, takes one look at Nolan's blown-off finger, and promptly faints.

In the chaos that ensues, Coco somehow gets everyone outside on the deck in the post-rain fresh air, drinking very strong, sweet tea and eating oatmeal cookies she made this morning.

"Wow, that was weird," says Julia. "I never fainted before."

"Another cookie, please," says Madeleine.

I'm surprised everyone isn't angrier. They should be furious. After all, I put them in probably the most severe danger they've ever been in. But they've just sort of understood and forgiven me, straightaway. I feel tearful with relief.

"I'll pay you back the money as soon as I can, Vic," I say. "I will ask my parents as soon as I speak to them."

"No hurry. Consider it a loan."

"No, I can't," I say, and quickly get up to grab a pen and paper from the kitchen. I sit back down, and start writing. "I owe Vittorio Bartolo $10,000," I write. "Signed, Pia Keller."

I fold it up and hand it to him, and he puts it in his shirt pocket.

"I promise it's coming," I say.

"Don't worry," he says, grinning at me. "I know where you live."

CHAPTER **31**

"Treat this as a war," says Julia. "You've done the recon, you have a battle plan, now put on some goddamn armor and go kick some food truck ass. All is not lost."

I nod obediently. It's 6:15 A.M., and Jules is standing at my door, fully dressed, gym bag over her shoulder, delivering a pep talk like a high school football coach.

She began said pep talk last night, after Vic had dinner with us, and hasn't really stopped since, except when I begged her to give me time to sleep. I think it's her way of regaining ascendancy after her fainting fit.

I'm sitting on the edge of my bed, pajamas on.

"This is your time, Pia. This is everything you've been working for. You look like shit, by the way."

"Thanks," I say. "I feel like shit." I haven't slept. I just kept replaying the Cosmo incident in my head. Then I'd think about the Lina meeting today and about my parents, and then just go straight back to thinking about Cosmo again.

"Regroup. Get your soldiers into—"

"But I don't even know what Lina is planning," I interrupt anxiously.

"I think she wants her boss to buy it. Simple."

"No," I say. "They own huge luxury hotels and restaurants. Buying a measly little food truck would be like Bergdorf Goodman buying a market stall at Brooklyn Flea. It doesn't fit."

Julia sighs. "Think positive visualization, Peepee. This is good. I can feel it in my waters."

"Last time you felt something in your waters it turned out to be cystitis," says Madeleine, poking her head around my door. She's off for her morning jog. "Want me to grab you a coffee on the way home, Pia? I'll be back in thirty minutes."

"Yes, please," I say. "Whatever you're having, plus an extra shot. Actually, two. Two extra shots."

"And, um, can I please borrow your blue dress tomorrow? The one with the high neck?"

"Yes, of course," I say. "For work?"

"No . . . I'm going to, um, go to this singing audition tomorrow night," she says, blushing. "I saw the ad on Craigslist. It's for a band over in Williamsburg. Last night I decided . . . life is too short to not do what you want." She pauses. "Within reason."

"Dude," I say. "That's awesome. Of course you can. We need to talk shoes, too."

Julia looks at her watch. "I've gotta run. Are you all set?"

"Just tell me one thing," I say.

"Shoot," says Julia.

"Will you keep Toto at your house in Rochester for me when I leave for Zurich? I can't bear to sell her. I'll come back to get her one day."

"Of course I will," says Jules. "But I won't need to. You'll be a huge success."

When I'm alone again, I take a second to send a SkinnyWheels tweet. *Sorry kids. No SkinnyWheels today. Exceptional circumstances . . . I'll make it up to you with 20% off tomorrow.* I texted Jonah last night, to tell him we wouldn't be working today. He replied telling me he had a call-back for another audition. Good for him. He's making his life happen.

That moment, my phone rings. It's my father's cell phone number.

I look at it for a second and press "silent" to let it ring out. Not yet. I am sure that today's meeting will be a waste of time, and tomorrow I'll have to borrow the ten thousand to pay Vic back, but I can't do it over the phone.

I take a very long, hot shower and dress, relishing the familiar creaky sounds of Rookhaven and the girls around me. Coco's singing along to some terrible old Nick Lachey song up in the attic, Angie's stomping around her bedroom in what must be five-inch wooden heels, and Madeleine has returned from her jog with coffees and is now doing her customary extra-long shower. I never spoke to her about the *UGLY UGLY UGLY* in the mirror. If it was even her. I figure it was just someone having a bad day.

What do you wear to go into battle?

I dress the way Lina does: charcoal pants, silk top, black blazer, black heels. Perfect. Professional, chic, and stylish. Hair chic and plain, makeup very basic.

I look in my wardrobe mirror one last time before I leave the house. This is it, I think. This is your chance to make something happen.

Whatever "something" is.

I'm at Forty-seventh and Lexington half an hour early. Like yesterday, the sky is cloudy and ominously gray. Oh, God, I hope that's not a sign.

Immediately, I start nervously pacing the nearby streets. I walk west down Forty-seventh, and then turn up Fifth Avenue, gazing idly in store windows, my brain buzzing with nervous energy.

When I'm on the corner of Fifth Avenue and Forty-ninth Street, waiting for the lights to turn green, I look across to the crowds of suits and tourists standing on the other side.

And that's when I see them.

My parents.

Here.

In New York City.

They're on the corner in front of Saks, facing downtown. I haven't seen them since the beginning of the summer, when I headed to Zurich for a week of compulsory family time before heading off to meet Angie. They look just the same as ever. My mother is looking into her purse for something and yapping away. My father is smoking a cigar, frowning into the distance and ignoring her. They're not supposed to be here till tomorrow!

I swivel 180 degrees and run into the store behind me. For a few minutes I feign interest in some deeply boring shoes. Next time I look out, my parents have disappeared.

Why the hell are they here early? Well, it's obvious, isn't it? They wanted to surprise me, so they had an extra day to force me to leave New York. This is really happening. I am going to have to leave Brooklyn and the girls and the life I feel like I'm finally, maybe, possibly making for myself.

Okay, breathe, Pia. Breathe. They don't know where my house is, don't know how to contact anyone's parents. They don't know my friends or anything about my life, in fact, they never have. Thank God for that.

How can I make sure I don't run into them today? Okay: they usually stay at the Carlyle, and right now they're probably out for their mandatory post-breakfast constitutional walk (something I was forced to do every Saturday and Sunday growing up and every single day on vacation, even though they walked two abreast and I had to walk behind them and they never even talked to me). My mother likes shopping at Bergdorf, my father likes to have a drink at the King Cole Bar in the St. Regis Hotel, and they both enjoy walking in Central Park while looking disapprovingly at people with dogs.

Tomorrow they'll call me. But I'll deal with that then.

Oh, God, now I feel even more sick. It's adding to my coffee-fueled anxiety.

I'll just put them out of my head. It shouldn't be hard, I've been doing it since I was about six. I have to focus on the meeting. I have to make the most of whatever Lina's planning.

I buy a banana and a bagel with cream cheese from a deli and eat as I walk the streets, doing the occasional 360 turn for recon to make sure my parents aren't following me.

Then, at exactly 9:45 A.M., I head for Lina's office. It's showtime.

CHAPTER **32**

More than four hours later, I'm still sitting in the lobby of Carus International, waiting.

Lina came down first thing this morning, and said, slightly mysteriously: "Our timing is perfect. But I can't guarantee anything. Can you sit tight for a little while?"

She then sent me a text message at about eleven saying, *I'm so sorry, don't leave yet!*

And another message at one saying, *Grab lunch, we're still talking.*

And now it's two. And I'm still here. Now, it's a nice lobby—spacious, light, with comfortable sofas and flowers everywhere. But come on. Four hours in one spot? It's mental torture.

I'm strangely exhausted from the hours of anticipatory nothing. My mouth tastes so sour that I am sure my breath must be kittenesque.

My head aches, my back is stiff, I've read every magazine and newspaper in the lobby twice, and I'd kick a puppy for a vodka on the rocks.

Worse, my cell—which is on silent—keeps showing missed calls from my father. Somewhere in New York, my parents are looking for me.

Why is Lina leaving me here to fester? I should probably leave. She's just too kind to tell me I'm wasting my time. Selling SkinnyWheels was a silly dream. I can't just sit here all day. I have parents to talk to, money to borrow, a loan to Vic to repay, and a flight to a frozen European city to catch. I'm just about to walk out, when—

"Pia! Forgive me!" Lina runs out of the elevator, a big smile on her face. "Come with me, I'll explain everything on the way."

"It's been a hell of a morning," she says, as we get into the elevator. "I have been in back-to-back meetings. I'm so sorry that I left you there so long. Were you dying of boredom?"

"No, no, it was fine! Great!" I say as brightly as I can. "Uh, good meetings?"

"I was setting you up," she says.

"Huh?"

"I'll explain everything in a moment," Lina says, grinning at me. She seems calm, yet excited, and suddenly I feel the same way. She's a natural leader. I might be going into battle, but I'm not alone.

I follow Lina down a hallway flanked with glass-walled offices with views over the city. This is the nicest workplace I've ever seen. There are calm dove-gray walls and dark shiny desks and soft, warm lighting. Very different from the cheap IKEA-chic of the PR agency and the fluorescent dankness of all those recruitment places. Wow, that seems like a lifetime ago.

We take a seat in an empty meeting room. I try very hard to act calm.

"So," says Lina. "Pia, before I tell you what I'm planning, I want to go over a few questions. Most of them we discussed at brunch yesterday, but I want to make sure I didn't miss anything so that when you talk the big guy through it all, we're clear."

"Go for it," I say. The big guy?

Lina picks up her folder and pad, and starts talking. When did I have the idea for SkinnyWheels? How did I start it? Why did I think it would work? What was my first step? What was my initial investment? What's my daily turnover? How did the idea develop? How would I expand if I could? How did I come up with the recipes? How did I evolve my social media strategy? ("My what? Oh, Twitter and stuff?") How do I feel I'm faring versus other food trucks? What do I think makes a food truck fail or succeed?

After an hour of interrogation, I'm re-energized. Talking about SkinnyWheels and how I've made the business work is genuinely thrilling, and I remember how much I love my job. In fact, I'm kind of proud of myself. I show Lina the photos that Angie took, and she's really impressed.

"I know it's only six weeks old," I say. "And that this growth trajectory"—a term I heard Lina use earlier and have used three times since, I should really stop—"isn't sustainable—I mean, of course profits picked up after I introduced breakfast; it's a whole extra meal and pancakes are incredibly cheap to produce, but from here I can only expand, time-wise, to offer dinner, which is far more complicated to do from a truck as old as mine, particularly since I haven't got much storage space left in the fridges. But I could offer SkinnyWheels delivery service to offices and gyms. I could have people dressed up like old school cigarette boys and girls walking around Union Square Farmers Market or the Brooklyn Flea or Central Park, selling the salads from those little trays."

"Damn, slow down!" says Lina, laughing.

"And I have ideas for different kinds of food trucks, too," I say. "Organic Italian, all-day breakfast . . ."

"I wrote them all down yesterday." Lina nods. "They're fantastic."

I'm smiling so hard my cheeks hurt a little bit.

"What really makes you unique," says Lina, looking at her notes, "is that you're not a jaded restaurateur doing this as a last resort, and you're not a seasoned food truck retailer, either. You're a genuine entrepreneur, with all the energy, enthusiasm, and blind bravery of youth. You saw an opportunity and absolutely nailed it. I think your instincts are stellar, your work ethic is obviously outstanding, and with the right management support and team behind you, you could really—"

Lina pauses, interrupting herself. I can hardly breathe, I'm so thrilled. She really thinks all those things . . . about me? But wait, what did she just almost say? I could really . . . I could really *what*?

"Best of all, you're not gimmicky," says Lina. "I was watching that Let Them Eat Cock girl, too, but her food got terrible reviews, she was all about appearances. . . . She's the kind of person who could really damage the food truck industry. If people don't trust food trucks, they won't buy from them."

"Right," I say, nodding. I wonder where Bianca is. I hope she's safe wherever she is.

"It's probably time I explained everything," says Lina. "I have been looking at new investment ideas for months. I've been focusing on hospitality start-ups that are finding new ways to target 'the personal.' You know: smaller boutique hotels with truly personal service, pop-up or seasonal restaurants and bars, experiences designed for niche audiences who'll know it's just for them and love it. Some people will always love mega-hotels and thousand-room resorts, and giant restaurants and clubs, but a lot of people don't anymore. A lot of people want something that feels genuine. That they can love."

"Something that feels more real, that's like a friend rather than a company," I say, continuing her thought almost unconsciously.

"Exactly! That's the perfect way of putting it," says Lina, looking thrilled. "So I met with the management team this morning, to discuss these other projects. And I talked about smaller investment opportunities, and how the market is changing, and asked them if they'd look at a new idea later today. They're finishing up everything else now, and we're meeting up with them at four. You're going to give a presentation to them about the food truck opportunity, focusing on niche, targeted, need-based ideas—like SkinnyWheels, like your organic Italian, like the all-day-breakfast. . . ."

"I'm helping you give a presentation to the board . . . on food trucks?" I say, my mouth suddenly dry. "So they'll what, they'll agree to sponsor SkinnyWheels, or something like that?"

"Something like that," she says, opening a laptop. "Now, I put a few introductory PowerPoint slides together last night, so let's put in those amazing photos that your friend took. She's very talented."

"Yeah, she is, but . . . I'm . . . I'm giving a presentation? To important people?"

"There are only eight of them," says Lina. "And they're friendly."

"Who . . . who are they?"

"The CEO, the COO, the CIO—that's the chief investment officer of development, and she's a key target for you, so make sure you impress her—the CFO, the VP of acquisitions and development, the VP of concepts and hospitality, and the VPs of hotels and restaurants, respectively." I don't even know what most of those acronyms stand for. "Okay, I'm getting coffees, would you like a latte? Great."

As Lina hurries out of the room, I stare blankly ahead of me. All those important people. All that experience, all that expertise.

And me.

My mouth is so dry that I can't swallow, my chest is seized with a tightness as though I'm being crushed, oh, God, why does no one call them pain attacks instead of panic attacks when they hurt this much.

I'm going to puke.

Somehow I make it across the room just in time, and start heaving into the bucket. Coffee does *not* taste as good in reverse. Then some not-very-well-chewed bagel drips down the plastic bag lining of the basket. Ew.

I sit up, forcing myself to take deep breaths. I will not collapse. I will not let Lina think that her confidence in me is misplaced. I will not fail.

I can do this.

Grabbing a bottle of water out of my purse, I swill a mouthful around my mouth and spit it into the basket, mentally apologizing to the poor janitor who'll have to deal with it, and quickly stuff six pieces of chewing gum into my mouth.

Moments later, just as I'm back in my chair trying to look serene, Lina returns with the coffees.

"Right," she says. "We'll put a simple script together for you to follow, and I will help you with the Q&A afterward. It's easy. You can do it in your sleep. Okay?"

"Okay," I say. "Let's do it."

CHAPTER 33

Less than an hour later, I feel like I've completed a crash course in Business Presentations 101.

Don't fidget. Put the pen down.

Stand up straight. Don't sway and bob like a drunk sailor.

Look everyone in the eye, one by one, slow and steady.

Feel confident enough to pause. You don't need to rush: everyone is interested in every single word you say.

Speak up. . . . No, don't shout like that.

Stop playing with your hair. It's distracting.

Be more enthusiastic. . . . Okay, now you just look like you're a cheerleader.

Smile. You're meant to be enjoying yourself. . . . Not like that. You're not in a beauty pageant.

She's so hard on me that at first, I almost feel like crying. But I don't, of course. I keep going. Even when I fumble my words, and panic-acid rises in my stomach, and I trail my sentences off into a tiny whispered helpless nothingness, I keep going.

At 3:50 P.M., Lina runs me through everyone's names and descriptions. Ken. Charlie. Judy. Louis. George. Cassandra. Gilbert. Jennifer. I'll never remember them all. Then she barks random, incredibly difficult questions at me. Her aggressive training tactics are working: I'm tougher and more confident than I've ever felt before. It does seem like a lot of effort for a tiny food truck that she's simply going to ask her company to sponsor. But I'm not about to complain.

Then we stand up, and head upstairs to the forty-fourth floor, to the big conference room where, apparently, everyone is waiting.

Lina walks into the room first, followed by me.

I say "room." "Amphitheater" would be more appropriate.

It's four times the size of the cozy conference room we practiced in, with a fifty-seat conference table. Award-filled cabinets line one side. The other side is entirely glass, floor-to-ceiling, overlooking Manhattan. I try not to gape at the view, and focus on looking confident.

Seated right at the other end are eight men and women, currently being served coffee and cookies. They're all in suits, aged between forty and that funny big-city sixty-ish that could really be eighty, but they'll never tell and you'll never ask.

"Good afternoon, everyone!" calls Lina cheerily.

They look up, smile at us briefly, and continue chatting with one another as Lina sets up the laptop. I bend over the laptop, trying to look helpful.

"Come with me," says Lina. I follow her to the other end of the room, and she introduces me to the team.

I try to repeat their names when I shake hands with them all, one by one. I focus on making eye contact and offering a genuine smile, with the firm handshake my father taught me, so inevitably names go in one ear and out the other. The only two I remember are Gilbert, the CEO, who looks impatient and testy, but has very friendly brown eyes, and Judy, the chief investment officer, who has extremely cold hands.

"I'll get started, shall I?" says Lina.

"Please," says Gilbert. "It's been a long day." He glances at me. "Not that we're not fascinated, obviously."

Obviously, I go to reply, smiling as brightly as I can, but my voice is gone. Completely gone, disappeared, vanished. Oh, Jesus. Not now.

"Thanks, everyone, for coming back, I know you've all been here since eight but I think this'll be a very interesting hour," Lina says, walking to the very other end of the conference table. She looks at me and taps a chair right in front of her.

I hurry to the seat and sit down. My chair bangs loudly against the table, and I go to say "sorry" but my voice is still gone. Then I feel my chest fluttering, oh, God, not another panic attack—

"Food trucks are more than a trend. They're the future of food retail. Year on year, the food truck industry is growing in double-digit percentages. . . ." As Lina talks I try to calm myself down.

Please, oh please, let me find my voice, please don't let me throw up, please help me to not disappoint Lina and the girls. . . .

Lina is midway through her speech. "With an investment of approximately ten thousand dollars, Pia has managed to turn a pale pink truck into a food phenomenon in just six weeks. She serves twelve hundred customers a day, and she's only hit that limit because the truck can't pack much more food in without getting a helicopter to drop supplies to the roof—"

Everyone laughs, and I open my mouth to laugh, too, but my voice still won't come out. *Come on, voice, come on. . . .*

"And now, I'd like Pia to talk about it a little bit in her own words. Pia?"

I smile and quickly stand up, knocking the chair over as I do.

"I've got it," says Lina quickly. "Go, go."

I smile and obey her, and take my place at the head of the conference table. It stretches out before me like a football field, unimaginably vast. I can't shout that far. I can't do it.

"Go for it, Pia," says Lina encouragingly. I look at her in anguish. She took a chance on me and I'm going to let her down.

"I—" My voice comes out as a tiny squeak.

There's silence in the room. Total, horrific, gut-churning silence.

"Speak up!" calls Gilbert.

Oh please, oh *please,* please let me find my voice. I have not come this far to fail now. And if Lina believes in me, and all my friends believe in me, then it's time I believed in myself. I can do this. I really can.

"My name is Pia Keller, and I'm twenty-two years old."

I see Gilbert leaning forward to hear me better, and I smile and raise my voice, talking from the very center of my being, as Lina told me to.

"I graduated from Brown a few months ago, and what became immediately, painfully obvious to me—and everyone around me—was that I was completely unemployable."

The crowd at the end of the table titters.

"No one wants to give you a job when you have no experience, and you can't get experience without a job. It's the catch-twenty-two for any graduate, and when you think that you've spent your entire life earning the right to be treated like an adult, it's tough to realize that the outside world doesn't see you the same way."

I pause. Everyone is paying attention to me. My voice is strong, I feel completely calm.

"But I needed a job. I needed to make money. I needed to pay rent, to buy food, to feel good about myself, to have a goal and strive to reach it. That's what the post-college struggle is truly about: finding a life worth living, and making it yours."

Judy is nodding. This is a good sign, and for a second I lose my train of thought. I clear my throat.

"And I wanted—well, I hoped—to do it in a job that I could be passionate about and make my own. I noticed that New York's food truck industry seemed to be a straightforward way to make cash. All you really need is a truck, and an idea. So I got the truck. And I had an idea."

I pause again. Everyone is still looking at me, no one is doodling, no one is checking their iPhone.

"SkinnyWheels is for every busy New Yorker who wants fast, filling, fantastic lunch options that won't go straight to their a—waistline," Thank goodness I didn't say ass. I clear my throat, and smile. "All my friends are in their first jobs, at the bottom of the ladder. They can't afford to spend forty dollars or take an hour off to go eat in a restaurant, and they don't want a carb-heavy sandwich that will send them to sleep, or fattening fast food. They want something delicious and nutritious that will fill them up and keep them going, so they don't hit that mid-afternoon lull and reach for a cookie or six."

Gilbert is nodding. Judy has just dropped the cookie she was about to eat. Oops.

"Naturally, I don't mean just the weight-conscious: people don't have to be on a diet to want to watch what they eat. Eating well is a way of life . . . or it should be."

Lina clicks through the photos Angie took yesterday. God, they look great. I take a slow breath, and keep talking.

"So I bought a very old food truck. Her name is Toto, she's more rust than metal, and she's gorgeous."

"Reminds me of an old Kombi I had in college," says Louis—or George, I can't remember.

"I started with two protein-rich, wheat- and sugar-free salads that had a low glycemic index. Salads full of taste and crunch, and smart fats, like almonds and avocado. I also made low-fat, low-sugar desserts, and within two weeks, expanded into breakfast, with gluten-free low-fat pancakes. I started Twitter and Facebook accounts . . ." I keep talking but I can see that their minds are wandering, so I get to the killer fact—at least, that's what Lina said it was.

"The most incredible revelation of the past six weeks has been this—" I pause, making sure I've got all their attention. "A food truck is its own best advertisement. You drive it around to and from your daily locations, people see you and remember you. You tweet or update your status with your location, people follow, and retweet. You sell food, people tell their friends or share it at lunch. . . . Everything you do increases your potential customers, every customer is an advocate, every time you drive anywhere, you're essentially marketing yourself. I didn't have the time, money, or know-how to invest in advertising, but it didn't matter. Food trucks are a low investment with a high payoff, if you're willing to do everything it takes to provide the best possible food . . . and it really is that straightforward."

I look up toward the end of the table, and see Judy scribbling something on a pad of paper and swiveling it over to the guy on her right. I think he was the CFO, I can hardly remember, oh, God, they're probably bored. My confidence puckers and drops. What was I going to say next? I can't remember.

"So, Pia, tell us about your other food truck ideas," prompts Lina with a smile.

"Uh, oh, yes," I say, and start talking about organic Italian, A Meal Grows in Brooklyn, packed lunch, and my all-day breakfast idea. This gets Mike's attention: he's nodding and smiling. "There are a lot of ethnic-specific or gourmet dessert trucks," I say. "What there's not—or at least, not yet—are trucks that are plugging the gap between feeling good, looking good, and doing good."

I sit down, nearly panting with relief, my heart racing. I did it! I spoke in public without freaking out! I nailed it!

Lina takes over.

"With SkinnyWheels, Pia created a brand that is so simple and real people responded to it immediately. Our lives are complicated, and even every food choice we make seems fraught with nutritional, financial, ethical, and even moral repercussions. But food trucks are simple. Food trucks make life a little bit easier, a little bit more real. They make food that you can love. And if it's food that loves you back, well . . . it's a no-brainer."

"I hope you're not going anti-restaurant, Lina," says one of the guys—I think it's Charlie—and everyone else chuckles.

"Of course not." Wow, Lina has a steely smile when she wants to. "I'm actively pursuing new avenues of revenue that can promote our brand in unique and innovative ways."

Gilbert nods, and Lina pauses for a very dramatic few seconds. "Every great idea needs a magic touch. With SkinnyWheels, Pia found it. And we believe she has the smarts and talent to do it again and again."

I'm staring at the table, hard, and trying not to look as thrilled and embarrassed as I am. But I can't help but glance up at Lina as she talks. She's beaming at me.

Lina clears her throat. "I'll take you through the financials quickly. . . ." She talks about ROI (I finally learned what it means: return on investment) and USPs (unique service proposition, as in, what makes Skinny-Wheels different from every other food truck), how much SkinnyWheels has earned, how much more it could earn if it were a slicker, stream-lined production line, and all that sort of thing.

"So, we won't keep you much longer," says Lina. Down at the end of the table, Gilbert is stretching restlessly. He looks a bit grumpy. I bet he had too many carbs for lunch and is having a sugar crash now.

She clears her throat. "What makes a good food truck great is the personality behind it. Any huge restaurant could sell food from a truck. It's the person running it who consumers make a connection with. It's Pia that they're responding to, not just the food. Pia's passion and vision are the key to her success."

I blush. It is?

Lina continues: "I propose that we back Pia to roll out Skinny-Wheels with three food trucks in the New York area, and when they're up and running, kick-start the organic Italian and all-day breakfast ideas, and then roll those brands out to Chicago, Boston, San Francisco, and L.A."

What?

"I get it," says Gilbert. "What's your time frame?"

"The problem with these initiatives is always finding the right personnel, which is where we're incredibly lucky. With Pia in charge, working with a small, trusted team of people to drive and sell the product, and backed up every step of the way, of course, by Carus management and support teams, we can start straightaway. We propose to invest in SkinnyWheels and expand immediately. A food truck empire within twelve months. It's the perfect Carus initiative: smart, forward-thinking, people-centric, and it has heart."

Thank hell I'm sitting down. Otherwise I'd collapse. Me in charge? Where the hell did that come from?

"We're going to have to discuss it," says Gilbert, exchanging glances with Judy.

"I should add that Pia has had another offer and has promised them an answer within the day," adds Lina smoothly. "Thus the rush. I didn't want to miss out on this unique opportunity to hit the ground running on a new venture that we know will pay huge dividends and really add value to our brand."

"Okay," says Gilbert abruptly. He clearly doesn't like to be given an ultimatum. "Thank you."

We all stand up and, following Lina's lead, I head to the end of the conference table and shake hands with everyone again. And I make sure to look into all of their eyes and smile as confidently and genuinely as possible.

"Thanks for coming in," says Gilbert. I can't read him at all—is he impressed? Unimpressed? His eyes are still friendly, but his face gives nothing away. I guess that's why he's CEO. Damnit.

"Well done," says Judy of the freezing-cold hands. "Very interesting."

I walk out of the conference room, tap myself a tiny high five that no one else can see, and then turn around to face Lina. She looks as gleeful as I feel.

"No cheering yet! My office!" shushes Lina, and I obediently follow her to the elevator and head down to her office. It's small but has a great view over Manhattan, and the desk is clear and devoid of all clutter, and as she closes the door we both grin manically. I almost want to jump up and down.

"Great job," says Lina.

"That was good? Really?" I know it was good, but I want more compliments.

"It was excellent," says Lina. "I've seen Gilbert walk out of meetings when he's bored. He just fakes a phone call and doesn't come back."

"Thank you! Oh, my God—I had no idea that was what you were planning—"

"I didn't want to psych you out," she says, laughing. "Nerves can ruin even the most surefire presentations."

"No kidding," I say. Suddenly I realize that my bubbling acid stomach has disappeared. I just gave a presentation to a crowd of important, accomplished strangers. I didn't lose my voice and I didn't sound stupid. I nailed it.

I'm so happy, I feel like I'm shining.

"Listen, you should head home," says Lina. "I'll wait here, I've got a few calls to make on other projects. I have a feeling that Gilbert'll call me sooner rather than later."

"Okay," I say. I suddenly feel slightly deflated. That's it?

"Don't worry," she says, looking me right in the eye. "I have a very good feeling about this. Just keep your phone on. I'll definitely be in touch."

As I walk out on the street, I look at all the people rushing around me and can't stop smiling. I'm one of you now. I had a business meeting. I belong here. New York is mine.

My phone rings: Julia. I smile to myself. I can't wait to tell her what's happened.

"Jumanji!"

"Pia!" says Julia in a cheerful voice.

"The one and only!" I say, equally cheerful. "You will not believe how great my day has been!"

"Your parents are here!"

Oh, my fucking God, how did they find me? How did they find Rookhaven?

"Surprise!" She pauses, as though listening to me. "Oh, okay, great. We're all here with them at Rookhaven right now, so you just come on home and they'll be here waiting for you. Buh-bye!"

She hangs up before I've even said anything.

There's a pause. My mind is racing. My parents. My parents who have come to force me to leave Brooklyn. And now I have to go home and deal with them.

CHAPTER 34

When I walk in our front door, Madeleine, Julia, Coco, and Angie are all sitting awkwardly in the living room. And so are my parents.

It's strange, even *wrong*, somehow, to see them in this house. This is my place. They don't belong here. My mother is sitting on one sofa, playing with her rings, and my father is on the other, talking to a very uncomfortable-looking Angie. Probably quizzing her about her recent career choices.

"How did you know where I was?" My voice is so tiny, it's hiding somewhere deep in my body.

"Pia," says my father, in the deep, disapproving voice that used to scare me so much. "I've been trying to get in touch with you all day."

"I've been busy," I whisper. "Working."

"What? Speak up."

"Working!" Jesus, how can they still make me feel like this? "I've been working."

He smiles wryly to himself at that—oh, the sarcastic disbelief of a facial expression! "You have a real job now. In Zurich. You can work as a PA to our neighbor, a banker at UBS. So go and pack."

"No." It's a knee-jerk reaction.

"Enough is enough. You can't stay here."

I shake my head, fighting to keep my voice as calm as I can. "My life is here." My voice sounds pathetically childish, even to me. I notice that the girls' heads are following the conversation back and forth like they're at a tennis match.

"What life? Partying all night? Sleeping all day?" chimes in my mother from the other sofa.

"I have a job," I say, ignoring her. "I'm making money."

"Yes, we heard," says my father. "A glorified lemonade stand. That's not a real job."

"It's a food truck," I say. "And it's successful. You don't know what you're talking about."

My mother blanches slightly, and I see my father's face crease in anger. Before he can respond, however, my phone rings. I glance at it: it's Lina.

"I have to take this," I say. Oh please, oh please let this be good news.

"How dare you—" snaps my father, but it's too late: I'm already out of the room.

"Hi, hello, Lina!" I say, trying to sound as confident and businesslike as I can.

"Pia, hi there," she says.

She sounds very serious. Oh God, I failed, it's all over, there's no way SkinnyWheels will ever be a success, she made a mistake, I'm going to have to ask my parents for the money for Vic.

Then she clears her throat.

"Pia, we'd like to officially offer you a role here at Carus International in a new division that we're calling Truck Eats. Your official title is head of new projects, you'll report to me, and your initial salary is seventy-five thousand. We also want to offer you forty thousand outright for a fifty percent share in the SkinnyWheels business, and in return, we'll back you to expand it, to a limit of five hundred thousand for the first year."

I make a little hiccup sound of shock.

"Now, that has to include additional trucks and permits, fitting out all the trucks, and hiring support staff, so it'll be tight. Very tight. Of course, we'll support you in every way you need—kitchens, food prep, storage, management strategy. . . ."

I am jumping up and down on the spot, but I can't get any words out. Lina pauses.

"I hope this is something you're interested in, Pia. We believe that it's the right time to invest in something small and real that will grow organically. And we believe that you are the right person to do it for us. Judy and Gilbert were particularly impressed with your commitment and passion."

"I . . . thank . . . you—" My mind is racing. I can't quite take it all in. "Lina, thank you—"

"Then, in six months, we'd like you to launch either the all-day breakfast truck or the organic Italian truck, depending on which proves the more viable investment in focus groups," she says. "I'll be working with you on those two. In the meantime . . . it's your baby."

Lina pauses, but before I can say anything, she lowers her voice. "I understand if you want to continue to go it alone, Pia, it's a fantastic business and I get it. I know that the corporate world can ruin small and perfect ideas, though I really think this would be different. But if you want to see how far you can go, Carus International is the place to do it. You won't be tied to a desk, though you will have one here of course, and you'll still have day-to-day autonomy."

"Yes!" I finally say. "Yes! Please! Lina, thank you, yes! Yes!"

"Oh, great!" she says, and I can hear the smile in her voice. "I am so thrilled to hear you say that! Can you come in tomorrow at nine and we'll go over everything?"

"Yes," I say. "Definitely. I'll be there. Thank you. Thank you so much!"

I hang up, and, almost in a daze, walk back through to the living room.

Immediately, I am hit by a wall of silent tension. I don't know why the girls are still sitting there—I mean, hell, they're not their parents. I guess that's the weird control my father can exert over a situation.

"You can't just walk out on us, young lady," says my father.

"I've just been offered forty thousand for half of the business I started six weeks ago," I say quietly.

"What? Speak up," he snaps.

"I've been offered forty thousand for fifty percent of the business that I started six weeks ago." My voice is finally loud and confident, but I feel completely relaxed. In fact, I'm not nervous, or worried, or in the least bit intimidated. I'm just me. "And I've been offered a permanent salaried position at Carus International. They're going to back me to expand my business idea."

"Awesome!" shouts Julia, and all the girls erupt into screams and wild applause. My parents don't move.

I turn to my parents. "Look, I'm sorry, I really am, that I abused your trust and let you down so many times. But I'm an adult now. You don't need to worry about me anymore."

"We have a room for you at the Carlyle," says my father, sounding less certain. "And you're leaving with us tomorrow night."

"No," I say as clearly as I can. "I'm not. I'm staying here. I have a job. I have a life. This is my home."

My father stands up, and turns to my mother, who is still staring at me, confused. "You're coming with us," she says insistently.

"No, I'm really not," I say. "Now, if you'll excuse me, I have some celebrating to do."

My parents stand up awkwardly and walk toward the front door. I stand up to follow them—more out of a desire to make sure they're really leaving than politeness. Just as they open it, my father turns around.

"If that's all true, then . . . well done."

And then they're gone, and I'm enveloped in a huge, whooping, screaming mess of girls.

"I can't believe you did it!"

"I always knew you'd do it!"

"I am so proud of you!"

"I am so happy for you!"

"Get me a bottle of wine," I say. "We're celebrating."

Moments later, the wine is open and we're all around the kitchen table.

"To Pia!" shouts Julia, holding up her wine.

"To me!" I echo. "And to you, for realizing that I could actually do something with SkinnyWheels—and for helping me do it!"

"Yay!" everyone cheers.

"To us!" says Coco.

"I don't know what I'd have done without any of you," I say. "And I'm so sorry my parents just turned up here, by the way. I wonder how they found me."

"Benny, your boss from the PR agency," says Angie, reaching for a pack of cards in the middle of the table. "He had your address for the paychecks."

"Of course," I say. "Well, I had to deal with them sooner or later. . . ." I pause, thinking. I wish that had ended better. I wish I'd earned their respect rather than demanded it. But maybe relationships can't be repaired in one day.

"So, head of new projects," says Julia. "What's your first order of business?"

"Drinking this. Then I'm going to smoke a cigarette."

Julia and Madeleine make disapproving sounds and Angie shouts, "Woo!"

"And I'm going to call Jonah and let him know the news. Then I'm going to introduce Lina to Phil and Lara, so they can talk about A Meal Grows in Brooklyn, and figure out how to buy the idea from them so we can set it up properly to launch, because that's an awesome idea and deserves another chance at success," I say. "And then I'm going to build the best little food truck empire in New York goddamn City."

"I'll toast to that," says Julia. "To building empires."

"To building empires!" we all chorus, and clink glasses.

Angie throws a cork at me. "Hey, I am so proud of you. Have I mentioned that?"

"You know, not everything worked out the way I expected it to, and yet . . . it's almost perfect. Bartolo's, Jonah, Bianca, Cosmo, Vic, Lina, even jail . . . it all happened for a reason."

"You took a hell of a lot of risks," says Angie, shuffling the deck of cards thoughtfully. "Maybe that's the secret to your success."

"That's what Marie told me to do," I say. "Take risks."

"To Marie," says Julia.

We all hold up our wineglasses.

"To Marie."

I take another sip of wine. "She also said that I'd survive with my friends and family . . . that's you guys. You're my friends *and* my family now. We can always rely on one another." I pause. "I sound seriously stupid."

"So now are you going to call Aidan, or what?" prompts Julia.

"Does anybody want any more wine?" I reply.

"Why are you changing the subject?" says Julia.

"Why don't you answer the question?" echoes Maddy.

We pause. They're all staring at me, arms folded. I get his business card out of my purse. *Aidan Carr.*

I stare at it for a moment and sigh.

"I know you've been thinking about him," says Julia. "You get that moony lovey look on your face."

"Moony?"

"It's true," says Angie. "You look kind of retarded."

I throw a wine cork at her.

"Call him!" says Coco. "What have you got to lose?"

"My self-respect?"

"You lost that a long time ago," says Angie.

"Be honest," says Madeleine. "Do you want to call him?"

"Yes, I want to, but . . ."

"But nothing!" shouts Coco. She clears her throat sheepishly. "That came out louder than I thought it would. Sorry."

"It would go wrong, he'd end up rejecting me."

"Why would you even say that?" says Madeleine. "No guy in his right mind would reject you."

"I can't put myself, you know, out there. I can't risk it."

"Isn't this exactly what you were just talking about?" says Julia. "Taking a risk?"

"What's the worst that can happen?" adds Coco.

"A blown-off finger behind the sofa?"

"Please, don't mention the finger," says Julia, looking sick.

"Let's put it to a vote," says Coco. "Who votes Pia calls him?"

Madeleine and Julia raise their hands. "We do!"

"Yeah, grow a pair and call him," says Angie.

"If you don't call Aidan, I will cry," threatens Julia.

"Then stock up on Kleenex, sweet-cheeks. Because it's not going to happen."

"How about this," says Angie. "We'll flip a coin."

Julia pulls out a coin from her pocket, flips it, and catches it under her hand.

"Call it, Pia."

I think for a moment. "Tails."

Julia pulls her hand away and looks.

"Suck it. You're calling him."

CHAPTER **35**

An hour later, I still haven't called Aidan.

Instead, I'm stretching out on my bed, still fully dressed, and reflecting on everything that's happened.

I did it.

I created a successful business from nothing, sold it, made a profit, got a job I know I'll love, and saved my home and the home of the people I love.

And this is just the beginning. I feel like I could do anything. I know how to fight for what I believe in, I trust my instincts, and I know what's really important to me.

I can't believe I'm saying this, but . . . I love my life.

Then my phone rings. It's an unlisted number.

"Pia speaking?"

"Pia, it's your mother."

I stiffen. What does she want?

She clears her throat. "I am just calling quickly while your father isn't here to say . . . I am so proud of you."

"Thank you," I stammer out. She's never said that.

"Don't tell your father I rang. You know what he's like."

"I won't."

"I love you," she says, and hangs up.

She hasn't told me she loves me in years, not since I was a kid, homesick and crying on the phone to her from my first boarding school. And she's never, ever told me she's proud of me.

Wow, I miss my mom.

For a second I wish I could go back in time to being six years old, and could climb into her lap and ask her to read me a story, so she'd wrap her arms around me and make me feel safe.

I vow to call her next week, just to talk. If I want a good relationship with her in the future, I have to make the effort.

Then my phone rings again. It's another unlisted number. Mom, again?

"Hello?"

"Pia, it's me." It's my father. I get a funny thudding feeling in my chest. What does he want?

"Hi."

"Your mother doesn't know I'm calling, so I need to be quick." He clears his throat. "Pia, I'm very impressed with everything you've achieved in the past two months. I have just been reading about Carus International and I looked up your food truck on the World Wide Web. . . . Well done."

"Thank you," I say after a pause. Is this really happening? And did he just say "World Wide Web?"

"You've really achieved something," he says. His voice sounds warmer and more relaxed than I've heard it in years. "I just want to say that I hope you're enjoying this bit. Building something, making it a success . . . I know how exciting and satisfying it is."

"I will, I am, it is—" I stammer. I'm stunned.

"Enjoy every second of it, *schatzi*."

"Yes, Daddy. I will . . . I am."

He hasn't called me *schatzi* since I was about ten. It means sweetheart. I get a lump in my throat.

"Well, good-bye. We'll call you next Sunday."

And then he hangs up.

I'm left staring at my phone, frozen with surprise.

Then, almost without thinking about it, I take out Aidan's card again, and lie back on my pillow. I stare at the card for a few minutes.

Aidan Carr.

Should I call Aidan?

Reasons yes: Because I like him, I really do, like I haven't liked anyone in years. Maybe ever.

Reasons no: Because I fucked up the date. Because I don't feel as confident about love as I do about SkinnyWheels. Because it will go wrong. Because it always goes wrong. Because I probably like the idea of him more than the reality. Because I don't even know if I'm capable of having a real relationship. Because I don't want to get rejected again. Because it's too hard. Because I'm scared of taking a risk.

With almost trembling hands—oh cliché of clichés!—I dial his number.

It starts ringing. I can feel my heart beating in my throat. God! How can something as simple as calling a guy be even more nerve-racking than presenting to a boardroom of high-powered executives?

"Hello?"

"Hi, hello, uh, Aidan? It's, uh, it's Pia," I say, trying to make my voice deep and calm.

"Hmm . . . Pia . . . Pia?" I think I can hear a smile in his voice.

"The girl who pressed the eject button and ruined an otherwise great evening? About two weeks ago?"

"Oh, *that* Pia," he says. "Well, how do you do?"

"I do very well, thank you," I say. "Actually, I was just, uh, calling to apologize for being such a freak at dinner. I wasn't quite myself. I ran into someone I used to know and it threw me."

"You don't have to apologize," he says quickly. "I'm sorry I shouted at you. I had no right to. I don't know what came over me. I've been regretting it ever since."

We both pause.

"I was wondering if we could redo the second half of that dinner?" I say, my voice catching in my throat.

"I'd rather not," he says. My heart stops for a second. I'm immediately flooded with a burning embarrassment. I knew it. I knew I would be rejected again.

Then he clears his throat.

"I'd rather just see you again. No explanation needed, no second takes of the first take. Just . . . more."

I jump up, off my bed, and punch the air a few times. *Yes!*

"Well, that is good news," I say, trying to sound as cool as I can.

"What are you doing right now?"

"I . . . can't think of a cute thing to say." My brain is empty, and I can't stop smiling.

"You live on Union Street, right? Just up from Smith? I'm taking my dog Ziggy for an evening stroll. I could call by in say . . . seven minutes."

"I'll be on the stoop waiting for you," I say.

We hang up.

I immediately scream at the top of my lungs, knowing I'll get everyone's attention. Within seconds, they're all in my doorway.

"What the hell is going on?"

"Aidan. I called him. Coming. Here. Seven minutes. Help."

Thank God for girls: within moments, Coco is back with my toothbrush with some toothpaste on it, Angie is standing at my wardrobe throwing clothes and shoes around my room, and Madeleine is brushing my hair.

"I'm not good at the preening stuff." Julia is sitting calmly on the bed, still holding her wine. "I'll give you moral support."

"Keep watch over the street! Look for a guy with a dog."

"Guy with dog, check," she says, bouncing over my bed to the window.

I apply bronzer and deodorant as I'm brushing my teeth, carefully rinse and spit into a glass of water also offered by Coco, and throw off my business meeting clothes and put on my favorite sexy-casual jeans and top, jacket, and big scarf.

"Where is my Kiehl's Original Musk?"

"In my room!" gasps Coco. "You brought it up last weekend, remember?"

I sprint up the stairs to the attic, bound into Coco's room, and glance around for the bottle. I find it sitting on her nightstand and pick it up, then glance into her trash can, and see an empty pregnancy test box. Huh? That makes no sense. Why would Coco need a pregnancy test? We got her the Plan B. . . . But if she had missed a period, she'd say something to us, right? She's probably just paranoid.

Making a mental note to talk to her about it tomorrow, I bound back down the stairs two at a time to my room.

"Do I look okay?" I'm breathless.

"Perfect," says Angie.

"Guy with dog! Guy with dog!" shouts Julia from the window. "This is not a drill! We are a go!"

I gasp, take a quick look at myself in the mirror as the girls dab my lips with gloss and fluff my hair completely unnecessarily, and then run out the door.

"I love you guys!" I shout as I run down the stairs.

"We love you, too!" shouts Madeleine.

I land with a thump in the front hallway and take a moment to compose myself and catch my breath.

Then I open the front door and casually step out, just as Aidan and his dog—a gorgeous Irish setter, carrying that huge rubber bone toy in his mouth—are walking past our stoop.

"Hey," I say casually.

He glances up and smiles, his face lighting up. "Why, hello."

The street is completely empty, no passersby, no cars, but every window is lit, giving it a cozy, calm, homey feel.

Smiling down at him, I'm suddenly filled with a warm feeling of . . . I don't know quite how to describe it. *Certainty*. I feel like I recognize him, like when you see a person you knew when you were very young and then see them again years later, and their face is just how you remember it.

I walk down the stoop slowly, smiling wider and wider with every step.

Aidan is smiling, too, and we don't break eye contact, not once.

And by the time I get to the bottom, I know what I'm going to do.

I stand directly in front of him, lift my face up to his. He's still smiling, too, and leans toward me . . . and then we kiss.

"Wooo!" I hear cheers from the house. I look up to see Julia, Coco, Madeleine, and Angie all cheering from my open bedroom window. "Yeah! Woo!"

I look back at Aidan and grin. "My roommates."

"I figured." He smiles back. "And this is Ziggy."

I look down at Ziggy, who is patiently sitting and smiling up at us in that happy doggy way. I offer my hand for him to smell, and he immediately starts licking it affectionately.

"He likes you," says Aidan.

"I like you," I say, without thinking about it.

"I like you, too," he says. "Can I interest you in a walk around Brooklyn this evening?"

"I'd love that."

We start walking up Union Street, automatically falling into step together. My hands are in my pockets, but within a couple of steps, he nudges my arm out and places his hand against mine.

Here's the strangest thing, and I cringe to admit it: holding Aidan's hand feels . . . perfect.

I've found home.

ACKNOWLEDGMENTS

Firstly, thank you for reading this book. I hope you enjoyed it.

Thank you to Jill Grinberg, for loving this idea and making it happen. You are my fairy godmother. Thank you to Laura Longrigg, for believing in me from the start. You are my fairy godmother, too. (I really hit the jackpot on the fairy godmother front.)

Huge, huge, huge thank you to Dan Weiss, for taking a chance on me when I said, "I want to write a series about twentysomethings that's like a cross between *The Group, The Best of Everything,* and The Baby-sitters Club, um, details to come," and for his constant encouragement and inspiration.

Thank you to Vicki Lame, editor extraordinaire, for her brilliance, humor, enthusiasm, and friendship, and for making the book sharper, smarter, and better in every way, and to Sarah Jae-Jones, for her help and support.

Thank you to Lucy Stille, for loving this manuscript, which made me fall in love with it again.

Thank you to Katelyn Detweiler, Kat Maher, and Fiona Barrows, for being emotionally insightful, honest, brilliant readers. (And the future leaders of the publishing industry in New York and London, if anyone is wondering.)

Thank you to Kirsty Richardson, for being the only thing between me and chaos after Errol was born; to Riikka Pirjala, for her amazing support and friendship when we moved to New York; and to Steve Clark, the best visa lawyer in the world, ever.

Thanks also to Jim and Tim, the bee guys; to the food truck people who patiently (and not so patiently) answered my questions and requested to remain anonymous (they're so mysterious!); and to Val, for helping me figure out how to get Pia arrested.

Thanks to Sasha Wagstaff for her friendship, counsel, and cheerleading. You are my kindred e-spirit.

Thanks to my wise, loving, funny parents for truly believing that I am, in fact, the next Jane Austen.

Thanks to all the readers who e-mail me and tell me that they're just like me. I hope so, because you guys rock.

Thanks to my friends who inspire me, particularly the ones who helped me survive the treacherous age of twenty-two: Bec, Sarah, Alex, Amy, Caroline, Vicky, Ali, Penny, Sass, Kate, Catherine, Devi, Bennery, Lorraine, Laura, Lydia, Victoria, Susan, Daisy, Mariana, Tanya, Andrea, and my sister Anika. You are all my homegirls. And to Conor, Matt, Mike, Max, Chris, Hawk, and Tim. You're my homegirls, too.

And most of all thanks to Fox, my love, and Errol, our baby. In the words of Bryan Adams: Everything I do, I do it for you.

TURN THE PAGE FOR A **SNEAK PEEK** OF

Brooklyn GIRLS

Angie

Coming **Spring 2014**

www.quercusbooks.co.uk

CHAPTER 1

I was really going to be somebody by the time I was twenty-three.

Have a career. Be good at something. Be happy.

But here I am, less than two months before my twenty-third birthday, in a tiny café with my mother, Annabel, "catching up" over waffles and fruit juice, because I am unemployed and have nothing better to do on a random Tuesday morning.

The waffles are organic, by the way, and the juice is organic lingonberry, a ridiculous Scandinavian fruit famed for its antioxidants. This is Brooklyn, where the greater the obscurity, the higher the cred. Personally, I haven't got a problem with SunnyD or good old full-fat Coca-Cola, but whatever fries your burger, right?

And of course, the waiter—who Annabel has already quasi-yelled at twice—rushes up with the jug for a refill, trips, and *boom*. Lingonberry juice all over me. So now I'm soaked. The punch line to an already (not so) delightful morning.

He's mortified. "Oh my! I am so sorry, let me clean that up—"

"You can forget about the tip!" My mother is furious.

"Don't overreact," I interrupt her. "It was an accident."

"But your top is ruined!"

"I was sick of it anyway."

"I don't know why you insist on coming to these ridiculous places." God, she's in a bad mood. Her phone rings. "Bethany! . . . No, darling, I'm still with Angelique. Somewhere in Brooklyn. I know, I know—"

The waiter has tears in his eyes, blotting and whispering frantically, "I'm so sorry. I keep spilling things because I'm so nervous. This is my first waiter job."

"Dude, it's not a problem," I whisper back. "Never cry over anything that won't cry over you."

He brightens. "That is such a good life philosophy! Can I take that?"

"It's yours. Get some T-shirts printed. Or a bumper sticker. Knock yourself out."

He starts giggling. "You are hilarious, girl! I'm Adrian."

"Angie."

Annabel hangs up, and blinks at me till Adrian leaves. She blinks when she's annoyed. Making friends with the waiter is just the kind of thing that would irritate her. "Well. I have some news. Your father and I are divorcing."

What?

That's why she came all the way from Boston to see me? I'm so shocked that I can't actually say anything. I just stare at her, a half-chewed bite of waffle in my mouth.

"It's all arranged." She examines her wineglass for kiss marks. "The papers are signed, everything is done."

I finally swallow. "You're . . . divorcing?"

"It's not a huge surprise, is it? Given what he's been up to over the years? And you're too old to be Daddy's little girl anymore, so I don't see why you'd be upset."

"Right on." I take out a cigarette and place it, unlit, in the corner of my mouth. I find cigarettes comforting. (Yes, I know, they're bad for you.) "You're divorcing. Gnarly."

My mother blinks at me again. Princess Diana had a formative influence on her maquillage philosophy: heavy on the navy eyeliner. *They're divorcing* is playing on a loop in my head. Why didn't my father tell me?

Annabel clears her throat. "You're single again, I take it? You broke up with Mani, did you?"

I don't answer. I told her about the guy I thought I was in love with in an unguarded moment of total fucking stupidity last year. Just before he dumped me.

"Unlucky in love, that's you and me," she continues blithely. "Perhaps we can go on the prowl, hmm? How's darling Pia? Why don't we get together and have a girls' night out?"

I stare at her for several long seconds. She's out of her fucking mind.

The minute she goes to the bathroom I make eye contact with Adrian and mime the international pen-scribble sign for "Check, please."

He hurries over. "I am so sorry again! It's on me, I really—"

"Don't be crazy," I say, handing over a fifty-dollar bill as I stand up and put my coat on. "No change. The tip is all for you."

"Oh, Angie, thank you!" Adrian looks like he's about to cry again, but then stares at me in concern. "Wait, are you okay?"

I nod, but I can't even look at him, or I swear to God I'll lose it. I need to be alone.

While my mother is still in the bathroom, I leave. She'll find her way back to her hotel in Manhattan, somehow. My mother is British, she lives Boston most of the time, and her only experience of New York was the year they lived here, on the Upper East Side, when she gave birth to me. She got so fat during pregnancy that she wouldn't leave the apartment after I was born in case she saw someone she knew. So apparently I didn't see the sun till I was five months old and she'd lost the weight. And that, my friends, sums up Annabel's whole approach to motherhood.

The moment I get outside, I light my cigarette. That's better. It's late February, and goddamn cold outside, but I'm toasty. I'm wearing my dead grandmother's fur coat that I turned inside out and hand-sewed into an old army surplus jacket when I was sixteen.

They're divorcing.

Well, finally, I guess, right? Dad hasn't exactly been the best husband. Not that she knows about any of that stuff. I wonder if he'll tell her now. Probably not. Why rock a boat that's already sinking, or whatever that saying is. For a second, I consider calling him. But what will I say? Congratulations? Commiserations? Better to wait for him to call me.

But how does this work? Like, where will we spend Christmas next year? How does divorce work when your kid is an adult? It's not like we can have visitation rights or custody battles or whatever, right? Will we simply cease to exist as a family?

When I was little, we'd go to my grandmother's house in Boston. I always emptied my Christmas stocking on my parents' bed, and sat in between them while they had coffee and I had hot chocolate and we shared bites of buttery raisin toast. I'd take each present out of my stocking, one by one, and they'd get all excited with me and we'd wonder how Santa knew exactly what I wanted and how he got to every house in the world in just one night.

A warmth washes over me as I think about it. I can still remember what it feels like, that sense of security and togetherness.

I just can't imagine feeling it ever again. There's a big hollowness in my stomach where that feeling used to belong.

Maybe I should grow the hell up. Our family hasn't felt like that for a long time. And I'm nearly twenty-three, the age that, to me at least, has always been the marker of true adulthood. It's the end of the carefree-unbrushed-hair-I'm-a-grad-winging-it early twenties, and the start of the matching-lingerie-health-insurance-real-career-serious-boyfriend mid-twenties. And I'm nowhere near any of those things.

They're divorcing.

I take out my phone and call Stef. He's this guy I know, a trust-fund baby with a lot of bad friends and nice drugs. And he's always doing something fun. But today he's not answering.

I share an apartment with four other girls in an old brownstone called Rookhaven, in Carroll Gardens, an area of Brooklyn in New York City. I'd love to live in Manhattan, but I can't afford it, and my best friend Pia hooked me up with a cheap room here after graduation.

I didn't think I'd stick around long, but it's the sort of place where you get cozy, fast. Décor-wise, it's a cheesy time capsule, but after six months of living there I even like that about it. What bad things can possibly happen in a kitchen that has smelled like vanilla and cinnamon forever?

I walk up the stairs to my room. "Is anyone home?"

No answer. No surprise. Everyone's at work. Until a few weeks ago I was working as a sort of freelance PA to Cornelia Pace, the spoiled daughter of some socialite my mother knows. Basically, I ran errands (dry-cleaning, tailoring, Xanax prescriptions) for her and she handed me cash when she remembered. She's in Europe skiing for the next, like, month. She said she'd call me when she gets back. I've got enough cash to survive until then. I hope.

And no, I don't take handouts. My folks paid my rent when I first moved in last year, and always gave me a generous allowance, but between you and me, they don't have the money anymore. A few investments went sour over the past few years, and my dad told me at Christmas that they were basically broke, which freaked me out completely. I'd never seen him look that defeated, and I can't be a financial burden on him anymore. Especially with the bombshell my mother just dropped. *They're divorcing*. . . .

Do you think that an empty, cold, gray house at 2:00 P.M. in February, with nothing to do and no dude to text, might be one of the most depressing things in the history of the fucking universe? Because I do. I feel like my toes have been cold forever.

Oh God, I need a vacation. I want sandy feet and clear blue skies and hot sun on my skin and that blissed-out exalted tingly-scalp feeling you get when you dive into the ocean and the cool seawater hits the top of your head. I crave it. We had the best vacations when I was little. My dad taught me how to sail and fish, and Annabel would stop wearing makeup and not worry about her hair for a few weeks. It was the closest to perfect we came as a family.

I flop down on my bed and look around my bedroom. Closet, drawers, bookshelf with back issues of *Women's Wear Daily* and Italian *Vogue*, an old wooden desk with my sewing machine and drawings and photos that I never get around to organizing, and clothes on every surface. Particularly the floor.

Clothes are my life, but not in a pretentious-label-whore kind of way. I honestly love H&M as much as Hermès (and my only Hermès was a present from an ex, anyway). Making clothes or styling clothes or thinking about clothes, or mentally planning how I could pick apart and resew my existing clothes, my future clothes, my friends' clothes, and sometimes, to be honest, total strangers' clothes—is my favorite pastime. I can lose hours just staring into space, thinking about it. Apparently, this sartorial daydreaming gives my face a sort of detached "fuck-off" expression.

I wonder how many of my problems have been created by the fact that I look like an über-bitch when I'm really just thinking about something else?

Sighing, I reach into my nightstand where there's always my latest Harlequin romance novel, M&Ms, cigarettes, and Belvedere vodka. I read a lot of romance novels; they're my secret vice. But they're not going to be enough today. All I want—no, all I *need*—is to forget about everything that's wrong with my life. I need to escape.

And I know exactly how to do it.

Cheers to me.

CHAPTER 2

"What's up, ladybitches?" I stride into the kitchen and do a twirl hello.

It's just past 7:00 P.M., and everyone's home from work. They've all assumed their usual kitchen places: Pia's texting her boyfriend, Madeleine's reading *The New York Times,* Julia is answering e-mails on her BlackBerry while eating pasta, and Coco is baking. How productive. La-di-dah.

"Angelface!" exclaims Julia. "You're just in time. Deal me in."

Julia's the loud, sporty, high-fiving, hardworking banking trainee, former-leader-of-the-debate-team type, you know the kind of girl I mean? I think her hair automatically springs into a jaunty ponytail every time she gets out of bed. We didn't get along that well at first, but actually, I think she's pretty fucking cool. She really makes me laugh.

Maybe it just takes me a long time to get to know people. Or for them to get to know me.

"Oh, I'll deal you in," I say, picking up the cards I always keep over the fridge. "I'll deal you in real good, just the way you like it."

Julia snorts with laughter. "You make everything sound dirty."

"Everything is dirty," I reply. "If it's done right."

"What's on your top?"

"Lingonberry juice. Duh."

"Have you been drinking?" asks Pia, looking up.

Pia's my best friend, and she used to be a reliable party girl, a high-maintenance and hilarious drama queen lurching from meltdown to meltdown, but then she went and got her shit together. Now she has a serious career in food trucks and a serious boyfriend named Aidan. She even looks after his dog when he's away, that's how serious it is. Serious, serious, serious. I'm happy for her—no, I really am, I've known Pia forever, she's so smart and funny and she deserves to be happy. But I miss her. Even when she's right here, it sort of feels like she's not really here. If that makes sense.

She stares at me now. She's absolutely gorgeous: mixed Swiss-Indian heritage, green eyes, and long black hair. "Seriously, ladybitch. Have you?"

"No! . . . Okay, that's a lie. Yes, I've been drinkin'. Actually, I've been drinkin' and sewin'," I say, shuffling the cards so fast they look like a ribbon.

Drinkin' and sewin' was actually kind of fun. One part of my brain was focusing on the sewing, the other part was skipping around my subconscious, thinking about movies and books and Mani—the fuck-puppet who dumped me last year—and what my grandmother taught me about pattern cutting and wondering when my father would call.

"Angie, it's a school night," says Pia. She's wearing her version of corporate attire: skinny jeans, heeled boots, and a very chic jacket that I may have to borrow one day. "Don't you have to work for Cornelia in the morning?"

"Cornelia doesn't exactly need me to be firing on all cylinders," I say. "Or any cylinders." I haven't exactly gone into details about my current job situation with the girls.

Pia narrows her eyes at me, and I ignore her.

"If you're all done, I'm taking the rest of this lasagne down to Vic," says Coco. Vic's our ancient downstairs neighbor, who has lived in the garden-level apartment for longer than I've been alive.

"Good idea, Cuckoo," says Julia.

Coco beams. Such an approval junkie. Coco is Julia's baby sister, and a total sweetheart. She's a preschool assistant, and whenever I think of her, I think of Miss Honey from that Roald Dahl book *Matilda*.

I take a swig of my drink and look around. How is it I can still feel alone in a room full of people? "How were your days at the office, dears?"

"Shit," say Julia and Madeleine at the same moment Pia says, "Awesome!"

"I'm on a project so boring, I may turn into an Excel spreadsheet," says Madeleine. She's kind of an enigma. (Wrapped in a mystery. Hidden in a paradox. Or whatever that saying is.) Accountant, Chinese-Irish, smart, snarky, does a lot of running and yoga and shit like that. Pia once described her as "nice but tricky." Recently Madeleine joined a band, as a singer, but she hasn't let us see them live yet. Who the fuck wants to be a singer but doesn't want anyone to actually hear them sing?

"At least your work environment isn't hostile. I sit next to a total douche who stares at my boobs all day," says Julia.

"To be fair, your rack is enormous," I point out. Julia frowns at me. Oops. That comment might have pissed her off. Oh well, if you can't laugh at your own boobs, what can you laugh at, right?

"Well, I'm happy. SkinnyWheels Miami has doubled profits in under a month," says Pia. SkinnyWheels is a food truck empire she started six months ago. You know the drill: tasty food that won't make you fat. Sometimes I think Pia has literally replaced our friendship with a truck. Well, a truck and a hot British dude who has his own place, so she practically lives there. But it's not like I can beg her to be my best friend again, right? I'm a grown-up. Adult. Whatever.

"Actually, I'm happy, too. My boss said 'great job' again today. That's the second time this year!" Julia looks insanely proud, and spills pasta sauce on her suit jacket. "Fuck! Every fucking time!"

"Does anyone want herbal tea?" says Madeleine, standing up.

I raise my glass. "Could you dunk the tea bag in my vodka?"

Madeleine gazes at me. "Is that a withering look?" I say. "Because it needs practice. You just look a bit lost and constipated. Maybe you should— Oh, no, wait. Now *that's* withering."

Madeleine ignores me.

"How about you, Coconut?" I look over at Coco. "Good day shaping young hearts and minds?"

She grins at me, all freckles and blond bob and oven mitts, and her usual layers and layers of dark "hide me!" clothes. "I got pooped on."

"Someone took a *shit* on you?" I pause. "People pay good money for that."

"Ew! Gross! He is four years old! And it was a mistake. I hope."

No one asks me how my day was, and they all go back to their own things, so I get up and open the freezer, where I always keep a spare bottle of Belvedere, and fix myself another three-finger tipple, on the rocks, with a slice of cucumber and a few crumbs of sea salt. My dad taught me this drink; we drank it together at the Minetta Tavern last time he was in Manhattan, about a month ago. But he didn't say anything about a divorce.

Cheers to me.

Several swigs later, I take a cigarette out of my pack and prop it in the corner of my mouth, and look around at the girls, so calm and happy together, so sure of one another and their place in the world. I can't remember the last time I felt like that.

My phone buzzes. Finally! A text from Stef. *Just woke up. Making a plan. xoxo*

It's weird the way he ends texts with *xoxo*, I think, making myself another drink. What is he, a nine-year-old girl?

"Oh, Angie, there's mail for you." Julia points at some parcels on the sideboard. "What the hell do you keep ordering?"

"Stuff." I start opening them. Buttons from a funny little button shop in Savannah, a bolt of yellow cotton from a dress shop in Jersey, and a gorgeous 1930s ivory lace wedding dress that I bought for two hundred dollars on eBay when I was drunk last weekend.

Julia screws up her face at the dress. "Wow. That is fucking disgusting."

This riles me up, for some reason, though the shoulder pads and puffed sleeves *are* a little Anne of Green Gables Does *Dynasty*. "This lace is exquisite," I snap. "And the bodice structure is divine, so I'm gonna take the sleeves off and make a little top."

"Good luck with that," says Julia, with a laugh in her voice, which again, really pisses me off.

"I'm not taking fashion advice from someone who wears a double-breasted green pantsuit to work."

"This pantsuit is from Macy's! And who died and made you Karla Lagerfeld?"

"You mean Karl Lagerfeld."

"I know that! I was making a joke."

"Really? What was the punch line?"

"Kids, play nice," says Pia, a warning in her voice.

"I am nice," says Julia. "Angie's the one living in a vodka-fueled dream world. I can't even remember the last time I saw her sober."

"That is a total lie! I was sober when I saw you this morning! As you headed out the door with your pantsuit and gym bag and laptop like the one percent banker drone that you are!"

"Okay, that's enough!" Pia says. "Both of you say you're sorry and make up."

"Fuck that. I'm out of here."

I slug my vodka, head upstairs, throw on my sexiest white dress from Isabel Marant, some extremely high heels, my fur/army coat, take a moment to smear on some more black eyeliner, and stomp down to the front door. I love wearing white. It makes me feel clean and pure, like nothing can touch me.

I can hear the girls talking happily again in the kitchen, ruffles smoothed over, conversation ebbing and flowing the way it should. Without me.

For a second, just as I close the front door, I'm overwhelmed by the urge to run back in and say sorry for being a drunk brat. To try to find my place as part of the group, with all the ease and laughter and fun that entails. . . . But I don't fit with them. Not really. Pia was my only tie to them, and she doesn't even act like she likes me these days. Though I don't like me much these days either.

Anyway, I already said I was leaving.

I call Stef from the cab. This time, he answers.

"My angel. Got a secret bar for you. Corner of Tenth and Forty-sixth. Go into a café called Westies and through the red door at the back."

He always knows the best places.

I quickly check my outfit in the cab; this is a great dress. I tried to copy it last week, but failed; I can't get the arms quite right.

And by the way, I tried to get a job in fashion when I first got to New York. I sent my résumé and photos of the stuff I've made and some designs I'd been sketching, to all my favorite New York fashion designers. No response. So then I sent all the same stuff to my second-favorite designers. Then my third favorites. And so on. No one even replied. I don't have a fashion degree—my parents wanted me to get (I quote) a "normal" education first—and I don't have any direct fashion experience at all. I thought maybe I could leapfrog over from my job with the food photographer I worked for last year, but then she fired me. (Well, I quit. But she would have fired me anyway.)

The problem is that when you're starting out, there's nowhere to start. And there are thousands—maybe tens of thousands —of twenty-two-year-old girls who want to work in fashion in New York. I'm a total cliché. And I hate that.

So I never talk about my secret fashion career dream. It's easier that way. Secretly wanting something and not getting it is one thing. I can handle that; I'm good at it. But talking about wanting it, putting it out there, making it real . . . and then not getting it? I couldn't deal with that much failure.

The café, Westies, is in Hell's Kitchen, an area of Manhattan I'm not that familiar with, but it seems aptly named today. The streets are freezing and empty, heaped with filthy, blackened snow. Manhattan looks mean in February.

Stef's car is parked outside. Predictably. It's his pride and joy, a red Ferrari 308 GTS. It's a gorgeous car, I admit, a little "look at me!" for my taste, but he loves it.

I stride into the empty café—past greasy counters and scabby red velvet cupcakes on a dirty cake stand—and open the red door, walk down some old metal stairs that smell strangely like cabbage and yeast, past a dark green velvet curtain, and find myself in a warm, dark, calm little room.

There's a ladder against a wall, where someone's been putting up wallpaper. A handful of small round tables, a bar area the size of a bed, candles, and the Ramones. The perfect secret after-hours bar.

Stef's the only person in here, and he's sitting at the bar. He's cute, though a little simian for my liking. Overconfident and overintense with the eye contact. You know the type.

"What's up?" I greet him with a triple cheek kiss, the way Stef always does.

"Nothing, my angel," he says, running his hand through his hair and lighting a cigarette. Wow, this must be a secret bar if they let you smoke inside. "How's life with Cornie? It's so cute that you work for her. Does she say *yoohoo* every morning when she sees you?"

"She's away." Stef is part of that Upper East Side Manhattan rich kid crowd that all know one another, always have and always will, and so is Cornelia. "I need to make some money, fast."

"You wanna split an Adderall?"

"Sure."

"Drug tales and dreams, baby. . . . This is my buddy's place. It's not open to the public yet, but the bar's fully stocked. Help yourself to a drink." Stef takes out his wallet, looking for his pills. He has a sort of cracked drawl, so he sounds permanently amused and slightly stoned. He probably is. "Fix me something while you're at it. I'm going to the bathroom. Unisex. Pretty nineties, huh?"

Two vodkas and half an Adderall later, and the world is a lot smoother.